Praise for *The Cosgrove Report:*

"Dazzling . . . A superior example of this genre."
—Nicholas Meyer, author of *The Seven-Per-Cent Solution*

"A humdinger of a mystery . . . transports us to a landscape at once familiar and as exotic as a sinister, murderous Oz."
—*The Washington Star*

"Compelling . . . a stunning conclusion." —*Grand Rapids Press*

"A gem . . . it truly takes the reader back to relive those days. But don't let anyone tell you how the book ends . . . that would be cruel and inhuman treatment." —*Memphis Commercial Appeal*

"Moves along at lightning speed . . . sprightly and intriguing . . . what gorgeous entertainment." —*Columbus Dispatch*

"Fascinating . . . an exciting chronicle of what might have been . . . ending with a twist that should satisfy the most fanatical mystery aficionado." —*Civil War Times*

"My hat is off to G. J. A. O'Toole. He has come up with an idea for a mystery so good . . . and he has brought it off with a flair that rivals Josephine Tey's *The Daughter of Time* . . . Ingenious and plausible . . . the research is meticulous."
—*The Baltimore Sun*

"If you think there is no more mystery surrounding *that* assassination, you are dead wrong. . . . A must for anyone to whom history is a wonderful old trunk in the attic, always full of dusty surprises." —*The Plain Dealer*

"A political thriller based on a careful reading of history that will make a thrice-told tale seem completely different."
—*The Boston Herald*

THE COSGROVE REPORT

OTHER BOOKS BY G. J. A. O'TOOLE

An Agent on the Other Side
The Assassination Tapes
The Private Sector
Honorable Treachery
The Encyclopedia of American Intelligence and Espionage
The Spanish War: An American Epic

THE COSGROVE REPORT:

Being the Private Inquiry
of a Pinkerton Detective into
the Death of President Lincoln

by Nicholas Cosgrove

EDITED AND VERIFIED BY
MICHAEL CROFT,
COL., U.S. ARMY (RET.)

AN ANNOTATED NOVEL
PRESENTED BY
G. J. A. O'TOOLE

Grove Press
New York

Originally published by Rawson, Wade

Published simultaneously in Canada
Printed in the United States of America

FIRST GROVE PRESS EDITION

ISBN-10: 0-8021-4407-1
ISBN-13: 978-0-8021-4407-2

Grove Press
an imprint of Grove/Atlantic, Inc.
841 Broadway
New York, NY 10003

Distributed by Publishers Group West

www.groveatlantic.com

09 10 11 12 13   10 9 8 7 6 5 4 3 2 1

For Mary Ann

Contents

·····━━◆━━·····

CONTENTS

THE COSGROVE REPORT

Foreword

BY MICHAEL CROFT

··•───◆───•··

Credentials are going to be an issue here, there's no doubt about that. I've rankled enough experts of various kinds in my time to know what to expect. Coroners, cops and criminologists resent amateurs poaching on their professional territory. I don't see why historians should be any different, especially when the interloper is someone so lacking in academic status as a private detective. So I want to make it clear at the outset that I did not volunteer for this assignment. I was hired to do it by someone who felt the job could be done better by me than by a professional historian. I'll let him explain why shortly. For my part, there was no point in trying to argue with my client about it. He couldn't change his mind; he died several weeks before he hired me.

About a year ago I found among my mail an envelope with the expensively embossed return address of the firm of Lawson, Hurley, Clinger and Osborn, Attorneys at Law. Most people quake at unexpected letters from law firms because they usually mean trouble. But in my profession they can also mean business, and as I slit open the envelope I recalled I had done some work for Raymond Lawson, senior partner of this firm, almost ten years ago. At the time Lawson was into his seventies, and I was surprised now to see he was still practicing law. But when I unfolded the enclosed letter and read it, I learned the old man had recently passed away. The letter was from one James Marsh, a junior partner. It was brief and not very informative.

Dear Mr. Croft:

    I have been appointed executor of the estate of Mr. Raymond Lawson, the late senior partner of this firm. It is necessary that we meet to discuss a matter that may be of considerable benefit to you.

    Please contact me at your earliest convenience.

Sincerely,
James Marsh, Esq.

Marsh wasn't any more enlightening on the phone, but his firm's offices in downtown Washington, D.C., were only a few blocks from my own. In person, Marsh turned out to be a young man with the meticulous air of a certified public accountant. He was the type that might have some trouble dealing with things that seem "a little irregular," which was how he described the matter that brought me to his office.

Mr. Lawson had left something for me, he explained. Not a bequest, exactly—a job. What kind of job? Marsh said he didn't know. He produced a sealed parcel of the same general size, shape and weight as the Manhattan telephone book, and a check in an amount that would pay my daily rate for almost a year. According to the terms of Lawson's will, Marsh was instructed to tell me only that the job was neither illegal nor hazardous, but that if I accepted it, I had to promise to give it my best efforts, priority over all other cases except those involving "life and death, or national security," and to work on it until either it was completed, or the fee had been exhausted. No report of progress or completion need be submitted to Lawson, Hurley, Clinger and Osborn. Under the terms of Lawson's will, the firm had no further responsibilities in the matter, after handing the parcel and the check over to me.

I don't usually take cases sight unseen, but I had to admit that this one certainly sounded like a good proposition. The "neither illegal nor hazardous" promise went a long way toward allaying my suspicions, and a year's solid booking is very attractive to anyone who freelances at anything. But I think my main reason for accepting the check and parcel from Marsh was curiosity; it seemed the only way to learn what had been on the old man's mind. And, of course, there was nothing to keep me from returning the money and the package to the law firm if, on finding out the details of the assignment, I decided it was something I didn't want to do. And that's exactly what I nearly did about forty-five minutes later.

Back in my office on Pennsylvania Avenue, I put the check aside and broke the seals on the parcel. Inside I found an envelope with my name on it, several hundred yellowing sheets comprising what appeared to be a book manuscript, and an assortment of very old photographs. The envelope contained a letter from Lawson detailing my assignment. I reread it several times because I couldn't believe what it said. There was no ambiguity in the late attorney's message however: Lawson had hired me to reopen the investigation into the assassination of President Abraham Lincoln.

Dear Mr. Croft:

First, permit me to thank you, for, if you are reading this letter, you have agreed to take charge of a matter that has been a vexing burden to me for most of my adult life. The time seems to have come for me to put my personal affairs in order and tie up the many loose ends left over from a life of more than fourscore years. But I could not do so with any sense of equanimity or peace of mind without first arranging for the proper disposition of this matter.

The problem in question concerns the enclosed manuscript, which I inherited from its author, my maternal grandfather, Nicholas Cosgrove, upon his death in 1914. During his lifetime, my grandfather had been wonderfully generous to my family, and especially to me. He made it possible for me to attend Harvard Law School, and saw to my earliest professional opportunities. In death, he was no less generous, and his bequest to my family has permitted us to live in moderate affluence, independent of the commercial exigencies of my law practice. Thus it hangs heavily upon my conscience that I have never fulfilled the single request that he made of me—to see to the publication of his manuscript.

It would not, of course, have been possible to publish the book in 1914; several of those who played roles in the account, or their immediate survivors, were still living. In fact, Grandfather Nicholas stipulated that I should wait until all involved had long passed from the scene before publication. But many years have gone by since that condition was met, yet I still find myself unable to do my grandfather's bidding. It is my hope that you, Mr. Croft, will enable me to discharge that obligation. Naturally, to do so, you will require some background information.

Nicholas Cosgrove was born in New York City in 1835 of Irish immigrant parents. For a few years in his early manhood he followed his father's trade of blacksmithing, but by 1855 he had joined the New York Police Department. After four years on the police force, he was assigned to assist in the investigation of a safecracking ring. The investigation was led by the famous private detective Allan Pinkerton, who had been hired by several of the victimized banks. Pinkerton was favorably impressed with the young policeman and offered him a job as a detective with his agency in Chicago. Grandfather accepted.

Two years after Grandfather went to work for the Pinkerton Detective Agency, the Civil War broke out, and Allan Pinkerton put his entire staff of detectives at the service of General George McClellan. Grandfather was sent to Cincinnati to establish a clandestine headquarters from which reconnaissance missions into the South could be mounted. Grandfather himself crossed the lines many times during the war in a variety of disguises. He narrowly escaped hanging as a spy on several occasions, and once made his getaway by means of an untethered observation balloon.

After the war, Pinkerton's agency resumed its private investigative business, and Grandfather had developed a special kind of skill. Pinkerton's had many ex-scouts who could track a bank or train robber through the wild, but Grandfather was one of the few detectives who knew how to track an embezzling employee who changed his name and fled from city to city, across the country, or even to foreign lands. Undoubtedly it was that talent that led to his involvement in the events he has recounted in his manuscript, which, if accurate, describes the most important missing-person case of the nineteenth century.

During the 1870s Grandfather made a series of shrewd investments in railroad and telegraph stocks. In fact, these ventures succeeded so handsomely that I must admit to the suspicion that they were actually elaborate mechanisms devised by some rich and powerful individuals to purchase his silence regarding the matters contained in this manuscript. I know that it is unworthy of me to voice such thoughts, but I do so to you because it bears on your assignment, in that it may tend to corroborate Grandfather's account.

In any event, Grandfather became a wealthy man and left Pinkerton's. He bought a seat on the New York Stock Exchange and hired a bright young man to run the stock brokerage for him. He married the daughter of a clergyman and moved to Newport, Rhode Island, where he built an elegant home. It was there that my mother, his one child, Penelope, was born.

His wife died in 1885, and four years later, Penelope met and married my father, Arthur Lawson, the young headmaster of a nearby academy for the sons of affluent New England families. Grandfather invited the couple to live with him in his mansion at Newport, and so that is where I was born in 1890.

My grandfather wrote the enclosed narrative during the early years of this century, using diaries he had kept during his detective days. As close as I can recall, he seems to have begun it in 1902 and completed it about

1905. He told us he was writing his "memoirs," and I remember often seeing him in his study, day and night, laboriously scribbling in longhand at his enormous rolltop desk. Every Wednesday a woman stenographer would come down from Providence to transcribe the foolscap sheets on a typewriter under my grandfather's close supervision. I remember that several different women were employed at this task during the years he was writing the narrative, and I later realized my grandfather had arranged things this way so that none of the stenographers would have read the entire manuscript.

None of the family was shown the manuscript. After it was completed my grandfather locked it away somewhere, and I had completely forgotten about it when, shortly before he died, he gave it to me. He asked me not to read it until after his death, and then to hold it and arrange for its publication at whatever time in the future I judged proper. I would never have agreed to do so had I known what it contained.

The manuscript purports to be a memoir of my grandfather's activities shortly after the Civil War—1868 through 1869 to be precise. In it, he writes that he was assigned by the Pinkerton Detective Agency to investigate the circumstances surrounding the assassination of President Lincoln, which, of course, had occurred only a few years earlier. According to this account, he discovered that the assassination conspiracy involved many more people than were caught and punished. My grandfather implicates some of the most important men in government and industry of the post-Civil War period.

After reading it, I realized that I, as my grandfather's literary executor, could not simply publish this memoir without taking a position regarding its authenticity. That is when I realized I was faced with an impossible dilemma. To offer this memoir as fact would be to assume the role of historical revisionist, a role I neither was qualified for nor wished to play. But to publish the manuscript prefaced by some sort of caveat as to its veracity would be to impugn the memory of a man who treated me with nothing other than kindness. The solution I have chosen may seem cowardly, but I believe that it is at least honest—to defer the matter a brief while longer until I too am gone, and to arrange to engage you at that time to investigate the memoir and, if possible, establish whether or not it is true. A former client of mine, who is a free-lance writer, has read it and has promised to see to its publication, regardless of what you may discover; he feels it is of some intrinsic historical interest, in any case, since its author was a Pinkerton's detective involved in the events of that period. His name is George O'Toole (I think you may know him) and I have enclosed his address with the manuscript. He will see that your findings are published together with the memoir.

Finally, you may wonder why I did not choose a professional historian rather than a private detective for this task. There are several reasons. First, professional historians are not disinterested in this matter; academic careers and professional reputations can be seriously affected by the challenging of historical orthodoxy. You, on the other hand, have nothing to gain or lose, regardless of your findings.

Second, investigation of a murder conspiracy is at least as much a professional specialty as is historical research. The dynamics of assassination plots do not change very much from one century to another, but the academic historian understands little of them. However, I know that you, by virtue of your past work for this firm, are well acquainted with such matters.

Lastly, the manuscript is the record of an investigation, by a private detective. It may be that one private detective is best suited to probe the mental workings of another of that profession.

In any event, I feel confident that I am leaving this matter in the best qualified hands.

Sincerely,
Raymond Lawson

P.S. You will find enclosed with the manuscript an assortment of photographs of some of the people, things and events involved in the matter you are to investigate. I have assembled this collection over the years out of curiosity. For me they have lent a kind of life to the long-dead affairs that are the subject of the manuscript. You are welcome to them for whatever help they may provide in completing your assignment.

I might have sent for a messenger just then, to take the check and the manuscript back to Marsh, had it not been for the photographs. Old photographs happen to be one of my weaknesses. The bookshelves in my study are filled with collections of the work of Daguerre, Brady, O'Sullivan, etc., and I often sit for hours looking at them. It's not that I'm especially a history buff; it's just that I'm fascinated by the accidental quality of antique photography. In one of my books there is a photo taken by O'Sullivan of a New York City street in the 1860s. The street is filled with wagons and horsecars, and teeming with humanity. An elegant coach is drawn up at the curb, its door standing open. The figure of a man, blurred by its motion before the slow film and shutter of the early camera, is stepping down onto the sidewalk. Who is he, and what business was he on at that moment eleven decades ago when the photographer chanced to open the camera's eye? We can never know. He remains forever frozen in time, like an ant in ancient amber, or the carcass of a mammoth buried in the Siberian tundra.

A while ago the Smithsonian put on an exhibition of old photographs. Kernan, the *Washington Post*'s reviewer, summed up my feelings better than I can.

"The great power in old photographs is the things going on around the edges: the true life of a lost time, all unaware that it is being stared at by the future."

The things going on around the edges. Exactly. Often a dozen mysteries, or more, and almost every one of them absolutely gone beyond any remote possibility of solution. And, for some perverse reason, that is what fascinates me, a professional solver of mysteries.

I glanced through the photographs Lawson had enclosed. Some of them were quite familiar; I'd seen them in history books. As I examined the pictures odd bits and pieces drifted to mind, learned no doubt in boyhood history lessons. There he was, John Wilkes Booth, handsome, dapper and self-assured. Son of a prominent theatrical family, he was already acclaimed a success at twenty-four, when he abruptly retired from the stage and entered the shadow world of the Confederate Secret Service. The proud and dashing pose he strikes before a stylized backdrop in some photographer's studio clearly proclaims he is prepared to accomplish everything. Even regicide.

Madame Surratt. The only known photograph of her, says a label Lawson has stuck to the back of the picture. A pleasant-looking woman in early middle age. There seems nothing of the zealot in her mild gaze. Her only crime may well have been owning the boarding-house where the assassination plot was hatched. It earned her the unenviable distinction of becoming the first woman hanged by the federal government.

Dr. Samuel A. Mudd, another victim of circumstances. A thirtyish man, prematurely bald, with a thick goatee. He treated Booth's leg, which the assassin had broken as he fled the scene of his crime, and nearly went to the gallows for his trouble. Sentenced to life in prison, he was later pardoned.

A contemporary view of Ford's Theater. I'm startled to see the familiar structure in a position of eminence on a muddy, unpaved 10th Street. Today it huddles among larger buildings on one of Washington's busiest downtown thoroughfares.

Here are the three conspirators who were hanged along with Madame Surratt. David Herold, a drugstore clerk, looks to be little more than a boy. History says he was a bit dull-witted. A stagestruck follower of the actor Booth, he shared his idol's twelve-day retreat in the swamps and wilderness of Maryland and Virginia.

George Atzerodt, drunkard and errand-boy of the Confederate underground in Civil War Maryland. Even in a whiskey bottle he could not find the courage to kill Vice-President Johnson, a mission which Booth unaccountably assigned to the man. A filthy, rodentlike face has been preserved for the ages by the camera.

Lewis Paine. At twenty, a Confederate veteran of a half-dozen major battles. Wounded and captured at Gettysburg in Pickett's charge. A seasoned killer with a huge frame and enormous strength, he slashed Secretary of State Seward and his son within an inch of their lives while Booth was engaged in the murder at Ford's Theater. He stares into the eye of the camera with passionate intensity. On some deserted battlefield where others have left arms and legs, Paine has left part of his mind.

There were other conspirators; eight in all stood trial for their crimes. Lawson had a complete collection in his rogues' gallery. Edward Spangler, the Ford's Theater stagehand. Michael O'Laughlin, a boyhood friend of Booth's. And Samuel Arnold, a young Confederate veteran. Because their guilt was judged to be less, they escaped the gallows but were sentenced to life imprisonment in Fort Jefferson in the Dry Tortugas off Key West. O'Laughlin died of yellow fever there. The others were pardoned in 1869.

The next photograph was not a portrait, and I stared at it, trying to identify the objects it showed. Eight dirty canvas sacks fitted with drawstrings. They looked like misshapen laundry bags. I turned over the print and read Lawson's caption:

On the orders of Secretary of War Edwin Stanton, the conspiracy defendants were forced to wear these hoods, or "headbags," to prevent conversation. The hoods were lined with inch-thick cotton padding and had no openings for the eyes or ears. The eyes were covered with balls of extra cotton padding which pressed down on the closed lids. One small hole was provided in each hood for breathing and eating. The hoods were worn day and night, except when the defendants were in court. One of the hoods was not used; Mrs. Surratt was excepted from the measure, although she, like the other defendants, was kept in irons throughout the conspiracy trial . . .

To prevent conversation! The seven male defendants were kept deaf and blind during the eight or ten weeks that separated their capture in April and their sentencing in July. From the moment the cell doors slammed shut behind them each day until the hour of the next morning when they were to be led back to the courtroom in the Arsenal Penitentiary, they lived in silent darkness. Why?

In the twentieth century, defendants in political trials have been subjected to similar ordeals. It's called sensory deprivation and it's based on the discovery that, when light and sound are cut off for hours or days, the victim loses touch with reality. He begins to hallucinate and eventually has trouble telling the difference between dream and reality. In such a state, his mind can easily be manipulated to think whatever his tormentors wish. Were such diabolical techniques known in the 1860s? I doubt it. Then why did Stanton order these cruel masks?

Was cruelty itself the purpose of the hoods? Perhaps. Certainly a good case can be made that Stanton was a sadist, but he would have had to have been a genius of cruelty to devise so simple an instrument to achieve such an exquisite combination of mental and physical suffering: claustrophobia, fear of impending death on the gallows, and the suffocating heat that often blankets Washington in May and June.

But as I read further into Lawson's gloss on the reverse side of the photograph I saw that Stanton's own explanation of the hoods—to prevent conversation—was the most plausible, for the hoods were only one of several measures taken to keep the defendants incommunicado:

Other elaborate precautions were taken to prevent the conspirators from conversing among themselves or with others. They were imprisoned in separate cells on the second and third floors of the Old Arsenal Penitentiary; empty cells separated each of the cells occupied by the conspirators. The guards posted at the cells were forbidden to converse with the prisoners. No individual guard was permitted to stand more than a single watch on any one prisoner, thus there was no possibility of a guard becoming acquainted with any of the prisoners. And the defendants' attorneys were not permitted to visit their clients in their cells; all conferences between lawyers and clients had to take place in the courtroom, under the watchful eyes of the guards.

I turned the photograph over to look again at the eight grim headbags. By themselves the grotesque items make a case for a larger assassination conspiracy. What other conceivable purpose for rendering the prisoners mute than to carry out a cover-up of some kind? Yet Stanton freely admitted the purpose of the hoods was to insure silence. Perhaps in some government archive he has left a perfectly legitimate explanation. The mystery began to pique my curiosity.

The next three photographs showed the hanging of the four conspirators in the courtyard of the Old Penitentiary. High noon on a bright July day, judging from the short shadows. Four nooses dangled over two long trapdoors; the prisoners were to die simultaneously. The condemned were seated and shielded from the blazing sun by great black umbrellas while the death sentences were read to them. Next they stood while the ropes were placed about their necks and the death hoods fitted over their heads. Lawson's lengthy captions on the pictures said that Mrs. Surratt was rumored to have been promised she would escape the gallows; many accounts say she believed she would not hang until the very moment she was led to the scaffold. Which, I reflect, might be as effective a way of insuring her silence as a headbag.

I was being seduced by Lawson's antique photos. Already I was spinning theories and filing them away for future reference. But there would have been no future reference—I would never have pursued the case—except for the next picture in Lawson's photo file.

It was a picture of a crowd on what I recognized as the steps of the East Front of the Capitol. It looked like a presidential inauguration, and judging from the Civil War era costumes, I guessed it was one of Lincoln's two inaugurations. I couldn't confirm this from the photograph, however, for the spot where the President would have been standing was obscured by what must have been a smudge on the photographic plate. I turned the print over and read Lawson's gloss.

It was, in fact, a photograph of Lincoln's second inauguration, on March 4, 1865, just six weeks before the assassination. The photograph had been taken by the well-known photographer Alexander Gardner, who made several exposures of the inaugural ceremony. Careless handling of the wet photographic plate caused the fingerprint smudge that obscured the central figures in the scene. The picture was filed away and forgotten for nearly a century, until it turned up in the Frederick Hill Meserve collection—some 200,000 pictures from the Lincoln period.

In all those years, apparently no one had bothered to look at the flawed view of the inaugural until its latter-day rediscovery. Then someone took the trouble to examine each figure in the crowd on the Capitol steps. The results were sensational.

The photographic experts identified five figures standing immediately below the speaker's platform where the President stood: Lewis Paine, George Atzerodt, David Herold, Edward Spangler and John Surratt, son of the boardinghouse keeper. Standing at a balcony railing above and behind the President is the top-hatted figure of John Wilkes Booth.

The great power in old photographs is the things going on around the edges: the true life of a lost time, all unaware that it is being stared at by the future.

Here, a century after the assassination of President Lincoln, was proof that several of the little band of conspirators involved stood within a few feet of their victim as he was sworn in for his second term. What did it mean? A suicide mission to kill Lincoln at the very instant he began his second term of office? Or a daring try at kidnapping the President from under the astonished eyes of the crowd?

Certainly either plan would have appealed to Booth's need for an audience. Whatever was intended, the action was aborted. An unexpected turn of events, a failure of coordination, or a flickering of the conspirators' courage—something thwarted whatever John Wilkes Booth planned for that day. Otherwise, what historic act might Gardner's photographic plate have recorded? Another dusty mystery. I gathered all of Lawson's antique photographs together and put them aside. They had done their work. I was hooked.

I visited the scene of the crime. Ford's Theater was restored in 1968, and, except for the addition of some modern lighting, it is exactly the same as it was on the evening of April 14, 1865. It is once again a theater, one of several stages for drama and music in the nation's capital. By day it is also a stop on the sightseeing circuit. In the basement the National Park Service operates the Lincoln Museum. Booth's nasty little derringer is on display, as is his diary with the mysterious pages still missing. The riding boot that Dr. Mudd cut from Booth's broken left leg stands in a glass display case. Virtually all the physical evidence in the case can be found here. One might expect that, after more than one hundred years, this collection could be of little value in shedding any new light on the mysteries surrounding the Lincoln assassination. But, as you will see, one item served to settle the most important question that can be asked about the Cosgrove manuscript.

Many of the discoveries Cosgrove reports regarding the circumstances of the assassination are confirmed by other disclosures made after the dates of his investigation. Other claims Cosgrove makes are not fully supported by such collateral historical evidence, but they are at least consistent with such records. But a few of Cosgrove's assertions remain entirely unsupported by other historical records; in a few instances, they contradict it. Therefore I have delineated the boundary between Cosgrove and history by interlarding the narrative with footnotes.

A few additional footnotes were needed to explain some of Cosgrove's references or locutions, which were current in 1868 or at the time the manuscript was written, but have since become obscure.

Such copious footnoting may distract the reader, and I apologize for it. However, I have assumed the reader would rather be distracted occasionally than baffled continually. Thus the frequent footnotes seem a necessary evil.

In trying to establish the authenticity of the manuscript, and the veracity of Cosgrove's report, I have drawn on the vast body of literature that has been written about the Lincoln assassination and the other events recounted in this narrative. I have included a bibliography of those books and other documents which are particularly relevant to Cosgrove's account.

I have saved my findings regarding the Cosgrove Report, and present them in an Afterword. Thus the reader is free to draw his own conclusions as he follows the narrative without being burdened or biased by my own.

The publishers favored revising the spelling of the Cosgrove manuscript to conform to presently accepted forms. In general this has been done, but I have persuaded the editors to retain the original spelling of a few words and so preserve a measure of the manuscript's antique charm. I trust this will not confuse the reader.

I'll say no more for now, but let the author of the Cosgrove Report speak for himself.

The True Account of a Confidential Inquiry
by Pinkerton's National Detective Agency
into the Circumstances of the Assassination of
President Abraham Lincoln
BY NICHOLAS COSGROVE

And now I will unclasp a secret book,
And to your quick-conceiving discontents
I'll read you matter deep and dangerous . . .
I Henry IV, ACT I, SCENE 3.

PART ONE

John Wilkes Booth, Dead or Alive

War Department Washington, April 20, 1865,

$100,000 REWARD

THE MURDERER

Of our late beloved President, Abraham Lincoln,

IS STILL AT LARGE.

$50,000 REWARD

Will be paid by this Department for his apprehension, in addition to any reward offered by Municipal Authorities or State Executives.

$25,000 REWARD

Will be paid for the apprehension of JOHN H. SURRATT, one of Booth's Accomplices.

$25,000 REWARD

Will be paid for the apprehension of David C. Harold, another of Booth's accomplices.

LIBERAL REWARDS will be paid for any information that shall conduce to the arrest of either of the above-named criminals, or their accomplices.

All persons harboring or secreting the said persons, or either of them, or aiding or abetting their concealment or escape, will be treated as accomplices in the murder of the President and the attempted assassination of the Secretary of State, and shall be subject to trial before a Military Commission and the punishment of DEATH.

Let the stain of innocent blood be removed from the land by the arrest and punishment of the murderers.

All good citizens are exhorted to aid public justice on this occasion. Every man should consider his own conscience charged with this solemn duty, and rest neither night nor day until it be accomplished.

EDWIN M. STANTON, Secretary of War.

DESCRIPTIONS.—BOOTH is Five Feet 7 or 8 inches high, slender build, high forehead, black hair, black eyes, and wears a heavy black moustache.

JOHN H. SURRATT is about 5 feet, 9 inches. Hair rather thin and dark; eyes rather light; no beard. Would weigh 145 or 150 pounds. Complexion rather pale and clear, with color in his cheeks. Wore light clothes of fine quality. Shoulders square; cheek bones rather prominent; chin narrow; ears projecting at the top; forehead rather low and square, but broad. Parts his hair on the right side; neck rather long. His lips are firmly set. A slim man.

HAROLD is a little slimmer, about quite a youth, and wears a very thin moustache.

· 1 ·

A Mystery Is Exhumed

I find myself in a strange world. The century in which I was pleased to reside for a matter of some sixty-five years is gone, like some mammoth steamship sunk to the bottom of the sea. The stately halls and ballrooms are hidden forever in the ocean depths, and live on only in the minds of survivors, such as myself. From time to time, books of memoirs appear, bits of flotsam broken free of the wreck that float to the surface. But soon even this decay will be complete, and the rusting hulk will have no more messages to send the world above. So, if ever I am to put in my own motto, I suppose the moment has arrived.

Unlike many of my fellow survivors, I write of events past not to celebrate my own importance as a witness to history. Rather, I write out of duty, and most reluctantly. I cannot take to my grave the Truth of which Chance and Fate have made me custodian. The late century was crowded with events that will bend the course of history for scores of generations to come, yet the true meaning of the most momentous act of those hundred years remains hidden. I seek only to lift the veil that enshrouds it. Thus, in adding to the growing burden of public reminiscences of the recently departed era, I have limited myself to an account of events that transpired during a period of only eighteen months, which began for me just outside New York Harbor on the bright, crisp morning of March 21, 1868.

I was aboard the *City of New London,* returning from a seven-month sojourn in England and the Continent. As the steamer waited a few miles south of Fire Island Light for the appearance of a New York Harbor pilot boat, I had a leisurely breakfast with my traveling companion, the cashier of a large New York bank. We shared this repast, not in the ship's dining room, as we had our other meals, but in the cargo hold. The man required some assistance with his knife and fork because, at my request, the master-at-arms had placed him in irons the previous night.

The banker had been the occasion for my European venture. He had absconded some eight months earlier with a large sum of his employer's cash. The bank retained Pinkerton's National Detective Agency, which it was then my honor to serve, and I was set onto the trail of the errant cashier. I tracked my quarry to Toronto and from there to Halifax, from whence he had boarded a steamer bound for Liverpool. The trail became warm when he bounded to Edinburgh, since an American is even less a Scot than he is an Englishman. When I flushed him from there to Paris, he was as good as caught, for he spoke not a word of French. Neither was he conversant with the celebrated wines of that country, and he failed to taste the few drops of chloroform that had been added to the glass of champagne served him by an avaricious lady in a Marseilles bordello. But when he awoke to the rhythmic pulsing of the *New London*'s engines as they churned Mediterranean water some hours later, he found himself once more among his countrymen.

He was moderately philosophical about his fate, however, not the least reason for which was his excellent position to negotiate a degree of clemency from the authorities. The majority of his booty remained unspent in banks from Toronto to Paris, and his cooperation in the recovery of these sums would save his former employer some considerable inconvenience. In making my hurried special arrangements for passage with the captain of the *New London,* I stipulated that my prisoner could have the freedom of the ship when it was out of sight of land. Until we rounded South Shoal lightship, the banker had worn irons only once before, when we stopped at Liverpool and I went ashore to cable ahead to Pinkerton's in New York.

The esteemed George Bangs, head of Pinkerton's New York Office, was surely waiting at dockside with a brace of New York policemen to take charge of the prisoner. Bangs would be there in person in anticipation of meeting the mysterious Cosgrove; few in the detective agency other than Allan Pinkerton himself knew my face, a precaution I forced on Mr. Pinkerton as a condition of my employment after the death of Timothy Webster. Tim, with whom I served in the New York constabulary before we both joined Pinkerton's prior to the War, was betrayed to the Confederates by a cowardly fellow detective and hanged. Since then, I have refused to be photographed, mastered the art of disguise and insisted that no one but Mr. Pinkerton himself should know my countenance. George Bangs was to be no exception. I sent for a porter to take my luggage on deck as soon as the sails of the pilot boat were sighted through the morning mists.

The schooner *James Funk* luffed to under our quarter, and launched a small boat. Some minutes later a man in a black suit and top hat climbed on deck and was handed up a small valise and a sheaf of papers. As I prepared to take his place in the boat for the trip back to the schooner, he stopped me.

"Mr. Nichols?" he asked, using the pseudonym with which I sign my reports.

I nodded, and he handed me a telegram, then went on about his business. I climbed into the boat, and as the seamen cast off from the *New London,* I ran a thumbnail beneath the flap of the envelope. The message was terse and emphatic:

TO: C. N. Nichols, aboard the *City of New London:*
      Urgent you join me in court.

                                              E. J. Allen

"E. J. Allen" was Mr. Pinkerton's favorite *nom de guerre,* which he had adopted while serving as General McClellan's Chief of Intelligence during the War. The "court" was a code word meaning Washington City. Since he hadn't specified otherwise, I knew that Mr. Pinkerton meant I should meet him at a certain house on K Street. The "urgent" was unnecessary; the pains that had been taken to deliver the message to me on the high seas was a most eloquent announcement that, whatever the reason for the summons, time was of the essence.

A brisk March wind filled the schooner's sails, and well before noon we had tied up amidst the forest of masts and smokestacks at the foot of Wall Street. A uniformed officer from the nearby Customs House inspected my luggage on the pier, and within twenty minutes I was walking through the crowded lobby of the Astor House, where I maintained a suite of rooms on a permanent basis. I stopped only long enough to pack a fresh valise and settle my accounts with the bewildered room clerk before hailing a cab to take me to the ferry landing at the foot of Cortlandt Street. I reached the railroad station in Jersey City with time enough to send a telegraph ahead to Mr. Pinkerton before boarding the noon train for Washington City.†

The cars were somewhat crowded, which was as well, since the human heat greatly abetted the work of the cast-iron coal stoves in driving off a late winter chill that had descended over the Jersey marshlands. Toward the front of the car I had selected, I recognized a cardsharp and his shill busily engaged in a game of three-card monte, before a fascinated audience of prospective pigeons. Before the sharp could glance up, I moved back to the next car and took a seat beside a well-dressed but gaunt man who seemed absorbed in a late morning edition of the New York *Sun*. Whatever he was reading seemed to disagree with him, or he with it, for he soon began to recite a *sotto voce* litany of sighs, exclamations and mutterings. Finally he cast the newspaper down and exclaimed, "The cowardly scoundrel!"

It was not clear whether this remark was addressed to me or to himself. I turned to him, lifted an eyebrow, and begged his pardon. He struck the folded newspaper with the back of his hand as though it were a despised adversary.

"The Great Criminal, Andrew Johnson," he said. "By this account he means to cower in the White House on Monday, instead of facing the bar of justice like a man."

My face betrayed my puzzlement.

"Can it be you haven't heard that Judas Johnson is to be tried in the Senate for high crimes and misdemeanors?" he asked.

---

† Until the railroad tunnels linking Manhattan with New Jersey were put into operation in 1909, travelers going by rail from New York City to Washington, D.C., had to make the first leg of their journey by water.—M.C.

The matter had received little notice in the European press, and the press had received scant attention from myself, busy as I was in pursuit of the errant banker. I knew almost nothing of the matter, beyond the meaning of the word "impeachment," which I looked up when I first heard it some months earlier.

"I believe I heard something of the sort, but I have only just returned from the Western Territories by sea. I haven't seen an eastern newspaper in weeks."

It transpired that my companion was in the employ of a newspaper, and one familiar to me, the Cincinnati *Gazette.* His name was Reed, and he was on his way to Washington to report on the Impeachment Trial, an assignment which he seemed to find eminently agreeable.† It struck me that the coming hours of enforced confinement with this student of political science provided me a splendid opportunity to come up to date on events in Washington City, and perhaps lend me some clew to the reason for Mr. Pinkerton's summons.

I introduced myself to my companion as Charles Nichols, a traveling canvasser for Hostetter Stomachic Bitters, a popular nostrum of the time.

"A wineglass full of these bitters taken three times a day is a certain cure for dyspepsia," I recited as I took a bottle of the product from my valise, drew the cork and offered it to the journalist. "It improves the appetite, prevents fever and ague, and removes all flatulency."

"Would that it could remove that flatulent Tennessee tailor from the White House and so spare the country the task of trying him," said Reed, after taking a long pull from the vessel.

Whatever else Dr. Hostetter added to his bitters, one part in four was pure grain alcohol, a fact that I, along with thousands of my comrades, discovered during the War. I cannot say whether the potion truly aided digestion, but I had often observed its effectiveness in loosening the tongue. And my disguise as a purveyor of the bitters

---

† Cosgrove's traveling companion was undoubtedly Whitelaw Reid. It is surprising that the author seems not to recognize him, since he later became editor of the New York *Tribune* and one of the most prominent journalists of his period.—M.C.

provided a natural occasion to administer it when the need for such loosening arose. But no hidden motive lay behind the hospitality I offered Mr. Reed, for it was clear even before the spirits reached his brain that he was making ready to deliver a disquisition on the high crimes and misdemeanors that had led to the impeachment of President Andrew Johnson.

The specific offense that led to the Great Criminal's impeachment, my companion explained, was his attempt to remove the Secretary of War in defiance of the wishes of the Senate. This was a brazen violation of the Tenure of Office Act, which had been passed only a year earlier by Congress. The act decreed that public officials appointed with the advice and consent of the Senate could only be discharged in the same manner. After the Senate voted thirty-five to six against the dismissal of Secretary Edwin McMasters Stanton, Johnson abandoned the rule of law that governs civilized men and sent one of his lackeys to evict the Secretary from the War Department. But, while this was the final outrage, the journalist declaimed, it was by no means the only one, or even the worst.

I do not involve myself in politics, but even I was aware of the ill will between the President and Congress that had been festering for more than a year. Andy Johnson was a Southerner, but never a Rebel. A man of humble origins who had earned his bread with his hands, he hated and resented the aristocratic leaders of the Old South. When the War came, he was serving in Congress, the Senator from Tennessee, but he resigned his seat to accept a commission as Brigadier General and Military Governor of Tennessee. He yielded to no man in his hatred of the Confederacy, and when he was nominated as President Lincoln's running mate in June, 1864, Senator Sumner of Massachusetts wished the ticket could be stood upon its head, with Johnson in the prime place. Sumner was one of the Radical Republicans who demanded the South be shown no mercy. But, ironically, he was one of the leaders of the pack now calling for the President's scalp.

Indeed, the Radical Republicans' displeasure with Andy Johnson was only a sequel to the umbrage inspired in them by President Lincoln, who looked upon the defeated Secessionists as strayed sheep returned to the fold. When Johnson suddenly ascended to the presidency, Sumner and his fellows believed this Rebel-hater would help them realize their dreams of plunder and vengeance. But within two months those dreams were shattered, when President Johnson ordered complete amnesty and pardon to hundreds of thousands of Confederate soldiers, and stipulated surprisingly mild terms for the reconstruction of North Carolina.

It was the first shot in the war between Andy Johnson and the Radicals. During the next three years he would be accused of everything from entreating with the enemy while Military Governor of Tennessee to conspiring with Booth in the murder of President Lincoln. In the end it would come down to the question of the President's power to discharge Edwin McMasters Stanton, the only ally of the Radicals within Johnson's cabinet. The articles of impeachment had been voted in the House of Representatives, and the Senate trial was to commence on Monday. The Washington City toward which we sped through that waning March afternoon was a city divided; a full battalion of troops stood guard at the War Department, where Secretary Stanton was completing his thirtieth day of continuous occupancy. In the White House, the five lawyers who would defend the President in the Impeachment Trial conferred with their client. Throughout the city rumors spread of Rebel sympathizers placing explosives in public buildings. There was intrigue enough for an army of secret detectives to deal with.

By the time Mr. Reed had completed his account of these matters in far greater detail than I have repeated here, we had gone through the cities of Philadelphia and Wilmington, as well as three bottles of Hostetter's Bitters. My companion discovered the medicine to be a most agreeable tonic, and had consumed the larger portion. As we departed the depot in Baltimore on the last leg of our journey, he was snoring in close harmony with the whistle of the steam engine that drew us toward our troubled capital.

The countryside through which we passed was now in the grip of a winter storm, and a thick curtain of snow dimmed the lights of the occasional farmhouse standing off in the early evening darkness. It was past ten o'clock when I felt the train slow to a crawl as it passed the city limits of Washington. I took out my watch and set it back twelve minutes.† Shortly I glimpsed the lights of the Capitol through the car window as we approached the old Baltimore and Ohio station at the foot of Capitol Hill. Leaving my traveling companion where he slumbered, I arose, picked up my valise and stepped out onto the rear balcony. It was a cloudy, moonless night and a few flakes of snow still fell, but the light coming from within the car illuminated the roadbed on either side of the train. We had slowed to the pace of a fast walk. I climbed down the steps and jumped to the ground, then made my way across the tracks to C Street. He who seeks to obscure his comings and goings is well advised to avoid railroad stations.

Some hundred yards from the station I found a young Negro lad dozing at the reins of a covered carriage parked just beyond the flickering aureole cast by a nearby street lamp. It was Patch, a footman in the K Street household of a close friend of Mr. Pinkerton. I wakened him and climbed into the vehicle.

Washington City had changed since the War. Gone were the throngs of soldiers, camp followers and peddlers who crowded the capital. It seemed that more of the streets had been lighted, but Pennsylvania Avenue, along which the carriage rattled, remained one of the few thoroughfares to have been paved. Just past the gas-lit facade of the White House, the War Department was bathed in torchlight. True to Mr. Reed's report, the building was ringed by armed sentries. We turned onto 17th Street, and the team slowed as the carriage wheels sank into the mud.

My journey ended in the doorway of a stately three-story mansion on K Street, where I was met by Mr. Pinkerton, himself. He solemnly shook my hand and ushered me into a sitting room at the front of the house. The drapes had been drawn across the windows, and Mr. Pinkerton quickly glanced about the empty vestibule before pulling

---

† In 1868 local time in Washington, D.C., was twelve minutes behind New York City time. The relative times of most major cities were published along with the timetables in the railway guides then in use, but to an experienced traveler such as Cosgrove, the adjustment of his watch would have been a nearly automatic action.—M.C.

shut the pair of doors separating it from our chamber. He strode across the room, seated himself and bid me do the same. When he spoke it was in hushed tones calculated to carry not even so far as the ornately papered walls.

"Thank you for your promptness, Nicholas. I feared ye would not arrive until the morrow."

When tired or anxious, Mr. Pinkerton tended to lapse into the idiom and accents of his native Scotland. I could see the fatigue engraved in his face, and he told me he had only just arrived that morning by rail from Iowa, where he and his son William had pursued the notorious Reno gang. He was nearing fifty, and a few flecks of gray had appeared in his black spatulate beard; soon he would have to leave such exploits to younger men. I waited for him to announce the occasion of our respective summonses to the capital.

"It is a very delicate business that we are about, Nicholas. I must ask your solemn word that you will never speak of it after it is done."

"You have it," I said.

"For my part, I have been forbidden even to instruct you in the particulars of the case. Those you must learn directly from our client, whom you will meet in a few moments. A word of caution before we join him: While we shall, of course, serve the man with complete loyalty in this matter, you are to tell him nothing of whatever you happen to know of any other case now under investigation by the Agency."

"Certainly not, sir!" I exclaimed, somewhat indignantly. "I believe that goes without saying."

Mr. Pinkerton gazed wearily at me.

"Of course, Nicholas. But you will see that this is a most uncommon case, with a most uncommon client. And circumstances have unavoidably put us in great jeopardy of being thought double-dealers."

He clapped his hands on his knees and arose.

"Come," he said. "You shall meet our client."

I followed Mr. Pinkerton upstairs to the second floor, where he stopped at the first of several doors facing the balustrade, and knocked. A man in an Army major's uniform opened the door and bid us enter. Inside, two junior officers were warming themselves at a fireplace in the corner, while behind a small oaken desk, a man in civilian attire was scribbling intently. As we entered, he put down his pen, carefully sanded the fresh ink, and summoned one of the lieutenants from the fire.

"See that this is in Congressman Butler's hands within the hour," he said, dismissing the officer and turning to us. As he arose his face emerged from the shadow and into the light cast from the chimney of the desk lamp. It was a countenance that bespoke great intelligence, as well as a kind of righteous intensity. There was, too, a bit of the middle-aged schoolmaster about the man, a quality that found amplification in the pair of spectacles that rested astride the bridge of his nose. His upper lip was clean-shaven, but a full beard cascaded halfway down his chest. It was a face I had seen countless times but never before in person. It was that of Edward McMasters Stanton, Secretary of War and eye of the political storm that now raged over Washington.

"You may leave us, now, gentlemen," he said to the major and the remaining subaltern. "Wait downstairs, but don't show yourselves unnecessarily in the street. We do not wish to advertise that the Secretary of War is away from the War Department."

When the officers had departed, the Secretary bid us be seated and began to read from a sheaf of papers he had picked from the desk. His eyes darted quickly over the documents, which seemed to pertain to me, for he repeatedly interrupted his reading in order to direct a quick glance in my direction. It took him but a minute or so to scan his way to the last sheet. He replaced the sheaf on the desk and turned to me.

"So you are to be our bloodhound, eh, Mr. Cosgrove? Tell me, how many men have you tracked down in your career?"

"I haven't kept count, Mr. Secretary," I replied. "About a score or so of those who'd never learned to hide. And perhaps half a dozen of those who had."

"Ah, yes," he said, "the sheep must not be counted with the foxes." He glanced at the topmost paper on his desk.

"During the War, you were chief of reconnaissance in Cincinnati, were you not?" he asked.

I paused.

"I'm sure the War Department's records of my service are correct, sir," I replied.

Mr. Stanton smiled slightly.

"Very good. Loquacity is not a desirable characteristic in a secret detective. I hope you will be equally taciturn regarding your involvement in this affair."

"He has been told nothing of the assignment yet," interjected Mr. Pinkerton.

Mr. Stanton nodded. He twisted a strand of his beard between thumb and forefinger and stared abstractedly for some moments at a point in space somewhere above my head. Finally he spoke.

"We have a fox for you this time, Mr. Cosgrove. Not a sheep, but a fox. He is skilled in the crafts of the secret agent, for he served the Confederacy in that capacity during the War. Like yourself, he is a master of the art of theatrical makeup, and can change his appearance at will. He can play almost any role he chooses, for he once was one of the most celebrated actors of our time. I thought him dead until recently, and I'm still not absolutely convinced I was wrong. But if he lives, you must find him and lead us to him. Here is one of his faces."

He passed a *carte de visite* across the desk. I held it up to the lamplight and instantly recognized the face, but I remained staring at the picture for what must have been near a full minute. Somehow, I thought, my eyes or brain were tricking me, and the man in the photograph was someone other than the person every detail of his physiognomy insisted he was. I looked to the Secretary and Mr. Pinkerton. There was not the trace of a smile on either of their countenances. I had no doubt they were in deadly earnest. And I was equally certain the face in the photograph belonged to John Wilkes Booth.

"I am sorry, gentlemen," I said, "but I do not understand this."

"Undoubtedly," commented the Secretary. "Your astonishment is perfectly natural. You, as did I, believe that Booth has been in his grave these past three years. But I have lately come into information suggesting otherwise."

"And what information is that?" I asked.

Stanton held up his hand, as if to ward off the question.

"That I cannot say. It comes from a highly confidential source, and a man of your profession will understand that such sources must sometimes remain anonymous. All I can tell you is the source is too reliable to warrant dismissing the report out of hand."

"You may recollect, Nicholas," Mr. Pinkerton interposed, "that at the time of the unfortunate business, there were rumors that the man taken at Garrett's Farm was not Booth."

"The sensationalist press made that charge," said the Secretary. "The Rebels wanted to believe it. They required a living hero to serve as a rallying point. Thus we could ill afford to give voice to our own doubts."

"Then you doubted the body was Booth?" I asked.

"I did not personally view the remains," the Secretary said, with a faint shudder, "but I was told they bore little resemblance to the man in life. You must understand that Booth had suffered the privations of a fugitive who had spent a fortnight in the wilderness, and a full day passed after his death before the body was brought to this city. Is it so remarkable, then, that the corpse did not appear to be Booth?

"I ordered Judge Holt to hold an inquest. He did his best to ascertain the dead man's identity, and obtained the testimony of a physician who had treated Booth. The surgeon said the corpse was his patient."

"Yet you remain uncertain," I said.

The Secretary shrugged and sighed.

"We cannot afford to exclude the possibility that they were mistaken. If Booth lives, I mean to know. How do you propose to begin your investigation?"

"By opening the grave of John Wilkes Booth, if I can learn where it may be," I replied.†

---

† The location of Booth's grave had been withheld from the public by the War Department for several years, presumably to prevent it from becoming a shrine to those who considered Booth a hero. However, Secretary Stanton had publicly revealed the general location of the gravesite on August 15, 1867. Cosgrove's ignorance of this may be attributable to his absence from the country in pursuit of the errant banker, which began about that date.—M.C.

A very strange expression came over Mr. Stanton's countenance. I would not have raised the question of exhumation so bluntly had I known then what I learned later. The Secretary suffered from a morbid mania regarding the dead. He was simultaneously obsessed with corpses and terrified of them. After his little daughter Lucy died many years earlier, he had her coffin exhumed and kept it in his room for two years. And when his brother took his own life, Stanton bolted from the funeral procession and ran madly through the woods, where he was overtaken and forcibly restrained by the other mourners who thought him bent on his own suicide.†

The Secretary's discomposure at my reply was momentary, and in a few seconds he regained his equanimity.

"I fail to see what you hope to learn from a corpse that's been in its grave for three years, that was not discovered by Judge Holt when the body was merely one day dead," he said.

"Perhaps the corpse has nothing more to tell us, but we may hope to find some clew in the grave. Tell me, please, the boot that Dr. Mudd cut from the broken leg of Booth—where is it now?"

"Why, it is in the custody of the Department of War," the Secretary replied. "It was entered as evidence in the trial of the conspirators."

"And where lies its mate?" I asked.

Secretary Stanton stared blankly back at me for a moment, then I saw comprehension dawning in his eyes. He thrust a balled fist into an open palm.

"Of course!" he exclaimed. "Booth was buried wearing the same clothes in which he was taken. If the body in the grave is truly Booth, it should wear one riding boot, the mate of the one we hold at the War Department."

"A brilliant observation, Nicholas," said Mr. Pinkerton proudly. "We must exhume the body tomorrow."

---

† In yet another incident, when Stanton was managing a Columbus, Ohio, bookstore in 1833, his landlady's daughter died of cholera and was immediately buried. On returning home and hearing of it, he could not believe the child was dead. To convince himself, he went to the cemetery and exhumed the body, then reburied it. Throughout his life Stanton suffered from intense headaches and asthma, which may have been symptoms of a deeper emotional illness.—M.C.

"No," countered the Secretary. "We must do so immediately! If Booth is not in his grave, I mean to know it tonight."

Secretary Stanton summoned the two officers waiting downstairs. The Major was dispatched in our host's carriage to the War Department to retrieve the boot. The Secretary, Mr. Pinkerton, the Lieutenant and I crowded into the Secretary's carriage and set out for the grave site, which, Mr. Stanton revealed, was in the Old Washington Arsenal Penitentiary.†

The Arsenal stood on Greenleaf's Point, the southern-most extremity of the Federal City, at the confluence of the Potomac River with the Eastern Branch.‡ It was within the grim stone walls of the compound that Booth's fellow conspirators were held and tried, and it was in the prison yard that four of them were buried, but a few feet from the place where they were hanged. It was a fitting spot for the grave of the assassin.

As we drew up before the ominous pile, we were challenged by a sentry. The Lieutenant stepped down and spoke with the man, while the Secretary, Mr. Pinkerton and I remained out of view in the carriage. Presently the Commandant appeared, apparently summoned from his bed. He was buttoning his uniform tunic and swearing softly as the Lieutenant escorted him to the carriage door.

"Who the hell are you?" he demanded. "And what are you doing here at this hour? It's the middle of the goddamn night."

The Lieutenant raised a lantern to the doorway, momentarily filling the coach with light. The Commandant snapped to attention as he met the Secretary's cold stare, and babbled a confused apology. Mr. Stanton made no response to this, but simply ordered the officer in frigid tones to enter the coach and be seated.

"I am here on a matter of utmost secrecy," the Secretary said. "No word of this visit is ever to pass your lips. To speak of it will be regarded as treason and punished accordingly. Your men are not to learn of the reason for this visit or the identity of the visitors. Therefore I

---

† The Arsenal no longer stands. Today the site is Fort Lesley J. McNair.—M.C.
‡ Now known as the Anacostia river.

shall require you to escort us personally to the place where the assassin Booth is buried, and to provide us with picks and shovels."

I could not see the Commandant's expression in the darkness. He sat in silence for a moment, then stammered his assent and stepped from the carriage. I heard the rasp of massive hinges and the coach lurched into motion. From the echoes that marked our progress I knew we had entered within the Arsenal walls.

Holding a lantern to light our way, the Commandant led us across the yard and into a forbidding dungeon. We stumbled after him through a labyrinth of narrow stone corridors sunk in a pitchy blackness relieved only by our escort's swaying lantern. Finally he stopped before a cast-iron door set into the stone. He drew the bolt and we followed him within.

It was a large, windowless room filled with kegs of gunpowder, boxes of ammunition, and the dank smell of earth. The Commandant hung his lantern from a wall hook and cautioned us regarding the explosives stored in the chamber. Then, with the help of the Lieutenant and myself, he cleared a pile of powder kegs from one corner.

"Here he lies, sir," he said. "Beneath this stone floor."

He lit a taper from the lantern flame and left us, returning in a few minutes bearing a pick and spade on his shoulder.

"Very well," said the secretary. "Now, return to the gate and wait there. A Major Harrison will arrive presently. Show him here. See to the matter yourself. Do not appoint a subordinate to do it."

It fell to the Lieutenant and myself, as the youngest and most junior members of the party, to do the digging. The most difficult task was the removal of the paving stones covering the grave. Each was of an enormous weight and required much effort to move. Beneath, the earth, petrified by the winter cold, resisted the thrusts of pick and spade. The Lieutenant and I took turns at the work. I was resting when the Major arrived.

Mr. Stanton examined the historic boot, then passed it to the rest of us for inspection. It was a cavalry-style boot designed to reach midway between hip and knee. Apart from the cut Dr. Mudd had made to remove it from his patient, it was in excellent repair. The boot was of superb workmanship, and I was certain its mate could survive a century or more in the ground.

We were interrupted by a cry from the Lieutenant, who was standing knee deep in the freshly dug pit.

"Here it is," he called out.

I stepped down into the depression and, using my bare hands, helped him to clear the earth from around the box. Booth's coffin was a wooden gun case. His name had been scratched on the cover. The Lieutenant and I lifted it from the shallow grave and placed it on the stone floor. As I wiped the earth from my hands, Mr. Stanton took the lantern from the wall and raised it over the box. A strange excitement shone in his eyes.

"Open it quickly, if you will, Mr. Cosgrove," he said.

Using the tip of the spade, I prized up the cover at each corner of the box. The coffin nails shrieked their protest. I lifted the cover from the case and set it upon the floor. Mr. Pinkerton and the Secretary edged forward and looked down into the box. Except for a few heavy stones, it was empty. Mr. Stanton stared at the coffin in horror.

"He lives." It was barely more than a whisper. He handed me the lantern.

"Bury it again," he commanded. "No one else must learn of this."

Abruptly, he stepped to the door of the ammunition room. The Major held a torch aloft and opened the iron portal for him. Mr. Stanton turned and looked back at me.

"Find him, Mr. Cosgrove. Find him and lead me to him."

Then, followed by the Major, he disappeared into the dark labyrinth beyond.

·2·

A Five-Cent Clew

"Aye, find the man. Find the man at all costs," said Mr. Pinkerton. "But it will be a bonnie trick for ye, Nicholas—to winkle out a trail as cold as the sod over that empty grave."

The gates of the Arsenal were shut behind us, and the snow had begun to fall again as we rode up 4½ Street in the brougham which awaited our convenience, Major Harrison having departed with Mr. Stanton in the Secretary's carriage. My chief's words were only an echo of my own melancholy reflections, but, as we were knee-to-knee with the young Lieutenant who shared the carriage, I held my tongue until we were delivered to the house on K Street. There, in the privacy of the parlor that had been the scene of our earlier conference, I confessed to Mr. Pinkerton that, for the nonce, I had not the vaguest plan of how to proceed with the task of searching for the assassin.

"You may recall, sir," I said, "that at the time of the tragedy I was abroad, and did not return to these shores until some months later.† As a consequence, I recollect only the most general facts of the case as I read them in the foreign press. It is not quite the same as though I'd been in Cincinnati or New Orleans‡ where I could read the dispatches . . ."

---

† Partial deciphering of Cosgrove's diary for the period January through August, 1865, confirms that he was in England and France, engaged in the apparently successful thwarting of the Confederacy's last-ditch attempt to secure more substantial aid from the governments of those countries.—M.C.

‡ After General McClellan's dismissal in 1862, Allan Pinkerton spent the duration of the War operating from New Orleans.—M.C.

"Of course, Nicholas, I had forgotten," Mr. Pinkerton interjected. "And had you been within reach when the hunt for Booth was on, I would not have squandered you in the reading of dispatches, and that box buried beneath the Arsenal would not be empty tonight."

I thanked my chief for this generous compliment, omitting to add that I would have much preferred the honor of being charged with catching Booth when the murder was but hours or even days old; but to be set upon the trail of a professional imposter who'd been permitted a three-year head start was the kind of tacit praise that could well prove my undoing. It was flattering to have been made legendary as a hunter of men, yet the price of such fame was to live up to the legend. He who aspires to the status of legend is well advised to arrange for such aspirations to be consummated posthumously. If Mr. Pinkerton had promised the Secretary of War that I would produce John Wilkes Booth, then it was my lot to chew that which I myself would have hesitated to bite off.

The day had been a long one, and I had taken no nourishment since my breakfast aboard the *New London*. Rather than awaken the household staff, I sought out the pantry and made myself a cold supper from the provender to be found there. As I ate, Mr. Pinkerton recounted some of the particulars of the pursuit and capture of Booth as he recalled them from War Department dispatches and accounts in the public press at the time.†

Within minutes after the assassination, Booth had coursed through the streets of Washington City, crossed the Navy Yard Bridge and was in Maryland. There he rendezvoused with David Herold, a young drugstore clerk and faithful follower of the actor. The pair fled down the road to Surrattsville, and there stopped to procure additional firearms and a supply of spirituous drink, the latter to

---

† Pinkerton's detective force was almost the only unit of its kind that was not involved in the hunt for Booth. Pinkerton himself didn't even learn of the assassination until he read of it in the New Orleans newspapers on April 19, five days after the event. He immediately wired Secretary Stanton, placing his entire detective force at the Secretary's disposal. In his reply Stanton merely asked Pinkerton to "watch the Western Rivers" for Booth, opining that the assassin might be headed for Texas or Mexico.—M.C.

bolster their courage and serve as anodyne to the pain which now assailed the assassin's broken limb.

It was the actor's injury which interrupted their flight and led them in the midst of the night to the door of Dr. Samuel Mudd, a physician of known Secessionist sympathies and, some say, a willing partner in Booth's murderous enterprise. There the pair spent some hours in repose, while Dr. Mudd fashioned a makeshift splint and crutch for Booth, and the physician's wife fed the fugitives and saw to their comforts. Yet the guilty duo knew their pursuers must be close upon their heels. Morning passed, then noon, but before the sun had set, Booth and Herold left the sanctuary of Dr. Mudd's farm and resumed their flight.

For the next nine days, Mr. Pinkerton explained, the pair remained *in perdue,* likely secreting themselves in the dense marshes that abound in that part of southeastern Maryland. A Government reward of $75,000 and a force of some two thousand Army troopers failed to turn up any sign of the fugitives, who had vanished as thoroughly as though they'd been snatched from the face of the earth. It was not until April 24 that the world again saw ought of Booth and Herold.

The pair appeared at Port Conway, Virginia, a fly-blown collection of warehouses huddled about a wharf, which pointed to the more fortunate hamlet of Port Royal, three-quarters of a mile across the Rappahannock River. While awaiting the ferryboat to take them across, they encountered three Confederate soldiers, to whom Herold, with reckless pride, introduced himself and his leader as "the assassinators of the President."

Without hesitation, the Rebels came to the aid of the fugitives, escorting them three miles down the road beyond Port Royal to the farm of Richard H. Garrett, an elderly man of Confederate sympathies, whose elder son had recently returned home from service with a Rebel cavalry unit. Booth and Herold assumed to be Confederate soldiers themselves, and did not disclose their true identities to the old man. Thus the pair were easily welcomed to the sanctuary of Garrett's Farm.

At nearly the very instant when Booth became safely ensconced in the Garrett farmhouse, a detective some seventy miles away was performing that which Mr. Pinkerton described with wry irony as "the greatest feat of deduction, or perhaps clairvoyance, in history." The detective was none other than Colonel (later General) Lafayette C. Baker, a person well known to both Mr. Pinkerton and myself, and a name illy suited to please us. Baker was then chief of the National Executive Police (Secretary Stanton's spy-catchers) and had earned himself the condign reputation of liar, thief, scoundrel and blackguard. The incident which Mr. Pinkerton here recounted was no restorative to his reputation.

Mr. Stanton had summoned Colonel Baker from New York City on the day after the assassination and placed him in charge of the search for Booth. For nine days Colonel Baker seemed singularly incapable of finding any trace of the fugitive. But suddenly, on April 24, on the strength of what he claimed to be sheer deduction, he summoned his deputies to his headquarters opposite Willard's Hotel and, spreading a map of Virginia upon his desk, drew a circle of ten miles radius around the town of Port Conway. Within that circle, said Baker, Booth would be found. It was, he said, "a sure thing."

It was a sure thing, Mr. Pinkerton agreed, but no feat of deduction. More likely the detective chief had obtained the intelligence from one of his informers, and carefully husbanded it until he could insure that the credit for the capture would go to none other than his detective force, and a large share of the reward money would be destined for his own pockets. Even the princely sum offered for Booth and Herold would come to very little if it must needs be shared with many of the two thousand troopers who had been dispatched for the search.

Late in the afternoon of the same day on which Colonel Baker received his inspiration, he dispatched a force of twenty-five cavalrymen, an officer, and a pair of his detectives to Port Conway. They traveled down the Potomac River aboard a tug to Belle Plain, and continued overland from there, arriving at the Rappahannock town the next morning. In Port Conway the detectives were told by the ferryman of the three Confederate soldiers and their two companions who had crossed the river on the previous day. The boatman chanced to know one of the soldiers, and that he might be found in Bowling Green, a town several miles south of Port Royal. The cavalry squad crossed the river and sped on to Port Royal, and presently had the hapless Rebel in custody. They swiftly prized the information they needed from the man, and, in the small hours of April 26, the cavalry squad had surrounded the barn at Garrett's Farm, wherein, they had been told, Booth and Herold were hiding.

The detectives called to the pair to come out. Presently David Herold emerged, Mr. Pinkerton recounted, but Booth, if it was Booth, refused. Baker's men then put a torch to the building.

The walls of the barn were loosely boarded and riddled with knotholes, and it was through these apertures the remaining occupant could be glimpsed by the light of the flames. And it was through one such hole that a cavalry sergeant, in defiance of orders, fired his revolver, striking down the man within. The detectives rushed into the burning barn and dragged the fellow out.

The bullet had passed through the victim's neck, entering below the right ear, smashing three vertebrae, and emerging on the left side. The detectives believed the wound to be mortal, although the man was still breathing. They were likewise convinced the dying man was none other than John Wilkes Booth. Whatever his name, said Mr. Pinkerton, he passed from this world as the sun rose on the morning of April 26.

The dying man regained his sense for a time, but said few words, none of which added to what was already known of the assassination of President Lincoln. Some commentary he had penned regarding his appalling act was contained in a small notebook found on his person, however. As dawn and the man's final breath approached, one of Baker's detectives took this diary, together with weapons and other items found in his possession, and departed in haste for Washington City, there to deliver news of the capture and death of Booth to his chief.

The cavalry squad, with their dead prize and their live prisoner, followed presently, arriving at the Potomac port of Belle Plain early that same evening. From thence they returned upriver aboard the tug that had brought them downstream two days earlier. The craft was intercepted midway by another tug, which had been commandeered by Colonel Baker on learning of the capture. Herold and the corpse were transferred to Baker's boat, and the detective chief delivered his prizes to the monitor *Montauk,* which was anchored in the Eastern Branch off the Navy Yard. The body was placed on deck beneath a tarpaulin, while Herold was taken below and placed in irons. It was about two o'clock in the morning of April 27, and the hunt was finished. The only thing yet wanting was an official pronouncement to that effect.

At midmorning an official inquest was held aboard the *Montauk.* Surgeon General Barnes performed the necropsy, while the Army's Judge Advocate General Joseph Holt examined witnesses brought on board to identify the body as that of Booth. These official proceedings were completed before 3:00 P.M., at which time Colonel Baker and his cousin Luther took charge of the remains. They hastily lowered the corpse into a skiff standing alongside the monitor, and made a great show of taking aboard the boat a chain and large iron ball, before casting off and rowing down the Eastern Branch toward the Potomac. The great throng of curious, who had crowded the Navy Yard Dock since news of the dead assassin's whereabouts spread throughout Washington City early that day, was thus impressed that the body of John Wilkes Booth was to be sunk deep in the mud at the bottom of the Potomac River.

However, Colonel Baker and his cousin rowed to a secluded spot along the Potomac shore, waiting there until darkness fell, at which time they brought their boat and its grisly cargo to Greenleaf's Point, and carried the body into the Arsenal Penitentiary, where, in great secrecy, it was buried.

When Mr. Pinkerton had completed this lengthy rehearsal of the pursuit and capture of the President's assassin, he fell silent for a long moment and a look of great sadness spread over his weary countenance.

"It may surprise you, Nicholas," he finally said, "that I can recite so particularly a story in which I, myself, was not a principal. It is, you understand, a case which I am compelled to study repeatedly and with great anguish. You, perhaps better than anyone else, know that their heinous plot was one that could have been within my power to avert. Had you and I been in Washington City in 1865, we could have done as well as did we in Baltimore four years before."†

"The safety of the President's person was the responsibility of the Secretary of War," I replied.‡ "Who should be blamed if he chose to use us for other tasks of grave import? If it was not Mr. Stanton's fault, it was certainly not your own, sir. It was the fortunes of war. Or, to put it plainer, it was bad luck."

"Bad luck, was it?" said Mr. Pinkerton with a weary smile. "Spoken like a true Irishman. And what is that thing you've been worrying these past ten minutes while I've rambled on? A lucky piece?"

While Mr. Pinkerton had been speaking I finished my repast and took from my pocket an item I'd found in the empty box at the Arsenal, the only thing in the makeshift coffin apart from the stones that weighted it. It was a five-cent piece, or a "nickel" as they've come to be called.

"It's from that box I spent the evening digging up and replanting," I said. "And it's small wages for such an arduous job of work."

"A souvenir from the grave of a felon!" Mr. Pinkerton exclaimed. "There's no good luck in such a thing."

"But the felon was not in the grave," I said.

"Then no doubt it is the property of a scoundrel," he said, meaning, of course, General Baker. "In either case it's a poor thing for a lucky piece."

"Perhaps," I replied, "but it may be a great thing for a piece of luck."

I handed him the coin, which I had polished on my sleeve so that the date had become visible. It was 1866.

---

† Pinkerton is here referring to the so-called Baltimore Plot, in which a cabal of Secessionists in Maryland planned and nearly carried out the assassination of President-elect Abraham Lincoln as he passed through Baltimore en route to his first inauguration in February, 1861. Pinkerton's agency detected the conspiracy and succeeded in preventing the murder.—M.C.

‡ Cosgrove may have been offering his own private opinion here, but it happened to be identical to an official opinion tendered by Lincoln's Attorney General, James Speed, in the wake of the assassination.—M.C.

"When that box was planted the nickel in this five-cent piece had yet a year to wait before it met the stamp of the United States Mint.†
If we can learn how it came to be in that grave, perhaps we shall also know how it is that Booth happens not to be."

---

† While Cosgrove could not, of course, have known the precise date in 1866 on which this particular coin was struck, he happens to be correct in this statement. The nickel five-cent piece was created by an Act of Congress on May 16, 1866, nearly thirteen months after the supposed burial of John Wilkes Booth beneath the Old Arsenal Penitentiary.—M.C.

·3·

The Custodian of Military Dispatches

Perhaps. Perhaps not.

Mr. Pinkerton showed me to the room which I had been assigned. Fatigue from the long day's events rendered me near oblivious to the chill which permeated the disused chamber and had even penetrated deep beneath the coverlet and blankets of the fourposter bed. The demand for sleep had become so powerful that I did not tarry to build a fire in the hearth for a little warmth before retiring. Yet before extinguishing the bedside lamp, I paused to examine once again my shiny discovery, the anachronistic five-cent piece that had been where it could not have been. However difficult the task I had been given, this early discovery of an important clew seemed to bode well for my prospects of success in the matter. Cheered by this happy presentiment, I sought and swiftly found repose.

It must surely seem a singular notion that the brain may labor while the body slumbers, but it has often been my experience to awaken with my mind filled by the fruits of mental labors that remained undone when I retired the previous night. The cold, gray Sunday morning of March 22 was one such occasion. The five-cent piece lying on my night table seemed to mock my nocturnal optimism as I now fully perceived its meaning. True, the coin was a valuable clew. But, as of that moment, it proved only one thing: the case was to be even more complex than first I had supposed. Like every coin, this nickel had two sides.

General Baker and his cousin had taken custody of a body and removed it from the *Montauk*. Later, General Baker claimed to have buried the body beneath the prison. Yet later, when the grave was opened, it was found to be empty. Given these data and no other, I could draw a simple conclusion and perceive my initial step. The Bakers knew why the body was missing, how it had been disposed of, and, perhaps, where it was now located. My first task, then, would have been to learn as much from them, through some means. The Bakers would have been the first step on the trail that would lead to Booth.

But now I perceived the constellation of new possibilities that had been bought for the bargain price of five cents. The grave had been opened and resealed since that April midnight three years ago. And what did I know of that exhumation? Why was it performed? Was a body removed, or did the earlier resurrectionist discover the same empty box we had unearthed last night? Alas, I had no answers to these questions. I knew but two things of my predecessor. He had done his work sometime during the past two years. And he was short five cents.

A body that may or may not have been the mortal remains of John Wilkes Booth was taken from the *Montauk.* It was sunk in the mud at the bottom of the Potomac River or otherwise disposed of by the Bakers, or else it was buried in the Arsenal as they claimed, and later removed by persons unknown after at least a year in its grave. At bottom my dilemma was simply this: I had been charged to find a fugitive, yet his trail had been so obscured by time and those who had preceded me, that I did not even know whether to begin my search for the man among the living or the dead.

These melancholy reflections oppressed me as I performed my morning toilet. The view from the window of my room did little to raise my spirits. K Street was encrusted with a thin layer of snow, already somewhat soiled by a few passing carriages, no doubt church-bound at this early Sunday hour. The scene was lit by the gray light of a lowering sky. It was, in sum, a reflection of my own dismal spirits.

I descended to the first floor and discovered the household not yet fully up and about. (I should explain that the house on K Street was the Washington City home of a distinguished gentleman who belonged to the Foreign Service and, at the time of the events herein recounted, resided with his family in one of our major European embassies. He was an old and intimate friend of Mr. Pinkerton, their friendship dating from the days when he, the martyred John Brown, and my chief worked together to aid runaway slaves in their north-ward flight. While serving abroad this gentleman put his house, to-gether with its servant staff, at the disposal of Mr. Pinkerton, who used it as a base of operations on his frequent visits to Washington City. To the immediate neighbors, Mr. Pinkerton was "Mr. Allen," a Chicago merchant whose firm sold a wide range of goods to the Government, and the strangers who, from time to time, visited or stayed at the house on K Street, were customers or business associ-ates. The servants knew better, but not all, of course. But they were trusted retainers of the diplomat's family, and they numbered only five.)

Mr. Pinkerton presently appeared, and we went to the dining room and sat down to a hearty breakfast. The food seemed to restore my flagging spirits, and as Cindy, the housekeeper's daughter, cleared away the dishes, I gave voice to some of the thoughts I'd earlier re-hearsed, in hope of learning my chief's analysis of the case.

"Perhaps," I offered, "this question of the empty grave is a need-less diversion at this stage. After all, the fate of the corpse after it was taken from the *Montauk* is not our client's primary concern. The pivotal matter is the identity of that corpse. If it was truly Booth, the present whereabouts of his bones is a matter of no great consequence. But if it was not Booth, the pursuit of his substitute's remains seems less than a promising means of tracing the living fugitive."

"Perhaps," Mr. Pinkerton agreed. "But you ignore the very im-portant question of motive."

"Motive? Whose motive?" I asked.

"'Whose motive,' indeed," said Mr. Pinkerton. "Consider it well, Nicholas. A body that is supposed to be in a grave is not. Where it truly is may be of less importance than why it is not where it was thought to be. Someone has lied, or someone has robbed a grave; we don't know which, but we know it must be the one or the other. But we have no comprehension of why anyone would do either. The motive behind a crime is often the key to the mystery surrounding it. Until you discover why the body is missing, a large piece of the puzzle is also missing. It may just be the piece that is needed to solve the rest of the puzzle."

Before I had time to reflect on Mr. Pinkerton's observation, Cindy returned to announce a caller.

"A Mr. Johnson is here to see a Mr. Cosgrove," she said.

At this I fear I dropped the cup from which I'd been sipping coffee while Mr. Pinkerton spoke. My chief caught my eye and made a subtle sign to me.

"Mr. Cosgrove is not here," he said. "I needed him at my office in Chicago. But this is Mr. Nichols, an associate of Mr. Cosgrove. Perhaps he will do as well."

The girl was too busy gathering the wreckage of my crockery and sopping up the spilled coffee to note my startlement. By way of covering it I made a small joke.

"A Mr. A. Johnson, perhaps?" I asked.

She stopped and withdrew a calling card from her apron.

"Indeed, that is his initial," she said quite seriously.

"Then we must not keep the President waiting," I bantered. "No doubt he is here to seek our advice on defending himself from his impeachers."

The girl tittered and presented the card to Mr. Pinkerton, who glanced at it and passed it across the table to me.

"Major Alfred E. H. Johnson," it read.

Our visitor awaited us in the parlor, and as I stepped into the room, I was illy prepared for the man who rose to meet us. It was not that he was a remarkable-looking fellow; quite the contrary. He was a remarkable-looking *major*, however, and I'd thought I'd encountered every variety of officer of that rank. It was not the fact that he wore no uniform, and was dressed quite conservatively in civilian clothes; many Army officers, including myself, had served from Sumpter to Appomattox and, owing to the character of their duties, never donned a uniform of any kind. It was simply that this man did not remotely resemble a military officer of any variety. The man looked like nothing so much as a clerk and, as I later learned, this was precisely what he was.†

Mr. Pinkerton introduced himself to Major Johnson, who shook my chief's proffered hand with some diffidence. He was a man of indeterminate age, appearing at first sight to be in his late forties. His hair was full, well barbered and parted at the precise geometric center of his forehead; it was nearly fully gray, with only a few traces of an earlier, youthful darkness. A thick mustache and goatee, equally grizzled, hid the lower part of his face as effectively as a mask, so that the only clew to the state of his countenance was offered by his eyes. But his gaze was mild and almost devoid of expression as he peered through a pince-nez which gripped the summit of a long, acuminated nose. A fine metal chain depended from the right frame of these spectacles and disappeared behind a lapel of his coat. As he turned to me I was impressed that his grayness was premature, and that, divested of beard and pince-nez, his face would look to be that of a considerably younger man.

"And this, I presume, is Mr. Nicholas Cosgrove," he said.

"No," I replied. "Mr. Cosgrove, like all good Roman Catholics, is at Sunday Mass where, I should think, he is thanking the Lord that the dailies do not publish on the Sabbath, else Secretary Stanton might have taken a first-page advertisement announcing he has hired a secret detective to conduct an investigation of the utmost confidentiality. After Mass I expect that Mr. Cosgrove will be embarking for Patagonia, so I

---

† Alfred E. H. Johnson had been a law clerk in Edwin Stanton's office before the war, when Stanton was a lawyer in Steubenville, Ohio. In 1862, after Lincoln appointed Stanton Secretary of War, Stanton brought Johnson to Washington to serve as his personal secretary. Johnson was undoubtedly Stanton's most loyal and trusted assistant, and closer to the Secretary than any other human being, with the possible exception of Mrs. Stanton. Johnson, for example, regularly drew the Secretary's wages for him at the Riggs Bank and held the money for his boss. Stanton never carried any cash on his person, and so he would bring Johnson along whenever he did the household shopping. In addition to these formal and informal duties, Major Johnson was Custodian of Military Telegrams from 1862 to 1869. A copy of every dispatch that passed into or out of the War Department was locked away in Johnson's safe. Thus, to use today's terms, Major Johnson had the highest level clearance and the broadest "need-to-know" of any officer in the War Department.—M.C.

shall take his place here. My name is Charles Nichols, a traveler for Hostetter Stomachic Bitters. I pray you do not forget it."

Major Johnson turned in bewilderment to Mr. Pinkerton. It was clear that he was as impervious to wit as he was incapable of perceiving that one of my lowly station might express, even implicitly, irritation with his master.

Mr. Pinkerton laughed politely.

"You must forgive Nicholas, Major," he said. "In the matter of confidentiality he is circumspect to a degree some might deem a fault. But that is one of the many reasons he is my most effective operative."

The Major drew himself up as though to recover some loss of dignity.

"May I assure you, sir," he said, "that I have the Secretary's complete confidence, and I am privy to every particular of his official business."

"Just so," I heard a Celtic devil use my lips to say, "but you have certainly served long enough in the Army, Major, to know that the privy is notorious as the means of spreading many dangerous things, not the least of which are rumors."

"Sir, I find that remark both vulgar and impertinent!" the Major exclaimed.

"Then I must regret making it," I replied, "when I might instead have quoted Samuel Johnson: 'The vanity of being known to be entrusted with a secret is generally one of the chief motives to disclose it.'"

The Major was, for a moment, speechless, but his eyes had expanded to congruence with the rims of his pince-nez. I cursed my errant tongue for having needlessly earned me an enemy. Mr. Pinkerton broke the silence with a conciliatory observation.

"I think it was Ben Franklin who said that three may keep a secret if two of them are dead. But keeping our own secrets is only a means to an end. We are in the business of discovering secrets, secrets that others wish to keep. And for that task the living are more often of aid than the dead. That, I am certain, is the reason Mr. Stanton has sent you, his most trusted deputy, here to help us, Major. Nicholas understands that as well as I."

"Certainly," I agreed contritely.

Apparently mollified somewhat by this, Major Johnson permitted the unaccustomed stiffness to depart his back, and his shoulders to resume their clerical slump. He removed his spectacles, withdrew a handkerchief from his vest and assiduously polished the lenses while he recovered his composure. After a moment he again clamped the pince-nez to the top of his proboscis, carefully folded the handkerchief and returned it to its assigned pocket, and drew in a long breath.

"That is quite correct," he exhaled. "The Secretary has sent me here to inquire of your plans for the investigation, and to offer whatever assistance it is within his power to furnish you."

Mr. Pinkerton turned a quizzical eye toward me.

"This is very fortunate," I exclaimed ingenuously. "You see, since our visit to the Arsenal last night I have discovered some evidence that the grave in question may have been recently disturbed. I must interview the Arsenal Commandant about this, but in the strictest confidence, of course, and before your arrival we were pondering whether it would be proper to disturb the Secretary for a letter instructing that officer to render us his cooperation. But I'm sure you can authorize this and save our troubling Mr. Stanton."

Major Johnson hesitated for a moment.

"Of course," he agreed. "I shall do so immediately."

Mr. Pinkerton went to an escritoire in the corner and pulled down the leaf, revealing a pen, inkstand and paper. The Major seated himself and looked up.

"Is this to introduce Mr. Pinkerton or Mr. Cosgrove?" he asked.

"It is to introduce Mr. Nichols, if you will," I said, as gently as possible.

"Oh, yes, of course," he replied, and began scribbling.

In a minute he had completed the order, signing it with a flourish.

"And if it is possible," I said, as he sat waving the paper to dry the fresh ink, "I should like to examine the official record of the inquest at which the body was identified."

"I can permit that," he said ostentatiously, "but only in the presence of the Secretary or myself. You are welcome to return with me now to the War Department to do so. The Secretary and I are in our offices today, you see," he added.

"Thank you, but the visit of a bitters merchant to the offices of the Secretary of War on a Sunday morning might strike the chance observer as quite singular," I said. "May I visit tomorrow?"

He looked startled, but said, "I see. Of course. Well then, if that is all . . ." He arose and prepared to leave, then abruptly stopped.

"I nearly forgot. The Secretary asked me to give you this. It is the official public record of the case, and he thought it might prove useful."

It was a book he apparently had deposited on a small table near the door while awaiting us. He handed it to Mr. Pinkerton, who passed it to me. It was Pitman's one-volume synopsis of the trial of Booth's accomplices.†

"Please convey our thanks to the Secretary," I said, with sincerity. "This will doubtless prove a useful reference work on the background of the case."

My chief and I showed the Major to the door. On the steps he turned back to us.

"Until tomorrow, then. I shall instruct the captain of the guard that I am expecting a Mr. Cosgrove to call."

"A Mr. Nichols," I insisted. "A Mr. Charles Nichols. Of Hostetter Stomachic Bitters."

"Nichols! Yes, of course, Nichols. Hostetter Bitters," he mumbled as he turned and picked his way down the icy steps.

After our visitor had departed we repaired once more to the parlor. Mr. Pinkerton discreetly avoided any reference to the contretemps between the Major and myself, a generous extenuation for which I was indeed grateful. He informed me that he had some other, unspecified business which would occupy him that day, and that he planned to depart for Chicago and thence to Iowa (to rejoin his son William in the pursuit of the Reno Gang) on the morrow. I picked

---

† Benn Pitman, cousin of the inventor of the shorthand system bearing his name, was chief of the team of stenographic reporters who recorded the trial. Pitman was commissioned by the War Department to write and publish an official summary of the trial. (See Bibliography.) —M.C.

up the introduction, which the Major had neatly folded and enclosed in an envelope, and placed it in my coat pocket.

"You're off to the Arsenal once more, then?" Mr. Pinkerton inquired. "What do you hope to find that we did not find last night?"

"An answer. The answer to one of the questions I now see as bearing great import owing to your own analysis of the case."

"And which question is that?" Mr. Pinkerton asked.

"Was there ever a corpse buried in Booth's grave?"

·4·

Dinner with the Devil

I did not send Patch to the hosteler's to fetch the carriage, but set out on foot. Few fully appreciate the salubriousness of this mode of progression. It accelerates respiration and circulation, increases the temperature and cutaneous exhalation, and excites appetite and healthful nutrition. As a post-prandial exercise (as it was in this instance) it is an unfailing means to promote efficient digestion. The secret detective especially is advised to choose this means of travel when time permits, and not simply because his profession often requires superior physical condition; he who rides shanks' mare is much less conspicuous than one who passes on horseback or within a carriage.

I was proceeding toward 7th Street at a quick pace in hope of encountering a streetcar† bound for the Virginia Ferry Slip, a scant half-mile walk from the Old Arsenal, when I espied the figure of a man approaching afoot. As he neared I could not fail to recognize him, although I had met him only once, and some years earlier, at that. He was much aged since then, his beard now graying and his countenance drawn as though from some illness or great fatigue, but the essential lineaments, etched idelibly on my memory, remained unchanged. My stride was momentarily broken by the force of an astonishment born of the singularity of such a chance encounter on a

---

† City streetcars of 1868 were, of course, drawn by teams of horses. Electric motors and cable propulsion systems were introduced later, necessitating the term "horsecar" to differentiate those public conveyances still powered by oats from their horseless successors.—M.C.

public thoroughfare in Washington City, after so long a time, with one I believed to be hundreds of miles from that spot. My amazement arose from the colossal improbability that he should be the first I met on this day of all days, for the approaching figure was none other than the self-proclaimed undertaker of John Wilkes Booth, General Lafayette C. Baker.†

Baker passed abreast of me without altering his pace or shifting his gaze, which was directed past me toward the quarter from which I had come. Thus it fell to me to choose the initiative I must take. Three choices presented themselves: I could continue on my course toward 7th Street and eschew this unexpected opportunity; I could slacken my pace and, when sufficient distance separated us, reverse my heading and track the man in hope of learning something more of the situation of affairs that caused our paths to cross; or I could hail him immediately on some pretext and engage him in a conversation that might reveal the occasion of his presence in Washington City.

---

† Cosgrove's reference to thinking Baker was "hundreds of miles" from Washington probably means he had heard the former detective chief was living in Lansing, Michigan, where he had made a considerable investment in a hotel venture undertaken by one of his brothers, Milo. In fact, General Baker was living in Philadelphia at this time, probably sadly pondering the swift decline of his fortunes during the past two years. As Stanton's chief spy-catcher during the War, Baker had been one of the most powerful men in Washington. However, in November, 1865, President Johnson discovered that Baker had placed some of his agents in the White House in what appeared to be an attempt to gather derogatory information about the President. The incident, which involved Baker's arrest and interrogation of a young woman of whom Johnson happened to be especially fond, led to the detective's indictment on charges of false arrest and extortion. Baker was separated from the War Department in January, 1866, and found guilty of the false arrest charge in March. Although a friendly judge limited Baker's punishment to a fine of one dollar plus thirty-five dollars in court costs, the detective's troubles did not end there. As the officer responsible for dispatching the force of detectives and cavalrymen to Port Conway, Baker expected to receive the lion's share of the $75,000 reward offered by the War Department for the capture of Booth and Herold; in fact his part of the prize was a mere $3,750. Then Brother Milo's Lansing hotel venture failed, costing Baker his investment in the business—$10,000 according to some reports, much more, according to others. Finally, in a bid to reverse these financial setbacks, Baker wrote (with the aid of a newspaperman as ghostwriter) and published his *History of the United States Secret Service,* which was a highly fictionalized account of his wartime experiences. But it, too, was a commercial failure.—M.C.

The first of these courses was quite unthinkable; a secret detective can illy afford to squander those rare gifts that Fate may send his way, for the greatest part of the intelligence he gathers is gleaned only through long and diligent application. The second prospect would have been foolhardy; Baker was a master detective, and a professional hunter knows instinctively when he has become the quarry. Without even glancing over his shoulder he would be aware of my pursuit before he reached 9th Street; I would have alerted him to myself and learned nothing in exchange. Thus I was compelled to follow the third course as the only practicable one. I turned and called after the retreating figure.

"I beg your pardon, sir, but are you not General Baker?"

The General continued on his way for several paces before halting abruptly and executing a swift half-turn. I could see that he had employed the interval to plunge his right hand beneath his coat. His left elbow was thrust forward slightly as he gazed at me over his shoulder. I knew that General Baker had many enemies, some near as deadly as himself, but I had not been aware he habitually armed himself when abroad.

"And who, sir, might you be?" he asked.

I spread my arms, as though in a gesture of surprise, but in fact for the purpose of keeping my empty hands in view, and took a few slow steps forward.

"Can it be you don't recall me? Have I changed so much in but a few short years?" I asked, closely watching his eyes for the faintest sign of recognition. There was none. He'd seen me but once, and I'd worn a different face then, yet it would be foolish to misprize the powers of one to whom faces were part of his stock-in-trade.

"Perhaps," he replied. "Has your name changed, as well?"

"Forgive me, General Baker. I am Anton Dumont," I replied, dangerously, for this was very close to the name he knew me by at our first meeting. Yet even this added piece of intelligence failed to stimulate General Baker's memory, judging from the constancy of his gaze.

"I don't recall that name," said Baker.

"Of course," I said. "It was presumptuous of me to have expected you might remember. After all, that which was a great adventure to a ticket-taker at the National must have been nothing more than a common job of work to a detective chief."

I spoke the name of an actress of minor distinction who once told me of being arrested by Baker on suspicion of spying for the Confederates, and was released a few weeks later, when it became obvious the charge was untrue. I claimed to have been introduced to General Baker by one of his detectives, who engaged me to report on the woman's activities. The episode was one of hundreds of almost identical cases, for the General seemed to have suspected every comely woman in Washington City of spying for the Confederacy, trading her charms for military intelligence provided by lustful Army officers. He had thrown so many women into the Old Capitol on the flimsiest of charges that he could hardly be expected to recall the particulars of the case I mentioned. And the number of paid and volunteer informers who carried their delusions, rumors, gossip and, often, malicious lies to Baker's detectives was truly legion. I had no apprehension that the General might be certain his whilom gang of liars and lunatics had not included the tattling ticket-taker I had extemporized.

"Of course," said the General. "I recall you now, though I admit your name and face had escaped me. Very grateful for your patriotic assistance however," he added. "And heartening to find a loyal Union man among the ranks of the theater-folk. Are you still taking the tickets at the National?" he inquired politely.

General Baker was not overly fond of "theater-folk," or, for that matter, of anyone else who dealt in earthly pleasures. During the War I think he believed all manifestations of wine, women or song were weapons of the Devil on loan to Satan's allies in Richmond for the duration of the hostilities. I had forgone offering him my disguise as bitters traveler, for the General, as every other member of the United States Army, knew Hostetter's Bitters as nothing but booze bearing an apothecary's label. In assuming to have been one connected, even in so superficial a manner, with the theater, I equally risked his brusque dismissal, but there was design behind this gamble. The General betrayed a faint impress of the shabby-genteel, which lent substance to reports I had heard that he had lately suffered some financial adversity. I knew he had tried, without notable success, to recoup his fortunes through the sale of his memoirs. A plan had sprung to mind whereby I might protract our colloquy and subtly lead it toward the object of my inquiry.

"I no longer take tickets," I said, "nor am I employed at the National. It has been my good fortune to ascend to a more remunerative calling, that of impresario."

This announcement evoked nothing more than a vacant stare.

"A theatrical broker," I explained. "I organize tours of performers, engaging them for a series of appearances in major cities. For this I receive a trifling percentage of the gate."

"Yet you find this kind of commerce remunerative?" General Baker asked, displaying some interest.

"With some clients more so than others," I replied. "I don't often profit so amply as I recently did with Charles Dickens. Would that I'd had a small share of his book sales, as well. I should be in a position to retire today if I'd had. At every stop on his itinerary the bookstores sold out his works and ordered more during his stay. I'll warrant you cannot find a single copy of *Great Expectations* or *Our Mutual Friend* at any bookseller's in Washington City, yet it's been more than a month since he visited here."†

"You arranged Mr. Dickens' tour?" remarked the General, clearly impressed.

"Yes, but he will soon return to England, so I must find myself a new personage to represent. That's what brings me to Washington City. I hope to find some prominent defender of the Union during the late Rebellion who can be persuaded to recount his adventures on the lecture circuit."

"Bah!" exclaimed General Baker. "You'd best devise a different plan. The public wants to hear no more of the War."

---

† Dickens was at this time near the end of his American tour, in which he lectured and read from his works. He had visited Washington in February, in the company of his American publisher, one Mr. Osgood, and his real business manager, whose name was George Dolby.—M.C.

No doubt the General had in mind the ill success of his own book of memoirs.

"Perhaps the *American* public has had their fill of it, but I was on the Continent less than a fortnight ago, and I assure you European audiences can't hear enough of the subject to satisfy themselves."

"Then your lecturer would require fluency in the languages of Europe, I'd imagine."

"Not so," I replied. "Certainly not in London or Dublin or Edinburgh. As regards Paris, Brussels, Berlin and those other capitals where English is not the common tongue, the public would be content to hear the lecturer's words translated on the spot by an interpreter who would stand beside him on the stage. The attraction, you understand, would be the opportunity to see the noted personage in the flesh, to hear his voice. And if, perchance, he had penned an account of his adventures, this could be translated into the local tongue and sold in theater lobbies. You can depend on it, sir, there is a fortune to be made this way in Europe if I can but find the right man."

General Baker had no immediate comment on this, but seemed to be reflecting deeply on what I had said. I coughed politely.

"General Baker, it may be a happy Fate that has caused our paths to cross today. Would you do me the honor of being my guest at luncheon? I should like you to consider a business proposition that could be to our great mutual advantage."

The General deferred his reply until he had taken his watch from an inner pocket, lifted the cover, and swiftly snapped it shut (but not so swiftly that I failed to observe it had either stopped or was running five hours fast). He allowed that he had time to join me at the meal, and we repaired to Harvey's for luncheon.

It was past noon, and the restaurant was crowded. The throng was composed of transients from the Kirkwood House and other nearby hotels, which, I learned from the General, were mostly filled to capacity by newspaper reporters and others attracted to Washington City by the occasion of the Impeachment Trial. I obtained a table in a secluded corner of the dining room for the purpose of continuing our discourse beyond ear-shot of the curious, but our transit of the chamber drew the notice of many diners, and the din which initially assailed our ears had dropped to a murmur before we reached our place. I do not know how many of our fellow patrons recognized General Baker—he had become a well-known figure in the city during the War—and how many were simply struck by his remarkable appearance. In manner and countenance he looked more the religious zealot than the retired detective chief

During our stroll from the Patent Office to Harvey's, I guided our discourse away from that subject which most interested me, and spoke instead of matters unrelated to my inquiry. I recall the General speaking of the recent disaster befalling the steamer *Magnolia,* which had exploded while departing Cincinnati the previous Wednesday, with 140 souls on board. This led him to a lengthy disquisition on the hazards of steam boilers in general. I was content to let him ramble in this matter, for I wished to defer any mention of Booth's burial until after we had enjoyed our meal. I knew the General to be a total abstainer from all spirituous drink, but I hoped that a full belly (the experience of which I think he had not enjoyed in some time) might be similarly effective in stimulating loquacity.

We had scarcely given our orders to the waiter when I became aware of a presence at my right shoulder.

"It's General Baker, is it not?" I heard a familiar voice say.

The General evidently recognized our visitor, for he displayed none of the wariness he had shown when I hailed him on G Street. But for my part, I was quite as disconcerted as my guest had earlier been, since I could not mistake the voice of our caller, having received more than ample exposure to it only a day earlier.

"Good afternoon, Mr. Reed," said the General. I affected to acquire a sudden interest in a potted plant which stood to my left, and so presented the back of my head to the reporter, while silently praying for his speedy removal to a safer quarter. My prayers were not answered.

"Come to town for the trial, I'll wager," Reed declared. "Tell me, sir, are you here simply to see justice done, or to testify and so insure it? Do you mind if I join you?"

Without waiting for a reply to either query, he drew a chair from a nearby empty table, placed it at ours, and seated himself. I knew reporters to be an ill-mannered lot in general, and had heard that the particular strain to be found in Washington City is especially so, but this was my first direct experience of the trait. However, it did not occur to me at that moment to resent Reed's rudeness, so thoroughly was I filled with dismay. Alas, the General was not equally unmindful of his manner.

"This is Mr. Dumont," he said, nodding in my direction. "Mr. Dumont, meet Mr. Reed, a journalist from Cincinnati."

Reed had deposited a large pigskin portfolio on the table and was engaged in undoing its straps. He stopped and turned to me with some startlement, as though I had at that very instant materialized at table. Abandoning all hope of continuing my personation, I looked him squarely in the face. His eyes were red and liquid, bearing evidence that the jugs of bitters he'd consumed during our journey had been succeeded by generous doses of undisguised spirits. His gaze riveted on my forehead, traveled quickly down to the point at which my vest was obscured by the tabletop, then made the return trip. It was as if he'd been presented with an item of merchandise by a shopkeeper, and was not entirely sure it suited his requirements.

"I think we have met, sir," he said.

"You may have seen Mr. Dumont at the National Theater," offered the General.

"Ah, a thespian," remarked Reed, with some mild interest.

"No," I replied, "a ticket-taker."

"I see. Well, it is a pleasure," said Reed, having turned back to the General before this utterance had fully escaped his lips. He withdrew a notebook from his portfolio, opened it, and moistened the tip of his pencil with his serpentine tongue.

"And are you here to testify at the trial, General?" he asked.

My relief was rivaled by my amazement. Here was one whose calling was that of observer and reporter of the passing scene. A scant twenty-four hours earlier, he had engaged me in conversation, albeit a rather one-sided discourse, which endured through all of the afternoon and most of the evening. Yet today he did not know me. But then I perceived the reason for my salvation. It was General Baker, himself. Had I entered Harvey's alone, the reporter would doubtless have recognized his traveling companion of yesterday. But in the company of

one of General Baker's celebrity, I was rendered invisible as the morning star after the sun has climbed above the horizon. Whelmed by the
presence of what he took to be one of the instruments that would bring
the Great Criminal in the White House to Justice, Mr. Reed had none
of his journalist's perspicaciousness left over to direct at his surround-
ings. Were someone later to insist that General Baker's luncheon companion had been a green-haired dwarf with two heads, Mr. Reed would
have no recourse but to take his word for it.

The waiter arrived with our meal and Mr. Reed ordered the man
to bring him a serving of steamed Rappahannock oysters, the house
specialty. The General didn't stand on ceremony, but dug right into
his serving. Mr. Reed, with equal disregard for the niceties of the table,
immediately undertook to regale him with his reporter's questions.

"Tell me, General Baker, have you returned to Washington City
to elaborate your testimony regarding Johnson's criminality?"

The query caught the General in the midst of mastication, and he
merely shook his head in the negative.

"You've brought us no further evidence against the man?" persisted
the scribe.

The General swallowed the morsel that had heretofore precluded
explication. He carefully set down his knife and fork and turned to
Mr. Reed.

"No," he replied, "nor have I done any other thing in aid of the
Congress's inquiry. If the Congress fail to recognize an honest man
speaking the truth, then I have little confidence they can remove a
scoundrel from the White House, and so I have not squandered my
time on thankless errands."

This discourse meant nothing to me at the time, but I later learned
its meaning. General Baker claimed knowledge of a letter written by
Johnson during the War, purported to be Johnson's acceptance of the
Confederates' proposal that he betray the Union and go over to the
Rebel side. A committee of the House of Representatives had been
appointed to investigate various charges that had been made against
the President and might provide grounds for impeachment, and its
members were understandably interested in General Baker's charge.
They summoned him to Washington City on two occasions to ques-

tion him on this and other matters. However, General Baker was unable to produce the letter in question, or any proof of its existence. The Committee's own inquiries failed to turn up any evidence of the letter.

During the course of his testimony before the Committee, General Baker sought to create some difficulties for Secretary Stanton, as well as the President. In his memoirs, the General disclosed that a diary had been removed from the body of John Wilkes Booth by one of his detectives and turned over to the Secretary of War by himself. The existence of this diary had not been disclosed previously by the Secretary. Mr. Stanton was compelled to surrender the volume, for the General's memoirs chanced to be published in 1867 at the very same time that John Surratt was standing trial for his life, and the defense insisted it be handed over as material evidence. When Mr. Stanton complied, it was found that a number of pages had been torn from the middle of the book. Mr. Stanton declared the diary had been in that condition when General Baker delivered it to him. Baker, in his testimony before the Impeachment Investigation Committee, swore no pages had been missing when he turned it over to the Secretary, thus implying Mr. Stanton had mutilated the book to serve his own dark ends. However, the officer who had actually removed the diary from the body and was present when Baker presented it to the Secretary, testified to the Committee that the pages were missing when he found it. The Committee seemed to prefer the word of the Colonel to that of the General.†

---

† This is a masterpiece of understatement. The Radical Republicans on the Committee would have dearly loved to accept Baker's charges against Johnson, but along with their colleagues, they had to admit that, taken as a whole, his testimony was a pack of lies capable of making even a Congressman blush. Of General Lafayette Baker, the Committee's final report states, ". . . it is doubtful whether he has in any one thing told the truth, even by accident. In every important statement he is contradicted by witnesses of unquestioned credibility. And there can be no doubt that to his many previous outrages, entitling him to an unenviable immortality, he has added that of willful and deliberate perjury, and we are glad to know that no one member of the Committee deems any one statement made by him as worthy of the slightest credit." Like most other nineteenth-century crafts, lying under oath was generally done with at least a minimum of style, and the Congressmen may have resented Baker's amateur efforts as an affront to their own professional skills. It was General Baker's unhappy fate to have been born a century too soon.—M.C.

"'. . . little confidence they can remove a scoundrel from the White House . . . !'" murmured Mr. Reed as he scribbled the General's words in his notebook. General Baker availed himself of this pause in the reporter's interrogation to spear a dollop from his plate and thrust it between his jaws. I seized the opportunity afforded by the temporary lull to guide the proceedings back in a direction closer to my own inquiry.

"Perhaps it would be anticlimatic, in any case," I offered.

General Baker raised a quizzical eyebrow at me as he munched.

"Driving scoundrels from public office, I mean," I offered. "After all, you have crowned an illustrious career of trapping traitors by commanding the force that brought the Greatest Criminal of the Century to Justice. You did not rest until you had personally cast his wretched carcass from the face of the earth into the ignominy of an unmarked felon's grave. After such deeds, the task of bringing an errant politician to justice would be an anticlimax, something better left to men who have yet to prove themselves."

At this General Baker nodded and chewed, both with great vigor. When he had swallowed he sat back in his seat and drew in a long breath. He did not fail to recognize the opportunity to rehearse something of the stuff I had assured him would mesmerize the capitals of Europe. I could almost see the reflection of footlights in his beady eyes as he sonorously undertook to recite a sample, no doubt for his own satisfaction, as well as my benefit.

"It will ever be impossible for me to forget," he began, "the tragic yet triumphant scene at the Navy Yard in the noon of that night. I ordered the tug on which we'd come upriver to lay to alongside the *Saugatuck* so that I might deliver the accursed assassin's remains to the Captain. Then I handed over Harold, his accomplice, and saw to it that he was ironed and taken below to join his fellow conspirators.†

---

† The name of the ironclad was not the *Saugatuck*, but the *Montauk;* Baker made the same error in his memoirs. He may have been confusing the ship with the *Saugus,* another ironclad, which was anchored nearby, and was the one on which most of the other prisoners were actually held. Referring to David Herold as Harold was a common error that can be traced at least as far back as a reward poster issued by Stanton shortly after the assassination. The time of the transfer is uncertain, but it

With that, my labors were complete. The whole villainous crew responsible for the foul crime had been accounted for. Except Surratt, of course, but he was in another country, beyond my reach."

"And except Jefferson Davis, as well," interjected Mr. Reed.†

"Of course," Baker agreed. "I meant only those hired to do the dirty work. We certainly did not have Davis in irons, or Andrew Johnson, either. Or General Grant, for that matter," he added, almost as an afterthought.

"General Grant!" Reed exclaimed. "Surely, man, you don't mean to imply that General Grant had a hand in the matter."‡

"If he had no foreknowledge of what was to take place in the theater that night, I should like to hear his reasons for sending his regrets and fleeing Washington City at the last moment, after he had accepted the President's invitation to share his box at Ford's," Baker declared.

"I'm confident General Grant had excellent reasons for his actions," Reed demurred.

"As am I," agreed General Baker, with a knowing wink.

---

was at least 1:45 A.M. However, it would be petty to cavil at a phrase so romantic as Baker's "noon of the night." Baker's essential claim that he delivered a dead body and David Herold to an ironclad at the Navy Yard in the middle of the night is well substantiated by other sources and not in dispute.—M.C.

† Davis and several other Confederate leaders were, in effect, found guilty of conspiracy in the assassination by the same Military Commission that tried Booth's alleged accomplices. However, soon after the trial it became obvious that all of the evidence against the Confederate leaders had been manufactured by Stanton's War Department, and none of them were hanged or sentenced to long prison terms. By the time this luncheon interview took place, only diehard Radical Republicans were still suggesting that Davis had a hand in the murder. Baker had testified to the Impeachment Investigation Committee that he knew of a letter implicating Davis in the assassination, but like the alleged Johnson–Davis correspondence, he failed to produce it.—M.C.

‡ It was obvious at this time that, whatever the outcome of the impeachment trial, Johnson would not be the Republicans' presidential candidate in next November's election. Grant was already considered a leading contender for the Republican nomination, and Reed had probably already decided this was the horse to back. According to the Washington *Star* of June 22, 1868, Reed had just completed a campaign biography of the General, a tract he had probably already begun to write when he heard Baker's accusation.—M.C.

Before this impromptu trial of General Grant could proceed further, I made an interruption calculated to prompt General Baker back to matters of more immediate interest to myself.

"But this midnight delivery of the assassin's corpse to the ironclad was not to be the last you would see of the wretched carcass," I offered.

"Not at all," the General agreed, composing himself to resume his lecture hall manner. "It was imperative that Booth's grave not become a shrine for unrepentant Secessionists, and it fell to me to see that the body be secreted in a place where it would not be found until Gabriel blew his last trump."

"And you chose for that place a deep pit beneath the stone floor of a cell within the Old Arsenal Penitentiary," I prompted.

"Yes, as it is now generally known through no fault of mine," the General replied.

General Baker then proceeded to recount, in his lecture hall voice, the story I had heard on the previous night from Mr. Pinkerton: the ruse calculated to lead onlookers to believe the body would be sunk in the river, the midnight visit to the Old Arsenal, and the secret burial. Suddenly he paused as though he had just noticed the meal now growing cold before him, and suspended his discourse in favor of another mouthful. Before Mr. Reed could resume his interrogation, I seized the moment to go to the heart of my inquiry.

"Tell me, sir," I asked, "did you thrust the wretch's bones into the pit as one would cast rubbish into a midden, or did you grant it the undeserved honor of a box?"

The General shook his head and swallowed.

"No box," he said. "Just a tattered and bloody horse blanket for a shroud."

"No box!" exclaimed Mr. Reed. "I seem to remember otherwise."

"I do not seem to remember that you were present," said the General, smiling ironically.

Mr. Reed burrowed in the depths of his portfolio and presently withdrew a pair of thick octavo volumes, well thumbed and bristling with bookmarks.

"I mean in your testimony before the Committee," he explained, rapidly turning the pages of one volume. The General stared with horrified countenance at the twin tomes as one possessed by Satan might regard a matched set of the Old and New Testaments.

"What," he demanded, "have you there?"

"Why, the testimony of all the witnesses before the Committee.† Here it is."

Mr. Reed then read aloud a portion of General Baker's testimony.

"'Question: Was the body put in a box?'" he read. "'Answer: Yes, sir, it was put in a box.'"

"Let me see that!" demanded the General. Mr. Reed surrendered the book, open to the page in question. The General stared at the page for a moment, then slapped the book closed, and cast it onto the table.

"Damned phonographers,"‡ he complained. "When they can't read their own notes they just go ahead and make something up. My answer was the exact opposite, and it would be ridiculous to suppose otherwise. It's a wonder they've failed to have me draping their supposed coffin with a Rebel flag and singing 'Dixie' over it, as well. We were not in that prison cell to conduct a state funeral, but to dispose of the stinking carcass of a felon. Ignore this so-called testimony, sir, and mark my words, instead. There was no box."

While the issue of box or no box had inspired a singular degree of heat in General Baker, it seemed of little consequence to Mr. Reed, who now resumed his line of questioning in a direction more suited to the defamation of President Johnson. The General, for his part, seemed pleased by the change of subject. Finding myself once again displaced from the axis of discourse, I risked being thought ill-mannered and

---

† The Impeachment Investigation Committee took its testimony in secret, but published it in November, 1867, at the same time it was delivered to the Senate. While it contained many diverting items, such as General Baker's allegations, it offered nothing with which to impeach a President, and so attracted little public attention. Apparently word of the publication hadn't reached General Baker in Philadelphia.—M.C.

‡ Stenographic reporters.—M.C.

picked up the volume from the table to see what other outrages the phonographers might have perpetrated on General Baker.

The General's testimony made interesting reading, for the subject of Booth's burial was raised repeatedly by the Committee members, and the transcript regarding this matter covered several pages. General Baker said he had never claimed to have sunk Booth's body in the ocean. In the next breath he allowed that it was likely he had said such a thing, although it wasn't so. However, the General disputed the characterization of this as a "lie." The General knew exactly where the body had been buried, although he could not say if it were beneath a cell or some other sort of room, or anything else more definite than that it had been buried within the Arsenal grounds, although he had seen the grave after it was dug, but was not present when the body was actually placed in it. The body, he testified, had been placed in a box after it had been taken within the Arsenal walls, but the General himself had not been within the Arsenal walls, he said, and so had not himself placed the body in the box. The General had viewed the scene from a distance he reckoned to have been some five hundred feet, presumably *through* the Arsenal walls.

Only two conclusions were possible. Either the General had suffered at the hands of a mad phonographer, or else he hadn't the slightest notion of whether the assassin had been buried in a box or stuffed and mounted. Unfortunately, the answer was obvious. General Baker couldn't tell me what I needed to learn of Booth's burial, for he knew less than I of the matter.

When finally I closed the book and set it down, I found General Baker and Mr. Reed in deep communion on the theme of Johnsonian transgressions. Swift as the journalist's pencil moved, it was hard pressed to match the fecundity of the General's imagination. Neither of my luncheon companions paused when I excused myself from the table. En route to the dining room exit I found our waiter and took him aside, explaining that the distinguished journalist who had joined us now insisted we accept his hospitality and would deem it a personal affront if the house presented the bill for our repast to someone other than himself. This arrangement seemed only equitable, since the wares offered by the General were of far greater utility to Mr. Reed than to myself, and I resolved they should be paid for by the Cincinnati *Gazette,* rather than Pinkerton's National Detective Agency.

I gave the waiter a coin and instructed him to deliver to the General a note, which I penned on the spot. It read:

To General Lafayette C. Baker

Europe has yet to hear a tale to match your adventures. I cannot praise your disquisitions too highly. I shall call on you later.

Very respectfully, your obedient servant,
Anton Dumont

· 5 ·

The Restless Remains

·····➤◆➤·····

I had opened the earth in a secret and dismal place said to be the grave of John Wilkes Booth. I presumed myself to be the first to disturb this unholy ground in the three years since the assassin was supposed to have been buried there. I uncovered a box, and within the box, found nothing but stones and a coin. The coin told a tale: whatever the true history of the box and its contents, the lid had last been nailed shut no more than two years ago, fully a year past the day on which the box was said to have been concealed in a place where it could not be discovered "until Gabriel blew his last trump." But the stones, as well, held a valuable message for one with the wit to read it.

Whoever had placed the stones in the box had expected the box to be moved. The stones were in the box to conceal from the shoulders of pallbearers the fact that the box contained no corpse. This much seemed obvious. Not quite so obvious, at least not to me, at first, was that this simple observation was the key to several important lines of deduction.

The first of these concerned the man who had lost the five-cent piece. Whoever he might be, it appeared he had not robbed the grave of its bones. If he had covertly entered the burial chamber in the Arsenal, prized up the floor paving, uncovered the box, and removed the body (for whatever mysterious motive), why add to his labors and risk of discovery by bringing along on this errand some hundred or so pounds of stones to place in the box before re-burying it? To deceive Gabriel?

The presence of the stones also, at first, seemed to absolve General Baker and his cousin of the suspicion that they had disposed of the body in some other manner than delivering it to the Arsenal. According to the popularly held version of Booth's burial, as recited to me by Mr. Pinkerton (and apparently promulgated by General Baker and his cousin in unofficial interviews where perjury charges were not a risk), the Baker cousins had removed the body from the *Montauk,* engaged in some maneuvers aimed at misleading onlookers, and took the body to the Arsenal in the dead of night, there to bury it in the presence of none but themselves. Now if this tale were largely true, except the Bakers had sunk the body in the river or concealed it elsewhere than beneath the Arsenal, why should they further add to their night's labors by taking a box of stones into the Arsenal and burying it there? If one ever were to doubt their story sufficiently to dig up the spot they claimed to be Booth's grave, he surely would have doubt enough remaining to prize open the box.

But now I'd read General Baker's recent sworn version of the event, in which he claimed to have delivered the carcass uncrated to the Arsenal grounds, outside the Arsenal walls. The boxing and burial were done by others, he testified. And, of course, I had just now heard his most recent version, which he had presented at Harvey's. This last was, in essence, the same as his first version, with the added particular that the body went into the ground unboxed and wrapped in a horse blanket. Obviously sheer deduction was not to solve this riddle. The truth must lie in the direction I had been traveling when I encountered General Baker in the street some hours earlier. As I departed Harvey's I turned again toward 7th Street, and there boarded a streetcar that delivered me to the vicinage of the Arsenal, where, I believed, the answer, if not the missing body, must lie.

As I walked southward from the ferry landing where the streetcar tracks terminated, I had an opportunity to view those details of the Arsenal environs that had been hidden by the darkness of the previous night. A long and stately avenue led toward the Arsenal, guarded on both sides by colonnades of towering trees, still winternaked against the leaden sky. A short way ahead to the right stood a small building on the riverbank. A short boat landing extended from the structure into the Potomac. To the left of the road a number of artillery pieces and many pyramidal stacks of cannon balls had been placed in orderly arrays. Beyond, on the left, stood the Old Arsenal itself, surrounded by a wall some twenty-five feet in height.

I stopped at the guard post in the West Wall and asked to see Brigadier General George Ramsay, which, I had been informed by Major Johnson, was the name of the Arsenal's commandant, whom I'd met, but to whom I'd not been introduced, on my visit of the previous night. To my surprise I was asked neither my name nor my business, but was immediately led inside the Arsenal walls and taken to a room in a building of modest size and great age. It seemed an unlikely office for a Brigadier General, and on entering I discovered that it was, in fact, the Dispensary. I was ushered into an office more medical than military, and met by an officer who wore the uniform of a major, and was certainly not the same man who had hosted my earlier visit. He introduced himself as Dr. Porter, a surgeon.† I identified myself only as Charles Nichols.

"General Ramsay was called away from the Arsenal unexpectedly. He said he was expecting some visitors today, and that I might be better able to serve them than he. He mentioned no names, but said it concerned an earlier visit here, last night. I frankly admit to confusion in the matter, Mr. Nichols. Are you of the party that visited here last night?"

I admitted that I was.

"Then how may I assist you?" he asked.

"I came to discuss a certain sensitive official matter with General Ramsay. As he has anticipated my visit and deputized you to meet with me, I assume I may reveal to you that the matter in question relates to the remains of John Wilkes Booth."

Dr. Porter turned away and paced the length of the small examining room. When he faced me again I observed a worried frown marring his visage. He tugged on his beard nervously and was silent for a long moment before replying.

---

† Dr. George Loring Porter. Dr. Porter held the rank of major, and was mustered out of the service on July 16, 1868.—M.C.

"'Sensitive' is precisely the word for that matter, Mr. Nichols, and I'm afraid even General Ramsay has not sufficient authority to order me to discuss it with you."

"Perhaps this will suffice," I said, withdrawing Major Johnson's introduction from my pocket and presenting it to him. Dr. Porter unfolded the paper, read the brief note, and handed it back to me.

"Of course," he said. "This is more than adequate. What do you wish to know?"

"Everything," I replied. "Every particular that can be recalled of the manner and circumstances in which the assassin's body was conveyed into this Arsenal and buried. And to whatever extent it is possible at this late date, I should like to hear it from eyewitnesses."

Dr. Porter nodded.

"I understand now why General Ramsay asked me to meet with you," he said. "The General was Commandant of this Arsenal at the time, but he had no direct involvement in the matter. I happen to be the only commissioned officer who was present at the event you speak of. Where shall I begin?"

"At the point at which the body was brought ashore, if you will," I replied.

"I did not actually see the corpse delivered," said Dr. Porter. "The first hint I had of its presence on this base was late in the afternoon of April 27th. Perhaps you noticed a summer house with a boat landing on the riverbank near the upper end of the Arsenal grounds when you came here."

I said that I had.

"Well, on the afternoon of the date in question, Mrs. Porter and I were boating on the river. When we returned late in the afternoon and approached the boat landing we were hailed by a sentry, who ordered us away. When I persisted he announced that no one was permitted to land at the pier and he would have to fire on us if we attempted to do so.

"I was astonished at this, for I had never even known of another instance in which a sentry had been posted at the landing, much less one with such harsh orders. I insisted the man summon the officer of the guard, which he did.

"The officer recognized me and ordered the sentry to permit us to tie up at the pier and land. As we came ashore, we passed through the little summer house at the foot of the landing, and I chanced to notice a bundle wrapped in a gunny sack in one corner of the building, but I failed to connect it with the presence of the sentry, at that time. As it transpired, of course, the sack contained the body of Booth."

"About what time was this?" I asked.

"I'm not sure," he replied. "At least an hour, and probably more, before sunset, if the Baker version of the midnight landing is behind your question."

"It is," I admitted.

Dr. Porter laughed.

"I'm sure General Baker and his cousin have their reasons for inventing their fantasies. The reasons may even be official, although I suspect they are pecuniary. However, you are authorized to be furnished with the facts in this matter, so I have no hesitation in telling you the Baker version of Booth's burial is a total fabrication. General Baker may have supervised the delivery of the body to the summer house. In fact, he probably did, although I cannot say so with certainty, since I was not present. But as to the time of that delivery, it was in the late afternoon, not the middle of the night. And as for the balance of the Baker account, it is completely untrue, and I have no reason to believe that General Baker or his cousin were even in the general proximity of the Arsenal grounds after sunset of that day."

"I had guessed as much," I said. "Pray resume your own account of events."

"Shortly after Mrs. Porter and I returned to our quarters I was summoned to General Ramsay's office. There, in addition to the General, I found Mr. Stebbins, the military storekeeper, and an officer from the War Department whose name, I seem to recall, was Colonel Benton. The General, at Colonel Benton's behest, asked for my pledge as an officer and a gentleman that I would reveal nothing of what I was to see, hear or do that evening. I believe Mr. Stebbins had been similarly sworn before my arrival. Since this was, by deputy, a pledge to the Secretary of War, I speak to you of these matters now only on the direct authorization of the Secretary, which you have shown me.

"Colonel Benton revealed to us the nature of the contents of the bundle Mrs. Porter and I had noticed in the summer house. He conveyed to the General the Secretary's order that the remains be buried within the Arsenal in circumstances of the utmost possible secrecy. General Ramsay ordered Mr. Stebbins and myself to report to the summer house precisely at midnight. We were then dismissed after again being cautioned to discuss the matter with no one, and I returned to my quarters.

"When I arrived at the summer house at midnight, I found a cart and mule team waiting on the lawn, and inside the building, Mr. Stebbins and four enlisted men. The four were of the Ordinance Corps and among the most trustworthy of the men stationed at the Arsenal. I believe they, too, had been sworn to secrecy.

"Two of the men lifted the gunny sack and brought it outside to the cart. One of the men brought out a lantern to light the way. I walked ahead with him. A second man led the mules and the other two placed themselves one on each side of the cart. Mr. Stebbins brought up the rear. In this fashion we proceeded down the avenue and were passed through the western gate into the Arsenal.

"Contrary to the Bakers' fanciful account, the body was not buried in a cell, but in a large storage room in the penitentiary building. The room was about fifty by forty feet, with supporting columns of stout cedar. There was a pair of enormous doors opening to the outside, and through these we drove the mules and the cart. We locked the doors behind us and drove the cart to the extreme southwestern corner of the room, where a shallow grave had already been dug, with a pile of earth standing beside it. Two of the men lifted the sack from the cart and placed it in the hole. Then the others joined with them in filling the hole with the loose soil and packing it down. The excess soil was placed in the cart. As the floor of the chamber was of dirt, there was little trouble in concealing the fact that a hole had been dug in it and then filled up.

"When all this was completed, the party left the room and Mr. Stebbins closed and locked the doors, which were the only means of entrance or egress.

"And that," said Dr. Porter, with a shrug, "is the whole of it."†

It was far less than the whole of it, in my view, for the agreement between Dr. Porter's description of the burial chamber and the place I had visited on the previous night ended with the general dimensions and the cedar columns. However, the doctor had been so definite about such things as the large double doors (which I would swear were not in the room I had seen) and the earthen floor (my back, as well as my brain, recalled the massive paving stones) that I saw no point in cross questioning him on these points. There were two particulars, however, on which he had not been absolutely specific.

"Did you examine the body?" I asked.

"Certainly not," he replied. "There was no need to. A necropsy had already been performed aboard the *Montauk* by Surgeon General Barnes, and the body had been identified by several witnesses, including Booth's physician. There would have been no reason to open the gunny sack, save to satisfy idle and morbid curiosity. I assure you, none of the party suggested such a thing, and I would not have permitted it if they had."

When goods come in a poke,‡ one should always look inside before accepting them, especially if the deliveryman is General Baker. I abstained from giving voice to this observation, however, since it would serve no purpose but to disclose the motive behind my inquiries.

"Was the sack placed in a box before burial?" I asked.

"I'm not certain. In the lantern light it was impossible for me to discern if a box had been placed in the hole. I think not, however, for I can definitely say no cover was placed in the hole before it was filled in."

"This room wherein the body was buried; may I visit it?"

---

† Dr. Porter was either telling the truth or had been well rehearsed; he wrote a virtually identical account of the burial forty-three years later in the April, 1911, issue of the *Columbian Magazine*. Dr. Porter died February 27, 1919.—M.C.

‡ A bag.—M.C.

"I am afraid that would be impossible. You see, the penitentiary building was torn down last year. This Arsenal, you understand, has not been used as a prison for many years, except briefly, when Booth's accomplices were incarcerated here during their trial. The penitentiary was no longer needed and had fallen into an irreversible state of disrepair."

"But what of Booth's grave?" I demanded.

"It was moved, of course. The body was reburied beneath the floor of a large storehouse at the other end of the Arsenal. That was last October, I believe, although I wasn't present at the time."†

At my request, Dr. Porter led me to the new grave site. The instant he raised his lantern and drove back the darkness of the chamber, I recognized it as the scene of my recent nocturnal labors.

"I'm afraid I don't know the exact spot," Dr. Porter apologized. "I only know that it is somewhere beneath this stone floor."

The Lieutenant and I had taken the trouble to pile cartridge boxes over the site, lest some peculiarity we failed to observe when replacing the heavy paving stones betray their recent disturbance. I asked Dr. Porter to produce someone who had witnessed the transfer, and after several inquiries he located a noncommissioned officer, one Sergeant Robert Flaherty, who filled the bill. The three of us repaired again to the Dispensary, and Dr. Porter apprised Sergeant Flaherty of my authority to hear whatever details he could supply of the exhumation and reburial.

"Tell me, please, Sergeant, exactly what you found when the grave beneath the penitentiary building was opened," I said.

"Well, sir," he replied, "when we cleared the soil from the spot pointed out by Mr. Stebbins, we found a bundle in a canvas poke. The poke fell apart when we tried to lift it from the hole, and inside it there were human remains wrapped in an Army blanket. The blanket was in better condition than the remains," he added with an expression of distaste.

---

† The body was moved on October 1, 1867, according to a current publication of the U.S. National Park Service entitled *Ford's Theater and the House Where Lincoln Died*, p. 17.—M.C.

"How was the body clothed," I asked, thinking again of the riding boot.

"I could not say, sir, as we did not unwrap the thing. I sent for a gun case and we lifted the blanket and put the whole business inside. The head had come loose and fell out of the blanket, but someone fetched it and put it in the box, as well. Then we marked the name 'Booth' on the cover and nailed it closed. I said a few Hail Marys over it, even though the man was not of the Faith and probably long since in Hell anyway, but it seemed a fitting thing to do. And then I told a couple of the lads to lug the thing over to the fixed ammunition storehouse."

"Was the box then buried immediately?" I asked.

"Well, sir, you see this was all done around midnight, so as not to attract attention. But when we got to the storeroom where Mr. Stebbins wanted it planted, I saw we'd need some bars and a few more strong backs to move the ammunition about and prize up the paving. Mr. Stebbins left me in charge and went off to get what we wanted. I let the lads go outside for a smoke while we waited. (Smoking's not permitted near the stores, you see.) I've never had the habit, and besides, I was ordered not to let the thing out of my sight, so I stayed until they'd all returned."

"And then the box was buried?" I prompted.

"Yes, sir. After that we all left and Mr. Stebbins locked up. The rest of us made for our bunks, and were damned glad to see them, if you'll forgive my language, sir."

"It sounds as though it were a long job of work," I offered.

"That it was, sir," the Sergeant replied, "but we were ordered to make morning muster, nonetheless, so none would wonder at our sleeping in."

"Then I imagine there was a little something extra in your pay," I suggested.

The Sergeant laughed.

"Begging your pardon, sir, but you don't know the Ordinance Corps. There was no bonus paid for this duty."

"Not a 'nickel'?" I asked, pursuing a sudden intuition. To one subsisting on a soldier's meager pay, the loss of five cents would not be immediately forgotten.

The Sergeant smiled wryly.

"Not even a 'nickel,' sir," he replied. "As a matter of fact, speaking of a 'nickel' . . ."

Sergeant Flaherty broke off his sentence, the smile fading from his face.

"Yes, Sergeant," I prompted. "What about a 'nickel'?"

"Nothing at all, sir," replied Flaherty. "I just thought of an old Army story, but it ain't fit for the ears of gentlemen."

At this Dr. Porter made an embarrassed cough.

"Thank you, Sergeant. You're dismissed. That is, unless Mr. Nichols has further questions."

"I do not," I said, "and I thank you kindly, Sergeant."

Before he turned to leave I added, "By the way, I think I've heard the story you had in mind. I never understood it before, but now I believe I do."

Dr. Porter seemed bewildered by this, but the Sergeant's face remained expressionless. As he turned to leave I withdrew my hand from my coat pocket, having palmed the mortuary coin. I affected to drop it by accident. It rolled across the floor and the Doctor made to grab it in mid-career. The Sergeant had spun about at the sound, but stood in place, his eyes following the course of the five-cent piece as it spiraled to a jingling stop at his feet.

"Well, speak of the Devil," I said jauntily.

The Sergeant's eyes never left my own as he bent and gingerly lifted the coin between thumb and forefinger. He walked up to me and gravely placed it in my hand.

"I think this is yours," he said.

"Thank you, Sergeant," I replied. "You know how hard I worked for it."

·6·

One of the Strangest Coincidences in History

A slightly bemused Dr. Porter escorted me to the West Gate, whence I had entered the walls of the Arsenal. I declined his offer of transportation to Washington City, offering as excuse my desire to enjoy as much of the grounds along the riverbank as the waning winter afternoon would permit. In fact, I did not tarry along the tree-lined avenue, but walked briskly until I came abreast of the summer house. There I stopped and went inside to wait. From my vantage point within I was concealed from the avenue, yet had an excellent view of those traveling along it. While I waited, I took stock of the afternoon's prizes.

A gunny sack that may have been delivered to the spot on which I now stood by General Baker was, after half a dozen or so hours, while presumably under constant guard, taken by Dr. Porter and his party and buried beneath the penitentiary, probably not within any sort of box. Approximately two and one-half years afterward, it was dug up by another party, which included Sergeant Robert Flaherty. Flaherty claimed the sack contained human remains, and this was probably so, or else Flaherty had reason to expect all of the others in the resurrection party would join him in the lie. I believed at least this much of Flaherty's report.

But I also believed of Sergeant Flaherty some things he had left unsaid, yet, in a sense, had told me. Whoever had substituted the stones for the remains in the gun box could easily have done so before it was replanted beneath the storeroom floor. I knew of only one man who had had the opportunity: by his own admission, Sergeant Flaherty. And since learning the remains had been re-buried less than a year ago, I'd changed my view of the man who had lost the "nickel." Now I saw that he likely was one and the same person who had stolen the body. And if I was any judge of human nature, the owner of the five-cent piece I carried in my coat pocket was Sergeant Flaherty.

There had been a body in that box, but it reposed therein only briefly, I believed. Sergeant Flaherty had prized open the casket while his comrades had a smoke outside the storeroom. It was he who exchanged stones for bones, concealing the remains elsewhere in the warehouse and nailing the cover down again, after losing a five-cent piece to the box during his hurried exertions. I could not prove it, as yet, but I knew it. And what was more, Sergeant Flaherty knew that I knew it.

Flaherty the resurrectionist must have had a client, for it was doubtful he took his trouble from a personal desire to collect the relics of dead felons. And now, if I knew my man, he would soon be off to warn his client that he'd been found out.

East of the Arsenal, and to its south and west there was water. If Flaherty planned to depart the Arsenal grounds by water, I calculated he'd use one of the boats tethered at the landing behind the summer house in which I was concealed. And if he left by land, he would go north along the avenue I watched. If Flaherty was my man, I reflected, I should be seeing him presently. As it happened, I hadn't long to wait before my prophecy was fulfilled.

I heard hoofbeats approaching and soon a lone rider came into view, mounted on a bay-brown roan. He flashed by at a full gallop, but not so swiftly that I failed to recognize Sergeant Robert Flaherty. He had soon put sufficient distance behind him that I was safe from discovery as I stepped out of the summer house and began my northward trudge. My kingdom for a horse, or any other means of divining Sergeant Flaherty's destination, for there I would find his client and, if not the missing corpse, at least the missing motive Mr. Pinkerton had urged me to discover. But there was nothing for it but to plod northward toward the streetcar tracks, while the mounted figure vanished into the distant reaches of 4½ Street.

I found a streetcar waiting at the ferry landing, but it continued to wait for some time after I boarded it, until the ferry from Virginia arrived and delivered a cargo of travelers bound for Washington City. Thus, it was nearly dusk by the time we approached the bridge over the Canal, and I had all but abandoned hope of seeing Sergeant Flaherty again that day, when, indeed, I did see him, riding beside an Army officer in an open buggy and headed in the opposite direction on 7th Street.

After the buggy passed, it stopped, turned and followed the streetcar. It pulled abreast, and Sergeant Flaherty caught my eye. He turned to the officer and the buggy dropped back, following a short distance behind. When the car stopped at Pennsylvania Avenue, I got off, and Flaherty and the officer drove up. The officer spoke.

"Mr. Nichols, would you please accompany me?" he asked.

"Perhaps," I replied. "Have you some particular destination in mind, or are you proposing a tour of the city?"

"We won't go far, sir. Please climb in," said the officer. Sergeant Flaherty permitted his cloak to fall open and I found myself staring into the hostile end of an Army Colt revolver.

"I find your invitation insolent," I replied as I climbed into the back of the buggy, "yet difficult to refuse."

Sergeant Flaherty laughed.

"I'm happy you saw fit to join us, sir," he said. "I'd hate to bury that 'nickel' twice."

Despite the dangerous flavor the situation had taken, I could not help but laugh at this, although the officer, who I now saw to be a captain, admonished the Sergeant to silence.

"I have no doubt of that," I said. "Burying it once has brought you enough bad luck. I would make you a present of the thing here and now, but if I did and then we should strike a hole in the pavement, causing your cannon to discharge, the curse might be passed to some unwary hangman."

Sergeant Flaherty seemed to appreciate this point, for he uncocked the Colt and returned it to some repository within his cloak. Without further conversation we proceeded westward along Pennsylvania Avenue. The buggy slowed as we passed the White House and, for a moment, I believed our destination to be the War Department, but then we turned left into 17th Street, stopping before a stately two-story residence on the corner of F Street, opposite the Winder Building. A massive American flag flew from a mast above the entablature that shielded the front door, and had I been a more frequent post-War visitor to Washington City, I should have recognized the house as the headquarters of General Ulysses S. Grant.

A private took charge of the buggy and I was led by the Captain up the steps and into the building, with Flaherty bringing up the rear. We walked down a long hall on the first floor and the officer opened a door and gestured for me to enter. Inside the air smelled of cigar smoke and whiskey. I recognized the particular variety of tobacco and spirits, for their combination was a familiar one, albeit an aroma I had not inhaled since the War. Thus, while General Ramsay's presence in the room was unexpected, I was not in the least surprised when I turned and saw the bearded man in Army braces sitting behind a huge desk that supported a pair of booted feet.

"So you are 'Mr. Charles Nichols,'" said General Grant, taking the cheroot from between his teeth. "I might have guessed as much."

He turned to General Ramsay.

"This *is* one of the men who called on you last night," he asked.

General Ramsay looked extremely discomforted.

"General Grant, I am truly sorry, but I must respectfully decline to reply to your question. I can say only that I have been ordered to silence by a higher level of command."

"Which can only be Stanton or Johnson, and you won't tell me which," said General Grant. "Very well, Get out of here. Sergeant Flaherty, close the door after you. 'Mr. Nichols' and I have some private matters to discuss."

After they had gone, General Grant took his feet from the desk and put his elbows in their place.

"Well, Colonel Cosgrove, are you going to tell me what the hell you're up to?"

"It's no longer 'Colonel,' and rarely 'Cosgrove' these days, sir," I replied. "I go by 'Mr. Charles Nichols' as you seem to have learned, and I am in the private employ of Mr. Pinkerton. I am at present conducting an investigation for one of his clients. Confidentiality regarding the identity of clients and the substance of investigations is a matter of policy in the Pinkerton's Agency, so I'm afraid that's all I can tell you."

"Cosgrove, I know a deal of this matter already," said the General. "I know you were down at the Arsenal this afternoon asking questions about Booth's carcass. I know that you are likely one of several men who visited the Arsenal last night and dug up his grave. I know that the grave was opened with General Ramsay's permission, so that can only mean you had authority from either Stanton or Johnson to do so."

"You left something out, sir," I said. "I think you also know what we found when we opened the grave."

General Grant accurately tossed his dead cheroot into a cuspidor beside his desk. He took out a fresh cigar, bit off the end and spit it unerringly into the same vessel. All the while he was studying me with angry eyes.

"I assume Allan Pinkerton knows of this business you're up to," he said.

"Since you know I have always reported directly to Mr. Pinkerton, that seems a safe assumption," I replied.

"Does Pinkerton understand what he's putting himself in the middle of?" he asked, stabbing the air between us with his yet unlit cigar. "Do you?"

I assumed the question to be rhetorical and waited in silence while he lit the cigar and puffed reflectively for a moment.

"In the event you don't know what's occurring in this city, let me tell you. The Government of the United States is damn near split in two. Right at this very moment Stanton is sitting across the street barricaded in his office, virtually under siege. Next door in the White House, Johnson is so busy with his lawyers he hasn't time to run the Government because up on the Hill the Senate has put him on trial. I've got the whole damn United States Army as my responsibility and I really don't know who I should be receiving my orders from."

"I can see your problem, sir," I replied, "although it seems to me that nothing is happening that has not been provided for in the Constitution. I should think you would find the answer to your dilemma there."

The General snorted.

"You're talking like a damned lawyer," he said. "I don't have a legal problem, I have a practical problem, and it's one hell of a problem."

"Yes," I agreed, "a problem in practical politics. How to ride out the impeachment storm and arrive at the Republican convention in June without having made any important enemies."

General Grant scowled at me through a miasma of smoke.

"You're very shrewd, Cosgrove," he finally said. "Very shrewd. I'm not saying you're wrong, but I'm not saying you're right, either.† But, believe it or not, I have some concern for matters beyond my own personal prospects. And at the moment the chief problem of that variety is the one created by your meddling."

"How so?" I asked.

"You know, of course," said General Grant, "that Booth paid his respects to Andrew Johnson at the Kirkwood House scant hours before he shot the President."

"I had heard something of the sort," I said.

"God alone knows what the madman had in mind, but it's a fact. He went to the hotel, asked for Johnson, and when he was told the

---

† Cosgrove was right. Grant knew very well that President Johnson was the Commander-in-Chief of all U.S. military forces and would continue to be unless and until he was removed from office. But he also knew Johnson was finished politically, and he himself was the leading contender for the Republican presidential candidacy. Instead of providing strong support to the Chief Executive during this time of crisis, he chose instead to walk a tightrope and keep his Army boots off the toes of anyone who might emerge from the Impeachment Trial as a power within the party. All but one of General Grant's finest hours were past. He had ceased to be a soldier and had become a politician. The very able military leader was soon to become a thoroughly incompetent President, who would, for eight years, preside over one of the most corrupt administrations in American history up to that date. He would not display any more heroism until his final days, when, almost penniless and dying from a painful throat cancer, he doggedly penned his memoirs to provide for the financial security of his family.—M.C.

Vice-President was out, he left his calling card. Now, for the past two years the Radical Republicans in Congress have been trying to prove Johnson was in cahoots with Booth and put him up to the murder."

"Do you suppose it's so?" I asked.

The General shrugged.

"If it is, there's no evidence except that calling card. The Impeachment Committee tried to get Annie Surratt and her brother to say so, and they could not. They even went down to Fort Jefferson and offered to turn Mudd and the others loose if they'd swear to it, but had no success. They finally gave up on it and left it out of the Articles of Impeachment. But, by God, if they learn Booth's grave is empty, they'll waste no time before they're all running about saying Johnson saw to his lackey's escape. If Stanton's the one you're working for, and you tell him what you found, you can mark my words that will be the outcome. But if Johnson is your client, you can rest assured his people will take the information and use it to call Stanton an incompetent who let Booth slip away, and Johnson has one more good reason for giving him the boot."

"Well, General Grant," I said, "should either of those exigencies come to pass, you shall be in a position to do your duty and disabuse the public of such notions."

"And so suffer for what was merely an act of simple Christian charity," said the General, piously.

"Suffer? How suffer, sir?"

"Suffer the scorn of an indignant public outraged that the assassin's bones no longer lie in a felon's grave."

"Then, General Grant, may I take it the body was disinterred on your authority?"

The General paused before replying.

"Cosgrove, I shall tell you what became of Booth's body if you give me your word as an officer and a gentleman that the information will go no further."

"I do not wish to share your burden, sir," I said, "but I will do so if you, in turn, will agree to favor me with an explanation."

"And what might that be?"

"You were due to share President Lincoln's theater box that night, but tendered him your regrets scant hours before the curtain. I should like to hear the true cause of your absence."

The General's eyes widened as he grasped the import of my question. He crushed his cheroot on the desk and flung it at the cuspidor, missing it.

"Damn your blazing insolence, Cosgrove!"

"My apologies, General, but if I am to offer my client nothing but my own assurances that Booth is truly dead and absent from his grave for excellent, but unspecified, reasons, I must be confident, myself, that I know whereof I speak."

The General opened a drawer in his desk and withdrew a book, slamming it down before me.

"If those are your terms, then here are mine. You have reminded me you are no longer an officer; now you have proved you are neither a gentleman. I shall require your oath of silence on this Bible."

"Certainly," I replied. "If that, as I presume, is the King James Version, I shall gladly put my hand on it and swear that the sun rises in the West, or that General Grant is neither a drunkard nor a graverobber."

"By Jesus!" Grant exclaimed. "I can see I was mistaken to think a brigand such as yourself would have any use for Holy Writ."

"On the contrary, General Grant," I replied. "I often keep a Bible near at hand, but I use it more often for reading than for swearing. I might recommend the same to you, as I perceive you can swear mightily without the Good Book's aid."

I did not know at that moment whether General Grant was going to summon the guard, blast me with further billingsgate, or run 'round his desk and attack me. As it happened he did none of these, but grabbed a whiskey bottle from his desk, poured out a generous potation and gulped it down. He sat perfectly still for a full minute, then filled his glass again. Before replacing the cork he pointed the neck of the vessel in my direction and lifted his gaze to my face. I shook my head, declining the offer.

"So be it," he said. "I have no choice but to risk your discretion. The incident is hardly a secret, anyway.

"Some weeks before the fateful theater invitation, Mr. and Mrs. Lincoln were my guests at City Point. I arranged for them to review the troops assembled there, and Mrs. Lincoln and Mrs. Grant rode to the assembly in an ambulance. When they arrived at the parade ground, the President and I were already there, as was the wife of General Ord, who had come on horseback. You may not know this, but Mrs. Lincoln was jealous of her husband to the point of madness, and difficult as it may be to believe, she permitted him the company of no other woman without first she approved of the lady. Well, on arriving at the parade ground, Mrs. Lincoln saw that Mrs. Ord was riding beside the President. She became furious and abused the poor woman in some of the vilest language I have ever heard from a lady's lips. Mrs. Grant, who is a friend of Mrs. Ord, attempted to calm this situation of affairs, and was rewarded for her trouble by a whopping share of Mrs. Lincoln's abuse. The incident embarrassed us all, and did little for the relations between Mrs. Lincoln and my wife, who were never the best of friends in the first instance. So, when I told Julia, Mrs. Grant, that we were to join the President and his wife at the theater that night, she resolutely refused to go. It is my everlasting regret that I did not simply go along with the Lincolns by myself and make Mrs. Grant's excuses as feeling indisposed. But to tell you the whole truth I had little fondness for the President's Lady myself, and so I begged to be excused to remove to New Jersey and visit my children early that evening."†

"And so, Mr. Cosgrove," said General Grant, "you have had your explanation. If it doesn't suit you, you can go to Hell."

"I do not doubt your word, General," I said.

---

† General Grant's explanation is confirmed by several other sources, including the memoirs of his secretary, Adam Badeau. However, he omitted to mention that Mrs. Lincoln's abuse of Mrs. Grant included the sarcastic, but prophetic remark, "I suppose you think you'll get to the White House yourself, don't you?" Grant also forgot to mention that he was urged not to attend the theater by someone else: Edwin Stanton.—M.C.

"Have I your promise, then, that what I am about to reveal to you concerning the whereabouts of Booth's remains will be kept by you in confidence?" he asked.

I promised him this. The General went to a safe in a corner of the room and unlocked it, taking out two letters, both addressed to the General, which he handed to me. The first was on the stationery of Barnum's Hotel in Baltimore and had been written the previous September. It was from Edwin Booth, the assassin's distinguished older brother.

The letter referred to a promise Booth said he had received from Secretary Stanton to the effect that, when sufficient time had elapsed, the body of John Wilkes Booth would be released to the Booth family. Booth said he had written to Mr. Stanton requesting the body on behalf of his heartbroken mother, but had received no reply. Therefore, Booth wrote, he was appealing to General Grant to release the body to him.

The second missive bore the letterhead, "Law Office of Scammon & Lincoln, No. 1 Marine Bank Building, Chicago," and was signed by the late President's son, Robert Todd Lincoln, who had recently begun the practice of law in that city. It, too, bore a date in September, 1867, about a week or so after the date of Booth's letter.†

Robert Lincoln's letter was brief and very much to the point. The disposition of the assassin's remains were a matter of supreme

---

† Edwin Booth's letter still exists and is in the collection of the Player's Club in New York City. Its full text can be found in Kimmel, pp. 278–279 (see Bibliography), and corresponds closely to Cosgrove's summary of it. Significantly, it was written only a few weeks before the date given by the U.S. National Park Service as that on which the body was moved to permit demolition of the penitentiary building at the Old Arsenal. It should also be noted that the letter was written, and the body moved, while General Grant was reluctantly serving as Acting Secretary of War *ad interim*. (Johnson had suspended Stanton from the post and asked Grant to take his place until Congress reconvened in November, 1867. On January 13, 1868, the Senate voted thirty-five to six to disapprove Stanton's suspension; Grant immediately resigned from his interim post and Stanton resumed his office in the War Department, setting in motion the events that ultimately led to Johnson's impeachment trial.)

If Robert Todd Lincoln's letter still exists, I have not been able to find a trace of it. However, the letterhead Cosgrove describes can be found on other letters written by Lincoln at this time.—M.C.

unimportance to him, he wrote. He added that he held no animosity toward the Booth family. But his closing sentence was so utterly astonishing the exact words remain etched on my memory. They were, "I welcome this opportunity to repay, even in this small part, the debt I owe Mr. Edwin Booth."

"What is this matter of a debt owed Edwin Booth?" I asked, as I handed the papers back to General Grant. "Does he make some grim jest, some bitter irony?"

General Grant shook his head. He returned the papers to his safe and locked them securely away.

"I would not risk the distrust of your detective's mind with this tale, if Mr. Robert Lincoln himself were not willing to vouch for its veracity. It is the habit of one of your profession to distrust coincidence, and the event Mr. Lincoln makes reference to is one of the strangest coincidences in History. I might doubt that it occurred, myself, were it not that through yet another coincidence, it was witnessed by my former secretary, Mr. Badeau, who reported it to me shortly after it happened. I immediately wrote to Edwin Booth, thanking him, and offering to serve him in any way, should he ever require my help. Booth had the grace to omit mention of that letter in his own, but I know he has not forgotten it. Little did I dream then of how I would finally make good my offer.

"It was in 1861, sometime in February or March, I think. Badeau was in the railroad station at Jersey City. The platform was crowded, but Badeau thought he recognized a familiar face, a young man standing beside the cars at the edge of the platform. Before he could approach him the lad was jostled by the crowd and fell between the cars, which at that very moment had begun to move. A man standing nearby dropped his valise, rushed forward, and grasping the fellow by the collar, hauled him to safety.

"The young man was Robert Todd Lincoln, and his savior was Edwin Booth."

The General poured another tumbler of spirits, and this time I accepted his invitation to join him.

"One Booth slaughtered the father after another had rescued the son. Fate keeps an ironic ledger," I observed. (Spirituous drink can inspire me to such rubbish. I blush to admit it, but I later had a discreet inquiry made by a Chicago confidant who was acquainted with Robert Lincoln. Mr. Lincoln confirmed this incredible tale as the truth.)†

"The body of John Wilkes Booth is in the custody of the Booth family," said General Grant. "Now that I have told you the 'wherefore' as well as the 'where,' I trust you will make good your word and keep the matter from your client. Robert Lincoln has suffered enough notoriety of late‡ and, to be candid, public knowledge of my role in the matter can do me no good and, perhaps, some harm."

"You may rely on that, General," I said. "But lest you think at some future time that I have broken my promise, I must now present you with some unhappy intelligence. It was the person of my client, and not his written authorization, that caused Booth's vacant grave to be opened last night."

General Grant rested his face in his hands for a moment, then looked up.

"Thank you for that advice, Colonel Cosgrove. Would that I had replaced the body with that of another, rather than put stones in its place as Edwin Booth requested."

Now that, I thought, was a curious request.

The General went to the door and summoned Sergeant Flaherty. The Sergeant entered and shut the door behind him.

"Flaherty," asked General Grant, "how many felons lie in unmarked graves at the Arsenal?"

"I could not guess," Flaherty replied. "But considering how many must have been hanged there during the long years the place was a prison, even Gabriel will have to pause to count them all on Judgment Day."

"Then he likely won't mind if you shift one about," said the General.

At this I arose and headed for the door.

---

† It is true. Robert Todd Lincoln verified it many years later in the April, 1909, number of *The Century Magazine.*—M.C.

‡ Lincoln had been devastated by the recent publication of a gossipy book written by his mother's former seamstress.—MC.

"General, I believe I am intruding on what should be a private conversation, so, if you will excuse me, I shall take my leave."

I turned to Sergeant Flaherty and handed him the nickel.

"This is yours, Sergeant. Try not to lose it this time." And with that, I departed.†

---

† Apparently Flaherty carried out his assigned task, although he made no mention of any of these picaresque doings while reminiscing on the guarding of Booth's grave at the Arsenal in a letter he wrote to the New York *Times* in 1909, published in the May 9 edition. But there *was* a body in the Arsenal grave when it was opened on orders of President Johnson on February 15, 1869. The exhumation was at the request of Edwin Booth, who had asked the outgoing President to release the body only a few days before that date, and who arranged for its burial in the Booth family grave in Greenbriar Cemetery in Baltimore. If that strikes the reader as curious, since Booth presumably had already acquired his brother's body, the Shakespearean's motives may become apparent as Cosgrove further unfolds his report.—M.C.

PART TWO

···→◆←···

Magic and Mystery

·7·

An Inquiry into an Inquest

$\cdots\!\!-\!\!\blacklozenge\!\!-\!\cdots$

When I returned to the house on K Street that evening, after my interview with General Grant, I was informed by the household staff that Mr. Pinkerton had already retired for the evening, having declared his intention to make an early start on the morrow. He was to depart on the 7:00 A.M. train to Baltimore, and had left orders for the carriage at 6:30 and a little breakfast before setting out. And so I spent the evening with the volume of Pitman the Secretary had sent for my edification.

It was interesting, if not entertaining, for it amounted to a concise summary of the testimony in the trial of Booth's accomplices, a requital of justice I had neither witnessed nor studied, having been abroad at the time. I was even unaware, until I opened this volume, that the trial had not truly been such, in the sense of a hearing presided over by a judge, resulting in a verdict rendered by a jury of ordinary citizens. It was more by way of a military court-martial, for a commission of senior Army officers acted in the role of both judge and jury (and, as I saw between the lines, prosecutor, as well). I had not realized that such a military tribunal had jurisdiction to try civilian defendants, but a learned opinion of the United States Attorney General was included in an appendix, wherein he argued the military's authority in the case.†

---

† The decision, which legitimized the commission, was certainly not universally accepted. The following year, the United States Supreme Court found that the military did not have such authority, in a similar case.—M.C.

Naturally, the testimony which won my closest attention pertained to the pursuit and capture of Booth. Unfortunately there was little here to enlighten the means employed by the pursuers to assure themselves the man whose body they bore back to Washington City was, in fact, the assassin's. Many pages of testimony reduced in this regard to a meager sum: the hunters captured a Rebel soldier who led them to a barn where they found two men. One they discovered to be David Herold; the other they shot to death. One Dr. May was said to have earlier removed a tumor from Booth's neck. The doctor did not himself testify, but a brief statement by Surgeon-General Barnes implied Dr. May had been shown the body and recognized his own handiwork. However, Pitman's book, like the "trial" it abstracted, was intended, not to establish the identity of a corpse, but to prove the guilt of Booth's cohorts. Surely the record of the inquest awaiting my inspection in Major Johnson's office would be more enlightening. I put Mr. Pitman aside and, as had my chief, sought an early repose.

It was not yet light when the faint reveille of breakfast preparations stole into my bedchamber and summoned me from slumber. I quickly dressed and found Mr. Pinkerton at table in the dining room. He greeted me and asked what luck I'd had at the Arsenal.

"In sum, I have learned this much," I replied. "The box we exhumed did, at one time, contain someone's mortal remains. The body was buried at the Arsenal by one who never doubted it was that of Booth, and so did not trouble to inspect it. It was later removed by another, who acted secretly, but in good faith and with legitimate authority. He, too, assumed it to be the assassin's remains and did nothing to confirm its identity. The body had been wrapped in an Army blanket which served as a makeshift shroud that obscured whatever footware it may have enclosed. The blanket was never opened before custody of the body was surrendered to one outside the Government."

Mr. Pinkerton, who had followed all this closely, gazed at me in expectation. He set down his silverware and quickly consulted his watch.

"'Good faith,' 'legitimate authority,' 'surrendered outside the Government,'" he repeated. "I'm to make the seven o'clock train, but

I surely have time to hear more than this. More particulars, if you please, Nicholas, and some names."

"The burial was presided over by Major George Porter, assistant surgeon at the Arsenal, and a Mr. Stebbins, the military storekeeper. As to the who, the why, and the wherefore of the resurrection, I regret to say I gained this information by trading my pledge of silence. But I am satisfied I have learned the motive for the removal of the body, and it in no way enlightens the mystery of whether Booth lives, or, if he does, where. Those questions must be answered by another line of inquiry."

Mr. Pinkerton arose and donned his coat.

"Very well, Nicholas. Then I, too, am satisfied of that much, for you're my best man, and I don't doubt your detective skill. But I'll admit to some reservations regarding your good judgment at this moment. At all events, I'm pleased to know I shall be some thirty miles from this city, at Baltimore, before you can repeat what you have just told me to Mr. Edwin McMasters Stanton. I expect his howl of outrage will be no more than faintly audible at that remove.

"Now I must hurry to the railroad station. Please go leisurely to the War Department."

He stopped at the door and turned to me.

"The best o' luck to ye, lad," he said, and then went on his way.

Mr. Pinkerton's words notwithstanding, I thoroughly enjoyed a sumptuous breakfast, reflecting that, while he apparently had observed Secretary Stanton at highest dudgeon, he likely never witnessed General Grant under a full head of steam. One scarcely can be expected to tremble at the rumblings of Vesuvius after gazing into the blazing mouth of Hell. After the morning newspaper and a cheroot, I betook myself to the Department of War. Ever obedient to my chief, I strolled there at a leisurely pace.

The War Department was quartered in an imposing, three-story structure on the southeast corner of Pennsylvania Avenue and 17th Street. In size and grandeur it was a worthy rival to the White House, its next-door neighbor on the Avenue. The main entrance, which faced the Avenue, was guarded by a row of six columns of the Doric order, which rose above the second story where they supported a broad, flat entablature that served as a balcony opening off the third floor. On the roof directly above the balcony was a gable of identical width, and from its apex rose a flagpole near as high again as the building on which it was mounted. From the top of this staff flew Old Glory in dimensions worthy of the edifice beneath.†

The building stood well back from the intersecting thoroughfares, being separated from the street by a generous sward, still winter-brown and muddy. It was further sheltered by many tall trees, of such age and haphazard arrangement to suggest they antedated the building and had been part of the virgin site selected for its construction. In a line that appeared to surround the building Federal infantrymen stood every few yards at parade rest. A pair of them stood at right-shoulder-arms on the portico, one to either side of the main entrance door. This was more than the military complement usually provided as martial adornment of the War Department; it was the full battalion sent by General Grant a few weeks earlier, when it appeared to many in the capital that the conflict between Secretary Stanton and Congress, on the one hand, and the President of the United States, on the other, might suddenly be reduced to a question of physical possession of this building.

As I approached the perimeter I was challenged by a sentry to whom I announced my pseudonym and assumed mission. He escorted me within, where I repeated myself to the Captain of the Guard. I was gratified to find that Major Johnson had managed to remember "Nichols" and "Hostetter." A sergeant was detached to escort me to the second floor and the eastern wing of the building, where I was ushered into the presence of the Major.

Major Johnson greeted me curtly, then picked a file of papers from his desk and went to a door that appeared to open into an adjoining

---

† A similar, if somewhat smaller, building housing the Navy Department was located behind the War Department building, just down 17th Street. In 1879 both were torn down to make way for a single, massive building to house the Departments of War, Navy and State. This gray granite building survives to the present, but it is now known as the "Old Executive Office Building," and houses part of the White House staff.—M.C.

office. He knocked and I heard Secretary Stanton bid him enter. The Major gestured to me to follow him.

The Secretary occupied an office in the corner of the wing, and so enjoyed a larger ration of daylight than did his secretary. A pair of windows opened on the Avenue, while another pair in the adjacent wall looked out to the east. But it may be less than accurate to imply these latter portals were a source of joy to Mr. Stanton at that moment, as the view they offered was the Presidential Mansion next door. Nevertheless, it was in this direction I found the Secretary gazing as I entered his office. He was standing with his back to us at a long table running the length of the eastern wall of his chamber. He turned as we entered.

"Good morning, Cosgrove," he said briskly. "Major Johnson informs me you returned to the Arsenal yesterday to make further inquiries. Have you discovered anything more of this matter? Do be seated," he added, pointing to a chair.

The Secretary remained standing. He was a man of short stature, and some say it was for this reason he preferred to interview visitors in such fashion. Others maintain it was habit acquired in the courtroom during his long career as an attorney. In this instance he lent support to the second theory by pacing to and fro as he conferred with me.

"I found nothing further to suggest that Booth lives, but instead a clew that argues he may well be dead," I replied.

"Oh, and what might that be?"

"A body thought to be that of John Wilkes Booth *was* buried at the Arsenal. It has since been exhumed and removed beyond hope of recovery for any purposes of identification. But I believe it to have been one and the same corpse that was the object of the official inquest. Thus, I've come today to review the inquest records. If they offer strong positive evidence the body was, in fact, that of Booth, I shall incline to suspect your informant is mistaken in reporting the man alive. But if they provide something less than reasonable certainty in the matter, I shall continue my inquiries."

"Exhumed and removed, you say!" he exclaimed. "Exhumed on whose authority? Removed to what place? But stay! We shall deal with those matters presently. You say a body was, in fact, buried at the Arsenal?"

"Yes. It was buried during the night, after the inquest. It was delivered to the Arsenal grounds wrapped in a blanket and bound in a gunny sack. Apparently the delivery was made by General Baker as he has most recently claimed before a committee of the House. But unless one can envision a plausible motive for Baker to exchange one body for another, I must conclude it was the same body he removed from the *Montauk*. Thus, it was the one the board judged to be Booth."

"Ah, Baker!" exclaimed the Secretary with distaste. "You ask for a plausible motive? That man needs none. Lying and deceit are ends in themselves to Lafayette Baker. He swore to the Impeachment Committee that it was I who ripped the missing pages from Booth's diary."

"Perchance Baker hopes to sell Booth's remains to Barnum," offered Major Johnson.

"I should not be surprised," commented the Secretary. "Tell me, Mr. Cosgrove, this body in the gunny sack, did you learn if it was booted?"

"Alas, the body was never wholly removed from its blanket shroud while at the Arsenal, so none there can say ought of the footware. I am afraid we must turn to the inquest for further enlightenment."

"Yes, the inquest," said Mr. Stanton. "Would that Holt had the wit to make so obvious a test as the one you devised, sir, while the body was yet in his custody. Here, Alfred, let me see the documents."

The Major handed the file of papers to his chief.

"I took the liberty of reviewing the depositions this morning, sir," said the Major. "There are a great many, but only one of true significance. I refer to the testimony of a surgeon, one Dr. May, who had removed a tumor from Booth's neck and was able to recognize the scar he left."

The Secretary rapidly shuffled through the pages of the files, stopping on occasion to bestow a more careful attention to some particular page. Invariably he would terminate his examination with a grunt and move on to the next sheet.

"Here we have one Charles Dawson, a room clerk, who sets great store by a tattoo of india ink upon the hand,"† the Secretary commented. "Major, if you were to go to my inkstand and put the same mark on your own left hand, and then showed it to Mr. Dawson, do you suppose he would believe that Booth's ghost walks?"

The Major cleared his throat.

"I believe Mr. Dawson also recognized Booth by his general appearance," he said.

Mr. Stanton gazed at him in silence for a moment, then said in a strangely quiet way, "Alfred, you are fortunate to be so innocent of the works of Death. Given a scant few hours he will add mockery to his theft."

The Major appeared bewildered by this, but said nothing. Yet his bewilderment was mute testimony that he had never been in battle, never chanced upon a fallen comrade after the guns had gone silent. The Secretary had resumed his brusk manner and moved deeper into the sheaf.

"Hah," he snorted. "Here's another who knew the body to be Booth's by its 'general appearance.' Yet we read further and find how well Mr. Seaton Monroe was acquainted with the assassin: he had met him once, some years earlier. Who was this Monroe, and how did he come to be aboard the *Montauk?*"

"He was the captain's brother," Major Johnson replied. "He happened to visit the ironclad that morning, and General Eckert asked his opinion."

---

† That John Wilkes Booth wore his own initials indelibly printed in india ink on the back of his left hand near the junction of his thumb and forefinger has been reasonably well established. In her memoir published in 1938, his sister, Asia Booth Clarke, recalled that he put them there himself, as a boy. Some writers who have questioned whether the body on the *Montauk* was really Booth have attached great importance to reports of various people placing the initials on his right hand, or arm, but invariably such reports were made from memory, often many years after the witness last saw Booth. Dawson, who had often stood by while Booth signed the register at the National Hotel and so had frequent opportunities to observe the tattoo, was quite specific about its location in his deposition aboard the *Montauk,* and none of the other witnesses deposed at the inquest placed the marks anywhere else. Stanton's point is well taken, however.—M.C.

"Hmmm. Eckert usually shows better sense," said Mr. Stanton.†

"It seems that you are right, as usual, Alfred," said Mr. Stanton. "Dr. May's is the only testimony taken at the inquest worth two cents toward establishing the body was Booth's. But it may not be worth greatly more than that," he added, perusing the deposition. "He tells us that Booth chanced to employ him to remove a carbuncle from his neck some two years earlier. Some weeks later he inspects the surgical wound when Booth's stage antics cause it to reopen. Yet two years later he can describe the precise shape, texture and location of the scar. Dr. May is surely a prodigy among physicians, for most would remember nothing more than the fee they charged for their work and how promptly it was paid. I find his testimony remarkable."

"I find his presence yet more remarkable," I offered. "I conclude that the doctor was not Booth's regular physician, since Washington City was not the actor's home. So the board of inquest seems singularly efficient in learning so quickly of a local surgeon's treatment of Booth."

"An interesting point, Mr. Cosgrove," said Stanton. He examined the deposition again. "Rendered even more so by the fact that the board apparently had not known of his work beforehand, for here I find he informs Dr. Barnes of the carbuncle incident in the midst of his testimony. We must send for Mr. Holt and learn how it was he summoned Dr. May in the first instance."

"It was General Baker who summoned him, sir," Major Johnson offered. "He went to the doctor's office and personally escorted him to the *Montauk*. As I recall his coming on board, he seemed

---

† Thomas T. Eckert, originally a telegrapher for General McClellan, joined the War Department's telegraph department, and soon became its chief. He rose through the ranks of Major and General to become an Assistant Secretary of War. Since the telegraph was the principal means of military communication during the War, Eckert was in almost daily contact with Lincoln and Stanton; his office in the Cipher Room, just down the hall from Stanton's, became, in effect, the North's national military command center from which the War was conducted. It has been said that Lincoln spent more of his waking hours in that room during the hostilities than in the White House. Eckert thus played an important role in most of the major military activities in Washington. In 1866 he left the War Department to become Supervisor of the Eastern Division of Western Union, and ultimately, through his services to Jay Gould, president of that company. As we shall see, Eckert played an important part in the events recounted in Cosgrove's narrative.—M.C.

almost in the manner of one who has found himself placed under close arrest."

"Then fetch him here in the same fashion immediately," commanded the Secretary, "for I have some questions to put to him."

"May I respectfully suggest you do not do so," I said. "At least not until I have had a chance to learn what I can from the man. If, out of some terror General Baker employed to threaten him, he perjured himself, then now he will fear the consequences of his perjury, as well. It may be that I can discover more through guile than you might by intimidation."

"Very well, Cosgrove," said Mr. Stanton, returning the doctor's deposition to the sheaf. "Your point is well taken. Now I would hear from you the details you've discovered concerning the removal of the body from the Arsenal.

"Wait," he interjected, before I could reply. "What is this?"

He withdrew a large envelope from among the depositions. I recognized the commercial imprint of Gardner's Gallery on the thing.

"What is this, Alfred?"

"The photographs, sir."

"Photographs? What photographs?" demanded Mr. Stanton.

"Of the body, sir," Major Johnson explained, almost apologetically. "I suggest you forgo inspecting them, for they are not pretty things."†

Mr. Stanton disregarded this warning and slipped the photographs from the envelope. There were several views, and they seemed to capture the Secretary's heed to a degree even the written depositions had failed to do. He seemed, in fact, to be overcome by some queer obses-

---

† It is a matter of record that Alexander Gardner, the famous photographer, and his equally celebrated assistant, Timothy O'Sullivan, were brought on board the *Montauk* during the inquest. While it is likely that both men were familiar with Booth and may even have photographed him in life, it seems reasonable to think they were there in their professional capacity, rather than as witnesses. In any case, no record of a deposition by either of them exists in the official government files. But neither does any photograph of the body, or any record that such photographs were taken. The New York *Daily Tribune* of April 29, 1865, reported that "a photographic view of the body was taken," and the fate of the reported photos has been one of the minor mysteries in the case. Cosgrove's narrative clears it up.—M.C.

sion, for he could scarcely take his eyes from one of the photographs, and then only to fasten them on its successor. There were four views in all, and only after what seemed at least a quarter hour had passed did he cease his repeated examination of them. During this extended silence Major Johnson's face betrayed concern as he watched his chief, while I made use of the pause to rehearse my claim of confidentiality in the matter of the exhumation, which now seemed surely the next item on our agendum. But when Mr. Stanton was done with the mortuary portraits, the matter of my inquiries at the Arsenal seemed to have escaped his concern, for he handed me the photographs and spoke in a strange manner, seemingly to neither the Major nor myself, but as though some other person had joined our conference.

"Could this have been the pretty fellow whose face was his fortune? The idol of women, the envy of men from Richmond to Boston?" he asked.

I looked at the photographs. The dead man lay grinning, nay leering, as though taking pleasure in the mystery he had become. But this was not the residuum of some final satisfaction enjoyed by the dying man. It was the all too familiar rictus I had seen stretching the face of many a corpse a few hours after death. The eyes stared at some private vision and the skin was stretched tightly across the dead face, making a beak of the nose, and transforming the countenance into one who looked to have eluded death for fourscore years or more. The grim visage bore no similarity to John Wilkes Booth, nor any of his illustrious brothers. Rather, it had taken on the lineaments common to the larger family its owner had joined. Whoever he may have been in life, he now had become one of the Dead.

"'Death's a great disguiser,'" I quoted,† handing the photographs back to the secretary.

Mr. Stanton stood before the fireplace beside his desk and, to my astonishment, cast the pictures into the flames. The glow from the

---

† This is from *Measure for Measure*, Act Four, Scene Two, and its appearance in Cosgrove's Manuscript is strange. As the reader must have noticed, Cosgrove is not especially modest in quoting his own wit and eloquence. Of course we can't know if he was actually so quick on the draw when it came to repartee, but if he did occasionally write his own lines after the fact, he did so in the diaries he seemed to

hearth glistened on his face, as if the faint heat from the modest blaze had made him perspire. But I quickly perceived that the man had been silently weeping, and tears, rather than sweat, dampened his countenance.

"He is the last enemy," he said. I marveled that the man could believe he recognized Booth's lineaments in the macabre mask the gruesome pictures revealed, and especially that the sight of a dead assassin could move him to tears. Then I perceived that the Secretary was gazing at the photograph of a lady that stood atop the mantel, and realized she was the more likely cause of his tears.

I sought to cover this embarrassing situation of affairs and distract Mr. Stanton from whatever private grief had so suddenly afflicted him by turning to the matter of the exhumation at the Arsenal and making my claim of confidentiality in the matter. To my amazement the Secretary responded to my words with unexpected mildness.

He turned his back on me and said, "Very well, Mr. Cosgrove, you seem to have matters well in hand. You are a secret detective and I am a lawyer, and I can understand that your profession, as mine, sometimes requires absolute confidentiality. But see to it that I am kept informed of the results of your continuing inquiries."

To my surprise and relief the interview was over, and Major Johnson silently indicated that I should depart. This I did without delay.†

---

have updated during his adventures, whenever a lull in the action permitted. The Cosgrove manuscript is generally faithful to the diary account of this period, but in this case it differs from the corresponding diary entry, in which Cosgrove quoted Ecclesiastes rather than Shakespeare. What he originally said was, "Make little weeping for the dead, for he is at rest: but the life of a fool is worse than death." But that still isn't bad for an ex-New York City flatfoot.—M.C.

† Cosgrove missed what actually happened during these final minutes of his interview with Stanton. He apparently did not know that Stanton's first child, Lucy, had died at the age of eighteen months in 1841, nor that his first wife died in childbirth three years later. While these tragedies occurred a quarter century earlier, and Stanton had since remarried and raised the surviving child of his first marriage, he never fully overcame the grief of his early bereavement, and was sometimes discovered by unexpected visitors to his office sitting weeping at his desk. Had Cosgrove known this much, the Bible-reading private eye would probably have recognized Stanton's paraphrase of 1 Corinthians, and realized the enemy Stanton referred to was not John Wilkes Booth, but Death.—M.C.

·8·

"The Preceptor of All Great Magicians"

···—◆—◈—◆—····

Major Johnson followed me from the Secretary's chamber and closed the adjoining door behind him with such gentle solicitude one might have thought we had departed a nursery full of snoozing babes, rather than the workshop of the Nation's Minister of War. I reminded him that I had come to inspect the sheaf of testimony he carried under his arm, and he nodded and led me across his office to another door that opened into a room identical in dimensions to his own.

There was a table in the center of the floor, and several desks arranged about the perimeter of the chamber. At one of these, beside the fireplace immediately to the right of the entrance, a lone clerk looked up from his meticulous labor, which I instantly recognized as the translation of a message from clear text into cipher. There were two other doors, one of which looked to lead to the corridor of the wing. From behind the other, which faced us as we entered, I heard the familiar chatter of telegraphy sets. That door stood partly open, and through it I glimpsed several men seated at marble-topped tables. Some were keying messages, while others were scribbling on foolscap sheets the intelligence clattering forth from the sounders beside them. This was the telegraph office of the Department of War, the nerve-center of the sluggish, mighty beast that stood guard over the Republic.

The Major stepped across the room and shut the door, but not before I'd heard enough to know that, at this particular instant, the wires carried dispatches in clear text, not cipher, and the messages concerned only such military trifles as boots and beans. He led me to a large desk beside a window and next to a massive peter† that bore

---

† A nineteenth-century slang word used by police and criminals to mean a safe.
—M.C.

the commercial mark of Thompson & Co. of New Haven, Connecticut. I made a quick appraisal of the thing and judged it likely a tough one to beat without the touch of a professional cracksman. Reflecting that it was a cut above the kind likely found in most banks, I said a silent prayer of thanks for the Grace that guided me from the paths of iniquity. It was a thanksgiving that many a banker should have joined me in offering.

"This was General Eckert's desk," the Major whispered in a manner that implied it was constructed of wood from the True Cross.† I seated myself and took the sheaf from Major Johnson, who returned to his office, stopping on the way to whisper with the cipher clerk, I suppose to caution him that I was of the Unwashed.

I took some considerable time to examine all of the depositions with care, and finally joined Major Johnson and Mr. Stanton in the opinion that none but that of Dr. May offered any persuasive evidence the corpse on the *Montauk* was Booth. And the Secretary had been generous to the surgeon in his analysis of the weakness in Dr. May's claim to have identified the body, for he clave to its obvious deficiencies, eschewing the subtler fragrances of equivocation which arose from the good doctor's deposition. I took out my notebook and copied some of the more doubtful passages.

Q. Have you, since you came on board this vessel, examined the dead body which is alleged to be that of J. Wilkes Booth?

A. I have, sir.

Q. Will you state whether, in your opinion, it is the body of J. Wilkes Booth?

A. I believe it to be, sir; I have no doubt that it is. I believe I have only seen Booth once since the time to which I have referred.

---

† Cosgrove might have been more impressed if Johnson had added it was used as often by Lincoln, during his visits, as by Eckert, who sat elsewhere on those frequent occasions. He might have been even more respectful of the desk had he known that it was while sitting at it that the President penned the first draft of the Emancipation Proclamation. But Cosgrove's description of the Cipher Room, the Telegraph Office, and the offices of Secretary Stanton and Major Johnson match extant records perfectly, and leave little doubt he visited the suite.—M.C.

Dr. May "believes," then has "no doubt," but immediately adds an afterthought that could not fail to inspire doubt.

> Q. Do you recognize the body as that of J. Wilkes Booth from its general appearance, and also from the particular appearance of the scar?
> A. I do recognize it, though it is very much altered since I saw Booth. It looks to me much older, and in appearance much more freckled than he was. I do not recollect that he was at all freckled. I have no doubt it is his body . . .

Far from assuring his questioner, Dr. May's teeter-totter testimony had raised, not merely doubt, but exasperation, that one can almost hear while reading the next question.

> Q. From the nature of this wound, even apart from the general appearance, you could not be mistaken as to the identity of the body?
> A. From the scar in connection with the recognition of the features, which though much changed and altered, still have the same appearance I think I cannot be mistaken. I recognize the likeness. I have no doubt that it is the person from whom I took the tumor, and that it is the body of J. Wilkes Booth.

The transcript was much crossed out and revised. This last answer had been in the original form of "From the wound, I think I could not be; but I also recognize the features," and the words, "I think I cannot be mistaken," looked to have been added later, as an afterthought.†

If Dr. May's interviewer was puzzled by his witness's vacillation, he might have found its cause nearby, perhaps in the presence of a glowering Lafayette Baker within vision and earshot of the timorous physician. But that was merely a theory, and one I had yet to prove.

---

† Cosgrove's extracts from Dr. May's deposition are accurate, as is his description of the crossing-out, the revisions, and the other indications on the handwritten original that Dr. May was something less than an ideal witness. The original document is on file among the War Department Records at the National Archives in Washington, D.C.—M.C.

At all events, the inquest records left ample room to doubt the identity of the corpse aboard the *Montauk,* and so my inquiries must needs continue.

I returned the documents to Major Johnson with my thanks and departed the War Department without having yet conceived a pretext upon which to interview Dr. May in hope of discerning the truth in the matter of his presence and testimony aboard the *Montauk.* Yet those were matters of which General Baker might know something. Would that I'd been curious to know of them yesterday, when I questioned the General from behind the mask of "Anton Dumont"!

General Baker! A strange coincidence to find him in Washington City now, at the very moment the shade of John Wilkes Booth had chosen to walk. As General Grant had pointed out, coincidences are things dissatisfying to secret detectives. Before I pursued Dr. May, I meant to learn the matter that had brought General Baker to town.

I established that the General was staying at the Pennsylvania House, a back-street hostelry of no great elegance that Baker would have more likely visited in his professional capacity, rather than as a patron, during his years as the War Department's chief secret policeman. Pennsylvania House was in the East Capitol section, on C Street. I betook myself there and inquired of the desk clerk whether General Lafayette Baker was in. He glanced at the boxes behind him and, presumably seeing the room key there, informed me the General was out. I penned a brief and inconsequential message concerning the matters we had discussed at Harvey's and handed it to the clerk, asking him to see to it that the General received it. The young man placed the paper in the box numbered "18."

I repaired to the hotel's public room, at which vantage point I could observe the desk and the clerk from behind the blind of a newspaper. When the lad left his post for a moment, I put down the paper and strode within the precincts of the hotel in the manner of one who had business there, as, indeed, I had. The lock that secured the door bearing the number "18" was of a quality and vintage consistent with the other appointments of the house, and it greeted the first skeleton key I placed in it with so warm a welcome one might have thought it to be its lawful mate.

I locked the door from the inside, leaving the key in place so that it could not be unlocked from without, and immediately stepped to the window to satisfy myself that an unobstructed route of egress was available, should it suddenly be required. A dim alleyway lay beyond the dingy pane, its muddy floor on the same level as the General's first-story room. Escape, if required, should be easily accomplished along this avenue. I turned my attention to the room.

It did not take long to search the place, for the General had left little in the dreary chamber. A swaybacked bunk, a washstand and a night table were the only items of furniture in the room. The empty closet testified that the only wardrobe the General had brought to Washington was that which he wore upon his back. Upon the night table I found several books. There was a copy of the *History of the United States Secret Service,* bearing his own name in the author's place on the cover, a well-thumbed copy of Pitman's account of the Conspiracy Trial (the same tome presented to Mr. Pinkerton by Major Johnson), and two fresh volumes comprising the testimony and report of the House Impeachment Investigation Committee. General Baker had wasted no time in acquiring these last items after learning of their existence during his interview with Mr. Reed the day before. Slipped between the pages of Pitman I found a letter from Commissioner Ashford of Washington City addressed to Baker at an address in Philadelphia. The letter informed him that a hearing was shortly to commence in the matter of the $20,000 that had been offered by the city in 1865 for the capture of Booth and his accomplices, which sum had yet to be awarded. General Baker had apparently laid claim to the prize, and the Commissioner invited him to Washington City to present his arguments in the case. I copied the General's Philadelphia address into my notebook for future reference.

As I returned the letter in its envelope to Pitman, a small scrap of paper slipped out and tumbled to the floor. I retrieved it and found it to contain a terse handwritten message, without either salutation or signature. It simply said, "Your lies have drawn your teeth. Do your worst, if you will. We have no fear. Not another cent."

I set the curious missive on the table and removed from my wallet a sheet of fine onionskin. Taking a pencil from my coat, I proceeded carefully to trace the handwritten words. I folded the copy and secured it in my notebook and replaced the note between Pitman's pages.

So, the General was a blackmailer, and he'd milked dry his victim. How many others still rented his silence? When the secret police chief departed Washington City in disgrace two years ago, how many of the guilty secrets of its most prominent citizens had he taken with him? Was Dr. John May's among them? Could it be the Doctor's hand had penned the desperate prescription I'd discovered?

I had given the room a final, hasty inspection, and was making ready to depart, when I heard the sound of key attempting entry of the doorlock, but thwarted by mine own. I crept silently to the door and placed my ear against it. From the corridor beyond came the familiar voice of General Baker muttering vile imprecations upon key, lock and house.

"Wrong damned key! He's given me the wrong damned one!"

Having achieved this fortuitous misapprehension, the General must have set out in search of the room clerk and the proper key, for I heard his tread attenuating in the hall. It would not do for me to follow him that way, lest I encounter General Baker and the room clerk making their return to the recalcitrant door. Thus I exited through the window. Once in the alleyway, I troubled to turn back and close the window behind me, lest the General or the clerk fathom the cause of the door's earlier resistance. I was completing this precaution when I was roughly seized by the back of my coat collar.

"Well, which one are you?" I heard a voice inquire. "A common burglar, or some gypsy who would be on his way without first settling his bill?"

It was a constable of the Washington City Police Department, and he'd come upon me with such stealth that one of my wrists was already shackled to one of his, before I could move to prevent it.

"Never mind," he continued. "Come along to the front door, and I'll have my answer from the fellow at the desk."

He was a large specimen, and I saw it would not be possible to take his key and free myself of him without doing the poor man some damage, and perhaps sustaining a bruise or two, myself. As a general matter, I am loathe to do violence to a fellow officer of the law, and especially not one of the Washington City Metropolitan Police Department, whose chief, Superintendent Richards, often cooperated with me on matters of mutual professional interest.† However, I could not permit this constable to do that which he intended, for I could think of no reasonable excuse to offer General Baker to explain my unauthorized presence in his room. He would be onto me immediately, and my inquiry would have met with disaster.

"A moment, if you please, Officer," I pleaded.

"What's that? Resisting arrest, as well?"

"Not at all. I shall come along quietly, but I suggest we go direct to Police Headquarters, and so save some embarrassment."

"Embarrassment, is it? Well there's more than some embarrassment in store for the likes of you, my fine fellow."

"I do not refer to myself," I said.

"Oh? Well, then, don't trouble yourself over the thing, man. It won't embarrass me at all to hear you explain to the manager of this house how it happens you prefer to leave it through a window."

"But I think it might. I am certain it would embarrass Mr. Richards."

These words brought up the constable sharply, and he turned and studied me carefully.

"Very well," he replied, at length. "Headquarters it is. But it will be the Blue Jug‡ next, if the Superintendent doesn't vouch for you. And you'll have a good, long look at the inside of the place before you ever see the outside of it again."

---

† Almarin Cooley Richards was appointed to the post by President Lincoln in 1864, and served as head of the Washington Metropolitan Police for ten years.—M.C.

‡ The blue stucco city jail, which stood on 4th Street, N.W., between F and G Streets.—M.C.

So saying, he led me to Police Headquarters on 10th Street. I managed to keep close to his side while we walked there, so to conceal the shackles that linked our wrists from the curious stares of passersby.

"I suppose, Mr. Nichols," said Superintendent Richards, "that you will refuse to explain what business you were about when my constable found you climbing through a window of the Pennsylvania House."

Mr. Richards was a trim, dapper man of some forty years, with an intense and serious mien. Yet he did not regard my predicament without a trace of humor. I think he may have found it somewhat more satisfying to have caught me out in my bungling than to have apprehended a true burglar. It was, at least, a more novel occurrence.

"I shall be obliged to inform you of the matter, should you insist on it," I replied. "But that would be a pity."

"A pity? Why a pity?"

"It would be a pity," I replied, "because the information would be of no value to you. Rather than supply you with a piece of worthless information simply because I owe it to you, I should prefer continuing to supply you, from time to time, with pieces of valuable information, which you are not owed, but of which I make you a present, nonetheless."

"So that's the way it is, is it?" Mr. Richards commented. "Very well, I take your meaning. But I won't let you off scot-free."

"What is it to be, then?" I inquired. "A night in the Blue Jug? Surely no more than that!"

"More, but also less," he replied. "I shall require your assistance in a certain matter this evening."

"Gladly," I replied. "I can comprehend that you might require my help; all your constables seem occupied guarding the city's alleyways."

"It is not an official matter, exactly," he said, declining the challenge to reply in a similar vein. "The owner of Wall's Opera House is a friend, and he has asked a favor of me. It seemed like a small thing when I agreed to it, but, now that the date has arrived, I should prefer to empty a saloon of a drunken crew without assistance than to keep my promise."

"You wish me to keep it in your place, whatever it is?"

The Superintendent shook his head sadly.

"I *wish* you to, but you cannot. It is something I must do. But you can come along and lend me moral support."

"Done!" I readily agreed.

Wall's Opera House, that night, was presenting Professor Haselmayer, "The Perceptor of All Great Magicians," who, so read the notices, would perform "Wonderful Feats of Music and Magic." Mr. Richards, it transpired, had promised his friend, the proprietor of Wall's, to lend his distinguished presence to the stage to assist in one of the Professor's wonderful feats. As I supped with the police chief, I suggested he take special pleasure of the food, as it might be the last time he would enjoy provender intended for human consumption. I speculated that henceforth he might dine on flies, as the magician might have in mind to transform him into a frog. But Mr. Richards seemed to find no pleasure in our supper until he learned that my present business required I interview Dr. J. F. May.

Dr. May no longer practiced medicine in Washington City, he explained, but had removed to New York City a year or so before. Thus, observed Mr. Richards, I was destined to spend a day aboard the cars going there. He then proceeded to recount in some horrifying detail a few of the more famous railroad accidents that had occurred in recent months, while expressing his confidence that the likelihood of my meeting with such a calamity was probably fairly small. More died of food poisoning than railroad crashes, he said, somewhat pointedly, as I dined on a plate of oysters.

Shortly before eight o'clock we repaired to Wall's, and took our seats in the front row of the house, which was already well populated with curious theater-goers, ready for a dose of wonderments. Presently the houselights dimmed, and the orchestra struck up a few bars to capture the attention of the audience and herald the imminent arrival of Professor Haselmayer.

He did not walk out upon the stage, but materialized there. Or, at least, he achieved the illusion of having done so. The proscenium had remained darkened until a small charge of flash powder was ignited. Then, as the footlights were raised, the Professor stepped forth through the resulting curtain of smoke. The effect was to suggest to the eye that the smoke had coalesced into the corporeal presence of the magician. It was, of course, an illusion, but one executed with such precision as to be completely effective.

Unlike other stage magicians I'd seen, Professor Haselmayer did not perform in the familiar costume of a wizard, bedizened with arcane astrological signs and the like, and replete with pointed cap. Instead the Professor appeared before the audience dressed as a fashionable gentleman out to some formal evening occasion. At first this departure disappointed me, for much of the delight I took in such magic shows was to persuade myself, at least for the duration of the exhibit, that I was witnessing a sample of true Black Art, and not merely a clever sham. But the reason for the Professor's choice of costume soon became clear. It was a mute proclamation to this effect: "Here, ladies and gentlemen! I need no spurious rainment to lay claim to the calling of wizard. You have come to see, not garments, but magic, and magic is what you shall see."†

If that was the magician's unspoken claim, it was one he made good, for during the ensuing hour he treated the audience to an astonishing progression of the most remarkable wonderments. He began with some preliminary feats of legerdemain, such as the production of birds and other living things, apparently from thin air, but soon moved on to even better marvels. He was aided in his performance by several male assistants. Unlike the Professor, they came onstage in costume, bedecked identically in uniforms reminiscent of the Zouave, viz., baggy red trousers, a short blue vest, and a black headpiece similar to a fez.

At one juncture in his performance, Professor Haselmayer approached the footlights to address the audience, first doffing his silk top hat to reveal a head completely devoid of hair. Still, he seemed a

---

† The now-familiar evening dress of stage magicians was an innovation of the celebrated French master of legerdemain, Jean Eugene Robert-Houdin (1805–1871), from whom one Erich Weiss of Appleton, Wisconsin, adopted the stage name of Harry Houdini. But Houdini never met Robert-Houdin, who died four years before the twentieth-century magician was born. Professor Haselmayer, on the other hand, had actually studied under the French master, as Cosgrove later learns.—M.C.

young man, of athletic build and stance. He spoke with a heavy Germanic accent from behind a thick, stylish goatee.

He informed the house that Superintendent Richards of the Metropolitan Police was present in the audience at his invitation, and asked Mr. Richards to join him on the stage. The Superintendent drew in a long breath and left his place beside me to brave whatever awaited him before the footlights.

The Superintendent's role in the performance now became clear. Mr. Richards was a man of unquestioned integrity, and his admirable reputation was known throughout Washington City and elsewhere. It was for this reason the magician desired his presence.

The magician was about to undertake a feat so remarkable that the choice of an assistant unknown to the audience, or a personage less celebrated for his integrity, might inspire suspicion that the wonder was accomplished with the aid of a confederate disguised as a theatergoer. But it was impossible to believe Superintendent Richards to be a confederate in any sense of the word.

The Professor removed his coat and gloves, unhooked the cuffs of his shirt, and rolled his sleeves well above the elbow. An assistant came forward and presented the Professor with a shallow wooden case of such size and shape that it might have held a brace of pistols, but when he opened it and tilted it toward the footlights, we could see that it contained five sets of wrist shackles resting on a bed of velvet. The Professor handed the case back to his servant, who took it to Mr. Richards and held it open before him. At the magician's request the police chief inspected each set of irons.

"So, Herr Superintendent, would you offer your professional opinion of these items?"

"Well," said the Superintendent carefully in a lower, yet audible tone, "they *appear* to be wrist irons."

"Ach, yes, they appear so," agreed the Professor, "but it would not be possible, even for one of your professional skill, to say, without more thorough inspection, they are not some kind of trick wrist irons meant for the stage and not the police station?"

The Superintendent readily agreed to this proposition.

"Nevertheless," said the Professor, "may I beg the Superintendent now to place these irons upon my wrists," and so saying, he extended his arms to Mr. Richards, who proceeded to do as he was bid. When he had completed this task the magician's forearms were locked in parallel by the five sets of shackles.

"Now," declared the Professor, "because it is impossible for even an expert to swear that these are not trick irons, I have asked the good Superintendent Richards to bring with him tonight a set of his own shackles, the same he might use any day of the week to restrain a prisoner. Have you remembered to do so, Herr Superintendent?"

Mr. Richards had remembered, and he produced from within his coat a set of irons clearly as formidable in appearance as any of the magician's collection.

"May I ask the Superintendent to add his own shackles to the ones I already wear?"

Mr. Richards complied, locking the sixth set of irons above the five he had already placed.

"And now," declaimed Professor Haselmayer, "the Sacred Mantle of Emancipation!"

At this, an assistant came forward bearing a square swatch of black silk, perhaps a yard in size, and draped it so as to obscure totally the magician's shackled arms. The assistant stood to the side and the Professor commenced to move his arms beneath the silken veil. After a moment, the Professor extended one hand from beneath the silk. It held one pair of shackles. The Zouave took the irons and lifted them aloft for the audience to see. Both wrist cuffs were unlocked and hanging open.

Meanwhile the Professor had busied himself again, and soon produced a second set of irons, which were duly received by his helper and exhibited to our view. These, too, dangled unlocked and open. The process was repeated again, and yet again, and once more, until the assistant held five sets of open irons. All the while the orchestra had been beating out a rataplan which began softly and slowly, but increased in volume and tempo as each set of shackles was produced. Now the music stopped for a moment, and the Professor stood frozen upon the stage, his outthrust arm still covered by the black mantle. Finally, an assistant stepped up to the Professor and, in one swift motion, wrenched away "the Sacred Mantle of Emancipation." Simultaneously, a deafening crash of cymbals burst forth from the orchestra. Professor Haselmayer dropped one arm to his side and raised the other high above his head. In his upraised hand he held the irons Superintendent Richards had applied to his arms. They no longer encircled his wrists, *but they were still locked!* Amidst a thundering ovation, the Professor approached Mr. Richards and presented him with the shackles, favoring first the police official and then the wildly applauding house with a brace of brisk Prussian bows.

Yet even this was not to be the finish of the wonderments the Professor held in store for us. No sooner had the tumult in the house died down than four assistants brought out a sturdy-looking trunk, which the magician climbed within, closing the lid on himself. More theater-goers were invited from the audience to help the Professor's Zouaves chain and lock the casket securely. Then the assistants brought forth a larger piece of black silk which draped the trunk completely. Again the orchestra added to the suspense, filling the theater with an alien and repetitive melody suggestive of Eastern lands. Finally the Zouaves uncovered and unlocked the trunk, tipping it forward so that all could see it contained neither the Professor nor any other thing. At the same moment the cymbals crashed once again and a Drummond light sprang to life, tunneling through the darkness of the house to conjure a circle of dazzling brilliance in the center aisle at the farthest point from the stage. And there, within the circle of limelight, stood the Professor.

There was to be more. I shall not endeavor to describe all of the wizardry witnessed in that hall. Suffice to say Professor Haselmayer demonstrated, beyond peradventure of a doubt, that the irons had not been forged, the rope had not been woven, nor the casket built that could restrain him. He was the unrivaled master of the art of escape. How he had accomplished these marvels, I could not guess. After each escape, my brain struggled with the new mystery he had posed. But I could not begin to divine the means he had used to accomplish his release from even one of the restraints that imprisoned him. I felt certain that every one of the Professor's escapes must have been accomplished through some practical means that evaded observation. My eyes argued otherwise, but my mind refused to accept the proposition that what had been exhibited that evening on the stage of Wall's Opera House was beyond the natural order of the universe. That the identical paradox plagued every other mind in the house I was certain.

At the consummation of what seemed to be Professor Haselmayer's final marvel of the program, the curtain was lowered, and for the hundredth time that evening, the house was brought to its feet. After the thunderous ovation finally attenuated, the curtain was raised again, and the Professor stood in the middle of the stage, which was now bare of his apparatus and assistants. The applause began to build once more, but the magician, after making several deep bows, raised his arms to beg for silence.

"Ladies and gentlemen," he declaimed, "I thank you for your generous response to my little tricks. And tricks they were, I assure you, for what you believe you have seen here tonight differs much from that which has actually taken place. My only power is one which enables me to disguise that difference. I claim nothing more than that.

"I am a conjurer, but a conjurer is nothing more than an actor playing the part of a magician. Yet an actor, like every other man, is something more than flesh. He is also part spirit.† 'Our revels now are ended,'" quoted the Professor, "and this actor, this spirit, is melted into air."

The man had begun to fade before our very eyes! The backdrop of the stage was becoming visible through him!

"Into thin air," said the specter. "Thank you again, and good night."

And so saying, *Professor Haselmayer vanished!*

---

† These words are generally attributed to Jean Eugene Robert-Houdin, who, as has been noted, was Haselmayer's teacher.—M.C.

·9·

The Blind Photographer

·····━━◆━━·····

Slumber nearly eluded me that night, for my brain pursued other quarry as I lay abed. How could a man escape from every confinement devised to restrain him, however inescapable it seemed to be? Would that Professor Haselmayer *had* claimed true magical powers; his performance made plausible such a boast. But in assuring his audience of the absolute contrary, he posed a puzzle, nay a damnable budget of impossible riddles, that cheated this theater-goer, for one, of a night's repose.

Downstairs a clock chimed thrice, and I twisted about on my restless couch, as though to turn my back on the Professor's riddles and so rescue what remained of the hours before dawn. But facing this new direction in the darkness, I found, not the welcome arms of Morpheus, but Dr. John Frederick May. Yet he was a better excuse for my sleeplessness, for it was the Doctor's secrets, and not the Professor's that I had promised to deliver to Mr. Stanton. Still, when four o'clock struck below, I had no better idea of how to swindle the truth from the surgeon than of how to vanish into thin air.

Sleep, when it finally came, did not bring oblivion. I was tormented by fitful dreams in which a man I supposed to be Dr. May (but who wore the countenance of Professor Haselmayer) stood in the midst of a stage beside a pine coffin, which had been securely trussed in chains and padlocked. I sat alone among the empty seats of the opera house. Dr. May beckoned me to come up on the stage and unlock the chains which bound the coffin. I found myself suddenly at the foot of the locked box, while the Doctor stood at its head, a mocking smile upon his face.

"Come, Cosgrove," challenged the dream doctor, "unlock this thing. You have the key."

But when I tried to reach my pocket I discovered my wrists were shackled. The key was in my pocket, but the shackles kept my hand from it.

"Come, Mr. Nichols. It is time."

It was not the surgeon taunting me now, but Patch, summoning me from my brief and troubled slumber.

"If you're to be at the station before seven, you'd best be up," he advised.

Before retiring I had packed my valise and asked Patch to see that I got aboard the cars before they departed for New York at seven o'clock. I bestirred myself and went to the washstand to perform my morning toilet. The shock of the icy water on my hands and face drove off the dream's lingering mood, but only for a moment. As I stood with my dripping arms extended before me and cast about for a linen to dry them with, I chanced to glimpse myself in this pose in the mirror above the basin. My arms were arranged exactly as they had been in the dream, exactly as Professor Haselmayer's had been beneath the black silk drape. All that the image wanted were the irons, the dream shackles, the magician's shackles and the shackles of Superintendent Richards. I stared at my wrists for a long moment, and then I saw it. I knew how Professor Haselmayer had shed the police official's irons. And that discovery betrayed the quintessential nature of the Professor's magic.

The magician had not claimed the five sets of irons affixed to him by his Zouave were true shackles. In fact, knowing his audience would certainly suspect they were trick devices, he gave voice to the doubt himself before that very mistrust could take seed of its own course in the minds of the onlookers. But he immediately made the point seem moot by submitting himself to a sixth set of irons that none could question, for they were produced and affixed by one of Washington City's most trusted citizens. Mr. Richards' irons must needs be authentic. Who, then, would trouble to doubt that the other five were not? But why involve the five other irons in the demonstration at all?

I saw the answer: Those other irons were placed on the Professor's wrists, not to make his feat more difficult, but to make it possible. They occupied those portions of the wrists and forearms where the police officer would otherwise have applied his irons, and left him no place to lock the true shackles but about the upper extremities of Haselmayer's muscular forearms. Locked at that greater circumference, the Professor could easily slip his lower forearms and wrists through their encincture *after he had first removed his own trick shackles*. And this, I now saw, was exactly how the feat was accomplished. And I saw more.

When Professor Haselmayer succeeded in accomplishing this trick, he escaped from something more than a set of police irons. He freed himself from the fetters of the audience's disbelief, which had cumbered him from the first moment he emerged onstage (however impressive his flash-powder entrance may have been). Unless some country bumpkin had wandered into Wall's for a taste of the notorious city's wicked stage, none in the house truly believed for a moment that he was to witness ought but a demonstration of the principle that the hands of some are quicker than the eyes of most. But Professor Haselmayer's performance was singular because in borrowing a true policeman and an authentic set of shackles to aid in one of his tricks, he tacitly convinced us that all of his other illusions were equally real. The real magic the Professor had performed was not an escape from Mr. Richards' irons, it was the transformation of several hundred skeptical onlookers into accomplices to their own deception. So well had he done his work that afterwards our credulousness was in jeopardy only once, and that was when he culminated his performance with the brazen proclamation that all we had seen was trickery, even as he vanished into the air before our very eyes!

These ruminations occupied me during a hasty breakfast and brisk carriage ride to the railroad station. I offer them here because they were the proximate cause of an inspiration which changed the course of my journey that day, and, consequently, my investigations. The Baltimore and Ohio station was already in view when I leaned forward and tapped on the glass. Patch immediately reined the team to a halt, and I thrust my head through the window and called to him.

"Forget the railroad, good friend," I said. "Take us to Mr. Brady's Gallery instead, if you please."

The lad evinced no surprise at my sudden change of plan, but simply turned the carriage about and drove back along C Street. More explicit instructions than the one I had shouted were unnecessary, for the Brady National Photographic Art Gallery was a famous and fashionable landmark on the Avenue, near 7th Street, where it occupied the upper three floors of a four-story building. As we pulled up before the building, I dashed from the carriage and vaulted the stairs, although I entertained small hope of finding anyone about at that early hour. But luck was with me, for not only was my knock answered, but the door was opened by a thin, bespectacled man of medium size wearing a precisely trimmed imperial† and dressed with equal care in a black coat, black doeskin trousers, and a vest of the finest merino wool. It was Mr. Mathew Brady, himself. Mr. Brady was an early riser, and he lived with his beautiful wife in a suite of rooms at the National, but one block down the Avenue from the Gallery. I learned later that it was his habit to come early to his establishment to prepare the day's tasks.

Mr. Brady seemed not to recognize me, although he knew me very well, albeit by another name, and of somewhat altered appearance. He could hardly have forgotten our first encounter in December, 1862, for a few minutes after we had been formally introduced, I declared my intention to hang him. Brady and his assistant, Tim O'Sullivan, had crossed the Rappahannock with the Army of the Potomac to make some views of the freshly conquered Rebel bastion of Fredericksburg, but he had not been as swift as General Burnside and his army in making the return trip after the tide of battle turned, and when he and O'Sullivan finally packed up their equipment and made for the pontoon bridge which they, and several thousand Federal troops had used to cross the river, they discovered the retreating army had taken up the thing, unwittingly stranding the pair in what

---

† Goatee.—M.C.

was once again enemy territory. Before the two could devise some means of escape, they were discovered by a Confederate patrol and taken into custody as suspected Northern spies. I, together with several other secret detectives, chanced to be in the area in Confederate costume on a wholly unrelated matter when I happened upon the scene. The Sergeant in charge of the Confederate detachment saluted and reported the situation of affairs. He was in the act of escorting his prisoners into Fredericksburg to turn them over to his superiors, who would determine what disposition should be made of them.

I well knew all that awaited them in Fredericksburg was a brief and perfunctory hearing, a quick trip up a short flight of steps, and a quicker one down a slightly shorter length of rope. I informed the Sergeant that in the interest of saving time I intended to see the matter to an immediate conclusion on that very spot. We repaired to a nearby fragment of stone fence upon which I seated myself, calling for the prisoners to be brought before me.

Mr. Brady coolly stated on behalf of himself and Mr. O'Sullivan that they were daguerrian artists present at this place for the purpose of making photographic views of the historic battle that had just been fought there. He entered as evidence of his claim his cameras and other paraphernalia. He stated that, while he had arrived in the company of the Army of the Potomac, he labored in the service of History. I asked him if he had anything further to say in his defense, and when he did not, I found him guilty of espionage and sentenced him and his accomplice to hang. I detached four of my detectives to escort the pair to a nearby tree, and ordered the fifth to scout the nearby farms and appropriate a length of rope. He inquired as to whether he should also procure a ladder for the ceremony, and I replied in the negative. I apologized to the captives for this omission and explained that, because such niceties were luxuries that could not be afforded during the harsh exigencies of war, there was nothing for it but to hoist them. Then, turning to the genuine Confederates, I acknowledged that they were to thank for the apprehension of this dangerous pair, and so were entitled to stay and watch the imminent conclusion of the matter, should they so desire. But they were unanimous in their immediate reply that their duty lay elsewhere, and they hastily betook themselves in the direction they deemed it to be located. Within minutes they were out of sight, and I hastened to commute the sentence I had so recently passed upon the dismayed photographers.

We escorted them to the river and, after some searching, located a small boat. After dark, I sent two of my men along with them to assure their safe arrival on the opposite bank. Before they pushed off, I penned a brief note for Mr. Brady to deliver to General Burnside. I can't recall the exact wording, but it was an objurgation for the indecorous haste with which he had departed Fredericksburg and its vicinage, and in it I observed that his fugaciousness had nearly cost the world a pair of aesthetes of far greater worth than his own wretched self. I believe I signed it "Robert E. Lee, General, CSA." After I became acquainted with Mr. Brady some years later, he confessed to me that, during the intervening period, he truly believed he had been the beneficiary of the noblesse of some Southern aristocrat, although he said he never accepted that I had, in fact, been General Lee.

"Good morning, Mr. Brady," I exclaimed. "How truly fortunate I am to find you here at this early hour. And to find you thus at your labors so hard upon the heels of the dawn bespeaks, I hope, a much more generous salubriousness than you enjoyed when last we met."

The photographer adjusted his thick blue spectacles and gazed at me with some confusion. It was apparent that he failed to recognize me, and this failure was due only in part to my penchant for wearing many faces. It was not well known at the time, for such intelligence would have adversely influenced the photographer's trade, but Mathew Brady, the pre-eminent daguerreotypist of the era, had been, for many years, nearly blind, and was constrained to resort to a staff of apprentices to execute most of the photographic portraits attributed to him. A bitter irony, perhaps, yet who can presume to fathom the Will of God in such matters. Would Beethoven have heard that voice which inspired his final works had he been able to hear ought else? Perhaps a keen-eyed Brady would be no better a photographic artist than his scores of imitators, some of whom mimicked him so thoroughly as to open establishments but a few doors away in the same block of the Avenue.

"I'm sorry," apologized the photographer. "Have you an appointment to pose?"

"No," I laughed. "I pose without appointment. At our most recent encounter, I believe I posed as a bitters traveler, while at our first meeting I was posing as a Rebel, who was, in turn, posing as a hangman. Posing, you see, is my profession."

"Mr. Nichols!" exclaimed the photographer, warmly grasping my hand and leading me within his establishment. "Do forgive me. I certainly could never forget you, but I fear these eyeglasses are no longer adequate to their task. Please come in and tell me if I can serve you in some way. Although," he added, "I doubt that one such as myself could offer much aid to a person of your profession."

"On the contrary," I replied. "It is precisely your own stock-in-trade that I require. You see, I have come to ask you to help me pose."

And so saying, I explained my plan, burdening him, of course, with only as much as was necessary to enable his collaboration in it. Mr. Brady readily agreed to help, and in aid of mapping the details of our little conspiracy, he led me on a tour of his establishment.

The first of the three storys occupied by his enterprise was his gallery. The walls were completely covered with his portraits, and I can think of no personage who had achieved even the most meager eminence during the two previous decades who had been omitted from this magnificent company. There were Presidents and poets, Congressmen and concubines, actors and assassins. There were many views of President Lincoln, and several of the band of brigands who slew him, including a proud and haughty Booth. Among the lesser stars of Mr. Brady's constellation I espied the glowering visage of a balding man of middle age, posed pensively with a bony finger thrust into one of a pair of bushy whiskers that beset, but did not conceal, a thin, petulant mouth. The inscription beneath the portrait identified the subject as Dr. John Frederick May. Mr. Brady, now witting of my interest, offered to remove the photograph and lend it to me. I thanked him, but declined. A moment's study had made the loan unnecessary, for I had etched a detailed copy of the picture in that little gallery I carry about in some remote region of my brain.

However, I asked the photographer if he might chance to have an example of the surgeon's penmanship. Mr. Brady consulted his records and found a brief letter from Dr. May ordering a quantity of *cartes de visite* displaying his portrait. I withdrew the onionskin tracing I'd made in General Baker's hotel room and compared the handwriting to that of Dr. May's letter. It was clearly the work of a different hand. If the Doctor was one of the patrons of Baker's silence, he was not also the exasperated author of the message I'd found in the General's Pitman.

Mr. Brady led me from the Gallery and we continued up the staircase to the floor above, where his vast workshops were located. None of his craftsmen was yet present at this early hour, and the tables, presses and other equipage used in the printing and framing of photographic views, and other steps in the manufacture of the Gallery's products, stood in silent abeyance in the vacant factory. Would that time had permitted the indulgence of my curiosity regarding the particulars of these instruments, for I knew the proud aesthete was eager to explain them, but these rooms were not to be elements of the action I had planned. The stage I had chosen for my conjuring was the topmost floor of Mr. Brady's establishment, and I asked him to take me there so I might be assured it was fully suited to my performance.

The studio was equipped with an ample skylight, for this feature was a necessity to the making of photographic portraits. While it was practicable to make views by gaslight, or other manmade illumination, such photographs required the camera's lens to remain uncovered over a protracted period of time, far beyond the interval most adults or any children could be prevailed upon to remain in a state of absolute immobility. Photographs made with artificial illumination were restricted to subjects that could endure protracted fixedness, viz., empty rooms and lifeless bodies. But Mr. Brady's studio was a place to photograph the living, and for this nothing would answer but God's Own daylight.

There could not be too much light, explained the photographer. The brighter the rays streaming down through his ceiling glass, the sharper the view produced, and the shorter the suffering of the rigid sitter. The sun, to Mr. Brady, was as oils to a painter. He did not plash its raw rays upon his subjects, but carefully manipulated the light by means of an assortment of screens and reflectors, which modulated both its direction and intensity. In this manner, he banished some shadows cast by his subject, while extenuating others to a pleasing dimness. These preparations comprised the art of photography, while the operation of the camera obscura itself was merely its mechanics, the practical means of preserving what the aesthetic sensibilities had prepared.

Apart from the screens and reflectors, the studio room was equipped with a pair of cameras, and an assortment of furniture from which various pieces could be selected according to the client's taste and arranged within the camera's perspective to create the simulacrum of some richly appointed parlor or drawing room. There were several curious stanchions of a variety of lengths that might have been taken for hat racks, except they were topped by curved bars, instead of pegs. These, Mr. Brady explained, were head rests, or more accurately, head clamps, used to enforce immobility of the subject's head while the lens was uncovered. These last items were arranged, of course, to be obscured from the camera's eye by the intervening presence of the subject. The wonders of the studio photographer, like those of the stage magician, were achieved, in part, through the judicious employment of sham. In all, the room was a sort of temple of trickery, and thus a most fitting place to enact the scenario I had composed.

I spent some time in the chamber with Mr. Brady, working out the particulars of the scene to be staged there on the morrow. When this was completed and he escorted me downstairs, I entreated him to pray that the sun would find a clear and cloudless sky when next it rose. As I departed he assured me that this was a regular element of his nocturnal devotions, except on Saturday, when he begged the Lord to deliver all the rain that Washington City might require on Sunday, when his gallery was, of course, closed.

While I had been visiting with Mr. Brady, Washington City had awakened and the Avenue had come to life. Passersby hurried along the brick sidewalk en route to their places of employment, while processions of streetcars, carriages and buggies seeking to make their way along the Avenue had been halted by a clutter of farmers' cans, livestock and early shoppers, all seeking entry to Marsh Market across the boulevard. The patient Patch waited at curbside with the carriage. I climbed aboard after announcing our next stop, Willard's Hotel.

The lad skillfully guided us through the pack and we were soon making headway along the Avenue. It took but a few moments to reach 14th Street and the lavish five-story hostelry, which was quite the most decorous hotel in Washington City at the time. The young fellow held the door for me, and I alighted and entered the place. As I strode up to the desk in the public room, Patch brought up the rear with my valise in tow.

Despite the reputed scarcity of accommodations in the city during the Impeachment Trial, and the unfashionable hour of my arrival, I had no difficulty securing a room at Willard's, owing, no doubt, to the parsimony of the editors of those distant journals that had sent correspondents to the capital for the show. I announced myself to the room clerk as "General Lloyd Christian Baker," and signed that name in the register, listing Chicago as my point of origin.

"Will you need the carriage anymore, General Baker?" inquired the ever alert Patch. I said I would not and dismissed him, while a hotel porter took my bag and guided me to my room. Before he departed the chamber, I inquired as to the nearest telegraph office, although I knew full well there was a Western Union station just across 14th Street on the corner of the Avenue. When he had so stated, I asked him to stay a moment while I penned a dispatch, and see that it was sent.

The message was addressed to Dr. John Frederick May at his New York City office and said simply:

> Your immediate presence here is required. Reply, advising your scheduled time of arrival Washington City.
>
> General L. C. Baker
> Willard's Hotel

I gave the porter a generous gratuity to see that it was dispatched without delay, and promised him an equivalent consideration to ensure the reply did not languish on the telegrapher's desk. As it transpired, I captured the attention of both the porter and the physician, for I had scarcely unpacked my valise and settled down with my copy of Pitman when there came a knock on my door, signaling the arrival of man and message. I paid him his bonus and told him to wait in case there should be need for further telegraphing. It happened that there was, for Dr. May's simple yet revealing reply read as follows:

> Impossible for me to comply at present. Please state price of goods. Will forward my draft on Riggs Bank.
>
>   J. F. May, M.D.
>   New York

So the surgeon was one of General Baker's "customers." I wondered exactly how dear were the "goods" Dr. May sought to purchase. I handed over another of Mr. Pinkerton's coins to the porter and sent him off with the following for Dr. May:

> Goods not for sale. Will be given away here in your absence. New York and Philadelphia cars depart your location for this city at noon and 7:30 P.M. Escort can be arranged if you require. Reply stating your choice.
>
>   General L. C. Baker
>   Willard's Hotel

I had not delved far into the record of the Conspiracy Trial before I had Dr. May's latest response in hand. It read:

> Your message received too late for noon departure. Will depart 7:30 P.M. as requested. Await further instructions per my arrival Washington City.
>
>   J. F. May, M.D.
>   New York

The dog knew its master. I donned my hat and coat and departed Willard's, striding down the Avenue in quest of the next ingredient of my plan. The 7:30 from New York would arrive in Washington City shortly before dawn, at 5:25 A.M. From frequent personal experience, I knew that securing a night's slumber while traveling aboard the cars was a difficult feat for even the seasoned railroad rider. To the traveler burdened with an uneasy mind, it would be impossible. Dr. May would arrive in Washington City fatigued to the point of exhaustion. The doctor's discomfort added to my advantage, for the more sluggish his wits, the better the chance my plan would succeed.

I went again to Brady's Gallery, but was informed by one of his assistants that the photographer had repaired to the National, as was his midday habit, to take dinner with his wife. Continuing yet another block along Pennsylvania Avenue, I arrived at the prestigious hotel, entered the hotel's dining room, and quickly located Mr. Brady, who was by himself, owing, he explained, to some slight indisposition afflicting his wife. I expressed my regrets at this news, but remarked that Mrs. Brady would shortly be able to consult Dr. J. F. May, who was among the Nation's most eminent, if perhaps not its most truthful, medical practitioners. Mr. Brady, in keeping with our plan, immediately called for writing materials, and dispatched a letter by messenger to General Lafayette C. Baker at the Pennsylvania House. The message stated that Mr. Brady had been commissioned, by one Anton Dumont, pending General Baker's consent, to execute a photographic portrait of the General in aid of arranging a proposed lecture tour. Mr. Brady added that he had not had the pleasure of General Baker's personal acquaintance, and, if such was both agreeable and convenient to the General, he begged the honor of the General's presence at nine o'clock the following morning to share breakfast with him at the National Hotel, and thence proceed to the photographer's gallery for the picture-making.

I joined Mr. Brady at lunch, and we had not yet completed our repast when the messenger was back with General Baker's reply. The General was honored to accept both the breakfast and the sitting. The cast of my scenario was now complete. Only the costuming remained, and, after our luncheon I took leave of Mr. Brady and proceeded to the vicinage of D and 9th Streets, wherein many dry goods shops could be found. In the end I was compelled to abandon these elegant establishments and resort to a pushcart near Marsh Market to obtain precisely those items of apparel I required.

These necessary purchases completed, I crossed again to the more fashionable side of the Avenue and entered French and Richardson's, a bookseller located a short distance from Brady's Gallery. There I found the pair of volumes containing the testimony heard by the Impeachment Investigation Committee, as well as Mr. Ben Perley Poore's more comprehensive record of the Conspiracy Trial, in three volumes.† With these entertainments in hand, I repaired to Willard's for an afternoon of heavy reading, followed by a light supper. Afterward I strolled over to the house on K Street for a brief conference with Patch. Thus were the final preparations for the morrow completed, and I had virtuously resolved to return to Willard's and pass another hour or two in lamplit study of my little library of assassination literature, then make an early evening of it, the better to prepare mind and body for my impending performance as conjurer. But instead I found myself once again before Wall's Opera House, wherein the master conjurer performed, and, yielding to temptation, I entered. Professor Haselmayer's magic was quite as absorbing when witnessed the second time, and only slightly less mysterious. I hoped to discover the means he employed to vanish into thin air, but though I was fully prepared on this second occasion when he climaxed his performance with this wonder, and I observed it with every sense fully alert, I failed to discern the trick he used to accomplish it. Still, I lost no sleep over the problem that night. The Professor remained an enigma, but he had become, as well, my inspiration.

---

† While Pitman's one-volume work summarizes the testimony given at the Conspiracy Trial, and arranges it according to a logical framework of the prosecution and defense of each defendant, Poore's is the complete, verbatim transcript of the trial, presented, without either a table of contents or an index, and in the exact chronological sequence of the eight-week proceeding. Poore was an eminent journalist who covered the Washington scene during a period of more than sixty years for such publications as the Boston *Journal* and *Harper's Weekly*. His three-volume record of the Conspiracy Trial was a rare item even in 1868. It found a small audience of readers who, like Cosgrove, had an insatiable appetite for facts and details.—M.C.

·10·

A Hand from the Dead

The train from New York arrived on time. We could hear it coming, Patch and I, for some quarter of an hour before it drew into the station. The sound of the locomotive and the rattle of the cars carried for miles in the chill night air, for dawn was yet a half-hour off, and no other sound competed as the rising voice of the cars insinuated itself into the silence of the sleeping city. The sudden drop in the tempo of the engine signaled the passage of the train within the city limits. I handed Patch the note I had prepared and sent him into the railroad station concourse, while I abandoned the carriage and concealed myself in the early dimness some distance from the lights of the station. Shortly I heard the shrill protest of brakes and a long sigh of steam escaping from the engine boiler. The glow climbing into the eastern sky enlightened one face of the station's clock tower. It was twenty-five minutes past five.

Within the station Patch would be circulating among the weary passengers as they entered the concourse, and calling for Dr. May. The note he carried I had penned with painstaking care in imitation of Baker's hand, a sample of which the General had conveniently provided in accepting Mr. Brady's invitation. The surgeon likely was not so frequent a recipient of holographic messages from General Baker to be familiar with his penmanship, but I preferred to assume the contrary, rather than chance to regret discovering it. The note Patch would present the surgeon read as follows:

Go along with the lad who gives you this. He will deliver you to the
National. Present yourself there and ask for Mr. Mathew Brady. The night
clerk has been informed that Mrs. Brady is indisposed, and your visit at
this early hour shall not be questioned. Mr. Brady will arrange for your
breakfast and other comforts. At precisely 9:15 A.M. you will betake
yourself to the hotel's public room and place yourself in a location from
which you can observe the dining room entrance. Shortly Mr. Brady and
I will emerge. If I should speak to you, it will be in the manner of a chance
encounter with one of slight acquaintance. Make no reference to our
confidential business or the occasion of your visit to this city. A minute
or so after Mr. Brady and I have departed, follow us. I shall meet you in
Mr. Brady's photographic studio, which is on the fourth story of 350–
352 Pennsylvania Avenue.

Surrender this note to the lad who delivered it after you have
committed these instructions to memory. Do not deviate from them in
the slightest degree.

L. C. Baker

Presently, the first elements of a straggling column of travelers
emerged from the railroad station and deployed to encounter a line
of carriages, some private, but most for hire, that had quietly assembled along New Jersey Avenue during the half-hour of our vigil.
Midway in this parade of weary wayfarers lumbered a sturdy and well-
attired gentleman, followed in close pursuit by Patch, now struggling
with a carpet bag of such generous dimensions and ample contents
that it might well have contained some other young fellow not much
smaller than himself. That Patch had found his man I had no doubt,
for I immediately discerned the peevish mouth, the glowering eyes,
and the bushy burnside of the ambrotype of Dr. J. F. May that claimed
its minor place among the eminent who adorned the walls of Brady's
Gallery. This churlish countenance notwithstanding, the surgeon
presented a beautiful sight to my eyes, for I viewed it by the light of
the sun, which had begun its ascent from beneath the horizon into a
cloudless sky. The Photographers' Orison had been heard, and the
supplication had been answered with the promise of a dazzling day.
Dr. May entered the carriage, and Patch, closing the door behind the
gentleman, climbed to the driver's bench and got underway. In a

moment the carriage had turned onto C Street and was out of sight. The clockwork had been set in motion.

Adversity, it seems to me, rarely calls upon those who have prepared for its visit. More often it prefers the company of those who do not expect it. I had allowed that it might be aboard the cars from New York, thereby not only placing a blemish upon the usually deserved reputation of the New York and Philadelphia Railway Line for punctuality, but disrupting my own careful planning, as well. Thus I had scheduled the breakfast of Mr. Brady and General Baker for the somewhat late hour of nine o'clock, against the chance that some minor misadventure would delay the cars en route. The train was on schedule, as we have seen, yet the price of the assurance I had purchased still needed to be paid in patient endurance of the hours that must pass before the next act of my little scenario could commence. But it was a price I cheerfully paid, for if the secret detective were to be guided by only one maxim, it should be this one: Be prepared.

I passed the time pleasantly enough, beginning with a stroll up Capitol Hill to inspect the Walter Dome.† From thence I proceeded down toward Pennsylvania Avenue, crossing the railroad tracks that bordered the Capitol grounds on their route to Virginia, and spent a pleasant half-hour or so searching out those clews to the imminent arrival of Spring as could be found among the grounds of the Botanical Gardens. I walked up the Avenue to 4½ Street and enjoyed a leisurely breakfast at Reuter's. About twenty minutes past eight I went to the Pennsylvania House and there seated myself with the newspaper in the public room, from which vantage point I could observe the anticipated egress of General Baker on his way to breakfast with Mr. Brady.

As I waited I perused the newspaper. The front page was, of course, filled with the Impeachment Trial. I found the report tiresome, not

---

† The familiar dome of the Capitol Building was still a novelty on the Washington skyline of 1868, having been completed only five years earlier in December, 1863. It replaced a less impressive dome which was removed in 1857 to permit construction of the new dome. The present dome was designed by Thomas U. Walter, who also designed the two wings of the building in which the House and Senate chambers are now located.—M.C.

that I failed to appreciate the moment of what was taking place in the Senate, but the Great Trial was hardly a feast prepared for those who hungered after the drama of History. Rather it was a plate filled with the sort of small, bland morsels lawyers love to chew upon, and the proceedings had settled into a petty pace that seemed calculated to lull those not passionately committed to the advocacy of either side into a drowsy stupor. Yesterday, so reported the paper, the House, in answer to the President's answer to the House's list of charges, had "considered the several answers of Andrew Johnson, President of the United States, to the several articles of impeachment against him by them exhibited in the name of themselves and of all the people of the United States, and reserving to themselves all the advantage of exception to the insufficiency of the answer to each and every averment in said several answers, or either of them, and for replication to the said answer do say that the said Andrew Johnson, President of the United States, is guilty of the high crimes and misdemeanors mentioned in said articles, and that the House of Representatives are ready to prove the same . . ."

The newspaper's correspondent was, of course, quoting the official record, and not indicting his own report. He may have wished his readers to share some small part of his own sufferings in sitting through this legal droning, or perhaps had been rendered into such a state of somnolence as to be unable to pen his own summary of events on returning to his desk at the newspaper. But, more likely, his editor permitted him to fill the first page of the daily with this lawyerly mumbling because the alternative was to grant the most important doings of the Nation's capital such meager cognizance as, "Yesterday the House of Representatives considered the President's reply to their accusations, found it wanting, and renewed their demand that he be impeached and removed from office." But if such pithiness bespoke an unseemly disregard for the historic momentousness of the matter occupying the magnificent deliberations on Capitol Hill, the reporter might have added, "The Senate has voted to adjourn the Impeachment Trial until Monday next. Subscribers to this journal may rest assured they shall read no more of the dreary business until that day has come and gone."

I turned to the next page, where the lesser eddies in the great current of History that flowed through Washington City found fleeting acknowledgment. One Brigadier General Benjamin J. Chandler, a retired cavalry commander, had passed away. The agency of his exitus was not disclosed in the report, which, however, did contain such other minutiae as the fact that the General's mortal remains were now in the respectful custody of the undertaking establishment of Harvey and Marr in F Street, and would be removed tomorrow to the Soldiers' Home, where former comrades and others of the public might visit to pay their last respects.

I found the most important item of intelligence contained in the newspaper buried near the bottom of its fourth page, beneath the caption, "Assassin's Slayer to Speak." The brief story read as follows:

> Our Rockville correspondent reports that Mr. Boston Corbett, the former noncommissioned officer of the New York Sixteenth Cavalry, arrived here yesterday to make one of his frequent stops along the sawdust trail. The former sergeant, who slew the assassin of our late, beloved President Abraham Lincoln, will speak tomorrow evening at the camp meeting now in progress at Washington Grove, near Gaither's Farms.†

So engrossed was I in this news of the fellow whom the world held to be the one who had dispatched the very man now feared to be alive by Mr. Stanton, that I almost failed to observe the arrival of my more immediate concern. It would have been virtually impossible not to notice him, however, for he was clad, not in the tatterdemalion hat and overcoat that I thought to be the extent of his Washington City wardrobe. No, Baker was now bedizened in the full dress uniform of

---

† Soon after the event, the cavalry sergeant who claimed to have been the trooper that shot the man in Garrett's Barn was much in demand for lecture appearances to give his personal account of the incident. However, Corbett was, to put it mildly, a religious fanatic, and, whenever admitted to such a public forum, he was more inclined to present his own version of the Word of God than to recount his exploits. After disappointing many lecture hall audiences this way, he found himself welcome only at revivalist gatherings and camp meetings, such as the ones frequently held at Washington Grove, a Methodist campground and summer colony north of Rockville, Maryland, near what is today the flourishing suburban community of Gaithersburg.—M.C.

a General of the Army, complete with a saber dangling from a fine pigskin baldric girded about his middle. From boots to buttons, the General had spared neither polish nor elbow-grease, and as he emerged from the hostelry into the sunlight, he sparkled and flashed like the mouth of Hell itself.

If the reader has not already guessed the sort of brummagem artifice I hoped to employ to swindle Dr. May out of his secrets, he will not also perceive that General Baker thus attired would bring disaster to my plan. Suffice to say that cached in a corner of Mr. Brady's posing room there was, at this moment, the closest relatives to the General's shabbier garments that yesterday's hunt through the marketplace could turn up, as well as a false beard, which, when added to my own modest whiskers, approximated the ample facial shrubbery sported by General Baker. I need not add that the same posing room did not contain the full dress uniform of a cavalry officer. Suddenly I found myself unprepared, with adversity knocking at the door. If the secret detective were to be guided by a second maxim, it would be one I later heard from the lips of a mechanical engineer: If there is anything that can possibly go wrong, it shall.

But my difficulties could not be laid at the door of bad luck. They were the result of bad planning, of failing to think through the matter with thoroughness. For who among us is so humble that he would be satisfied to have his portrait made for posterity by the pre-eminent photographic artist of the Age dressed as some hapless mendicant? The General was a military man, and it was natural that he should wish to be depicted as such by Mr. Brady's camera. How and where he obtained the raiment he now wore, I did not know, but I should have anticipated that such would not lie beyond his resources. My immediate problem was how and where, during the next sixty, and perhaps some odd, minutes, I could do the same.

The General had disappeared around the corner of 6th Street, bound for the National and his appointment with Mr. Brady. I could think of nothing better to resort to than the tailors denizened near the intersection of 9th and D Streets, and I made off in that direction at a rapid pace which soon progressed to a full gallop. During the next half-hour I satisfied myself that there were no ready-made

Army officers' uniforms to be had, and that it was impossible to create the simulacrum of such in the brief minutes remaining.

Next it occurred to me that, if the theater had been the inspiration that led to my present predicament, it might also provide my salvation. I stepped into a newsdealer's, purchased a copy of the same daily I had perused in the Pennsylvania House, and searched the theatrical notices for sign of some production likely to require martial costuming. Unfortunately, there seemed to be none. Of course, reposing within a trunk in a dressing room of one of Washington City's many theaters there was undoubtedly some approximation of General Baker's attire, but a systematic search for the necessary apparel would take hours, if not days. I was about to discard the newspaper when my eye fell upon an item I had earlier read while awaiting the appearance of General Baker. Immediately I tossed away the paper and betook myself to F Street, near 10th, at which location I found the undertaking and embalming establishment of Messrs. Harvey and Marr.

I entered the place and was met by a soberly attired young man of professionally somber mien who inquired if he could be of assistance. I looked about furtively, then identified myself as an official representative of the Washington City Sanitary Commission, an institution that, for all I knew, might well exist somewhere in the labyrinth of the local government. I explained that I had come on a matter of the utmost confidentiality, and that any undue disclosure of my visit might result in an unfortunate public panic. I could say no more, I said, except that it was imperative I be shown the remains of General Chandler.

The fellow stared at me for an instant with widening eyes, then quickly led me into one of the rear chambers of the establishment and opened the ornate casket contained therein. Inside the box there was the full dress uniform of a cavalry general. Inside the uniform, inconveniently, was a general.

"There is no time to lose!" I declared. "Quickly, help me remove this attire. It must be taken to the city's laboratories for a thorough examination." I did not wait on the fellow's reply, but commenced to undo the brass buttons securing the late officer's tunic.

"Here," I demanded of the frozen mortician, "help me with the boots."

The young man finally found his tongue.

"But, surely you know the cause of the General's passing," he said.

"*I* know it very well," I replied, a momentary uneasiness assailing my nerve. "What did they tell *you?*" I inquired meaningfully.

"Why that be died of apoplexy," replied the undertaker.

"Exactly!" I agreed. "But the Surgeon General has in hand a recent communication from his colleagues at the University of Heidelberg informing him that some varieties of apoplexy may be contagious."

"Contagious?" remarked the young man, wonderingly.

"It may be catching!" I shouted, at which juncture the fellow departed, leaving me to my labors unaided. No matter. In a trice I had the General down to his undergarments, and made a handy bundle of his uniform, including his boots, and the Army hat that had rested upon his stilled breast. I grabbed my prize and departed as I had come, glimpsing along the way the young mortician in another chamber, stripped bare and standing by a basin, scrubbing himself with horse soap and a stiff wire brush. The look upon his face offered persuasive evidence to the validity of my thesis: apoplexy *might* be catching. In fact, I felt a touch of it, myself.

I ran all the way to Mr. Brady's Gallery, and as I turned the corner from 7th Street onto the Avenue, I espied in the distance the photographer and his resplendent client. I turned into the doorway and vaulted the four flights to the photographic studio. Without pausing to recover my breath, I stripped off my own attire and donned the uniform of the departed warrior. All this I did without a word to the startled young man who, according to plan, was waiting in the sunlit room.

He was Edward Murphy, a local phonographer. Mr. Brady had arranged for his presence at that place and time,† offering him a mini-

---

† Edward V. Murphy, like his two elder brothers, Denis F. and J. J. Murphy, was an official stenographic reporter for the U.S. Senate. Apparently he was also a trusted friend of Mathew Brady, although I have found no record of their relationship. However, the Senate was in adjournment on March 25, 1868, the date of Cosgrove's masquerade as General Baker, and Murphy would have been one of the few stenographers in Washington available for this outside job.—M.C

mum by way of explanation. Thus one can easily understand his startlement at the spectacle of a blown madman stumbling into the studio and immediately commencing to disrobe.

"Here, you," I commanded, "help me with these boots." But it seemed I was to have no accomplices in the matter of General Chandler's boots, either in stealing them or in donning them, for Mr. Murphy stood gawking, temporarily stunned beyond the capacity of lending a hand. Fortunately, I was not a man who could fill the General's boots, and they slipped on quite easily. Unfortunately, the remaining items of his dress uniform were of a consistent largeness, and hung from my body as though I had suffered some long illness or other privation. This imperfection could be disguised by arranging myself appropriately in a chair, but the General's campaign hat was another matter. I stood before one of Mr. Brady's reflectors and tried to adjust the hat to sit astride my own head, which, like my other physical components, seemed to be considerably smaller than the late officer's.

The inner circumference of the hat was so great that it descended about my head without encountering the sides of my cranium. In fact, the only point of contact I could achieve between hat and head was the top of my skull, which stopped the hat's descent only after the brim had dropped midway down my ears and obscured my forehead to the bottoms of my eyebrows. The effect was so ridiculous as to threaten further contagion of the late General's apoplexy, if that malady can be induced through the convulsions which may result from excessive stimulation of the risibilities. It would hardly do to afflict Dr. May with a fatal case of cachinnation, and so permit him to escape into the next world, taking his secrets with him. I appropriated several sheets of foolscap (an appropriate appellation, in the circumstances) from Mr. Murphy, crumpled them into a ball, and thus filled the crown of the campaign hat, elevating it to a more dignified altitude.

Below, the sound of footfalls on the stairs signaled the arrival of Mr. Brady and the General, and their ascent to the second-story gallery. Dr. May would be coming along shortly. The photographic studio, I saw, had been prepared according to plan. A long conference table had been placed to run the length of the room, with one end near the door, and a pair of straight-backed armchairs had been positioned, one at either end. To one side, in the corner farthest from the door, a screen had been placed, and behind it, a chair and inkstand. Here Mr. Murphy would conceal himself and record the dialogue. On either side of the long table Mr. Brady had stationed one of his reflectors, and I adjusted them to channel the beams of the mid-morning sun so that they bore directly on the chair intended for my visitor. A third reflector cast its brilliance upon the door through which the surgeon would enter. Hearing Dr. May's foot upon the stair, I made one final inspection of my costume in the nearest reflector, attached the false beard to my own, and seated myself at the end of the table farthest from the door. When the knock finally came I had recovered suffi-cient wind to call out to my visitor to enter.

Dr. May opened the door and stepped into the glare cast by the reflector. He turned his head to the side and threw an arm across his eyes, like some rendition in a cathedral mural of a damned soul con-fronted by the Beatific Vision.

"Close the door and take a seat," I commanded, mimicking the General's tone and manner. Baker spoke in the nasal twang of west-ern New York State, accents familiar to me since my nonage, which was passed near that region, and, so easily imitated by myself. The surgeon shut the portal, then, shielding his eyes against the light, found his way to the chair opposite me.

"Can't we dispense with this wretched glare?" whined my visitor.

"We could, but we shall not," I replied. "You will become some-what accustomed to it shortly."

"But why must I?" asked the surgeon.

"Dr. May, I know of several methods to aid in obtaining the truth. Brilliant light is the gentlest of them, I assure you."

"You've brought me here to interrogate me, then?" asked the Doctor, summoning up a degree of indignation.

"I've brought you here to see if you can shed some light of your own on a matter of considerable importance to us both."

"And what matter is that?"

" 'What matter is that?' " I mimicked. "What matter do you imag-ine fits that description, sir? For one who claims to recall the exact character and location of every surgical operation he has ever performed, your memory seems in a poor state of repair this morning, Doctor."

"Booth? You mean Booth?"

"Secretary Stanton has heard reports that the body you identified on the ironclad was not that of the assassin," I said.

"Well, he surely has heard nothing of the sort from me. Why should I impugn my own testimony and hazard my own professional reputation?"

"Perhaps because you have heard some reports yourself, and think the wisest course may be to raise such questions before they are raised by others."

"I fail to follow this," said the Doctor.

"The assassin is still at large," I said.

"Great God!" exclaimed Dr. May. "But I had your assurances."

"My assurances?" I prompted. "What assurances?"

"Man, you know very well what assurances. Those you made to me that morning when you forced me to accompany you to the warship and say the dead wretch on deck was Wilkes Booth."

"I recall no assurances," I said.

"You said that you had the assassin in custody, that you would dispatch him after you were satisfied you'd gotten the names of all his accomplices from him. You said it was essential the public think him dead so that those who were in the affair with him would not take flight."

"Ah, yes," I said mockingly, "I'd quite forgotten that I appealed to your patriotic sentiments to secure your cooperation."

"You blackmailed me!" exclaimed Dr. May. "You made me out a traitor because I was faithful to the Hippocratic Oath I've taken, because I'd clung to my Christian principles, even in time of war," he added piously.

"You mean the medical supplies you sold to the Rebels?" I inquired, taking a modest gamble.

"I mean the quinine," Dr. May agreed.

I shuffled through a sheaf of papers before me on the table, and withdrew one, holding it up to my eyes as though for closer inspection. The doctor could not see that it, like all its fellows, was blank.

"And the cotton?"

"You know of the cotton?" exclaimed the Doctor, in dismay.

"I know of it all. I suppose you say the cotton was to bandage our own wounded. But there was quite a lot of cotton, fully enough to swathe every officer and man in the Army of the Potomac from head to toe, to judge from the quantity in which you dealt."†

The Doctor made no reply.

"You need not fear that you'll swing for your treasonous trade. If every scoundrel who made his fortune at the cost of our soldiers' lives was to hang, we'd empty the clubs of New York and Boston and fill the countryside with gibbets. But aiding the assassin's escape is a hanging offense, so I advise you to keep your own counsel and pray that Booth has chosen to play a new role in some distant place."

"Perhaps you should heed your own advice, General Baker," said Dr. May. "In the matter of Booth, none can accuse me of worse than an error of professional performance. You, however, seem to be the one who turned the assassin loose."

"And there's none can accuse me of *that,*" I replied, "but a self-confessed charlatan and demonstrable traitor. If I ceased my search for Booth, it was only after you swore the carcass aboard the ship was his. But, no matter. Your skin and repute shall both remain intact unless he should make an appearance. I beg you," I mocked, "should he consult you again for the removal of a pistol ball, or a tumor, or whatever, pray do not denounce him to the authorities."

Dr. May arose and went to the door. Before taking his leave he left this parting shot:

"You have a queer sense of humor, General Baker. You know very well, as I told you that morning, I have never in my life set eyes upon John Wilkes Booth."

---

† Cosgrove had not suddenly added mind-reading to his magic act. Many a fortune was made in the North during the Civil War by trading with the Confederacy. The selling of medical supplies and the buying of cotton (generally for delivery to European markets) were two of the most popular forms of commerce.—M.C.

PART THREE

Riddles Within the Mystery

·11·

The Shadows Gather

My suspicions were fully confirmed and remained only to be documented. I summoned Mr. Murphy from his hiding place and asked if he had succeeded in making a complete record of my colloquy with Dr. May. He replied, with a touch of injured professional pride, that he, of course, had done so, and he exhibited a sheaf of foolscap covered with the cryptic markings of his trade. I was eager to see them translated into a more useful form, and asked him to accompany me to a room amidst the workshops on the floor below, where he might immediately commence this work. At all events, we must needs vacate the photographic studio promptly and return it to the photographer's use, before General Baker's interest in the diversions of the Brady Gallery, and his patience, as well, were exhausted. But first I sought assurance that the Doctor had indeed departed the building, else risk the embarrassment of encountering him while still attired in my outsize uniform. I went to a window, poked my head out, and espied the surgeon's figure retreating up the Avenue, doubtless bound for the railroad station, where the last train of the day to New York City would depart at 12:30. As I turned away I chanced to note a pair of gentlemen standing before a watchmaker's shop across the way.

Two things about the duo captured my attention. First, there was something of the secret detective about them both. I cannot say precisely how, but when one has made a career of surreptitiousness, clandestine observation and studied unobtrusiveness, he recognizes a faint reflection of himself in others engaged in the same craft, much as the first encounter of a cousin one has never before met discloses certain common familial lineaments that mark him as a relation. This pair and I belonged to a common fraternity, though likely did not share a common employer.

The second cause for noting the two was the aim of their gaze, which seemed to follow Dr. May as he hurried along the Avenue. As I watched, one spoke briefly to his companion and then departed in the same direction as the surgeon. The other fellow remained in his place, his attention now turned to the shops below the window from which I observed him.

Much as I should have preferred to investigate this latest development, there was no immediate opportunity to do so. Mr. Murphy and I removed to the third-floor workroom lent us by the photographer, and while he set about converting his phonographic notes to a precise and pleasing longhand, I changed from my borrowed costume and donned my own duds. I folded the General's uniform neatly, taking care that when it was returned to him, he would not be set in the earth somewhere to await Gabriel's reveille in rumpled finery.

I instructed Mr. Murphy to execute his transcript in the form of a legal deposition, stating the identities, to the best of his knowledge, of the two participants in the conversation he had recorded. To this end I offered to borrow Mr. Brady's ambrotype of Dr. May for identification purposes and request the photographer to swear out his own affidavit averring the picture he exhibited to Mr. Murphy was a true likeness of Dr. John Frederick May. Mr. Murphy replied that such would not be necessary, as the former resident of Washington City was well known to him by sight, but that he could not state the same to be true of myself. I told him, for the purposes of the deposition, that it would suffice to refer to me as "one who called himself Charles Nichols," and so he did. Mr. Murphy made two identical copies of the transcript, and appended to each his signature, which was witnessed by Mr. Brady, after turning General Baker over to his assistants for the picture-taking upstairs.

Before dismissing the phonographer, I asked his word that he would speak to no one of what he had heard in the photographic studio. I did this purely as a formality, since I expected no less from him by way of professional confidentiality. To my surprise, however, he demurred.

"Mr. Nichols," he said, "if that is your true name, when I accepted this assignment from Mr. Brady, I did not anticipate the nature of the intelligence I would be called upon to record. But in the performance of my task I have become the unhappy possessor of sure knowledge of Dr. May's perjury and trade with the Confederates, hearsay testimony that General Baker suborned the Doctor's perjury, and evidence that yet another crime of infinitely greater magnitude may have been committed. You have presented me with a hard choice: to remain silent, and so become an accessory to these crimes, or to report what I know immediately to the proper authorities. The former is unthinkable, so I am constrained to the latter. Unless you, sir," he added, "represent the Government in this matter."

"You have my assurances that I am acting under color of law," I replied. "Unfortunately, I can offer you no more than that."

"Pray take no offense, sir," apologized the phonographer, "but that is not sufficient to satisfy either the moral or legal imperatives involved. While it may be that what you say is so, you have shown me no document or other material evidence of your office, and even in the matter of your true name, your words are somewhat ambiguous. I am certain such is not the case, but should ever I be called upon to do so, I could not prove that your true aim is not the extortion of Dr. May, rather than to accomplish the ends of Justice."

I took no offense. I had not anticipated this development, but I could not fail to see Mr. Murphy's point. He was perfectly right. Unhappily, not only was I unwilling to confide in him the particulars of my assignment, I should be unable to show him one scrap of paper in support of my claims even if I could take him into my confidence. It is my practice, in the interest of secrecy, to avoid carrying on my person anything that might serve to reveal my true role. I certainly bore no badge or other credential of the Pinkerton National Detective Agency, and Major Johnson's letter of authorization in the matter of my inquiry at the Arsenal reposed at that moment in a strong box concealed in the house on K Street.

"I can see your predicament," I said, "and I regret, for your sake, as well as my own, that I have put you into it. There seems to be nothing for it but to take your report to the authorities. May I inquire as to which authorities you intend to inform?"

"Why, the police," replied Mr. Murphy.

"The Washington City police? They will simply refer you to the Bureau of Military Justice in the War Department, for the crimes in question are Federal matters."

At this Mr. Murphy seemed sharply taken aback.

"Of course, you are right," he said. "I had not thought of that."

It was clear from his manner that the prospect of reporting what he had learned to the War Department authorities caused Mr. Murphy no little dismay, but the reason for this was not equally apparent. Whatever the cause of his discomfiture at the idea of taking his intelligence to the Bureau of Military Justice, it worked in aid of my own interests, which included the protection of my client's confidentiality. While the Department of War was Mr. Stanton's bailiwick, the Secretary obviously wished the matter of my inquiries kept to himself and his trusted Major Johnson. But if the phonographer were to report to the Department, it would be to the office of the Washington District Provost Marshal, and from thence the startling disclosures would swiftly ripple throughout the Government, and eventually reach the press. Apart from whatever embarrassment this might cause Mr. Stanton, it would surely make my own task infinitely more difficult, if not impossible. The weight of the evidence now argued that Booth was alive and at large, and if the hue and cry were raised, my prey, wherever he might be, would surely go to ground. I began to see a solution to the dilemma.

"I can see from your hesitancy," I said, "that you appreciate the sensitivity of this matter. Permit me to make a suggestion as to how you might handle it with commensurate discretion."

"Pray do so," Mr. Murphy eagerly replied.

"Although you should be perfectly correct if you were to go to the Bureau of Military Justice and make your report to whatever underling has charge of dealing with such unsolicited tidings from the public, I can easily envision that this course could lead you to a somewhat embarrassing position. Dr. May is, after all, an eminent physician who enjoys an excellent reputation in Washington City. Other than yourself, I am the only witness to his admissions of wrongdoing, and, as you have noted, you do not even know my true name. Thus unbolstered, your accusations might easily rebound to your own disadvantage, rather than aid the ends of Justice."

"I had not seen that," Mr. Murphy admitted. "What do you recommend?"

"That you seek a private interview with General Grant and make your report to him in person. General Grant will know the name 'Charles Nichols,' and so take your story seriously. I can also assure you the General will keep your own role in the strictest confidence."

Dr. May's guilty secret lay too close to one of the General's own to tempt him to meddle. If there was one man in Washington City I could count on to hear Mr. Murphy's report and do nothing about it other than keep his mouth tightly shut, it was Ulysses S. Grant.

"Then General Grant is your principal!" exclaimed Mr. Murphy.

"I did not say so," I replied.

"You need not," said Mr. Murphy. "Nor need I inform him of that which will doubtlessly be contained in your official report to him. I thank you, sir, for you have lifted a great burden from my mind."

Mr. Brady had departed the workroom after placing his signature on the transcripts, and before Mr. Murphy voiced his dilemma to me. Now I heard the photographer on the stairs, evidently seeing his celebrated subject to the door of the Gallery, the portraits of General Baker having been made. When they had passed to the floors below I went to the window to see if the watcher still kept his vigil before the watchmaker's shop across the Avenue. He was there, and his companion had rejoined him, likely having seen Dr. May off at the railroad station. As I watched, the same drill I had earlier witnessed was repeated. The pair observed General Baker as he made his way up the Avenue. Next, one of the two, the same as had done the earlier footwork on the path of the surgeon, set off again on the trail of the General. This betrayed ignorance of either his craft or the identity of his quarry, for, as I have previously remarked, to stalk one equipped with General Baker's professional instincts is worse than futile. The fellow might just as well have donned cap and bells and danced along the Avenue beside his prey. I wondered if the General had his shooting iron tucked beneath his coat today. I guessed he likely had.

As I returned from the window, Mr. Murphy was making preparations to take his departure, having assured himself (albeit inaccurately regarding particulars) that the matters to which he had become witting were in competent official hands. But yet, as he gathered together his kit of pens and pencils and foolscap sheets, I could see he retained something yet unsaid, and was struggling with the question of whether it should remain so. When finally he strapped his portfolio closed and looked up, I saw he had resolved it should not.

"Mr. Nichols," he began, "this is by no means the first time in my career as amanuensis that I've found myself recording the words of someone involved in the melancholy events proceeding from the tragic death of our late President. I was one of the several phonographers who assisted Mr. Pitman in recording the trial of those accused in the assassination conspiracy.† But even before the trial, I had become professionally involved in the matter. There had been a short session of Congress in 1865, as you will recall, and after adjournment I accepted a temporary position to serve as private secretary to Provost Marshal General Fry. I was in that post on April 14, 1865, when President Lincoln was assassinated. During the three weeks that followed, I worked day and night, every day, recording the statements and depositions of witnesses, suspects, and many others thought by Colonel Baker's detectives to have some material knowledge of the circumstances surrounding the murder. And through some ironic fate, it happened that one of the principal witnesses in the case, one who shared roof and table with Mrs. Surratt, her son and daughter, and the other occupants of that boardinghouse where the dastardly plan was said to have been hatched, was a personal friend of mine for many years, an erstwhile school chum from Philadelphia, where I was raised. I refer to Louis Weichmann.

---

† Assisting Pitman at the Conspiracy Trial were Edward Murphy and his elder brothers, Denis F. and J. J. Murphy, both of whom were, as Edward, reporters in the U.S. Senate, and two other stenographic reporters, R. R. Hitt and R. Sutton.—M.C.

"I tell you these things, Mr. Nichols, not to make idle conversation, nor to remark on the singular coincidence that has today once more drawn me into the lamentable affair. My point is simply this: Chance, Fate, Destiny, the Lord's Hand—call it what you will—has made me the reluctant intimate of the particulars of this tragedy. I know all that the public has been told of it, for I sat at the phonographers' table every day of the Conspiracy Trial. But I also know much more, intelligence that was collected by the War Department's detectives and remains to this day locked away from public view in the secret files of the Bureau of Military Justice. And with that knowledge comes a dreadful, yet ineluctable, certainty: President Lincoln was not the only innocent whose life was taken by this conspiracy, and Booth, if indeed he lives, is not the only conspirator still at large."

Mr. Murphy had made his recitation with obvious apprehensiveness and discomfort, and his final words were uttered in little more than a whisper.

"That does not sound like a tale you've had much practice in telling," I remarked. "I wonder why?"

"There are few I'd trust with it," he replied. "And until this moment I've found none armed with the authority to act upon it."

The phonographer thought me General Grant's agent. I wondered if he'd heard Baker's theory that Grant himself was a conspirator.

"You speak of conspirators still at large," I said. "The Military Commission, as you surely know, found the Confederate leaders to be part of the plot, yet they walk free. There are some in Congress who say Andy Johnson had a hand in the killing, but he has been formally charged with nothing more heinous than discharging his Secretary of War without congressional assent. General Baker has, in my presence, accused General Grant of the crime, but I perceive from your confidence in General Grant you do not share this opinion. So I must therefore put it to you: If some conspirators other than Booth are, as you say, still at large, I beg you to name them."

"To offer you their names without presenting you with some of the evidence against them would be to invite your incredulity," Mr. Murphy replied. "Indeed, my charges are so shocking that even I have rejected them fully a hundred times, but a hundred and one times have I sought and found no escape from the secret knowledge it has been my Fate to acquire, and no alternative to the awful conclusion those hidden facts demand."

He was a likable young fellow, but he was beginning to try my patience.

"Mr. Murphy," I began, as gently as possible, "if you wish to impart to me some intelligence material to the assassination of Mr. Lincoln, you have my ear. My appetite for information in the matter is neigh impossible to sate, and I do not care if you prefer to serve your secret knowledge as the main course and hold the names of those you think involved to present as dessert. But if the appetizer is to be a dish of mysteries, I must pass that up, for I've already had a glut of mysteries."

"You have my apology," Mr. Murphy said most earnestly. "Please do not think I meant to dramatize my disclosures, for they are dramatic enough without added artifice.

"If it's facts you crave, you shall have them. I've hoarded them too long awaiting the occasion when I should find the proper person to share them with. No, not to share, to make a gift of them," he corrected, "for they are a burden of which I'll happily rid myself by placing them in your hands. But this is not the occasion. I have more than my own utterances to offer. I have documents, exact duplicates I have made of secret records. I shall give you them and let you arrange them to suit yourself. Perhaps you can assemble them in some pattern other than the dreadful mosaic they form for me."

"If this is not the occasion, then name the time and the place," I said.

"Do you know the Crypt beneath the Capitol?"

I said that I did.

"Then meet me there at midnight," said Mr. Murphy. "I shall deliver the documents to you then."

A midnight journey to Capitol Hill was not especially tailored to my comfort or convenience, but I agreed to the rendezvous, partly to satisfy my curiosity regarding Mr. Murphy's dark documents, but largely of a desire to be rid of him. The latter aim was immediately consummated, for the phonographer departed without further words.

It was my intention to do the same after thanking Mr. Brady for his invaluable cooperation. But before doing so I took a moment to look into the latest of the budget of mysteries I had complained of. I went to the window and viewed the clockmaker's shop across the Avenue.

The lone watcher remained at his post, his companion doubtless still occupied in the formidable and hazardous business of trailing General Baker. As I observed the observer, he abruptly came to life and started off along the Avenue. I thrust my head out the window to see if I could discern his prey. The apparent object of the man's attentions was Mr. Murphy, who was striding away in the direction of Capitol Hill. The phonographer had done me an unwitting service, for the observation post at the watchmaker's shop was now abandoned, and I was free to depart the Gallery unobserved. This I did forthwith, after making a brief call on Mr. Brady to express my gratitude.

My course lay opposite to that traveled by General Baker, Mr. Murphy and their respective trackers. I set out for Willard's, making one stop along the way at a florist's shop. There I purchased a magnificent funereal garland and ordered it sent to the Soldier's Home, where General Benjamin J. Chandler was to lie in state. I paid the florist's messenger an additional stipend to deliver the parcel containing the General's uniform to Harvey and Marr's on F Street, together with a note I hastily penned in my best imitation of the special language written by minor government officials, to the effect that the late General's garments had been found free of any trace of the deadly strain of galloping apoplexy. Before setting down the florist's pen, I wrote a brief message for delivery with the floral tribute: "In deepest sympathy," I inscribed the card, and signed it "Ulysses S. Grant." I felt certain this would not duplicate a garland already dispatched by the Chief of Staff, for he was not likely to have thought of such a gesture. If I misjudged General Grant, there would be no harm in it. General Chandler's bereaved would doubtless be comforted that Grant had felt a single tribute insufficient to the regard in which he held the departed. I knew nothing of the military career of the late officer, but I was confident the posthumous service he had rendered his country this day was the equal of any performed while in more active status. That he should receive some token reward for this was essential, and it fell to me to see that such was done. It was an obligation I gladly discharged, notwithstanding the inevitable discussion I foresaw as a consequence of this item on my bill of expenses when I presented it to the distinguished Scotsman for whom I labored.

These formalities concluded, I hurried on to Willard's with the object of paying my room bill and removing myself from that conspicuous establishment at the earliest possible moment. My stay at the illustrious hostelry had been most comfortable, and necessary to the successful accomplishment of the sell† I worked on Dr. May, but there was one too many General L. C. Bakers in Washington City at the moment, and that I was the surplus officer could jeopardize the obscurity so essential to the work of a secret detective. Thus I hastened to Willard's, but in the event, it transpired I had not hastened enough.

As the room clerk handed me my key he greeted me by name in so stentorian an exhalation that bystanders might have thought me deaf. But it happened that a bystander, or rather a by-sitter, was the apparent instigator of the man's vociferousness, for I noticed the clerk was looking, not at me, as he spoke, but over my shoulder. I followed his glance and there, seated in a pose of studied indifference to us both, was the same fellow I'd last seen striding up the Avenue hard on the highly polished heels of the original General L. C. Baker.

That he had survived his task apparently unscathed was surprising. That he had somehow managed to learn of the presence in Washington City of a second L. C. Baker, and further to discover the duplicate's lair, was astonishing. It was also disconcerting in the extreme. The fellow was something more than a detective. In the matter of L. C. Bakers, he was a collector.

I accepted my key from the dirty hand of my tracker's hired accomplice and went to my room. I shut the door behind me and immediately undertook an examination of the place for any sign that my nameless admirer had made a professional visit during my absence.

---

† In the parlance of police and criminals of the time, the word "sell" denoted a deception, hoax, or swindle.—M.C.

The chambermaid had, of course, been in to make up the bed and otherwise refresh the room. Thus, I thought it unlikely I might find conclusive evidence of an unauthorized intrusion, but, in fact, I did.

Before I departed for the railroad station early that morning, I had locked my valise. This I did more from habit than out of any particular concern, for the bag contained nothing of great value: a few personal items and my small library of assassination literature. The bag was still locked, but it now bore evidence that it might not have remained so during the full duration of my absence. The metal plate surrounding the keyhole bore a tiny scratch that had not been there when last I handled it. As Dr. May claimed to have done, the picklock signed his handiwork with a scar.

I unlocked the valise and quickly confirmed that the intruder had been successful in his assault upon its lock. He had attempted to disguise his tampering when replacing the bag's contents by arranging them exactly as he thought he had found them. However, he erred in the matter of Poore's three-volume record of the Conspiracy Trial. These I found arranged as though they had been taken down from a bookshelf and laid in the valise, with Volume One on the bottom of the stack, Volume Two in the middle, and the final volume on top. But I had barely gotten through Perley Poore's introduction contained in the first of the set, and so had placed Volume One on top of the stack when I returned it to the bag that morning. The other two tomes of Poore's set I had not even removed from the valise during my brief stay in the room at Willard's. But nothing had been taken from the bag, or from the room. My intruder had gotten only one thing for his trouble, but that was the one possession in the chamber I most wanted to keep: the secret that I had a singular interest in the matter of President Lincoln's assassination.

I sat down and considered the mystery of the two watchers, who had now acquired primary importance among my collection of question marks. General Baker, Dr. May, and even Mr. Murphy were all figures of intrigue, each involved in his own assortment of machinations. Thus, the presence of the watchers at their post across from Brady's Gallery was a development I found interesting, but not obviously connected to my own maneuvers.

Their paths had not intersected my own before I entered Brady's. I knew that with the same certainty I knew my own professional instincts would have alerted me to their presence had they followed me to the railway station that morning, or tracked my various peregrinations which culminated in my breathless arrival at the Gallery. I could not swear they were not at their clockshop post when I hastened into Mr. Brady's establishment, but I was certain they had not galloped along in my wake as I rushed there from the undertaker's parlor. Thus, I concluded I had only recently become an object of their interest.

The fellow I had just now observed in Willard's public room I'd last seen setting forth on the trail of the true General Baker. He may have tracked the General the three blocks to his lair in the Pennsylvania House, but how came he so quickly to learn that a second General Baker stayed at Willard's? There seemed but one answer: The fellow *expected* Baker to go to Willard's, and when he discovered the General was, in fact, a guest at another hostelry, he came here to investigate the duplicate. From this but a single conclusion appeared to proceed: Somehow the fellow had read my exchange of telegrams with Dr. May. He knew the messages summoning Dr. May to Washington City had been sent by a General L. C. Baker at Willard's Hotel. Presumably he and his companion had been among the passengers emerging from the railroad station this morning, and had managed to secure a carriage and trail Patch and Dr. May to Brady's Gallery. But when the pair spied upon the apparent rendezvous of Baker and May at Brady's, one discovered that the true General Baker was ensconced in the Pennsylvania House, and so wondered who the imposter at Willard's might be, and what was his game. Thus he proceeded here, inspected my room, and bribed the desk clerk to announce my arrival.

What had the fellow earned through his pains? The knowledge that an imposter had summoned Dr. May from New York, and that this mysterious fellow had taken a great interest in the assassination of President Lincoln. He also had seen my face. But, unless I was greatly mistaken, he did not know of my presence at Brady's Gallery, and he must suppose it was the true General Baker who had met there with Dr. May. If his partner was successful in discerning Mr. Murphy's identity, he would shortly have evidence that the meeting at Brady's required the services of a phonographer. And what would he have when he assembled all of these hard-won scraps of intelligence? A mystery, and so also, my sympathy. Alas, the rules of the game forbade it, but would that I could simply invite the fellow to sit down with me and strike some sort of bargain: "Tell me why you spied on Baker and May, and I'll tell you why I did the same. Throw in the name of your client, and I'll present you with a copy of Dr. May's revelations." But if mysteries could thus be bartered away, there would be no need for secret detectives to prize them loose. Nicholas Cosgrove would be a trusted clerk in Pinkerton's General Store, or remain a constable protecting the streets of New York from sneaks, pickpockets and confidence men.

My immediate problem, however, was not to discern the motive behind the fellow's interest in me, but to devise some means of ridding myself of him. I had planned to settle my account at Willard's and proceed to the War Department, there to apprise Mr. Stanton of Dr. May's disclosures, and furnish the Secretary with a copy of Mr. Murphy's affidavit. This latter had been rendered impossible for the moment, for I should compromise my client's confidentiality if I were to visit the Department while casting this unwelcome shadow.

I re-locked my valise and, taking it in hand, left the room and went to the front desk. There I settled my bill with the treacherous room clerk, and requested that any messages addressed to me should be forwarded in care of Mr. Gustave Kindt of Alexandria. Having completed my business at the desk, I strode quickly into the street. A streetcar was approaching along the Avenue, bound for the Capitol and, ultimately, the Navy Yard. I hurried across the boulevard and boarded it. As the car started off, I glimpsed my pursuer climbing aboard the rear of the vehicle. I settled back and enjoyed the crisp March air, until we stopped at 7th Street. There I got off to wait for one of the cars that ran to the Virginia Ferry Wharf on the Potomac. My shadow did the same and made an admirable effort to look in every direction save mine until the 7th Street car arrived. I held up my side of the play by endeavoring not to notice that he, too, boarded the car bound for the ferry slip.

To something less than my utter astonishment, my shadow chanced to be bound for Alexandria and followed me aboard the ferry boat, which was waiting at the slip when the streetcar arrived. I settled down on the deck to enjoy the sunshine, while he made a great show of turning his back on me to lean against the railing and study the distant bank of the Potomac. I remained in repose, my eyes shut as though in a shallow drowse, but my ears sharply tuned to the activity on the wharf. Presently the sound of other sojourners boarding the craft ceased. Next came a pair of splashes as the deckhands undid the hawsers and cast the shipboard ends of the lines into the river. In a moment the sidewheels began to churn the waters around us, and I felt the first movement of the ferryboat as it started its journey across the river. I sprang to my feet, grabbed up my valise and, taking a long running start, leapt from the deck onto the slowly retreating ferry slip. I turned to watch the craft as it moved away. It was a full fifty yards into the Potomac before my shadow chanced to face about and discover I'd jumped ship. I waved him a cheery farewell and climbed aboard the 7th Street car, which was preparing to depart on its return run to the city. I calculated we'd be across Pennsylvania Avenue before the ferry was halfway to Alexandria.

As we proceeded up 7th Street, I wondered if my erstwhile companion would return on the next boat or take an hour or so to seek out my Mr. Gustave Kindt in Alexandria. For all I knew Kindt might be there, or anywhere else, for that matter. The last I ever saw of Kindt he was climbing aboard the Cortlandt Street car, while I watched in dismay from the deck of a ferryboat bound for Jersey City. The maneuver I had used to rid myself of my shadow was the last of many valuable lessons Kindt had taught this secret detective, and I recited a silent prayer of gratitude in his behalf. May he ever evade human justice and find God's Grace and Mercy!†

---

† Gustave Kindt, aka Frank Lavoy, was a Belgian-born toolmaker who became one of the most successful burglars in America. Apparently Cosgrove had encountered him in the line of duty, and his contacts with the ingenious crook may have been the source of the detective's own considerable skill at locksmithing.—M.C.

·12·

In the Crypt

As the hour of midnight approached I ascended the Hill. Behind me, the street lamps of the Avenue shone through the mist, twin torchlight processions, halted and stretching back to converge in the distant dimness. The shops, the boardinghouses, the restaurants, all of the respectable north side of the boulevard was in darkness, save for a faint constellation of windows scattered along the way, where oil or taper still lighted some nocturnal venture. On the south side of the Avenue, several blocks away, where the city's voluptuaries were denizened, a cluster of illumination gave proof through the night that the pursuit of happiness had not been abandoned early, confirmed by the distant sounds of steel strings, reeds, horsehair on catgut, and the rippling murmur of merriment. But this hubbub was attenuating, and even such as sought the comforts of softer arms would shortly lie in those of Morpheus. The city would soon be asleep.

At the summit before me stood the empty Capitol, a beacon amidst the midnight gloom. Its marble face shone by the glow of illuminating gas, a recent addition to the majestic monument of the Republic. (Gas was, of itself, no novelty to the structure, but the gas that had long been commonplace in both chambers of Congress rarely illuminated anything.) Somewhere about I was certain a watchman watched or slept, but I found no sign of him as I circled the building. When I was certain the shadows about the Capitol were free of that particular shadow I'd last glimpsed on the ferryboat's deck, and of his companion, or any other watcher, I entered the passageway that runs beneath the Inaugural Steps and picked my way through the darkness toward the Crypt.

Few who visit or dwell in Washington City know that the large, circular room that lies beneath the Capitol Rotunda was meant to be the final resting place of the Father of Our Country. The chamber, which rises some thirty feet to a ceiling of groined arches supported by a ring of columns, was to be the vestibule to a small room beneath, wherein the sarcophagus of President Washington was to repose. But it was the wish of the first President's family that he should sleep in the soil of his native Virginia, doubtless a providential decision, for the great man would hardly find peace in this dreary basement, what with the shenanigans that take place upstairs. Even at the remove of some dozen miles in Mount Vernon, General Washington must twist his shroud at least a half-dozen times on days when Congress is in session.

It is said that the Gaels are a superstitious lot, and even those transplanted to lands far from the Emerald Isle take along this trait and pass it on to their heirs. This may be so, but I can speak only for myself, and while I've seen more than my share of dead men, and even on occasion have assisted the odd rascal in securing early membership in their company, I have yet to see one who has gone to his grave make a round trip of it. And until that midnight visit to the Capitol Crypt I never for a moment supposed I had. But as I groped my way through the darkness toward the dim glow of lamplight within the ring of pillars, I came upon the pale white countenance of Abraham Lincoln.

"What do you think of it, Mr. Nichols?"

The voice from the darkness was distinctly feminine, thank God, else I might have expired on the spot. Its owner stepped into the dim circle of the lantern, and proved to be not only one of the living, but an especially sightly example of the gentler sex. She was a very young woman, dressed as though ready for a stint in the scullery, and, from her elbows to the tips of her fingers, as chalky white as the life-sized rendition of the martyred President. After a moment I gathered my scattered wits together.

"I regret you have the advantage, Miss?" I ventured.

"Not at the moment, I haven't," she said, "but I had it just before, when you blundered into the light without first exploring the darkness. I could have shot you like a sitting duck, had I a pistol and the inclination. Mr. Murphy says you spy for General Grant, but I should think a spy would be more cautious.

"My name is Vinnie Ream," she added, as an afterthought.

"Well, I am honored to make your acquaintance, Miss Ream," I said, "and grateful that you did not shoot me. Is this your work?" I inquired, referring to the plaster likeness.

I did not suppose that it was, having had a moment's opportunity for closer inspection of both the statue and the young woman. The former was a striking depiction of Lincoln rendered in plaster, showing the late President in a melancholy pose, his head bent in a thoughtful, downward gaze, and a bundle of papers in his right hand, while his left held a trailing robe. It appeared incomplete, but the work thus far accomplished was obviously that of an experienced hand. Yet the lovely apparition sharing the lamp's aureole with Abe looked to be little more than a child, and despite the chalky evidence that clung to her fingers, I doubted that one so young could be more than 'prentice to the author of this magnificent likeness. However, in answer to my question, she averred that she was the sculptress of the yet unfinished work, having been commissioned by Congress to create a statue of the late President.† I did not dispute her claim, but merely observed that she was mighty faithful to her art to be found thus laboring at it at this late hour.

"Art answers to no timekeeper," she said. "I often come here in the night, for I can see Mr. Lincoln best when the Capitol is still. But tonight I came for another reason, to meet you, Mr. Nichols. Mr. Murphy asked me to do so."

"I am grateful he sent so charming an emissary," I replied, "but how is it that Mr. Murphy did not come in person?"

"He thinks he is being followed," she said.

"By whom?"

---

† Vinnie Ream was about twenty years of age at the time of this meeting with Cosgrove. She completed the plaster model, took it to Europe, where she supervised its rendering in Carrara marble, and delivered the final version to Congress in 1871. It can be seen today in the Capitol Rotunda beside the western entrance, just upstairs from the scene of her midnight encounter with Cosgrove.—M.C.

"He does not know, but he is very frightened," she replied. "Mr. Murphy is a man of high principle, but there is little gallantry in his soul." She spoke these last words rather sadly.

"Did he give you a message for me?"

She shook her head.

"No, only that he cannot meet with you because he is being watched. Is he being watched, Mr. Nichols?"

"Who might watch him?" I countered. "Does he know?"

"He said not. He said only that he was followed after he left you today. Was it you who had him followed?"

"No. I was followed, too, as were others who visited the place we met today. A pair of men did the following. I do not know who they may be, or what their aim, but I doubt that Mr. Murphy is the principal object of their interest. Did he give you something for me?"

"The papers? No, he has secreted them. He feared those following him would follow me, as well, and wrest them from my custody before I should have delivered them."

This news sparked my ire. I had not asked the wretched fellow for his mysterious documents, he had all but demanded I receive them. It was he who had insisted upon this penny-dreadful midnight meeting in the Crypt. Then some bumbling snoop enlivened the puling lad's melodrama, and so terrified him that he sent a wisp of a girl in his place, while he, himself, remained *in perdue.*

"Well," said I, "I am confident Mr. Murphy will summon up sufficient courage to crawl out from beneath his bed in a day or so. If you chance to see him, I would be indebted to you if you would tell him he can leave his precious documents with Mr. Brady, if he wishes me to read them. But if he prefers to keep them hidden in his mattress, that may be as well, for it will save me the trouble of reading them.

"And now, may I escort you home?" I asked. "It is a very late hour for one such as yourself to be abroad."

She shook her head.

"No, thank you kindly, but I believe I shall remain and work some on Mr. Lincoln. But you must not think too harshly of Mr. Murphy, and I think you should endeavor to learn what is contained in his documents."

"You recommend them, then?" I asked, my irritation yielding to amusement.

"I think them important to your mission," she replied.

"I see," I replied. "Then perhaps Mr. Murphy should take them directly to General Grant."

"Do not jest with me, Mr. Nichols," she said. "Mr. Murphy may believe you work for General Grant, but I know better."

"Indeed," I replied. "Whom do you say I work for?"

"'Mr. Nichols,'" she said, "I know that is not your true name, and I know for whom you work. I tell you this with great reluctance, but it seems I must, else you will not take what I have said seriously. Both you and I serve the same man."

"And what might his name be?" I asked.

"Allan Pinkerton, of course," she replied.

·13·

A Charming Secret Detective

Miss Ream proceeded to prove her claim by uttering a code-phrase then in use by secret detectives of the Chain of Agencies to identify themselves one to another. I was pleased to hear it, for, had I any doubt that she was, in fact, in Pinkerton's employ, her knowledge of my own association would have been cause for considerable distress.†
When I inquired how it was she knew of my service to the Agency, while I had been ignorant of hers, she quite properly reminded me that it was Mr. Pinkerton's policy to provide his detectives with only that intelligence required to perform their tasks. As this is a policy of

---

† The use of women as clandestine operators is a practice as ancient as the business of spying, and many women served as spies, informers and couriers for both the North and South during the Civil War. However, the employment of women as private detectives seems to have originated with Allan Pinkerton. The first female private detective on record was Kate Warne, whom Pinkerton hired in 1856. Ms. Warne was, according to Pinkerton, one of his best detectives, and she played an important role in thwarting the "Baltimore Plot" to assassinate President-elect Lincoln in 1861.

Pinkerton had a genius for recruiting capable people to his detective agency, and it is not surprising that he chose Vinnie Ream to work for him. Despite her tender years she was not only an accomplished poet, painter and sculptor, but a resourceful and courageous young woman with a gift for intrigue. That she played an important role behind the scenes during the Impeachment Trial is a matter of historical record, although the extent of her involvement is in dispute. Absolute discretion was one of her qualities, and she never revealed her role with Pinkerton's Agency, even in a memoir she wrote and privately distributed in 1908. Neither is there any reference to it in any of her biographies, nor in her *curriculum vitae* in *The National Cyclopedia of American Biography*. She seems to have taken the secret to her grave in 1914, and we have it here for the first time in Cosgrove's narrative.—M.C.

which I heartily approve, I perforce had to admit that her answer was as good as my question deserved.

Regarding Mr. Murphy's documents, Miss Ream had never seen them, but she heard enough of their contents from the phonographer to be convinced he was justified in his general conclusion that much evidence material to Booth's movements, motivation and associates had never been brought out at the Conspiracy Trial, and so, could not be found in Pitman or Poore, or even in the volumes of testimony taken by the Impeachment Investigation Committee. Whatever weakness Mr. Murphy might suffer in the vicinage of the spine, said Miss Ream, it did not seem to afflict his head, and she knew him to be a man of meticulous accuracy in word as well as recollection. From those fragments he had elected to recite to her, she was certain the circumstances of the assassination involved a vast labyrinth of intrigue that, for whatever reason, remained hidden from the public.

This seemed plausible in view of my discoveries of the past few days. The simple task of tracing the route of the presumed cadaver of J. Wilkes Booth from the empty grave in the Arsenal back to the deck of the *Montauk* had unlocked the guilty secrets of so many private lives that I shouldn't be surprised if Mr. Murphy's packet of unauthorized copies contained a rich harvest of like furtiveness. Recalling that Mr. Stanton had set me on the trail of the missing assassin armed with nothing more substantial than Pitman's synopsis of the Conspiracy Trial, I wondered now why he had not, instead, laid open to me the War Department's complete archive regarding the assassination. Perhaps there were some personal matters of his own, the disclosure of which he deemed too dear a price to pay even to learn the whereabouts of Booth. Viewed in such perspective, Mr. Murphy's mysterious packet looked a sight more covetable. But how was it to be prized from the grip of its timorous custodian?

I learned from Miss Ream the whereabouts of Mr. Murphy's rooms, but when she perceived my intention she urged against it. I doubted the fellow to be so shrewd as to have secreted the papers other than within the walls of his own diggings, and I was certain a brief visit thereto while the phonographer was off scribbling in the Senate chamber would quickly yield the prize I sought. But Miss Ream believed she could accomplish the same through suasion, by convincing the timid fellow that in delivering the packet to me he would thus also rid himself of his shadow. She would then bring the item to me at the house on K Street, with which it transpired she was familiar. And so, as I took leave of the sculptress in the Capitol crypt, that was the way we left matters.

The next morning I was up with the sun, my late night sojourn notwithstanding, for I had much to do. After a quick breakfast, I retired to my room and penned a report to Mr. Pinkerton. Because it was to be sent by telegraph, and therefore must needs be translated into cipher, I made it brief, and recounted only the major developments: The body buried in the Arsenal had not been Booth's; Dr. May had perjured himself aboard the *Montauk,* and I had his witnessed confession in hand, which implicated General Baker in the fraud; Mr. Edward V. Murphy claimed to possess papers implicating important personages in the assassination, and I hoped shortly to have these papers in hand; and because some unidentified agents had taken an interest in my movements, I had eschewed visiting our client to deliver my report. Pending Mr. Pinkerton's further instructions I planned to continue my inquiries regarding Booth's present whereabouts. The message was directed to Mr. E. J. Allen at an address of convenience used by the firm for that purpose in Chicago, and it was signed C. Nichols.

Next I retrieved my code and cipher materials from their hiding place and painstakingly translated my report into this impenetrable language. The system was based on the rearrangement of some words of the message, and the substitution of others in a standard codebook used by the Chain of Agencies. The encoding process required that the words comprising the message be arranged in a rectangular array of certain prespecified numbers of columns and rows. Then, each word was selected from the rectangle according to a particular pattern of diagonals drawn through it in a certain order. The first word of the message indicated the dimensions of the rectangle, and the selection pattern, as well. The result was a perplexing string of words certain to confound all but one equipped with a matching set of code and cipher instructions. Each individual word remained intact, however, to facilitate its reading and copying by the telegraphers. Yet the message, as a whole, was gibberish to them.†

I gave Patch the message, together with the necessary funds, and dispatched him to the Western Union office on the Avenue at 14th Street. I knew that such coded messages would seem no novelty there, for similar encryption schemes were used extensively by large commercial enterprises, many of which housed their Washington City representatives at Willard's or other nearby hotels. Nonetheless, I cautioned the lad to be watchful while returning to K Street lest some curious observer strive to discern the origin of the cryptic telegram.

I had no inkling of how much time must pass before the telegram would overtake Mr. Pinkerton and I would receive further instructions from my chief. I must, perforce, lay my plans guided only by my own best judgment.

The confidentiality of our client was of paramount concern. Mr. Pinkerton had premonished me to a special measure of prudence in this. But the case had reached an important juncture, and Mr. Stanton should have been consulted. If John Wilkes Booth had been alive, in custody, and under intense interrogation while the actor's lifeless understudy lay on the deck of the *Montauk,* then either Baker later executed the assassin in secret and secretly disposed of the body, or else he set him loose. But the veteran secret detective could not be tricked out of his secrets. If he would yield them at all, it would only be while under arrest and threat of prosecution. This was beyond my legal power, but it was most surely the measure Mr. Stanton would take immediately upon hearing my report.

Yet I stickled at the prospect of calling upon the Secretary at the War Department building, surrounded as it was by a perimeter of troops and a larger encincture of newspaper reporters and others of

---

† This combination of code and substitution cipher was essentially the same used by the Union Army during the Civil War, and its success can be attributed to the fact that the Confederates were even more naive than their enemy in the matter of codes and ciphers. (The War Department broke the simple cipher used by the Confederates early in the game and easily read every Rebel dispatch that was intercepted during the war.) Cosgrove used an even simpler form of the technique when enciphering his own diaries, so firm was his conviction that the basic scheme was "impenetrable."—MC.

the curious. I had been watched and followed by I knew not whom, or for what purpose. Nor did I know whether the pair of shadows that had stood before the clockmaker's had accomplices. Whoever the secret watchers might be, they already knew too much of my mission to fail to guess the name of my principal were they to see me enter the War Department. But if I were to confer with Mr. Stanton, the conference must needs take place in his office, for there he remained, night as well as day, lest he arrive some morning to find one of Andy Johnson's squatters had laid claim to the place.†

Of course, it would not be impossible for me to attempt to reach Stanton's office in disguise, or I might attempt a ruse to get past the troops unchallenged. But should I fail, I would have drawn the notice of all of Washington City. Covert maneuvers have this in common with the classical ballet: when executed adroitly they are beautiful things, but the merest stumble transmogrifies them into the lowest variety of comic opera.

Major Johnson, the Secretary's faithful lackey, must leave his master's side now and then, if only to run such errands as fetching victuals for Mr. Stanton and himself. But, although doubtless an excellent clerk, the Major seemed slow-witted when he ventured any distance from his desk. He was not the means with which to contact Mr. Stanton unobserved. As I could think of no other, I put the matter aside and turned my attention to less vexing problems.

First among these was the paucity of information in my possession regarding Lafayette C. Baker, the custodian of the secrets I craved. It was Baker who presided over the search for Booth, Baker who miraculously deduced the locale wherein the assassin had secreted himself, Baker who dispatched a brace of his secret detectives (including his cousin) and a cavalry troop to apprehend Booth, Baker who confiscated the presumed carcass of Booth in midstream near Alex-

---

† Johnson had already tried this tactic once, on the morning of February 21, when he sent General Lorenzo P. Thomas to Stanton's office with orders to kick him out and take his place. Stanton refused to leave, and except for the brief absences we know of only through Cosgrove's narrative, he remained continuously in the building until after the Impeachment Trial was over.—M.C.

andria, Baker who delivered a cadaver to the *Montauk,* and Baker who
suborned Dr. May's perjured identification of the dead man. General Baker seemed to dwell in the heart of the riddle of whatever became of John Wilkes Booth, yet while a wealth of particulars was known by everyone regarding the assassin himself, there was scant intelligence to be had of Baker.

I consulted the records which Mr. Pinkerton kept locked in a vault within a hidden room in the cellar of the house on K Street. This extensive collection included the biographies of those denizens of Washington City, the high as well as the low, whom Mr. Pinkerton anticipated as potential objects of his professional attentions. As I expected, there was an extensive assortment of intelligence regarding the former chief of the National Detective Service, but most of it pertained to his occupancy of that position, and there was little of the man's pre-War history. He had been born October 13, 1825, in Stafford, New York, had served in some unspecified capacity under General Winfield Scott during the Mexican War, had been a farmer in New York State, a mechanic in Philadelphia, and he removed to California in 1856. There he resumed his mechanical business in San Francisco and Sacramento, and joined the notorious Vigilante Committee. Later he served in the capacity of constable and catchpoll. He was the proprietor of the Mercantile Agency of San Francisco until he departed that city on January 1, 1861, returning to New York, and from thence to Washington. At the commencement of hostilities he volunteered his services as secret detective to General Scott, operated as such behind Confederate lines in Richmond, and returned to Washington to serve Secretary Seward as chief of the Treason Bureau. After Mr. Stanton became Secretary of War, Baker came under his command and became chief of the National Detective Service.

I could not say, of Baker's pre-War career, that the record was totally blank, yet my own professional instinct insisted there was much of interest which was not in Mr. Pinkerton's file. Had Baker spent his years in California in the quiet pursuit of his business as mechanic or merchant, then Mr. Pinkerton's information might seem complete. But the man had been busy at less placid work, as well, and had served both sides of the law, first as vigilante, then as constable. And then, most abruptly, on the eve of hostilities, he betook himself to Washington, as though Fate, or some other agency, had called him to readiness to serve as Stanton's spy-catcher. No, there was a much longer story to be told of Baker's years in California, and I'd warrant some of it was well known in San Francisco and Sacramento, however obscure the tale might be at so distant a remove as Washington City. I recalled the name of a young brevet major from the Ninth Indiana Infantry whom I had befriended well enough to know that he now lived in San Francisco and where a letter might find him. When last I'd had a word from him, he was engaged in the newspaper business, and so it seemed likely he'd heard much of the lore of the city's earlier days. I composed a letter asking him what gossip he might have heard or could unearth regarding the California doings of one Lafayette C. Baker.

By the time I had completed the missive and turned it over to one of the household staff for posting, Patch was back from the telegraph office. I told him I was bound for the Maryland countryside, where I understood some hellfire and brimstone were being ladled out in tents north of Rockville, and I inquired if he'd like to come along for the sake of his soul. He allowed that he would, and I could see in his eye the certainty that something other than a dose of preaching was on the agendum. He was, as usual, correct. My theological persuasions were of a different brand than those hawked on the sawdust trail, but Boston Corbett was to preach at the camp meeting at Washington Grove, and, as matters stood, I was prepared to withstand a round trip of some thirty miles and unwanted blasts of Methodist thunder for a glimpse of the man who said he had killed John Wilkes Booth.

·14·

Conjuring in the Countryside

Patch and I went to the local stables where the mounts and carriages of the house on K Street were quartered, and drew a phaeton and a pair of warm-blooded steppers for our excursion. We proceeded out the Avenue to Georgetown, from whence we took High Street† and were soon moving briskly northward through the country on the Rockville Road. We passed through the village of Rockville and stopped near Mulligan's Store, a few miles farther along, to enjoy the basket lunch Cindy had packed for us.

As we sat thus beside the pike while having our mid-afternoon repast, I could not but remark on the number of buggies, wagons, and even travelers afoot on the Rockville Road. There were many more than one might hope to see in the midst of a farming region of a Thursday, and most headed north, in the direction of our own destination. I concluded that the denizens of Rockville were thus roweled from their usual workaday preoccupations by the prospect of seeing Mr. Corbett, if not out of a hunger for the spiritual fare being served in Washington Grove. But as it soon transpired, after we completed our meal and regained the road, the throng shared neither our interests nor our destination.

It caught Patch's eye before my own, and he exclaimed as we topped a rise and the distant spectacle first came into view. Even at that remove we could see the thing was immense, for its lower parts were

---

† Today's Wisconsin Avenue.—M.C.

obscured by a grove of trees, themselves of impressive height. It seemed, in fact, to stand taller than any building one might find in Washington City, although it was clearly something other than a building. Patch inquired if this might be the Methodists' tent, and I assured him it was not, if for no other reason than the riot of color that engauded it. Yet it was a kind of tent, but of pongee, not canvas. It was a balloon, not the first of my experience, as it happened, but by far the largest and most spectacular.

When the trees no longer intervened, we saw that this had been the destination of the many who shared the road with us, for a crowd of several hundred souls was gathered around the apparition. The craft was tethered to the earth by a dozen lines, and a large wicker gondola was suspended beneath it, beside a raised platform that stood a half-dozen feet above the heads of the throng. Nearby there were three truck wagons, two of which bore a pair of large wooden cases I recognized as the apparatus employed to produce the gas which filled the balloon. The third seemed a kind of caravan, with a door on one end, windows on the sides and even a short chimney projecting above the roof.

Some distance off, beyond the fringes of the crowd, there was a tent, but clearly of the kind more likely employed at carnivals than camp meetings. If any doubt remained as to its function, it was dispelled by the words printed large across an enormous banner strung between its twin poles: "Professor Haselmayer's Magic Show." The conjurer who entranced Washington City audiences by evening was, it appeared, delighting their country cousins with matinee performances. And whatever wonderments the magician planned for the beguilement of the countryfolk, it seemed at least one was to be included which he had not shown his city following, some marvel involving the balloon.

Patch and I drove the phaeton into a nearby field and tethered the team to a farmer's fence. Washington Grove and the Methodist camp lay only a mile or so ahead, and I estimated that the afternoon was likely allotted to the small-bore fulminations of 'prentice divines, while the heavier pieces, such as Boston Corbett, would not be brought into action against the Evil One until after sundown, which was yet sev-

eral hours off. So it seemed a harmless truancy to postpone our northward advance for a while, and see what marvels the Professor planned
to offer the rustics. Patch seconded the motion without hesitation,
and we joined the throng to gawk at the aircraft.

It promptly transpired, through fragments of conversation overheard as we pressed forward for a better view, that a sizable contingent of the crowd was composed of deserters from the camp, their
appetite for wonderments doubtless having been whetted by several
days of reports of miracles of Biblical vintage. Their hungers were
soon to be fed, for as we approached the platform, I espied the formally frocked figure of Professor Haselmayer ascending its wooden
steps, followed by one of his Zouaves, and an elderly fellow I guessed
to be some species of local dignitary.

A hush descended as the Professor doffed his top hat and took a
step forward. In his rich teutonic accents, he introduced his illustrious guest as one Judge Bowie,† an announcement that was redun-
dant to all save such outlanders in the gathering as the Methodist
refugees, Patch and myself. When the Professor's Zouave produced
the case of trick irons, the Judge's role in the coming performance
became apparent to me. He was to serve the function Superintendent Richards had performed in Wall's Opera House, to wit, lend
his repute and a pair of genuine shackles to the magician's act.

There was to be some variation in the Professor's escape from the
irons in this performance, however. First, he omitted the black silk
"Sacred Mantel of Emancipation," a well-advised dispensation, at least
regarding language, considering that Montgomery County was still
strongly Secessionist in sympathy, and many in the audience were
former slaveholders only recently introduced to the salubrious benefits of working their own fields.

The second innovation involved the balloon. When the Professor's
five sham shackles were in place, and the good Judge had wrapped
the authentic set immediately beneath the magician's elbows, Professor Haselmayer, aided by his Zouave, climbed into the swaying
gondola of the craft. The Professor, after gaining the wicker carriage,

---

† Undoubtedly Judge Richard Johns Bowie of Rockville.—M.C.

clasped his hands together and raised his manacled arms above his head in a salute to the onlookers. Then, on some signal, a dozen of his Zouaves working in unison untethered the lines that secured the envelope of gas to a circle of stakes, leaving the craft moored by a single rope depending from beneath the gondola to a great iron windlass resting on the ground directly below. A pair of the Professor's Zouaves were unwinding the winch and so lengthening the balloon's remaining tether. As the ship ascended, the body of the gondola obscured more and more of the Professor, until, at a height I reckon to have been some hundred yards, he was no longer visible. The ship was permitted to remain there for a few minutes, drifting about in obedience to the zephyr's whim, and straining at its line, as though yearning to soar into the blue world far above. After the onlookers had been treated to a sufficient dose of this spectacle, the Zouaves on the windlass reversed direction and began drawing the craft down once again.

The return to earth was accomplished more gradually than the ascent, for the men at the windlass were now working against the buoyancy of the colossal gas bag. The pair were joined by several other Zouaves who lent their backs to the task, and after much sweating and straining around the winch, the balloon was brought within a half dozen yards of the earth. One of the Professor's men seized the rope and began to climb it sailor-style, adding his weight to the gondola and so easing the task of those toiling at the winch. The Professor was not visible above the rim of the gondola.

When the wicker carriage was brought within reach, several of the Zouaves who had climbed to the platform leapt across the intervening space and clung to the craft, then climbed into the gondola. Their added weight increased the speed of descent, and the basket was shortly brought to earth and tipped on its side. As the Zouaves crawled out, we could see the gondola was empty. All that it contained were the shackles, which one of the Professor's men displayed to the crowd. The carriage was turned in a full circle so all could see it no longer contained Professor Haselmayer. A few skeptics, including the incredulous Judge Bowie, inspected the basket carefully in search of a false bottom or some such compartment in which the Professor might yet be found. Their search was interrupted by a loud cannonlike report from the direction of the tent. The crowd turned as one to observe, standing amidst a drifting curtain of white smoke, none other than Professor Haselmayer!

The general gasp of astonishment was quickly followed by a thunderous ovation, and the throng abandoned the balloon and gondola to the Zouaves and crossed the pasture to gather before the tent, where the Professor now stood atop another pulpit. Patch and I led the pack. When all had arrived and found places as near as possible to the wizard, he raised his unshackled arms in a bid to speak. An expectant silence spread speedily throughout the gathering. Professor Haselmayer began a brief oration.

"Ladies and gentlemen! What you have seen, or, rather, what you believe you have seen, is only one of my little tricks, a free sample. I hope it has entertained you."

He paused, and a ripple of applause grew into a second ovation. The Professor bowed several times, then again held up his hands to beg for silence.

"You do me too much honor," protested the wizard. "I am only a simple peddler, a vender of illusions. I sell sweets, although my confections are meant to delight the eye, not the palate. You have had a sample of my wares. Those who would taste more of them I invite inside my humble shop. I shall begin serving a full dish of tasties in a quarter hour."

And so saying, he withdrew to his tent. Most of those assembled hankered for more of the Professor's confections and soon had assembled in a long queue to purchase admission to the canvas playhouse from one of the Zouaves stationed at the entrance. The tariff he demanded was less than the price of admission to Wall's, but whether this was in consideration of rustic thrift, the matinee hour, or for some other reason, I cannot say. I cheerfully parted with the coins required to admit Patch and myself, and we were among the first to find our seats, which we chose from those closest to the wooden platform on which the performance was to take place.

The Professor's sweets were much of the same selection he had dished up in Washington City, but they had not gone stale, even in this third serving. I had divined the means he used to escape the shackles, but all else eluded my comprehension, and so remained both mysterious and delightful. But the balloon ascent had been a novelty absent from his earlier performances, so, as he proceeded with his marvels, I watched in anticipation of some additional innovation. Thus it was that when the shots rang out, I thought them the herald of some new wonder. It was only after I turned about to look behind me that I discovered the gunplay was not a part of the program.

At first sight, in the dimness of the great tent, the audience seemed, for the most part, to have disappeared, a wonder that was surely beyond even the powers of Professor Haselmayer to work. Then I saw that most were crouched close to the earthen floor in the doubtful shelter of the rows of wooden chairs, while those nearest the periphery of the tent were struggling indecorously with each other for precedence of opportunity to escape beneath its skirts. Those who had been near the entrance were nowhere to be seen, having already accomplished their egress. The whole chaotic mazurka was accompanied by a chorus of ragged ululation.

A lone figure stood erect near the last row of seats, and the smoking revolver in his hand left no doubt that he was the author of the disturbance. He was a slight fellow of moderate years, dressed shabbily, and, apart from the hardware he held, remarkable in but a single aspect: the look of stark, staring madness in his face.

"Sorcerer!" he screamed. "Devil's whelp!"

He got off two more shots, and I joined the multitude on the tent floor. I hazarded a glance stageward, and saw that Professor Haselmayer remained where he stood. Yet the magician's seeming indifference to the gunman evoked no suspicion that the fellow was some species of sham supplied to enliven the ceremonies, for the velvet backdrop to the rear of the stage was now a tattered ruin, and, if further proof was required that real lead had been loosed, it was to be seen in the jagged scars of naked wood that pocked the polished casket the Professor had been on the point of entering.

"Beelzebub!" ranted the marksman, punctuating this salutation with another blast from his weapon, and precipitating a renewal of the general exodus of those near the canvas hem. One resourceful fugitive facilitated his escape by slashing an exit with his knife and diving through it. Daylight poured in through the rent and enlightened the bizarre tableau.

I arose, stepped into the aisle and hastened toward the madman. Lest I be thought uncommonly dauntless or foolhardy, I must explain that the daylight had confirmed what my ears already suspected. I thought I had recognized the familiar voice of an Army Colt, and that is what the fellow's shooting iron now looked to be in the light of day. Whatever its species might be, I was certain the genus was that of the large-bore percussion revolver, and none of that class, in my experience, held more than six rounds. Six was the number of shots I had heard, and so I concluded the lunatic's weapon was spent. As I raced toward him, the sound of the pistol's hammer striking a dead chamber confirmed my deduction, but to my dismay he tossed away the useless iron and immediately produced a second revolver from within his coat.

To my great good fortune the mad fellow was oblivious to all save the magician, and it was in Haselmayer's direction that he proceeded to empty this sequel. A more miraculous Providence seemed to guard the Professor, however, for though all of the dozen balls struck near him, he remained unharmed, and, I hasten to add, unfazed. As the cloud of gunsmoke drifted into the distant reaches of the tent, the madman and the magician stood staring at each other, a pair of human superlatives: the coolest man in the world faced the worst marksman in History. Here was a miracle to beggar the best of the magician's conjuring. I had seen his face in Brady's Gallery and there was no doubt in the matter: The mad gunman was Boston Corbett.

The "Glory-to-God" Man

··· ⟶ ◈ ⟵ ····

There was talk of stringing him up then and there. He had not likely done more than fifty dollars' worth of property damage, and no injury at all to life and limb, but he had scared the wits out of a couple of hundred solid citizens, and roweled a few into an exceptional state of dudgeon. I pinioned Corbett's arms from behind after he had spent his second Colt, and promptly satisfied myself that there was not a third tucked somewhere beneath his tatterdemalion coat. Thus disarmed and restrained, he looked mild and in no way dreadful, and I incline to believe this added insult to injured dignity. Those most vociferous in demanding immediate hempen retribution were, I suspect, the ones who had run the farthest and the fastest when the first shots were fired. The only true victim of the onslaught was Professor Haselmayer, and he seemed in no way disposed toward vengeance. The only sentiment he evinced as he approached the captive was amazement.

"But why?" inquired the magician. "Why have you done this? I do not think I know you. Have I ever done you injury?"

Corbett struggled in vain to free himself of my grasp.

"Belial!" he hissed. "Satan! Lucifer! Apollyon! I know all your names, Foul Fiend, Prince of Darkness! By your fruits do I recognize you, Arch-Enemy!"

"He thinks you're Old Nick, himself," I panted, striving to keep the wriggling fellow from getting loose and making more mischief. "Seems to have been impressed by your show."

"Ach, so!" exclaimed Professor Haselmayer, the situation of affairs becoming clear to him. "But I have explained, even before I began, that these are nothing more than clever tricks."

The mood of the onlookers was becoming increasingly wrathful, the more ductile bystanders inflamed by the demands of a few of their irascible associates that the fractious fellow be strung up forthwith. The hoisting enthusiasts were local folk, of course. The truant Methodists seemed to want no more of the matter, and were swiftly vacating the tent, presumably bound for the more familiar terrors on exhibition at Washington Grove. There were two exceptions, a pair of sturdy fellows who seemed to know Corbett, and ignoring the hostile circumambience, placed themselves beside me and tried to calm their friend, or, at least, shut him up. I admired their pluck, but they weren't having much success, for Corbett continued to wriggle and rant at the bemused magician.

"Professor Haselmayer," I said, "I don't believe you can talk him out of it, but if you hold no grudge against the poor fellow, you might try talking these people out of hanging him. It seems to me you're the only one about with any legitimate claim to his neck."

The Professor quickly comprehended the situation and, spinning about without further colloquy, returned to the platform and called what remained of the house to order.

"Ladies and gentlemen," he announced, "if you will forgive this unfortunate interruption, I shall continue my conjuring."

The knot of humanity that had gathered around us dispersed and its members regained their seats. The departure of the Methodists left many choice vacancies, and there was much maneuvering for improved positions as the Professor executed a few sleight-of-hand tricks to set the mood of the company before resuming his main-course miracles. Eventually even the most bloodthirsty of the locals could resist the allure of his conjuring no longer, and Corbett, his two loyal stalwarts, and I found ourselves alone in the rear of the tent.

Professor Haselmayer's Magic Show had been received with a chorus of superlative encomiums by the Washington City dailies, but no greater endorsement could the Professor be granted than that with which the gentry of Montgomery County had regaled him: His act was more diverting than a hanging.

With the aid of his two allies, I steered Corbett from the tent and further mischief. The perspicacious Patch, having evaporated during the confrontation with the hemp-minded hot heads, was waiting with the buggy in readiness, having anticipated the necessity of a swift departure. We boosted the former cavalryman aboard and sat him between us, where he continued to mutter regarding the satanic doings he'd witnessed in the tent, but was now otherwise docile. His two companions, who identified themselves only as "Joe" and "Will," retrieved their own mounts, and Corbett's, as well (it transpired the trio had come to the show on horseback), and escorted us up the Rockville Road to the Methodist Camp at Washington Grove.

The encampment of the Methodist Tribe was comprised of some dozen wigwams erected in a congenial glade not far from the pike. Few of the faithful were to be seen, but the voices of many could be heard from within the tents, lifted in hymns, exhortations, invocations, testifications, abnegations, and other varieties of pious noise. A few prodigal stragglers returning from the conjurer's sinful pleasure dome were about, but none paid us any heed, even when our passenger startled Patch and myself by rearing back and roaring a boisterous "Glory to God!" heavenward. I incline to believe they did not recognize Corbett or realize he was to be the evening's Main Attraction.

After we had tethered the team and repaired to a group of benches likely used for al fresco devotions when the sun was higher than at that moment, our guest first seemed to take particular notice of Patch and me.

"Bless you, stranger, for delivering me from the hands of the Evil One and his Legion," proclaimed Boston Corbett.

We were joined by Corbett's allies, Joe and Will, who added their own thanks for rescuing their friend.

"You done the country a service, as well," observed Joe, "when you helped talk them fools out of stringin' this man up. You probably didn't know, but this is a genuine national hero, the trooper who shot down the man who murdered the President of the United States. This here's Sergeant Boston Corbett."

I assumed to be awed by this news, and insisted on shaking the hand that had fired the historic shot, omitting to observe that the marksmanship exhibited by the distinguished organ on that occasion seemed to have since fallen into a state of desuetude.

"The Lord rewards good works in astonishing ways," I remarked, easing into the mood of the occasion. "I only thought to rescue a fellow pilgrim from the profane clutches of the infidels, but He has requited my labors by deeming I should hear of an infinitely more glorious service to God and Country from the lips of the very one who performed it."

If this smacks of blasphemy to those who share my religious convictions, I can only say that the theory was not far removed from that which I truly believed: I think Corbett was presented to me so conveniently by Divine Providence that I might be spared listening to an evening of Protestant heresy, and, instead, get right down to business. If I stretched things a bit, it was in aid of this very purpose, and it put the two-gun evangelist in a position from which he could hardly refuse to repeat his oft-told tale.

"Sergeant Corbett ain't a prideful man," said the one called Joe. "He don't like to boast about the thing. It's all right, Bos', go on and tell the man. Tell him how you come to shoot John Wilkes Booth."

"It was not I who slew him," said Corbett. "The Lord told Moses, 'Thou shall not kill.' Vengeance belongs to the Lord, not to man. Bless the Lord!"

"He don't mean it like it sounds," interjected Joe. "He shot him, all right. I know, I was there. He means the Lord told him to do it. Ain't that right, Bos'?"

"The servant of Satan was struck down. The Lord used my sword and my arm to strike him. I was but an instrument of the Lord's vengeance," proclaimed the ex-Sergeant.

"Your sword, you say," I remarked. "I'd heard he was struck down by a bullet."

If memory served, both Pitman and Poore quoted Sergeant Corbett's testimony at the Conspiracy Trial to the effect that he shot the man in the barn. Yet, in view of the recent exhibition of the cavalryman's marksmanship, it was easier to believe he had skewered him with his saber.

"Bos' don't mean that literal," explained Joe hastily. "He's speakin' in a sort of parable, ain't you, Bos'?"

"The servant of Satan was shot," Corbett allowed.†

"And Bos' were the one what shot him," declared Joe. "I can tell you that 'cause I was there. I was servin' in the Sixteenth New York at the time, and I was one of the troopers the Lieutenant picked to go after Booth and Harold. Ain't that so, Bos'?"

Corbett acknowledged that it was so, but omitted to clarify whether his endorsement covered all, or merely part, of Joe's declaration.

"I heard you plugged him through a crack in the barn wall while you were standing some ten yards off," I offered.

"Well, it weren't exactly a crack," Joe supplied. "Matter of fact, it was big enough to ride a horse through it."‡

"Still in all," I insisted, "that was a fine piece of marksmanship."

"It certainly was," Joe agreed. "Bos' was a better hand with a gun back then," he added in obvious reference to the futile fusillade we'd witnessed in the magician's tent. "'Course, like he says, the Lord guided his hand that day when he shot John Wilkes Booth."

---

† Cosgrove is correct in saying Boston Corbett testified he had shot Booth (see Pitman, pp. 94–95; Poore, Vol. 1, pp. 323–326). However, in a letter written to a Mr. S. B. Harrington of Hudson County, New Jersey, on May 11, 1865—two weeks after the event—Corbett states only that "Booth was Shot." In another letter, written in 1887, Corbett again resorted to the ambiguous passive voice: "A single pistol shot from a Colt's revolver brought (Booth) down . . ." Such evidence, together with the sheer improbability of Corbett's reputed marksmanship and the general consensus that Boston Corbett was insane, have caused even some of the most conservative historians who have considered the question to doubt that Corbett fired the shot that killed the man in Garrett's Barn. One popular revisionist theory is that Booth took his own life when faced with the inevitability of capture. This version would probably have achieved complete respectability by now were it not for the official medical report that the fatal bullet entered the right-rear quarter of the victim's neck.—M.C.

‡ In his testimony, Corbett described the size of the crack: ". . . you might put your hand through it." (Pitman, p. 94; Poore, Vol. I, p. 324).—M.C.

"It was not Booth," Corbett suddenly proclaimed.

"'Course it was Booth!" Joe shouted. "Don't go saying things like that, Bos'. There's no tellin' what some might think."

"It was not Booth," Corbett insisted. "It was the Son of Satan."

"He sure was possessed by Satan, I guess," Joe allowed, "but it was Booth, all right, Bos'. I can tell you that 'cause I met him once down to New Orleans, while you never laid eyes on him. Not until you shot him, I mean," he added hastily.†

"Satan may take whatever human form he chooses," proclaimed Corbett. "It was in the guise of Booth he slew Our Leader, and it was in the same guise he was struck down by the wrath of the Lord. Praise the Lord!"

"Praise the Lord!" I echoed. Joe did the same, but his discomfort with his friend's revisions was apparent. At that moment I supposed his concern was with the mental state of his former comrade, who was quite obviously afflicted by a condition of religious mania.‡

---

† Corbett had testified at the Conspiracy Trial that he had never seen Booth before, but was certain the man he shot was Booth because he had a broken leg and made "desperate replies" to the Federal officers who called out to him to surrender. (Pitman, pp. 95–96; Poore, Vol. I, p. 325).—M.C.

‡ Boston Corbett was as mad as a hatter, which, in fact, happened to be his occupation when not fighting Confederates or the Legions of Satan. Born Thomas P. Corbett in England in 1832, he was raised in Troy, N.Y., where he was apprenticed as a hat finisher. He married early, but his wife died in childbirth as did his newborn daughter. After this tragedy, Corbett drank heavily, but was "born again" into the Methodist Episcopal Church. The place of his spiritual rebirth was Boston, Mass., and Corbett adopted the name of that city to mark his salvation.

Whether his insanity can be blamed on his genes, grief, alcohol, or the mercury which was used in the manufacture of hats (and afflicted the reason of so many who practiced that trade as to link it with madness in the familiar expression) cannot be said with certainty. There is no question, however, that he was "afflicted with a condition of religious mania" long before his meeting with Cosgrove, and even prior to the Civil War. In 1858, while preaching in Boston, Corbett became sexually aroused by the blandishments of a pair of prostitutes, and immediately went home and castrated himself. He spent a month recovering from the operation in Massachusetts General Hospital.

If it was, in fact, a bullet fired by Corbett that killed the man in Garrett's Barn, his success may be considered one of the most extraordinary firearms' accidents in history. He was never again to duplicate his historic marksmanship.

In 1886 he was appointed Doorkeeper of the Kansas State Legislature, in consideration of his heroic service in the Civil War. On the morning of February 15,

I thanked Sergeant Corbett for sharing his recollections of the historic moment with me, and for the new insight into the theological side of the affair, which I truthfully declared I had not theretofore suspected. He was clearly gratified by this acknowledgment, but seemed to have no inclination to discuss the matter further, and shortly begged to be excused to join the holy hollering within some nearby canvas cathedral. I confess I was pleased to see his back, for his deranged assertions were of absolutely no aid to my inquiries, and his departure permitted me to pursue the subject with his former comrades, who claimed to have witnessed the death of Booth. I was reflecting on how best to raise the more temporal side of the incident, when Joe saved me the need.

"I hope you don't take the wrong idea from what Bos' just said, mister," he implored. "I mean all that stuff about him not shootin' Booth and how it weren't Booth, anyways. Ole Bos' gets carried away with his preachin', sometimes, and he says things that ain't strictly truthful. He don't mean to lie, exactly; he's just speakin' in parables, sort of. Trouble is, some might not understand that."

"You say you were present on the occasion?" I ventured.

"I surely was, and I seen Bos' do the thing with my own eyes. We was all drew up 'round the barn while Booth and one of Baker's men—Colonel Conger by name—parleyed back and forth about who were we, and that he wanted to take us on one at a time, and such. If you ask me, Conger let it go on too long, but he finally told him to come on out or he'd fire the barn, and that's just what he did. Well, the barn weren't put together so tight, and we could see Booth movin' around inside. The place got to burnin' pretty good, but Booth still hadn't come out, and old Bos' figured the man had made up his mind to die then and there, but likely not afore he took a few of us along

---

1887, he entered the legislative chamber, locked the doors behind him, and announced to the assembled lawmakers that he was subpoena-ing the lot of them to the Hereafter on the instructions of the Lord. He then proceeded to empty two revolvers at the statesmen, who, it must be stated in fairness to Sergeant Corbett's marksmanship, were at that point moving targets. He failed to dispatch, or even to wound, anyone.

Boston Corbert was sent to the Kansas Asylum for the Insane in Topeka. On May 26, 1888, he vanished from that institution, and from the pages of history. —M.C.

with him. So Bos' just hauled off and plugged him afore he could do us any damage. It were against orders, but Bos' did the right thing, under the circumstances, and no one ever claimed otherwise."

"Sergeant Corbett wasn't brought up on charges of disobeying an order?"

"No, sir. I think there may have been some talk of it at the time, as there were many who were looking forward to see-in' Booth hang. But everyone knew there weren't no justice in punishin' a man for doing his duty as he saw it. Even the Army's got that much sense."

"It was lucky for Sergeant Corbett that the fellow turned out to be Booth. I think I heard you say Corbett had never seen the assassin before."

"Oh, it were Booth, all right. I can tell you that for sure, and Will can back me up. You see, it just happens we knew the man. Made his acquaintance back in '62 when we was both in New Orleans with the First Artillery."

"You say you knew John Wilkes Booth?" I asked.

"Well, we weren't real close pals, or nothin' like that, but we met him once or twice, and we knew him to speak to. So when I saw this man dragged out of that barn, there weren't no doubt in my mind, or in Will's either, that it were Booth. And, a' course, that's just what the Army said when they brought his carcass back to Washington City and gave his friends a look at it. I hear they even got his sawbones who once had worked on Booth to take a look and say it was Booth. So it don't matter what Bos' or anybody else says, it were Booth, and they ain't no 'maybe-so' about it."

Joe's assurances regarding the identity of the man Corbett shot were delivered with increasing heat and voice, as though such emphasis were demanded by some serious challenge to his claim. Yet I had voiced no doubts in the matter, and Corbett's remarks could only find serious consideration among those prepared to believe that the person felled by his bullet might truly have been Lucifer disguised as the actor. I asked Joe his view of this theory, but he merely smirked and shook his head.

He and Will, Joe explained, did not share Sergeant Corbett's species of worship, and were in his company at Washington Grove as former comrades, not co-religionists. He explained that he had chanced to be in New York City a few days earlier, where he saw an announcement that his whilom sergeant was to speak at the Attorney Street Methodist Church in that city. He attended the occasion, and there encountered Will, whom he had not seen since the War, and who also happened to be visiting New York City and had come to the church out of the same motive, to wit, to renew an old acquaintance. Neither veteran had any pressing need to return home, and so, on impulse, both agreed to accompany Sergeant Corbett along some part of the sawdust trail as a sort of holiday. But as to Corbett's theory, Joe allowed that Satan might well have been in the vicinage of Garrett's Farm waiting to collect Booth's immortal soul, but the mortal remains he left behind were those of John Wilkes Booth, beyond peradventure of a doubt.

The matter of who it was that Sergeant Corbett had dispatched, and whether he had, in fact, dispatched anyone at Garrett's Barn seemed of much lesser significance to Will, who remained silent for the most part, speaking to endorse Joe's averments only when specifically called upon for such by his companion. But to Joe, the issue was one that demanded to be argued, even in the absence of contradiction. He could be diverted briefly from the theme, but would resume it ere long, and with heightened emphasis. He was, in fact, protesting too much. I was even less committal on the question than Will, and Joe finally could contain himself no longer, but came right out and asked me if I believed him.

"With all due respect to Sergeant Corbett," I answered, "I can assure you I give no credence whatsoever to his religious fantasies. But," I added, "I must confess I am mystified by the importance you seem to attach to the opinion of a stranger, and why you insist on that which has not been seriously challenged."

Joe was taken aback by this reply and lapsed into a state of momentary confusion.

"Well," he offered, "it's just that there is some what say it weren't Booth. Some newspapers wrote that at the time. I didn't mean to work up such a head a' steam over the thing. But I know what I know, and it riles me to hear that story."

"You'll never hear it from me," I assured him. "In fact," I added, glancing at the sun's reddening orb, now low in the western sky, "it's past time I should return to Washington City. I had not intended to stay so long in the countryside."

Patch took the cue and went for the phaeton.

"I don't believe I got your name," said Joe.

"Charles Nichols," I replied, and waited for him to supply his own surname in exchange. My wait proved in vain.

"Well, it certainly has been a pleasure makin' your acquaintance, Mr. Nichols, hasn't it, Will?" And thanks again for helpin' us and Bos' out of that difficult situation."

By choice or oversight, they were to remain simply "Joe" and "Will." Yet I was grateful to Joe for the more important intelligence he had imparted, albeit only through his frantic efforts to do the opposite. There was yet much to be learned regarding the incident at Garrett's Farm, but of two things I was now certain: First, Boston Corbett had proved he would have been fortunate to hit the side of Garrett's Barn, let alone a moving target within. And second, the dead man Corbett hadn't shot was not John Wilkes Booth.

·16·

"Stand and Deliver!"

·⋯⟶◆⟵⋯·

We were just past Mulligan's Store on the Rockville Road, yet a mile or more short of Rockville, when first I heard it, the drumming of a pair of mounts, hard-ridden through the twilight stillness. They were behind us and closing fast, and we were hardly overtaken by the hoof-beats when we were overhauled by the riders themselves. The two horsemen passed us, then reined about and stopped in the road, compelling us to do the same.

"Hallo," I called, "I had not expected to see you gentlemen again so soon. Have you abandoned the Methodists' hellfire for the gaslights of Washington City?"

"No," replied Joe. "Me and Will fancied palaverin' with you so much we decided to up and come after you for more of the same thing."

"I'm flattered," I said, "but afraid I'm already overdue at an engagement in the city."

"Well, that's bad enough," laughed Joe, "but it would be worse to miss it entirely. There's more than one way a feller can be late."

If there was any doubt of the menace behind these words, it was dispelled by Will, who unlimbered a Sharps' rifle from his saddle holster and cantered his mount to a position behind the phaeton. Joe drew a large revolver from within his coat and gestured with it.

"Let's all of us just ride on a ways, nice and slow, till we spot a good place to stop and have a little more talk."

So saying, he turned his mount and ambled on ahead. From behind came the familiar click of a Sharps' back-action lock. I took the reins from Patch and drove forward. We were alone on the road with the pair, and unarmed, so there was little else we could do, for the moment.

We had proceeded perhaps a quarter-mile in this fashion when Joe halted the procession at the juncture of a narrow lane leading from the main road. He dismounted and unpacked a lantern from his saddlebag, filled it from a small tin, and lighted it. Then, holding the lamp to light the way, he went afoot, leading his horse along the wooded pathway. The lane was barely wide enough to permit the phaeton to follow, and brush and branches clawed at the sides of the carriage as we passed. Even the dim twilight that still parted shape from shadow in the countryside did not penetrate into this wood, and I could make out nothing but the swaying lantern ahead. Behind us, I was confident, Will rode with his Sharps at the ready.

Our little procession moved slowly down the narrow lane. When we had covered a few dozen yards, I felt Patch tap me upon the shoulder. I turned, but could not make him out in the darkness. Indeed, I should not have discerned him in the blaze of noon, for, without a word or any other sound, he was gone. I heard no shot or cry from our rear guard, who must have passed within a few feet of the lad, now hidden by the night and the thicket.

Presently we seemed to have entered a clearing of some invisible dimensions, for the forest no longer pressed in upon us. Joe brought the parade to a halt and carried the lantern back to where I now sat alone on the carriage seat.

"Where's the darkie?" he demanded.

"He seems to have vanished," I replied. "Perchance if we betake ourselves to Wall's Opera House, we will find him within Professor Haselmayer's hat."

"Damn you, Will," exclaimed Joe, "you let him get away. You been asleep back there?"

Will, who had ambled his mount into the ring of lamplight, glanced into the phaeton with no show of concern.

"I ain't no cat, Joe," he replied. "You're lucky they didn't both of them make off back there. I could scarcely make out the rig, let alone spot a darkie. Anyways, the kid don't matter none. This here's the one you're so set on talkin' to."

Here was some reassurance. The Sharps and the Army Colt suggested Joe might have a more violent aim than "palaverin'," but his partner's offhand comment implied this was indeed the reason for the pursuit and abduction. Still, it is one thing to be offered a penny for one's thoughts, and quite another conversational gambit to be accosted by a pair of highwaymen and ordered to stand and deliver them.

At Joe's armed invitation I stepped from the carriage, and Will tethered the team beside their own mounts, just beyond the lantern's ambit. When he returned from this chore I saw he had not left the Sharps in his saddle.

"First off," Joe began, "I'd like to hear what business you're in, Mr. Charles Nichols, if that's your true handle."

"Why, I travel for Hostetter Stomachic Bitters."

"A booze drummer?" inquired Joe, who had served in the Army.

"Hostetter's Bitters is not 'booze,'" I objected, with feigned indignation. "I don't deny that ardent spirits may be one of its ingredients, but the formula is intended to promote salubriousness, not intoxication. It is a certain cure for dyspepsia, a bolster for the appetite, and a prophylactic against fever and ague."

"Yeah," Joe snorted, "and don't leave out snakebite. Booze is booze. Speakin' of which, where are your 'bitters,' if you claim to be sellin' 'em?"

"I am not a peddler," I announced with injured dignity. "I am a commercial traveler, I solicit wholesale orders from druggists and physicians."

"Is that what took you out to Washington Grove?" asked Joe. "Tryin' to sell a few cases of booze to the Methodists?"

"You know very well why I was there," I replied. "I was helping you keep your unfortunate friend's neck out of a noose. I decided to put business aside today and take an outing in the country with my helper. We saw the magician's tent and went in for the show. You know the rest."

"Aw, come on, Joe," interjected Will. "Let the man get on his way. You heard his story, and it sounds all right to me. You got no call to say it ain't so, and he sure helped us out of a fix."

"That's the part that started me wonderin'," said Joe. "The way he handled hisself and Bos'. That weren't like no drummer I ever seen. A drummer'd a been outta that tent and halfway to Rockville afore old Bos' was done fir-in' the first Colt. A drummer'd been lookin' for a piece of rope to sell to them sodbusters, 'stead a facin' 'em down that way. I don't believe this man is no drummer. I think he's some kind of lawman."

"A lawman!" I repeated incredulously. "You are a singular sort of road agent to chase me halfway across the country in that mistaken belief. If you restrict your 'clientele' to one profession, you'd be better advised to specialize in bankers, rather than constables. It happens I am neither, but you'll find my meager purse more closely resembles that of the latter than the former. I am, as I have told you, a bitters merchant. When you relieve me of my purse, as you doubtless intend to do, you will find my calling cards, which identify me as such."

So saying, I slowly opened my coat and removed my pocketbook, which I offered them.

"Here," I said. "You'll find ought else but a watch on my person, certainly no constable's badge, or shackles, or firearms, or the like. Only this slender wallet. As I said, I have made this lamentable sojourn into the countryside without thought of commerce, so it contains little beyond the evidence of my trade, and certainly scant reason to rob me. But take it, and the watch, as well, if you must, and permit me to be on my way."

Joe accepted the pocketbook, removed one of my cards, which identified me as Charles Nichols, a representative of Hostetter's Stomachic Bitters, and squinted at it in the guttering glow of his lantern. Giving a grunt, he returned the card to the wallet and the wallet to my hand.

"You got us wrong, Mr. Nichols," said Will. "We ain't no road agents. Seems like Joe got you wrong, too. Take your poke, we don't want it. I guess you can be gettin' along."

"Not so fast," said Joe.

"Now what in hell is wrong?" demanded Will.

"Maybe this feller is a drummer, like he says," Joe allowed, "but I'll tell you what he ain't. He ain't no fool, but maybe we are. You were in his shoes right now, what do you suppose you'd be thinkin'?"

"You speak for yourself 'bout bein' a fool, Joe," exclaimed Will. "Whatever he's figured out for hisself, he done with plenty of help from you and none from me. If you'd just let things alone back there, you wouldn't have no problem right now."

Whatever the particulars of Joe's "problem," its general outline was increasingly obvious. The corpse at Garrett's Farm had not been Booth. He knew it, and he knew that I knew it. Why his inadvertent revelation so distressed him, I had yet to fathom. But of this much I was certain: The truth, when it fully transpired, would implicate him in a crime. It was his conscience and not his acumen that caused him to doubt my disguise. The guilty flee when no man pursues.

"Maybe," said Joe, "but if that's what you've been thinkin', you've waited mighty long to say so. And it ain't me that has the problem, Will, it's us. Or don't you recall where you got all that cash money I seen you spendin' some of lately?"

"Don't matter what I recall or don't recall," replied Will. "I ain't done nothin' they can hang a feller for, and I don't aim to ever do such, if I read what you got in mind. Could be I should a spoke up sooner, but I'm telling you now, Joe. I say you turn this feller loose, and if you're fixin' to do otherwise, you're gonna do it by yourself."

So saying, Will turned away and started off in the direction of the horses. He had scarcely passed beyond the ring of lantern light when a sudden commotion arose in the darkness ahead of him, and the stillness was broken by the noise of equine startlement and a ratamacue of hooves fading swiftly into the night.

"Our mounts!" Will exclaimed. "The darkie's makin' off with our mounts."

He swung the Sharps to his shoulder and fired into the blackness, then groped at the cartridge box on his belt to reload. Joe ran past him, firing his Colt wildly, but promptly saw the futility of their gunfire.

"Come on, Will! Stop fiddlin' with that damn carbine and help me with the buggy! We gotta ketch him 'fore he reaches the road."

Will dropped the Sharps and the cartridge box and rushed after his friend into the darkness. I could hear the pair of them cursing at each other and the frightened team as they thrashed blindly about, trying to unhitch the steppers and give chase in the phaeton.

"Where's the goddamn path? I can't see a goddamn thing!"

"Oh, it ain't no use. That lane's no wider than the buggy. We ain't gonna make no headway even if we could see where we're goin'. The kid's likely got a mile on us already."

The two veterans continued in this vein of disputation for a minute or so, during which interval I retrieved the Sharps and cartridge box Will had discarded and withdrew from the lantern's reach. I opened the breech, replaced the spent cartridge with a live round, and stationed myself in the sheltering darkness. After a moment the pair reappeared.

"Damn it, Will, now the other one's made off, too!" Joe exclaimed.

"On the contrary," I said. "It would be unmannerly to take my leave without a word of adieu. Besides, I don't think we have completed our 'palaver.'"

Joe tugged the Colt from his belt and swung about, blinking at the circumambient blackness.

"Please, gentlemen, remain near the light. And you, Joe, place that hog's leg on the ground. There's been too much gunplay as it is, and the next round will likely find its target."

I punctuated this last remark by drawing back the Sharps' action, producing a note the two old Army hands apparently found both familiar and persuasive. Joe set the Colt on the ground at his feet, and, at my suggestion, backed away several paces from the weapon.

"What're you fixin' to do, mister?" asked Will. "Remember, it weren't me, but Joe here, who was talkin' about pluggin' you."

"I haven't forgotten that, Will," I replied. "You were so opposed to the idea that you refused to watch. I gather the sight of blood distresses you. Don't worry, you're not going to see any."

"You mean that, mister?" Will inquired, visibly relieved.

"Absolutely. If you behave yourselves, there'll be no need for bloodshed. If you don't, well, I'm a pretty good hand with a Sharps, and I think I can likely reload it so fast I can plug you before the hole I'll have to drill in Joe here starts to bleed."

"Take it easy, mister," pleaded Will. "I ain't gonna bet you can't. But what're you fixin' to do with us?"

"Wait and see," I answered.

They had not long to wait. In a few minutes Patch emerged into the lamplight. I was relieved to see him unscathed by the wild gunplay, not only as I was fond of the lad, but also because it would have been distasteful to shoot the pair, regardless of how ardently they had labored to merit it. Patch retrieved the Colt and the lantern, and, at my suggestion, we removed to the edge of the clearing.

Contrary to the belief of Joe and Will, Patch had not made for the Rockville Road with their mounts, but, instead, paused after galloping some little distance, and waited in patient confidence for me to avail myself of the opportunity offered through his diversion. Thus, the two saddle horses were tethered nearby, and I asked Patch if he had chanced to notice a rope among the mounted service of either animal. It transpired that he had, and he immediately went to the place he had secured the mounts and shortly returned with a generous coil of the desired commodity. As this brief transaction was carried out in the proximity of a stately old tree, the two ex-troopers quite naturally believed they had divined my aim, and that they were on the verge of meeting the Fate both knew they richly deserved.

"You ain't gonna hang us, Mr. Nichols," cried Joe, obviously believing the contrary.

"Please don't hang me," Will implored. "Remember, I was the one that was for turnin' you loose."

"I am grateful for that," I replied, "and even more so for the loan of your Sharps, which was the true instrument of my manumission, I believe. No, I shan't hang either of you. I'm content to leave that task to someone who is paid to do it, for I'm confident that you shall sooner or later provide one of that calling with an occasion to collect his fee. For the moment I have no other plans for this rope than to insure your presence while you experience an unfamiliar, yet worthwhile, exercise."

"What kinda exercise you mean?" Joe inquired uneasily.

"Telling the truth," I informed him.

I had the pair stand on opposite sides of the tree, each with his back against the bole, while Patch bound them securely to it by passing the rope repeatedly about the trunk. When this was completed, I approached Joe with his revolver in my hand.

"Joe," I said, "you were correct in surmising I'd guessed your tale of the events at Garrett's Farm is a pack of lies. Since you've made such an issue of it, and put me and my associate to some considerable bother over the thing, you've sparked my curiosity, and now I want to hear the truth."

"What I told you was the truth," Joe insisted. "I swear it."

"You swear it? Then I ought to believe it, I suppose," I said. "The sworn word of a man who may be facing his Maker shortly ought to be taken seriously."

"What d'ya mean? You said you wasn't gonna hang us."

"I'm not going to hang you. I'm not going to shoot you either, unless you keep on lying."

"For God's sake, tell the man the truth!" cried Will from the other side of the tree.

"You shut your mouth!" Joe called back to his comrade.

I held up Joe's Army Colt before his eyes, half-cocked it, and spun the cylinder.

"Ever played the game of roulette?" I inquired.

Joe warily allowed he had.

"Fine," I said, "for I have in mind that we should play it now. As you know, several of the chambers in this revolver are empty. You, in fact, emptied them in the general direction of my associate a few minutes ago. However, I do not think they are all empty. I think there may be one or two still loaded and capped. What is your opinion?"

Joe admitted I was likely correct in my belief.

"Very well, then," I said, "this is how our game will go. I shall ask you a question, and you will answer it. If I disbelieve your answer, I shall put the Colt to your head and pull the trigger. If the hammer falls on a spent chamber, I shall ask you the question again. Otherwise, the game is over."

"But I told you the truth!" Joe howled.

"Wait! I haven't asked you the question yet. Now here it is: Who was killed at Garrett's Farm?"

"Please," pleaded Joe. "I've told you the truth. It was Booth."

"John Wilkes Booth, you say?"

"Yes!"

"I don't believe you," I said, and taking care that the hammer should fall on a spent chamber, I placed the Colt to Joe's head and pulled the trigger. The sound of metal on metal seemed so loud in the country stillness that, for an instant, I thought the weapon had truly discharged. I think Joe experienced the same fleeting impression, but when he opened his eyes and found himself yet among the living, he bleated loudly.

"Tell him, Joe! Tell him," cried Will from the dark side of the trunk.

"Shut your mouth, you damn fool!" Joe replied. "He's bluffin'. He ain't gonna murder a man in cold blood outta pure curiosity, so shut your mouth."

"You admit you're lying, then?" I asked.

"No," Joe insisted, "I say it was Booth. John Wilkes Booth."

"Oh," I said. The next chamber was live. I cocked the Colt, pointed it at the trunk a few inches from Joe's right ear, and pulled the trigger. The report shattered the night, the ball shattered the bark, and the startlement shattered what remained of Joe's composure.

"He's kilt me!" he wailed, and fainted, as dead, for the moment, as though I'd truly shot him. I left him and circled the bole to the place where his comrade waited. Patch followed, bringing the lantern.

"No!" screamed Will. "Don't shoot me, Mr. Nichols. I'll tell you the truth, but don't shoot me."

I agreed not to shoot the man and, after gathering some degree of composure, Will began to speak. After a few words, however, his voice attenuated to an unintelligible croak, and I realized the poor fellow's mouth was arid with the taste of terror, so I fetched his canteen and held it to his lips, while he swallowed thirstily.

"You wouldn't happen to have none of them bitters you was speakin' of afore?" he inquired when he had regained his speech. I assured him I had not, and suggested he get down to cases.

"I surely will. I'll tell you the God's honest truth, so help me."

"Fine. The first question, as you may have overheard, is who was killed at Garrett's Farm?"

"I don't know, Mr. Nichols, I swear to you I don't, and neither does Joe. But it weren't Booth. Joe and I did know Booth from New Orleans—that part of what he told you was a fact. And whoever it was that got shot at Garrett's place, it weren't John Wilkes Booth."

"Very well. If it wasn't Booth, why did Joe insist it was? And why did you back him up?"

"On account a the money, the reward. Joe took his share of it along with the rest of 'em. Came close to fifteen hundred dollars."

"And what of yourself? Didn't you receive your share as well?"

Will shook his head.

"No, leastways not from the Army. See, the reward went to them as was actually present at Garrett's place, like Joe. I never did get there. Y'see, I was in the First Artillery, and so was Joe. That's how come we know one another. But Joe's hitch was up afore mine, and he re-enlisted and joined the Sixteenth New York, a cavalry outfit. Near the end of the War, we both turned up bivouacked near Washington City, him with the Sixteenth at Vienna and me still in the First Artillery, at Arlington Heights.† But it was a squad from the Sixteenth, includin' Joe and Bos', that was sent to Garrett's place.

"One day, whilst the hunt for Booth was goin' strong, I happened to be detailed to take a dispatch from my company commander to the Sixteenth. Whilst I was there, I stopped to visit a spell with Joe. We was passin' the time in the company barracks when Bos' came bustin' in—I didn't know him then—with a lieutenant. Well, the next thing was they was soundin' 'Boots and Saddles,' and Bos' and the Lieutenant rounded up a couple a dozen troopers to go down the river and look for Booth. I told the Lieutenant I was from the First Artillery, but I wouldn't mind goin' along with them anyhow as I wasn't expected back in Vienna till the next day. The Lieutenant said it didn't matter either way to him, and if I wanted to come, the squad

---

† Vienna and Arlington are today part of the northern Virginia suburbs of Washington, D.C.—M.C.

was leavin' on a tug from the Sixth Street Pier. So I got myself down there, and by and by, the cavalry squad showed up and went aboard, mounts 'n all. There was, like I say, maybe a couple a dozen troopers, Bos' and another sergeant, the Lieutenant—I believe name a Doherty—and two a Baker's Rangers, includin' a cousin a Colonel Baker's.

"We went some forty-five mile downriver to a place name a Belle Plain on the Virginia side. By this time it was the middle of the night, but the squad went right ashore and took off a lookin' for Booth and his buddy. As I didn't have no mount, not bein' in the cavalry at the time, I was left behind, aboard the tug, which was fine with me, 'cause when I volunteered to go along with 'em, I didn't guess they meant to spend the whole night beatin' the bushes. But that's just what they did. Fact is, I didn't see hide nor hair of any of 'em again for near two days.

"On the mornin' of the second day—it were a Wednesday as I recall, Bos' and one of Baker's Rangers came ridin' up hell-for-leather. The Ranger—Colonel Conger, by name—had the captain a the tug hail a mail boat that was headin' toward Washington City, and he got aboard it and was on his way. Bos' stayed behind to tend their mounts and wait for the others, and he told me they had cornered Booth and this other feller, Harold, in a barn somewheres beyond the Rappahannock, and that he shot Booth dead hisself. He said the Ranger was taking the news to the Army and Joe and the others was some ways back, bringin' along the body and their prisoner.

"Well, to make a long story short, they all finally showed up around sundown and we went back aboard the tug and made for Washington City. I was itchin' for a look at the famous murderer, and I managed to see the carcass afore it was took below. I knew right off it weren't Booth, but afore I could say a word, old Joe takes me aside and tells me to keep my mouth shut. He says the Harold kid was worth twenty-five thousand by hisself, and the carcass was worth twice as much long as it was thought to be Booth, but it wouldn't bring a penny if I gave things away. See, he was fixin' to get his piece of the reward money, and he promised to share his take with me if I kept quiet."

"But you are certain the body was not that of Booth?"

"I knew the man, I tell you, and even if his face got changed about somehow, there wasn't no way he coulda got them letters off'n his hand. I know that from the man hisself, 'cause I recollect him tellin' Joe and me he regretted puttin' 'em there, but there weren't nothin' he could do to get rid a them, on account a he'd been trying for years. He said they just wouldn't come off. 'I'm gonna take 'em with me to my grave,' I recollect him sayin'."

"The body had no tattoo on the hand? Are you sure you looked at the left hand?"

"Looked at both hands. There weren't no letterin'. It weren't Booth, I tell you."

"Who else knew this?"

"Don't know for sure. Them what knew weren't sayin', as they was lookin' forward to the reward money, just like Joe. But anybody what got a good look at the fella coulda told it weren't Booth."

"Everyone in the party knew Booth by sight?"

"I don't think any a them did, 'ceptin' Joe and I. But we all knew we was lookin' for a feller with a broken leg, and neither of this man's legs was broke."

"You examined the legs?"

"Had no call to. Joe told me he saw the man through a chink in the barn afore he died. He was steppin' back and forth just as nice as you could ask, and he didn't have no crutch, neither. Joe says it was plain to see neither a his legs was broke."

"Was one leg booted?"

"Nope, this feller weren't wearin' no boots, just a pair of yeller Rebel brogans."

"What of Harold, then. Didn't he deny that his companion was Booth?"

"That's the funny part of it. Accordin' to Joe, Harold were the one to first say it was Booth. Baker's men and the Lieutenant pressed him about it, but he stuck to his story and said it was Booth, even though anyone could see it weren't. I think that's where they got the idea, the officers. I think they said to themselves, 'What the hell, if this man is goin' to claim it's Booth, what're we doin' arguin' with him over it? Let's take the carcass back and pick up the reward money.'"

"And that's what they did?"

"Well, they turned it over to General Baker late that night. He came down the river in another tug and met us. Took Harold and the carcass away with him. That's the last I seen of either of 'em. We was a year gettin' our money. Natchurly, the officers got the biggest shares, but Joe got fifteen hundred dollars, same as the other troopers, and he gave me a third, five hundred, like he promised, so's I'd keep my mouth shut."†

"And what of Sergeant Corbett? Did he receive a bonus for shooting the man?"

"Hell, no!" snickered Will. "Ole Bos' didn't get no bonus, on account a he wasn't the one that shot the man. That's the one part of the whole shebang that was really turned inside out. See, the story the officers been tellin' has Harold givin' hisself up, and this other feller—the one what's supposed to've been Booth—makin' a fight of it, and gettin' hisself shot by Ole Bos'. Joe says that's all purely hogwash."

"What actually occurred?"

"What truly happened was just the opposite. When they got the barn surrounded and the officers called out for them what were inside to give themselves up, this other feller—the one they say was Booth—was all for surrenderin', but the kid, Harold, he was the one what said 'nothin' doin'.' Joe says they could hear them arguin' about it. That's when one a Baker's men fired the place, and I suppose the man decided he'd take his chances on gettin' shot rather than stay there and burn for sure. So he opened the door, as Joe tells it, and came out with his hands over his head, this feller they say was Booth."

"And who does Joe say shot him?"

"Why, his own buddy shot him down afore he'd taken two paces from the doorway, accordin' to Joe. The man wasn't shot by Old Bos', he was shot by Davy Harold."

---

† Each of the enlisted men in the squad received $1,653.85. Apparently Joe short-changed his accomplice.—M.C.

·17·

A Profitable Bargain

...◄───◆──►...

"That's a damn lie! I never said no such thing!"

Joe, having recovered his sentience during my interrogation of Will, seemed also to have regained his voice, which he exercised vigorously, alternately cursing his whilom comrade as the lowest species of blabberer, and resolutely denying that even a scintilla of truth was contained in that which had been blabbed.

"Joe!" cried Will. "I thought you was dead."

"You're the one what's gonna be dead when I get loose," Joe replied.

"Don't turn him loose, Mr. Nichols," pleaded Will. "Please don't, least not till I get a good head start outta here."

"I'm not going to turn either of you loose," I replied. "Not until I have your deposition, that is."

"What's that?" asked Will.

"He wants you to put what you just told him in writin'," declared Joe. "Don't you do it, Will!"

"I'll do whatever you want, Mr. Nichols," Will promised. "Just don't let that man get at me."

"Fair enough," I said. "We'll leave your friend here, securely trussed, while you accompany me into Rockville and repeat your account before a constable or judge, or some such local officer, have it recorded by an amanuensis, and, after you have put your signature on the paper, you may be on your way."

"Whatever you say, Mr. Nichols. Just don't let that man get at me!"

"Now, wait just a minute, Will," called Joe in a gentler tone than he had lately employed. "Don't you do nothin' foolish on account a what I may have said when I was riled. I didn't mean what I said just then about killin' you. I don't aim to harm you at all, 'cause I got no reason to do any such thing."

"Yeah?" Will responded uncertainly. "What about what you just heard me tellin' this feller?"

"Hell, that don't mean nothin'," Joe replied. "It's just his word against ours that you told him anything. He ain't got no witnesses, 'cept that darkie. But if you go swearin' out a paper, then you're truly gonna be in trouble."

"How's that?" asked Will.

"Well, if anyone believes you, which ain't likely, you'd be admittin' that you was what they call an 'accessory' to a hangin' offense, which happens to be the punishment for helpin' the murderer of a President of the United States go free. See, that's what you'd be sayin' you done, if you swore you knew the man weren't Booth. You'd be puttin' your own neck in a noose, as well as mine.

"But if they don't believe you, you'd still be in a mess, account a swearin' to a lie is a jailin' offense. And when you finally got outta the pokey, you know who'd be a waitin' for you?"

"You?" asked Will, timorously.

"No, sir," Joe replied. "Wouldn't be no need for me to settle up with you, after General Baker got done with you. That's who's gonna be waitin' for you, Will, Lafayette C. Baker. What d'ya think a that?"

"Oh, my Lord!" moaned Will.

I took up the lantern and circled the tree to Joe's side.

"And why should General Baker concern himself with the matter?" I inquired.

Joe snorted.

"Seems to me you're sharp enough to figger that one out fer yourself," he replied.

"Are you suggesting that General Baker might also be what you call an 'accessory' in this matter?"

"An accessory?" Joe remarked. "He sure weren't no accessory, not as I understand the word. An accessory is a feller what helps out someways in a crime, he's helpin' some other feller that's truly doin' the crime. Now, I don't happen to know what you want to call *him*, the one what's being helped out by the accessory, but whatever he's called, that's what Lafayette Baker happens to be, as ought to be plain to you, even if you're only a drummer, like you claim. If it ain't, I'll spell it out for you. The carcass we turned over to General Baker didn't have no tattoo, and neither a its legs was broke. The carcass *he* turned over to the cap'n a the ironclad *had* a tattoo and one busted leg, which is why they believed it was Booth."

"And you say that General Baker tattooed the corpse's hand and broke one of his legs?" I asked.

"Well, I sure as hell don't claim the dead man went ashore to get hisself tattooed and busted his leg on the way back," declared Joe. "There ain't no doubt it were Baker what done it, and what's more, he busted the wrong leg."

"The wrong leg?"

"Yep. I heard it from a corporal of Marines who was right there on the ironclad and saw the dead man. You see, the real J. Wilkes Booth busted his left leg after shootin' the President. We already knew that for a fact afore we set out for Belle Plain, on account a this sawbones what took care a him said so, and he had the man's left boot, which he had to cut off the busted leg 'cause it was swole so bad. But this corporal, who got hisself a good look at the carcass on the iron-clad, he said that this here dead man's left leg was fine, but that his right leg was busted."

"Maybe the corporal was mistaken," I offered.

"Well, maybe so," Joe admitted, "though most Marines I've met can tell a right foot from a left one, on account a that's one a the first things they have to teach 'em. But it don't matter which leg was broke, 'cause the carcass we handed over to Baker didn't have neither one a its legs broke."†

---

† If the unnamed Marine corporal was mistaken, Dr. May made the same mistake in a memoir he wrote some years later, in which he recounted his identification of the body on the *Montauk* as that of John Wilkes Booth. According to Dr. May, "The right lower limb was greatly contused, and perfectly black from a fracture of one of the long bones of the leg." However, the physician wrote those words in January, 1887, and the discrepancy might be attributed to a memory lapse. None of the testimony recorded at the inquest aboard the *Montauk* specifies which of the dead man's legs was broken.—M.C.

"That's very interesting," I observed. "I wonder what General Baker would say about the matter."

"Well, why don't you just go out to Michigan, or wherever he is, an' ask him about it."

"An excellent suggestion. As it happens, General Baker is, at the moment, visiting Washington City and staying at the Pennsylvania House. I should be able to go there and fetch him back in a couple of hours' time. I'll leave my associate here with you gentlemen to insure that the rope doesn't somehow come loose while I'm gone. When I return with the General, you can share your reminiscences with him. I'm sure he'll enjoy that."

"Oh, my Lord!" moaned Will, from the dark side of the tree.

"Simmer down, Will," Joe called out to his friend. "This here feller's bluffin'. Baker's gone West. He ain't nowheres near Washington City."

"No, Joe," Will replied. "Baker's in the city, just like the man says. I heard one of the pilgrims mentionin' it to Bos'. Said he read it in the papers."

"Mr. Nichols," said Joe, "or whatever your name is, I don't know what your game is, but I don't reckon you're gonna get whatever you're after by bringin' General Baker here—that's assumin' you truly could—anymore than you can by shootin' us or scarin' poor Will here into signin' a paper. Now, I know you ain't no drummer, 'n I believe I was correct when I took you for some kind of lawman. Only now I don't think you're out to catch them what took the reward money without deservin' it. I think you got bigger fish to fry than us. I think you're after John Wilkes Booth hisself. Am I right?"

"Suppose you were," I said. "What have you in mind?"

"A little swappin'. Will and me just want to get outta here. We don't want to sign no papers and we surely don't want to meet General Baker. All's we want's to get turned loose, be given back our mounts, and let go."

"And what are you offering in exchange?"

"Somethin' that maybe you can use, iffin it's Booth you're after. Y'see, when Baker's men dragged that feller outta the barn, they knew it weren't Booth, just like Will told you. So when they set him down on the porch, they asked him, 'Where's Booth?' It happens I was standin' close enough to hear what he told 'em. Now, Will here can't tell you what the man said, on account a he weren't there. And I don't think any a the other troopers overheard, 'cause the feller's voice was near gone. And I surely didn't tell 'em. Fact is, I never let on to no one that I heard anythin', so what that feller said is somethin' known only to me and to Baker's men, and I don't think they'd tell you, if you was to look 'em up and ask 'em about it. Now, I can't say that it's gonna be worth anythin' to ya, but it maybe will. Anyways, if you give your word to turn us loose, let us have our mounts, and ride outta here, I'll promise to tell you the God's honest truth a what the feller said. How 'bout it?"

I had no reason to believe that Joe would deliver his part of the bargain, and every reason to suspect he had invented whatever tale he proposed to trade for his freedom. Yet, he was right in his esti-mate of the situation of affairs. Will's deposition would be worth-less, even if I could prevail upon him to make one. What he could testify to was, in the largest part, hearsay, and there was likely not any official record to support even his claim to having accompanied the expedition as far as Belle Plain. A deposition signed by Joe, even less likely to be forthcoming, would be worth little more than Will's. In sum, could I prevail upon them to swear to their account of mat-ters, it would be their word against Baker's detectives and the other cavalrymen, while if I could not compel them to repeat what they had told me, it would be my word against theirs. What they had fi-nally said, I was inclined, for the most part, to believe, and it was, in fact, ample profit for my time and trouble. I had already concluded they could likely be of no further use, and had resolved to set them free. Thus, while I doubted Joe had truly heard the dying man's last words. I saw nothing to be lost in listening to what he proposed to offer as the price of his freedom.

"Very well," I said. "Let's hear it."

"Now, you promise to keep your end of the deal?" Joe insisted.

"I promise you this: If I believe what you say, I'll do what you ask.

But if I think you're lying, I'll tighten that rope, leave the pair of you here, and send a note to General Baker at his hotel recounting what you have said and where you can be found. But I've wasted too much time on the pair of you as it is, and one way or the other, I shall be gone from this spot within five minutes. Unless you have acquired a fondness for this place, I suggest that, whatever you're about to say, it had better ring true."

"Tell the man the truth, Joe!" wailed Will. "Please God, tell the man the truth!'

"I'm gonna tell him the truth," Joe insisted. "Now here it is, 'n remember I didn't say I knew for sure it'd be any use to you, but this is the God's honest truth. When the detectives asked this feller where Booth was, he says, 'With Dr. Stewart.'"

"'With Dr. Stewart?'" I repeated.

"Yep. That's what he said."

"That's all?"

"That's all."

"And who might Dr. Stewart be?"

"I never heard the name afore or since the feller mentioned it," Joe replied. "Now, remember, I told you I couldn't make no guarantee it'd be worth anythin' to you. I only promised I'd tell you the God's honest truth, and that's what I done. I'd swear to that on a Bible."

There was no need for Joe to endorse his claim with Holy Writ. He was too inept a prevaricator to have invented anything so artfully artless. Had he claimed the dying man put Booth in Mexico or Canada, or some such likely story, I might have wondered whether he was telling the truth. But Joe lacked the acumen to perceive that his claim to ownership of a tiny fragment of the truth would be far more plausible than a pretense to more valuable goods. As barter for his freedom, perhaps his life, as well, Joe had offered me the smallest scrap of intelligence bearing a face value of nought. There was no need for him to swear to its truth on the Holy Bible. I would do that for him, were it needed. Joe, I was convinced, had made good his part of the bargain, and, without further discussion, I did the same.

I loosened the rope sufficiently to enable the pair to work themselves free after an hour or so of vigorous struggle. Meanwhile, Patch and I regained the phaeton and set out once again for Washington City. The day's pastoral interlude had proved, to an unexpected degree, both arduous and profitable. John Wilkes Booth, I now knew for a certainty, was among the living. And his trail, wherever it might end, began at some place where resided one Dr. Stewart.†

---

† Joe and Will may have been Joseph Zisgen and Wilson D. Kenzie. According to Izola Forrester (p. 299), a pair of Civil War veterans Joseph Ziegen (sic) and Wilson D. Kenzie executed affidavits on March 31, 1922, stating the man killed at Garrett's Farm had not been Booth. I have not been able to locate the affidavits or any other evidence to confirm their existence. Forrester's granddaughter informs me she can find nothing in her grandmother's papers to indicate the source of the reference. However, War Department records list Joseph Zisgen as one of the cavalrymen who took part in the capture at Garrett's Farm and later shared in the reward for Booth and Herold. The April 20, 1898, *Daily News* of Beloit, Wisconsin, reports an interview with a Wilson D. Kenzie of Beloit in which Kenzie recalls the incident at Garrett's Farm in details which closely approximate those recounted by Will to Cosgrove. However, the *Daily News* story contains so many major errors of historical detail (and minor errors; Zisgen is misspelled "Zisjen") that if it is an accurate report of Kenzie's statements, it seriously reflects on the Union veteran's memory or veracity. The Wisconsin Historical Society seems to know nothing further of Wilson D. Kenzie. Kenzie, Zisgen and the anonymous *Daily News* reporter are likely dead by now; Izola Forrester certainly is. Thus the identities of Joe and Will must remain a loose end that can't be tied up at this late date.—M.C.

PART FOUR

Dr. Stewart's Secret

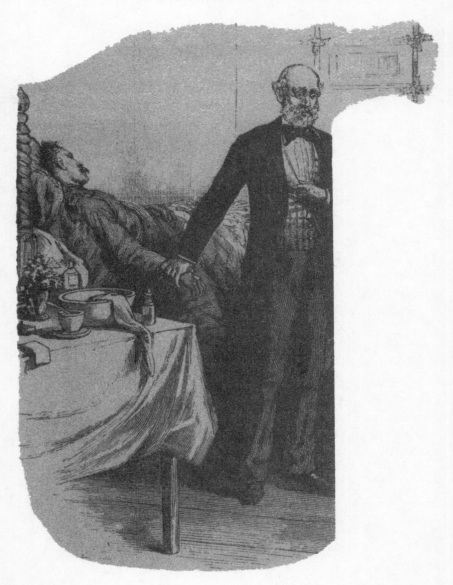

·18·

A Theft Is Investigated

"Burglar!"

The alarum wrenched me from my slumber.

"House-breaker! Thief!"

I was out of bed, and standing barefoot upon an icy floor in the midst of a freezing chamber. What bed? What frozen bedchamber? Never mind! First, seize the intruder before he makes good his escape. Time enough then to gather scattered wits.

"Unhand me, sneak!"

The voice was female. The softness of the form struggling in my grasp confirmed her gender. A salient of lamplight from the hall, where stood Mrs. Baxter, the housekeeper, in a state of great agitation, revealed my intruder to be Vinnie Ream. It was, quite literally, a rude awakening, yet, I blush to add, not an altogether unpleasant one. I released my captive. I gathered my wits. I found myself within my room in the house on K Street, adorned in my nightshirt, and in the company of a comely maiden who had, a moment earlier, been resisting my embrace. The gray, predawn dimness beyond the leaded panes of my window advised that the time was fully as inappropriate as the place for a gentleman to receive a lady caller. My costume would have rendered an improper situation indecent were it not for the housekeeper's presence.

"I'm sorry, Mr. Nichols," fretted Mrs. Baxter. "I told this, this, *woman*, that you were not yet up, but she would not wait while I called you. I could not restrain her from bursting in upon you."

"Do not disconcert yourself, Mrs. Baxter," I replied. "This is Miss Ream, and she is a sculptress."

"Oh, I see," murmured the housekeeper, who then departed. I do not know precisely how the word invoked the withdrawal. It may be Mrs. Baxter believed all artists mad; or, perhaps, Mrs. Baxter perceived that one who practiced sculpting must, perforce, already possess a more extensive familiarity with the masculine anatomy than my modest if unheroic nightshirt revealed; or it may simply be that the housekeeper believed that all aesthetes enjoyed a Bohemian disregard for the normal standards of propriety, and, therefore, Miss Ream's objectives in calling upon me at so unseemly a time and place might prove, upon sustained examination, to be grossly indecent and a threat to Mrs. Baxter's blushes. If so, I shared the housekeeper's suspicion that Miss Ream's motives were immoral, although I perceived them more a threat to my life and limb, than to my chastity.

Whatever the reason for my visitor's umbrage, it seemed to derive from the conviction that I had been guilty of some species of larceny. After she had cooled to the point where discourse was feasible, it transpired she believed me guilty of sacking Mr. Murphy's rooms in quest of his wretched documents.

"How did you come here?" I inquired, with some urgency, before getting on to the task of disabusing her of my guilt.

"I was not followed," she snapped. "You may have no fear of *that*.

Her emphasis clearly conveyed that the risk of her compromising Mr. Pinkerton's secret offices should be the least of my worries.

"I have not burgled your Mr. Murphy, Miss Ream. Now, if I may beg you to wait downstairs in the parlor, I shall take a few minutes to make myself more presentable, and then join you to discuss the matter further."

She complied, albeit with visible skepticism. Her suspicions remained unabated a quarter-hour later, when I made good my promise. I closed the doors behind me to guard our discourse from curious ears.

"Now," I said, "what is this of your Mr. Murphy and burglary?"

"Someone has done that very thing you proposed to do, when last we spoke," she said pointedly. "They have burgled Mr. Murphy's rooms in search of his documents."

"'In search of,' you say. Then they failed, and he retains possession of the things?"

"He does."

"Then I misprized Mr. Murphy's shrewdness, for I did not think
he had wit enough to conceal them ought but within his own
diggings."

"Oh, Mr. Murphy hid them in his rooms," she replied with hau-
teur. "He was just cleverer than the burglar."

"Miss Ream, I am offended. Not by your accusation, I hasten to
add, for, as you pointed out, I did have in mind to do the very thing
you accuse me of. But to suggest that, having broken into his rooms,
I should fail to find what I was after, that I might, in fact, have been
outwitted by a callow scrivener, is an affront to my professional
competence."

"I am very pleased to learn that," she replied.

"Oh?"

"Yes," she said, with the trace of a sly smile. "You have implicitly
admitted that you are a second-story man; I have perceived you to be
the sort of rogue who would break his promise to a lady; but I am
reassured to know that Mr. Pinkerton has not commenced to hire
bunglers."

Having thus smartly put me in my place, Miss Ream suggested
we remove to that of Mr. Murphy.

The phonographer occupied a suite of rooms in a boardinghouse on
Capitol Hill. He was fully awake and dressed when he answered our
knock. Mr. Murphy appeared to be an early riser, a trait that seemed
especially useful to those of Vinnie Ream's acquaintance. He ushered
us into his sitting room, which was in a lamentable state of disarray.

The storm, like a prairie twister, had demolished some parts of the
chamber, while sparing others. The greatest damage seemed to have
been inflicted upon a secretary desk: every drawer had been removed
and turned out onto the floor, strewing the carpet with sundry items
ranging from a set of silver-backed hairbrushes to a pair of opera glasses
and a full company of chessmen, black and white. All of the volumes
from one of the bookshelves above had been scattered about the room,
although the tomes aligned on the two remaining shelves were

apparently unmolested. A costly mantel clock was in its proper place, and an equally salutary fate protected the mirror which hung behind it, within a magnificently carved wooden frame. As I looked into the splendid glass, while standing a bit to the side of it, I saw the face of my host looking out at me. We both turned, and our eyes met again, now in direct confrontation.

"When did you discover your rooms in this condition?" I inquired.

"Late yesterday, when I returned from my desk in the Senate Chamber," he replied.

"And your landlord? Did he see or hear ought of the intruder?"

"He says not."

"And the men who followed you? They were no longer on your heels when you departed the Capitol yesterday?"

"How did you know that?" he demanded suspiciously.

"I surmised it," I replied.

"Mr. Nichols denies he was the burglar," said Miss Ream in an offhanded manner. The remark thrust Mr. Murphy into stammering embarrassment. Clearly, he shared her suspicions, but not her boldness, and so hesitated to put the matter to me.

"What is missing?" I asked.

"Nothing, quite fortunately," he replied. "I have spent the night making an inventory of my belongings, and I can account for them all."

Hundreds of sheets of the phonographer's scribblings reposed in several orderly stacks upon a large walnut table, where Mr. Murphy had placed them, presumably having rescued them from the carpet.

"You are certain?" I persisted.

"Nothing of any import is gone, of that much, at least, I am certain," he replied.

"By which you mean your documents regarding the assassination," I said.

"The thief never found them," said the phonographer with some satisfaction.

"The thief was not looking for them," I informed him.

"How can you know what the thief sought?" demanded Mr. Murphy.

"I do not claim to know what he sought, although I can guess," I replied. "I only claim to know that he did not enter your rooms in quest of those documents you have spoken of. I can also tell you that, whatever he sought, he found."

"You seem very well informed of the matter for one who claims innocence of any hand in it," said Miss Ream.

"I know only that which I have been told and that which I can plainly see. You believe your thief came in search of some document, and in this I agree. Clearly he was no common burglar, for he has left you many items of considerable monetary value which he could easily have taken off when he departed. His search was restricted to the vicinage of your desk, suggesting that it was, indeed, some paper he sought. He opened your desk and examined everything contained therein, depositing each scrap on the floor when he had satisfied himself it was not his prey. Next he searched for the document in the desk drawers, emptying the contents of each on the carpet as he proceeded. Then he searched among the books on the bottommost shelf of your secretary. But he left those on the other shelves untouched. He came and went undetected, so we may assume he was not interrupted by a hue and cry. Thus, I believe he found what he was after, and it was on the bottommost bookshelf, in or among the volumes standing there. And that, Mr. Murphy, is where you must have chanced to place your phonographer's notes from our recent interview with Dr. May. I'll warrant they are not among the tidy piles of foolscap you have arranged on your table."

"Good Lord!" exclaimed the phonographer, "I think you are right. But how can you tell?"

"You were followed when you left Mr. Brady's establishment. I gather from Miss Ream that you were further shadowed that day. Yesterday, while you were at the Capitol, the thief did his work, and last evening you discovered your shadow gone. I think it likely was he who visited your rooms while you were out."

"That is quite plausible," Mr. Murphy admitted. Then after a moment's reflection, he asked, "But if the thief wished to learn what Dr. May told you, would he not have been even more interested in the documents I hold, which bear on the same matter?"

"He might well have been interested in them, had he known of their existence. I am doubly grateful he did not, for it is bad enough that your service to me has brought this regrettable disorder to your rooms. Had he coveted your documents, I fear he would have swept away that pretty little clock which adorns your mantelpiece and smashed that magnificent mirror which conceals their hiding-place."

"How did you know?" demanded the stunned phonographer.

"I should have guessed," I replied, "but there was no need, as you have disclosed their location to me yourself. Since I entered this room, you have looked toward your mantelpiece no less than a half-dozen times. Even were you an unusually vain gentleman who enjoyed such frequent consultations with his looking-glass, you would first place yourself in a position from which you could study your own reflection, but I have observed you looking at the mirror from places where you could not possibly see yourself. Of course, you might have some pressing engagement imminent, and your interest was not the mirror, but the clock standing before it. However, were that the case, you would not fail to note that the clock reads ten past two, as it did some ten minutes ago when you admitted us to this chamber. I think it likely your natural vexation with events has made you forget to wind it, or even see it wanted winding. But, even so, I suspect you would have seen the clock had stopped were it located anywhere else in the room except the place where you have concealed your hoard. At all events, had I been your burglar, I should have begun with the mirror and not the desk, for such is a favorite place among those with little practice at hiding and none whatsoever at seeking. Were I to go this instant and fetch that which reposes behind the mantelpiece mirrors in this single block of Washington City, you could examine a goodly part of the wealth of your neighbors and learn many of their deepest secrets."

Forgetting his usual punctilious manners (Miss Ream was standing), Mr. Murphy sat himself down upon a side chair amidst the rubble of his room and was silent for a while, reflecting, I presume, on the situation of affairs. Finally he arose, went to the mantel, and carefully lifted down the mirror, uncovering a rent in the wall through which the chimney bricks could be glimpsed. He reached within the crevice and withdrew a metal manuscript case. This he presented to me.

"Please take this," he said. "The cobbler should stay at his last, and the phonographer who plays detective invites calamity. I am thankful my folly has not brought even more dire consequences to me."

"In point of fact," I observed, "this unfortunate incident owes to your service as phonographer, not your efforts at detection. Were you not a collector of such things, you would have sent your notes up the chimney, and not held them to add to the store you hide in back of it. And had that been your course, the wreckage of your rooms would be complete, for your burglar would not have stopped until he was satisfied that which he sought was not here. No, I cannot dispute your logic: The cobbler should stick to his last. But, had you followed such excellent reasoning, it would have cost you dearly. Life seems filled with such ironies."

"Nonetheless," said Mr. Murphy, "I am done with meddling in the case, and I am pleased to turn these papers over to you. I hope that will put an end to the matter, so far as it concerns me."

"Stay a moment, if you please," I said, weighing the manuscript box. "You have bestowed a mighty present on me. I reckon it will want the investment of a good dozen candles to profit from it. Perchance you will first lend some light from your purloined fire. What evils will I find imprisoned in your Pandora's box?"

"Treason," replied the phonographer. "Treachery in the highest places. Conspirators still at large."

"Aye, so much I've gathered already," I said. "But can you not be more particular about it? Can you give me no names, dates, places, acts?"

Mr. Murphy reflected for a moment. When finally he spoke, he chose his words with great care.

"That which you hold in your hands," he began, "is evidence. It consists of verbatim copies of secret documents that can be found in the files of the Bureau of Military Justice. Most of these papers are sworn statements. I can attest to the authenticity of them all, for it was I who recorded them as they issued from the lips of the witnesses.

"Some of the statements are accusations; others are confessions. They reveal complicity in the most grievous crimes, the self-same crimes for which four are imprisoned, and four were hanged. Yet the statements offer names you've likely never heard, for those who bear them have not been punished in any way, nor even brought to trial.

"There are other statements among those documents which are neither explicit accusation nor confession, but they disclose curious and remarkable circumstances of the crimes, circumstances which implicate persons who also were never tried or punished, or even pressed for a full accounting of their roles in the case.

"But the whole of what is contained in that box is greater than the sum of its parts. When you have read all the documents, when you have learned all the 'names, dates, places and acts' you speak of, I think you, as did I, will perceive a dreadful mosaic that allows of but one, horrid, yet ineluctable interpretation.

"I shall not draw that picture for you. I wish you to do it for yourself, free from the influence of my own conclusions. I pray that you may find a different pattern, one less hideous than that which I perceive. I pray that you will show me, as one would show a frightened child who imagines horrors amidst the darkness, that my specters, as well, are nothing more than dark imaginings that vanish in the light."

"Then I am to have no clew whatsoever?" I asked. "I am to sift this ore by the panfull, without even so much as the knowledge of what species of nugget I may expect to find?"

"No, I decline only to offer you my conclusions. I am quite willing to tell you of some of the facts upon which those conclusions rest, if doing so will ease your task, or encourage you to pursue it."

He hunted about in the rubble on his carpet for a moment before stooping to retrieve one of the volumes scattered by the intruder.

"This is Pitman. *The Assassination of President Lincoln and the Trial of the Conspirators.* Are you familiar with the book?"

I told him that I had perused a copy of it.

"Fine. You then have seen that Mr. Pitman performed an excellent service in summarizing the trial testimony, and rearranging it from the haphazard sequence in which it was actually given, to produce a coherent account of events from the day of the assassination until the capture and death of Booth. But, if you study the book closely, you will find a gap in the account. The book, as the testimony itself, tells us nothing of the whereabouts of Booth and David

Herold from the time of their departure from the home of Dr. Mudd on April 15th until their appearance at the Port Conway ferry landing on the Rappahannock River on April 24th. Nine days, and not a word as to where the fugitives hid, how they lived, or how they came to Port Conway."

"I had noticed the omission," I remarked, "but I assumed it was for want of information. I imagined the pair were hiding in the wilderness along the river, subsisting as they could off the land, and that there was none but themselves to give an account of it."

Mr. Murphy opened the book to a page near the front and showed it to me. It bore a map of the Potomac River and environs from the vicinage of Washington City southward to Port Royal and Garrett's Farm. A line had been drawn linking the former with the latter, meandering in between through several counties in Maryland and Virginia and crossing the Potomac and Rappahannock Rivers.

"Observe this line," said the phonographer. "It is supposed to be the route the fugitives traversed on their way to Garrett's Farm. Here, follow it from the Navy Yard Bridge to Surrattsville, then on to Dr. Mudd's house. That is based on testimony. And here, follow it from Port Conway across the Rappahannock to Port Royal and on to Garrett's Farm. You will find testimony to support that, as well. But here," he ran his finger along the line as it wandered from Dr. Mudd's to Port Conway, then snapped shut the book and handed it to me. "Show me the testimony that supports that leg of their journey, that nine-day sojourn in the wilds."

"Perhaps it is based on conjecture," I offered, opening the volume and turning to the map.

"No, it is based on lies," he rejoined. "Here," he said, pointing to a place on the questioned segment marked with the name "Capt. Cox." "Who is 'Captain Cox'? Have you seen ought of him anywhere in the testimony?"

I confessed I had not.

"Nor shall you, even were you to search every page of Pitman, even were you to read the full transcript of the trial. That his name appears even on this map is remarkable, a tiny flaw in the otherwise perfect job of suppressing the truth. But you will find him in there," he said, pointing to the manuscript box. "And you will read his own words and the testimony of others that mark him guiltier than any now imprisoned at Fort Jefferson, and fully as guilty as some of those who were hanged."

"And what was Captain Cox's crime?" I asked.

"The same as that of Thomas Jones, and of Elizabeth Quesenberry, and of William L. Bryant. I take it those names are no more familiar to you than that of Samuel Cox?"

I admitted they were unknown to me.

"You ask what their crime was. I shall tell you. You imagine that Booth and Herold wandered for nine days in the wilderness, subsisting on what meager provender they might scavenge in the swamps of Maryland and Virginia. The truth is far different. The assassin and his helper did not miss a single meal during those nine days. They were fed, sheltered, and supplied with such comforts as spirits, and even newspapers, so that they might enjoy reading of their heinous act. They were hidden from their pursuers, and provided with the boat they used to cross into Virginia."

He took the book from my hands and placed it on the desk, open to the map page. Taking a pencil in hand, he placed the point on "Capt. Cox."

"Booth and Herold arrived here about midnight on April 15th, some hours after departing the home of Dr. Mudd. Cox provided them food and shelter for the night. Early the following morning, he arranged to have them secreted in a pine thicket about here."

Mr. Murphy drew a line from "Capt. Cox" to a point about a mile to the west.

"Here they remained, enjoying the solicitude of Cox's foster brother, Thomas Jones. Jones saw to their wants and shielded them from their pursuers for five days. On Thursday, the 20th, he guided the pair to the riverbank here," Mr. Murphy's pencil traced the route, "and provided them with a boat to cross to Virginia. This they did, landing here," the pencil traversed the Potomac and followed the course of a small tributary marked "Gamble's Creek."† "Here they concealed themselves, and Herold sought and found succor at the home of Mrs. Elizabeth Quesenberry and her daughter, who provided them food and a guide in the person of their neighbor, Mr. William L. Bryant.

"Bryant lent a pair of horses to carry the crippled assassin and his cohort, and he led them to the house of a physician near King George Court House."

The phonographer's pencil traced the route southward to the point he had mentioned.

"There they were fed and further guided to the cabin of a Negro, where they spent the night. And it was from that point the two journeyed to Port Conway," Mr. Murphy's pencil completed the journey as he spoke, "where they arrived, as the official account admits, on the morning of April 24th."

"And all of these persons took a guilty hand in aiding the fugitives?" I inquired.

---

† The creek was actually called "Gambo Creek," and the point identified as "Capt. Cox," should have read "Colonel Cox," since that was the title he used; however, Cosgrove's references are accurate inasmuch as these are among the errors to be found on the map in Pitman. The map was hastily drawn and included in the book as an afterthought, as a consequence of Benn Pitman's own misgivings regarding the gap in the official account he was writing for the War Department. He suggested the map in a letter of August 14, 1865, written during his labors.

"The testimony," he wrote, "relates to Booth and Herold at Dr. Mudd's on the 15th and at the ferry on the Rappahannock on the 24th and contains no word relating to the flight of the conscience-stricken fugitives in the interval. I think the Appendix ought to supply this in the way of a good map, showing the ground over which they traveled."

That Pitman suggested such a map be drawn implies he was aware of the evidence the War Department held detailing the movements of Booth and Herold during the nine-day gap. However, he may not have known how damning a case could have been made that the individuals Murphy named had aided and abetted the fugitives. Extant War Department records reveal there was indeed enough testimony to hang Cox, Jones, Bryant and Quesenberry, although Murphy seems to know more of the details, e.g., that the fugitives were supplied with liquor and newspapers, than can be found in the records; the full story of how the pair were aided in their flight seems to have emerged only decades later, when those involved, or their heirs, felt it safe to speak. On the other hand, Murphy seems ignorant of other accomplices, e.g., Colonel John J. Hughes, who also had a hand in helping the two on their way.—M.C.

The phonographer nodded.

"All save the physician of King George Court House. He refused to treat Booth's wounded leg, and did little else than feed them and tell them to begone. Booth was so angered by this use he penned an insulting note and sent it back to the doctor with money to pay for the meal, as though the man were nothing but an innkeeper. In truth, that note may well have saved the doctor from the rope or Dr. Mudd's fate. Here," he said, taking the box from my hands and opening it, "it is worth reading, for, while it was written by the same hand that slew our President, it must have been inspired by Providence."

Mr. Murphy sought for the sheet among the contents of the manuscript box.† He found it and read it aloud.

"'Forgive me,' the brazen fellow wrote, 'but I have some little pride. I cannot blame you for want of hospitality; you know your own affairs. I was sick, tired, with a broken limb, and in need of medical assistance. I would not have turned a dog away from my door in such a plight. However, you were kind enough to give us something to eat, for which I not only thank you, but, on account of the reluctant manner in which it was bestowed, I feel bound to pay for it. It is not the substance, but the way in which kindness is extended, that makes one happy in the acceptance thereof. The sauce to meat is ceremony; meeting were bare without it. Be kind enough to accept the enclosed five dollars, although hard to spare, for what we have had.'"

"A prickly sort of thanksgiving," I observed.

"Yes," agreed Mr. Murphy, "but one worth a man's life or freedom. Had he bestowed as much on Dr. Mudd, that poor innocent would not today be rotting in some dungeon in the Dry Tortugas. Booth signed his note 'Stranger,' and so this doctor was able to prove to the authorities, not only the limit of his aid to the assassin, but his ignorance of the man's identity."

"An extraordinary piece of luck," I agreed. "And what, pray tell, was the name of this fortunate physician."

"Dr. Stewart," replied the phonographer.

---

† The original was written on a page Booth tore from his notebook for the occasion. Murphy's copy of the text corresponds to that contained in the official War Department records.—M.C.

·19·

An Honest Man

·····➤◆◄·····

His full name was Dr. Richard H. Stewart, and I had not hoped to learn it so soon. Not a dozen hours had passed since Joe revealed that it was one Dr. Stewart who harbored Booth while his personator lay dying at Garrett's Farm. But the dawn had scarcely risen on a new day when I heard that name again.

Dr. Stewart was the most fortunate of men. He was rescued from the rope or the dungeon by the happy chance of Booth's impulse to interrupt his flight and pen a churlish and insulting note, which proved the physician unwitting and innocent. Or so it seemed. But the truth, I suspected, was somewhat different. Dr. Stewart's great good fortune derived, not from Booth's note, but from the benevolent Fate that saved him from the scrutiny of all but the most credulous dolts ever to serve in the Bureau of Military Justice.†

I did not know what might have been docketed beneath the name of Dr. Richard H. Stewart in the bowels of the Department of War, but here is some of the intelligence compiled by Pinkerton's National Detective Agency and held (I found) in the cellar room of the house on K Street:

---

† Cosgrove is unduly harsh in his verdict. While Dr. Stewart and Booth's note were not known outside the War Department's secret files at the time, they became public knowledge around the turn of the century and have been available to every student of the assassination since then. However, not one writer that I am aware of, including such revisionists as Eisenschiml and Roscoe, has ever been suspicious of Dr. Stewart and his good luck.—M.C.

Dr. Stewart was one of the wealthiest and most prominent Confederate sympathizers in Virginia. That he was highly regarded among the Confederate leadership cannot be doubted, for none less than General Robert E. Lee entrusted the care of two of his daughters to Dr. Stewart during the War. But the physician also played host to less gentle Secessionists, and often sheltered Confederate spies and couriers as they made their way between Richmond and Washington City. For the latter service, Dr. Stewart was twice imprisoned during the hostilities by the Federal authorities.

Consider, if you will, the likelihood of this tale: Ten days have passed since the murder of the President, and the countryside of Maryland and Virginia is alive with thousands of Federal troops. A prize of $100,000 has been posted, and word that the man with the highest price on his head is one with a splint on his foot has reached even the tiniest and most obscure hamlet in the region. Yet, somehow this news seems not to have found its way to the manse of Dr. Stewart, although it is but a half-mile from the main road near King George Court House. From out of the twilight come a pair of travelers in the company of the doctor's neighbor, William Bryant. One of the pair is lame and complains of a broken leg.

"I was suspicious of the urgency of the lame man. He desired to tell something I did not care to hear."†

Perhaps the good doctor did not need to hear it.

"I then went out to Mr. Bryant who brought them there & asked him if he knew anything about these men. He said no; they had come to him out of the marsh & asked him if he could send them to my house. I said, 'It is very strange; I know nothing about the men; I cannot accommodate them; you will have to take them somewhere else . . .'"

Whereupon, the pre-eminent healer and Southern patriot refused shelter or medical care to the pair, and sent them on their way after grudgingly bestowing a few morsels upon them.

---

† Cosgrove is here quoting from the statement of Dr. Stewart, which he gave and swore to on May 6, 1865, in Washington. Apparently this deposition was among the documents copied by Murphy and shown to the detective.—M.C.

"They were in my house not more than a quarter of an hour," swore Dr. Stewart. And that may have been the letter of the truth, if not fully in keeping with its spirit, for the "they" of the good physician's deposition designated Booth *and* Herold, and it may have required no more than fifteen minutes to select an understudy from Dr. Stewart's ample household ("My family was large," the Doctor deposed, "my house was full . . .") and send him on his way with the assassin's acolyte to decoy the pursuers.† That might be the *whole* truth.

But, on the other hand, it might not be.

Coincidences, as General Grant observed, are discontentments to detectives. Yet the General offered a stunning example of innocent coincidence. Had I found another? How many Dr. Stewarts lived in the world? How many might a fleeing assassin (or his pursuer) hope to encounter? Could the Dr. Stewart whose name was uttered by the dying man at Garrett's Farm be one other than the physician on whose doorstep Booth stood a scant two days earlier? I thought it most unlikely. But secret detection is not a game of chance. I must be certain.

Five men (at least) knew the truth, but two, Herold and the man who died at Garrett's Farm, were beyond my inquiries. Booth, himself, could say, but, if the prize were at hand, there would be no need for the game. Dr. Stewart of King George Court House knew, but could hardly be expected to make a gift of the answer. There was but one remaining, William Bryant.

It was Bryant who guided the pair to Dr. Stewart's home, and Bryant who led them away from it to seek a night's shelter in the cabin of the colored man. By Mr. Murphy's account, Bryant was but a poor dirt

---

† That decoys were, in fact, sent out by the local Confederate sympathizers to throw the Federal troops off the track is now a matter of record, but was probably not known to Cosgrove at the time. For example, a Port Tobacco farmer, one Richard M. Smoot, recalled years later, "When Booth and his party dismounted at Dr. Mudd's house, a man on crutches, accompanied by a second man, was put in the road to make tracks to decoy the searchers in the wrong direction." And the War Department files record that, on the night of April 25, when Booth was supposedly at Garrett's Farm, in Virginia, Federal troops were checking out reports that a man on a crutch and a youthful companion had been seen on the fringe of a swamp two miles north of Bryantown, Maryland.—M.C.

farmer, who struggled to wrest a meager living from his marshy glebe near Gamble's Creek, a pathetic fellow who could scarcely read or write. But I reflected, this bumpkin was likely a dedicated Confederate agent, shrewder by half than any scrivener to be found on Capitol Hill. Still, if I must needs resort once more to guile in aid of my inquiries, better to match wits with the bog-trotter than the physician. Bryant, at least, had not been possessed of such foresight and ingenuity to procure in advance a pardon signed by the assassin himself!

A plan came to mind, and I betook myself to the Georgetown Wharf to set it in motion. There I found, as expected, a half-dozen coastal packets moored. Some were newly arrived, and not yet rid of their cargo. But there was one, the steamship *John Brooks,* that was taking on casks of flour, and to judge from the depth of her keel in the river, she would soon be underway. I went aboard and sought out the master. His name was Captain Bayard, and he was a surly fellow, some species of New Englander to judge from his speech. I found him on the afterdeck supervising the loading, and was briskly informed by the man that he carried no passengers. I expressed my disappointment at this news, remarking that I had in mind only a short journey and inquired if he knew of some other ship's master who might carry me. As I spoke I displayed a handful of double eagles,† taking them from my pocket and casually passing them from hand to hand. The gleam of the metal caught his eye, and he suggested we repair to his cabin that he might give the matter more deliberate consideration.

How short a journey had I in mind? It transpired he was bound for New York and due to sail that evening. I informed him the evening would suit me perfectly and asked if he had a map of the river. He produced a pilot's chart of the Potomac, and I soon found a "Gambo Creek," which, to judge from its location, was one and the same as the "Gamble's" Creek of Pitman's map. I pointed out the place to Captain Bayard and explained what I wanted and how much I was prepared to pay.

---

† Twenty-dollar gold pieces.—M.C.

It was a singular sort of request, but Captain Bayard evinced no curiosity regarding my aims. This may have owed to his New Englander's reserve, but likely derived in no small part from his suspicion that, while what I proposed was of no apparent illegality, it might not withstand closer scrutiny. At all events, what the Captain lacked in curiosity, he made up in cupidity, and he directed his energies at discovering, rather than my true objectives, the amount I should be willing to pay to achieve them. After some dickering we agreed on a price, which included the cost of some items he would need to execute my plan.

I returned to the house on K Street to make preparations for my journey. Foremost among these was the inditement of a summary of my progress for Mr. Pinkerton. The man killed at Garrett's was not Booth, I wrote. He had been killed by his companion, Herold, to seal his lips. General Baker, his two detectives, and some of the cavalrymen were accomplices, in on the sell, all apparently motivated by a pecuniary interest in the reward money. I had some evidence that Booth made good his escape through the aid of one Dr. Richard Stewart of King George Court House, Virginia, and I was removing to that vicinage to continue my inquiries. I had received the documents mentioned in my last dispatch from Mr. Murphy, but had not yet had any opportunity to examine them. (I had, in fact, entrusted them to the custody of Miss Ream, while I advanced my quest for Booth.) Meanwhile, pending instructions from Mr. Pinkerton, I had made no report to our client.

Next I transcribed my report into code and cipher for telegraphic transmission, and dispatched Patch to the Western Union office with the impenetrable result. This task accomplished, I completed my other preparations, which consisted of equipping myself with the following items: an extra complete suit of clothes, of the roughest cut and material; a map of King George County on which Mr. Murphy had noted the precise location of William Bryant's farm and other landmarks; a compass; a Bowie knife; Joe's Army Colt, which I loaded and capped; a candle lantern; and a watertight tin matchbox. I stowed all these items in a carpetbag, and made my way once again to the Georgetown Wharf.

The *John Brooks* had already built up a full head of steam when I boarded her, and we shortly got underway and headed downriver. The sun was low in the sky over Arlington Heights, and had set before we came abeam of Alexandria. From then onward, our way was guided by the scant glow of a quarter moon and a knowledgeable pilot. About ten o'clock the moon set, and the engines were throttled back, as the pilot picked his way through the darkness between the navigation lights along the riverbank.

It was near two o'clock in the morning as we drew close to my destination. I needed no announcement of our arrival, as I had kept my own watch by means of the compass I carried. From Washington City downstream, the river follows a generally southern direction, until it nears Mathias Point, at which place it turns and flows northeast for a short distance, until the Point is passed. Then it resumes its southward flow and shortly passes, according to the charts, the inlet variously marked as Gamble's or Gambo's Creek. I had been watching the compass needle slowly registering our changes of heading, and when we swiftly turned from the northeast back toward the south I knew we were past the Point, and that the Creek was but a short way farther. My reckoning was soon confirmed, when the engines were stopped, and the *John Brooks* lay to.

I had not followed our progress simply for my own amusement; in fact, I should have preferred to pass the journey in slumber. But I did not altogether trust Captain Bayard, by which I mean to convey that, of whatever traits of personality he chanced to possess, I judged his cupidity to be the solely reliable one. Yet the Captain had halted his craft exactly where we had agreed he should, and I was nearly persuaded I had sinned against charity in my appraisal of the man, when he came to where I waited on the afterdeck and resurrected my mistrust.

A dinghy had been put in the water, and Captain Bayard informed me he would personally take me ashore. I thought it singular that the master of a steamship would assume such a labor, when there were abundant hands aboard to do the job. Nonetheless, I took up my carpetbag and joined him in the little boat.

The running lights of the *John Brooks* retreated, and we were swallowed by the darkness that covered the face of the deep. But for the sound of the oars and the Captain's exertions, I might have thought myself alone in the craft. Presently Bayard shipped the oars and announced our arrival on the riverbank, yet the whispered greetings of the shore to the stream issued from a remove of some hundred yards. I recalled the sheath knife that the Captain carried on his belt and reflected that I had done him no injustice.

I did not reply to Captain Bayard's announcement, but, instead, withdrew the Army Colt from my carpetbag and held it before me at eye level, with the business end pointed in the oarsman's direction. The dinghy rocked gently as Bayard crept toward me, but he was brought up sharply in the darkness when his nose (I should imagine it was that organ, or one in close proximity to it) encountered the barrel of the revolver. Lest he be puzzled by the nature of the obstacle, I drew back the hammer in hope that the sound of the mechanism would provide him clew enough to render a verbal description superfluous. Apparently nothing further was required, for the next sound to disturb the stillness was that of the oars, as Bayard resumed his exertions. Captain Bayard realized he had misjudged his position.

I thought it best to light the candle lamp before we reached the bank, while Captain Bayard's hands were both fully occupied with rowing, and I could still safely dedicate my own to the task, having stuck the Colt in my belt. The light revealed the expressionless countenance of the veteran poker player, and he eschewed any comment whatsoever regarding his recent miscalculation. For my own part, I had no wish to make an issue of the matter, and, when the bottom of the dinghy finally scraped the sandy shallows near the riverbank, I spoke my agreement with his earlier announcement of our arrival as though a full five minutes had not separated our respective utterances.

A fleeting flash of the eye betrayed his stoic visage, however, when I produced the agreed-upon half-dozen double eagles, but whether this owed to an instinctive reaction to the metal, or surprise at seeing any sample of it, under the circumstances, I cannot say. I presented him with the coins, and, picking up my carpetbag, I stepped into the shallows.

"There is your money," I said. "If I owe you more, I shall meet you in Georgetown next week to pay you, as I recall you make this trip regularly."

He gazed lovingly at the golden coins I'd placed in his palm.

"You owe me no more," he said. "This is the amount we agreed on."

I reached out through the darkness and withdrew the knife from the sheath at his hip.

"Yes," I said, "it is the amount we agreed on. Now, if you keep the rest of our bargain, I shall owe you nothing more."

I cast the knife downward so that the point buried itself in the bench on which he sat, forming a kind of nautical pommel. Captain Bayard leapt backward and landed on the bottom of the dinghy, with his boots on the bench, one to either side of the knife.

"But if you fail to deliver what you have agreed, I shall owe you something more, and you may depend on collecting it the next time the *John Brooks* puts in at Georgetown Wharf."

Without wasting more conversation on the fellow, I grasped the prow of the dinghy and pushed it out of the shallows and back into the river. The little boat was instantly beyond the ambit of my candle lantern, but I could hear the dip of the Captain's oars attenuating in the direction of the steamer's running lights. He seemed to have struck up a quicker tempo for the return trip.

I waded ashore and crossed a sandy beach to await developments. Shortly I heard the wheels of the *John Brooks* churning the water, and the constellation formed by its lights began to move downriver. It was nearly out of sight, and I was on the point of concluding that I should, indeed, have an engagement the following week in Georgetown, when Captain Bayard finally commenced delivery of his end of the deal.

It began with a blast from the ship's artillery, which consisted of a single three-pounder mounted on the afterdeck. This was fully sufficient for my purpose, however, as I wished to fill the night with sound and fury, rather than destruction. (It was, as I recall, a Whitworth breech-loading gun, and not a trifling piece at all, despite its small bore.) This initial detonation was sequeled by a succession of identical ones at frequent and regular intervals. Meanwhile, the *John Brooks* came about and steamed upriver. A pair of Drummond lights mounted fore and aft were lit and their beams danced a duet between ship and shore, lighting every drop of the Potomac that flowed between the keel and the riverbank as the steamer moved along.

The steamship reversed course and traversed the same stretch of river several times, and each time it came about, it launched a signal rocket which turned the night into noon for a few seconds, and climaxed its ascent with a detonation of such intensity as to be felt, as much as heard, moving the entrails quite as much as the eardrums. The show was impressive beyond my expectations. I had hoped to create the impression that a prisoner, in transit by steamer on the Potomac, had made good his escape, and to convey this idea into every household within a mile or so of the place I'd landed, an encompassment I reckoned to include the abode of Mr. William Bryant, the object of my interest. But Captain Bayard seemed to have been roweled into an excess of enthusiasm for my project (perhaps inspired by an aversion to any future transactions with me in Georgetown or anywhere else), and the quantities of noise and fire he furnished would provide credible support to the theory that two vast armadas had met in combat upon the river during the night, and provoke such speculation among the wakened occupants of churchyards as far off as Fredricksburg.

When, at last, the show was over, and the lights of the *John Brooks* disappeared into the distance, I picked up my satchel and started southward along the riverbank. I had gone no more than a quarter-mile when I encountered a small tributary I (correctly) judged to be Gamble's (or Gambo's) Creek. I turned inland and followed the stream with some difficulty, owing to the marshy character of the terrain through which it coursed. At length I found a place where the stream was both shallow and narrow enough to ford, and this I did. Frequent employment of the candle lantern and reference to Mr. Murphy's map and my compass guided my now sodden feet to the modest cabin of William Bryant.

It was yet more than an hour short of sunrise, but a lighted window and column of whitish smoke climbing into the predawn dimness bespoke an early wakefulness within, but whether this proceeded from Mr. Bryant's habit or the recent commotion on the river, I cannot say. Having located the abode of the one I sought, I prepared to introduce myself to him. This necessitated retracing my steps some hundred yards or so to a brook I had encountered in my path from the creek to the farm. There I took the suit of clothes from my carpetbag and immersed them in the icy flow, then wrung most of the water from them, leaving them about as wet as one might expect to find them an hour or so after their owner wore them while swimming in the river. Next I removed my comparatively warm and dry garments and donned the cold and damp ones. My footware was, as I have noted, authentically soaked in consequence of my wading, and required no additional dampening, but the hair on my head was suspiciously dry, so I thrust my head into the frigid flow in the interest of authenticity. This move I instantly regretted, for it was only after I had added this touch that I began to feel truly cold. I was, in fact, shivering truly and uncontrollably, and it was all I could do to stuff my dry clothing, the revolver, and all my other possessions (save the Bowie knife) into the carpetbag and secrete it in some bushes along the lane leading to Bryant's farm. When I arrived on the man's doorstep I felt fully as desperate as the character I assumed to be.

My advent was heralded by the scolding of a hound of considerable vintage, who emerged from somewhere to the rear of the cabin, limping upon the scene with obvious reluctance tempered by an apparent sense that the occasion demanded a few obligatory howls. When his master had come to the door and taken appropriate note of the situation, the dog seemed to think his duty fully discharged, for he abruptly subsided and trotted within.

The householder was a match for his mongrel in length of tooth; more than a match, for while his age was indeterminate, he must have been an old dog when the old dog that now hid behind his heels was yet a sprightly pup. But his eye was keen enough, and it needed but a moment to survey my condition as I stood shivering in the early dimness. Without requiring a word from me, or offering one of his own, he indicated with a gesture that I should enter his cabin.

I thanked him and went directly to the hearth, placing myself in the path of its welcome warmth. The old man added a log to the fire, augmenting its heat so much that my anterior was soon sufficiently dry and I turned about to warm my dorsal parts in the friendly glow. The cabin, I now saw, encompassed a single room, which, to judge from its rude and meager furnishings, served as parlor, kitchen and bedroom. My host was sitting at a crudely wrought table, immersed for the moment in a book. It was the only book in sight, and it looked to be a Bible. As I turned, he glanced up.

"Want a drop of likker to warm your innards?" he inquired.

I said I would, and privately welcomed my good fortune; if Mr. Bryant was a drinker, he likely was a talker, as well. But it transpired I was incorrect in my premise, for, to judge from the difficulty the farmer displayed in locating his supply of spirits, they were not often consumed beneath his roof. He had uncorked a half-dozen dusty jugs before inhaling what he seemed to decide was evidence of the sought-for potation. I hoped the fragrance was sufficiently familiar to him that he could distinguish it from turps, for it seemed I was destined to sample the liquid alone. Mr. Bryant poured out a single glassful and handed it to me. Whether it was, indeed, a distillate intended for human consumption I cannot say with certainty. It did, however, accomplish the stated objective of warming my insides. I think a second helping of the stuff would have combusted them.

"You're the feller they was tryin' to blow outten the river last night," he said. It was not a question.

"You're welcome to dry off here and have a bite. Stay as long as you like. But I ought to warn you: If they send someone to look for you, this here's likely one of the first places he'll stop at."

"I imagine they'd start searching on the bottom of the river, were they to search at all," I replied. "And I can scarcely believe I'm not to be found there."

Mr. Bryant nodded.

"From the look of you I'd say you brought a good piece of river along in your pockets. But it's been rainin' a mite lately, so they're not likely goin' to miss it."

The old man set about creating a breakfast that would have done justice, if not put to shame, the kitchen of the National Hotel. He stepped outside his cabin for a few moments and returned laden with provender from his smokehouse and chicken coop, then fell to work at the hearth. Within a remarkably short interval he had spread his table with a savory array of bacon, ham, eggs, pancakes and a steaming pot of coffee. Mr. Bryant was, in his way, a greater wizard than Professor Haselmayer, for he worked his miracles in full view of his audience, yet betrayed no clew that would account for the means he used to produce so magnificent a repast from the humblest instruments and materials. When I suggested that such a magical performance deserved theatrical exhibition, he replied that while he'd practiced conjuring up breakfasts, he had not yet perfected a way to make them disappear, and hoped now to learn such from my example.

I did my best, and my host seemed nearly as gratified by my performance as was I by the meal. He joined in, but ate quite sparingly. Clearly he was a man who found great joys in food, but the least of his gustatory pleasure was taken in the eating of it. Orchestrating gastronomical symphonies such as the one he set down that morning was, I think, more satisfying to him. But his true delight seemed to lie in witnessing one possessed of a commensurate appetite encounter one of his culinary extravaganzas.

When I had engulfed as much of the banquet as I dared without abandoning myself completely to the toils of gluttony, I pushed my chair back from the table and turned my thoughts to the pressing matters on my agendum. I must confess that I did so with profound distaste.

If one discounts the ends and examines only the means, there is little substance to distinguish the work of a secret detective from that of a common swindler. While I chose the former as my profession, Nature equipped me equally well to perform either role. Deception is not only my talent, it is my pleasure.

I am not, I pray, a misanthrope. But I have found in the general run of humankind, in the good as well as the bad, a certain measure of selfishness, cowardice, deceit and stupidity. I have always believed this to be a natural consequence of Original Sin, and, so, part of the

Human Condition. It is not something I am often moved to reflect upon, but it provides me aid and comfort in my work. The greedier a man is, the craftier, the more cowardly—in precisely the same measure, the easier he is to bamboozle, and the less likely am I to be troubled by a bad conscience afterward. I have heard it said that an honest man cannot be swindled, but I cannot say if this is so. I had resolved to test the theory if ever I should encounter one of that rare species in my work. But until the day I met William Bryant, the opportunity had never been presented to me. Now that it had been, I was loathe to avail myself of it.

I had concocted a tale calculated to steal the man's confidence, and had set the stage for my scenario with a measure of elaboration that should inspire envy in the heart of the most lavish theatrical impresario. The nocturnal commotion upon the river I devised to create the impression that a prisoner had escaped from a ship. What prisoner? And whither sailed the vessel he escaped? I had not neglected such particulars in hope of extemporizing them when needed. No, I had prepared them with care, selected them from among those I thought most likely to capture the man's sympathies, to embezzle his trust.

Grenfell and several of his fellow convicts had made good their escape from the Dry Tortugas a few weeks earlier.† Their fate was unknown, and I thought them likely hiding in Cuba or feeding the fishes in the Gulf of Mexico, but, in any case, unlikely to appear on Mr. Bryant's doorstep and deny the tale I planned to tell him, to wit: that I was a Canadian who had aided in the escape, had been re-taken, and was, myself, bound for Fort Jefferson when I plunged from a Federal prison ship into the icy waters of the Potomac. This, then, was the lie

---

† Colonel George St. Leger Grenfell, a British soldier of fortune, who fought on the side of the Confederacy, had been convicted of taking part in a plan to free the Confederate prisoners held at Fort Douglas in Chicago in 1864. He was sentenced to hang, but the sentence was commuted to life in prison at Fort Jefferson in the Dry Tortugas (the same Federal prison to which Dr. Samuel Mudd and the other defendants not condemned to death by the Conspiracy Trial were sent). On March 6, 1868, during a storm, Grenfell and several other inmates escaped the island prison in a small boat and were never heard from again. Cosgrove seems to have expected Bryant to know of the escape, but it is entirely possible the farmer had never even heard of Grenfell.—M.C.

I prepared for my host, even as I sat beneath the shelter of his roof, warmed myself at his fire, and partook of his splendid hospitality. But when the moment arrived, I found I was not knave enough for the task, and the story stuck deep in my craw, buried beneath my breakfast.

Mr. Bryant perceived that I was wracked by some dilemma, although he did not comprehend it was a struggle between conscience and treachery, or that he, himself, was the cause of it.

"I ain't particularly curious about what you done, or why they're after you," he ventured, "if that's what's on your mind, and I can plainly see somethin' is. Fact is, unless you want to tell me, I'd rather not hear about it. Sometimes the less a feller knows, the better off he is."

"You're not apprehensive that I might be a common criminal?" I asked.

The farmer shrugged.

"That ain't my business. Might be, if I was a lawman or a judge, but I ain't. Don't matter none to me if you're a criminal, common or otherwise, or if you just got yourself into some kinda scrape through no fault of your own. I'd feed you and give you a place to rest your bones just the same."

"You might be putting yourself on the wrong side of the Law," I ventured.

"Maybe," Mr. Bryant replied, "but if the Law's goin' to hang a man for bein' a Christian, that's somethin' the Law's got to answer for. I got a clear conscience. Besides," he added with a laugh, "the Law seems to reckon me too old for hangin'. They didn't hang me for the last feller I helped out, and, whatever it is you done, it's surely small potatoes compared to what he done."

"You were called to account for helping him?" I asked.

"I was. But I told them I didn't know who he was or what he'd done, which was the truth. That seemed to satisfy them, 'cause they turned me loose." Mr. Bryant gazed into the fire for a while and then mused. "Might have been better if they'd caught up with that feller while he was here."

"Why do you say that?"

"Well, it ain't for me to judge. I can't say if he was a bad man or a good one, but the thing he done was terrible, and what's more there wasn't no point to it. That was before he came here. After he went on, he made another good man lose his life, although that wasn't his fault. Still, it wouldn't have happened if they'd a caught up with the feller while he was here!"

"Well," I prompted, "if it wasn't his fault, it might have happened anyway."

Mr. Bryant shook his head.

"No," he said. "No, it wouldn't have happened. It's kind of complicated, and I didn't mean to get into it, but, you see, I took this feller to a doctor, him and his partner (there was two of them, y'see), on account of he was hurt some. Well, the Doc says the feller ain't in no shape to keep running, but the Federals, they was hot on his heels. So another man took his place, went along with the feller's partner so's he could stay and get doctored. But the Federals caught up with the other man. They took him for the one they was after and killed him. But that never would've happened if the feller had got caught here, or if I hadn't a taken him to the Doc. I guess I feel bad about that, even though there wasn't no way I could've known what was goin' to happen."

"He must have felt worse," I said, "the one who changed places with the man who got killed."

"I suppose he must have," Mr. Bryant replied. "I never heard what happened to him. Never asked the doctor about it. Like I say, sometimes the less a feller knows, the better off he is. I would surely feel a sight better if I didn't know what I do. Still, I got no business tryin' to second-guess the Lord. He must've had some reason for sendin' this feller to my doorstep, just like He had some reason for bringin' you here. All's He wants from me, as I figure it, is to lend a helpin' hand. I suppose I ought to leave the whys and wherefores in His hands."

At that moment I wished I might do the same. I hardly need add that, on taking leave of this good man, he gently declined my offer to reimburse him for his kindness. It was not in his nature to take, only to give.

As to the question of whether it is possible to swindle an honest man, I had no answer. Of that which I had come to steal from him, William Bryant had made me a present.

·20·

Edwin Stanton's Secret

I stopped briefly at King George Court House to make some simple inquiries regarding Dr. Stewart. From thence I made my way back to Washington City, first, by shank's mare as far as Acquia Creek, and from there up the Potomac by R.F.&P.† steamboat. When I arrived once more at the house on K Street the sun had set and darkness had brought a clandestine caller. The household staff was in a state of extreme consternation, and I was quickly ushered to a room on the second story where I found my visitor, watch in hand, pacing between a brace of Army captains. It was my client, the Secretary of War, and he was in a condition of considerable pique. He spun about to face me as I entered the room.

"It is seven o'clock, Cosgrove," said Mr. Stanton, without any other preliminary, "seven o'clock *in the evening.*"

"And I bid you a good evening, sir," I replied.

"Seven o'clock of a *Saturday* evening, Cosgrove," continued the Secretary. "The Saturday following the Monday when last you reported to me. Can you recall my instructions to you at that time, Cosgrove, or was it too long ago?"

"I believe I recall them exactly, sir," I replied. "I was to keep you apprised of the progress of my inquiries."

---

† Richmond, Fredericksburg & Potomac Railroad, which operated daily steamboat service between Washington and the railroad station at Acquia Creek. If the boat was running on schedule that day, it departed Acquia at 2:35 P.M. and arrived at Washington at 6:00 P.M.—M.C.

"Exactly, Cosgrove. I am pleased that you troubled yourself to encumber your memory with them, even if you have taken no other trouble over the matter. Am I to conclude, then, that you have made absolutely no progress after a week? Or have you simply ignored my instructions to report?"

"Oh, the latter, sir, I assure you!"

Mr. Stanton's wrath yielded to astonishment, and he shook his head in wonderment.

"You hasten to assure me that you have disobeyed my orders," he said. "I believe that to be by far the most amazing sort of assurance I have ever been granted."

"I meant to assure you that I had made no little progress in my inquiries," I said. "I regret that you have remained unapprised of my discoveries, but to do otherwise would have risked disclosure of your interest in the matter. And the confidentiality of your patronage is, so Mr. Pinkerton has informed me, of paramount importance."

I then explained that my own inquiries had, in turn, become the object of curiosity of several unidentified persons, and while it had been impossible to prevent them from learning the nature of my investigation, I thought it feasible to forestall disclosure of the identity of my client through the expedient of avoiding him. These words mollified the Secretary, but did not completely satisfy him.

"You are the detective, Cosgrove," he said. "How is it that you have not discovered the identities of these spies, and the name of the one they serve."

"Mr. Secretary," I replied, as gently as I could, "I can easily obtain this intelligence, if you wish it. I should prefer to know who they are, myself, and would have found it out by now, were I serving a different client in a less delicate matter. A word to Superintendent Richards, and these fellows would be arrested as suspicious persons and thrown into the Blue Jug, and by tomorrow I would know the names of their grandfathers. But Superintendent Richards would know as much, and he would also know whatever these fellows know of my errands, and I think he is possessed of sufficient curiosity to wish to know even more.

"There are, of course, other means of dealing with the problem. I might send off a dispatch to Chicago addressed to whomever

Mr. Pinkerton has left in charge of matters in his absence, and request assistance. Tomorrow's train from New York would deliver a squad of additional secret detectives to be set on the trail of the fellows who are on my own. But I cannot warrant that would be the end of the matter, for the next day's trains might bring yet more secret detectives sent to shadow the ones I had summoned. Soon Washington City would be filled with secret detectives, and not an alleyway from Capitol Hill to Froggy Bottom could be found that did not shelter some fellow lurking about to watch some other fellow lurking about . . ."

"Enough!" cried Secretary Stanton, holding up his palms. "I think you have made your point quite adequately, Cosgrove."

"Thank you, sir," I replied, with modesty.

"But you claim to have made some progress in your inquiries," he said. "Pray let me hear what it may be."

"The man killed at Garrett's Farm was not Booth," I said.

"You are certain?"

"I am. Dr. May lied. He was made to do so by General Baker, who had evidence the Doctor had traded with the enemy, and threatened to expose him. The General counterfeited the grosser features used to confirm the identification, and several of those who were at Garrett's know of it. They remained silent out of pecuniary motives, and I think the General himself may have acted out of greed. At all events, the man killed was not Booth, but an imposter, a decoy. And he was shot, not by Sergeant Corbett, but by David Herold, to forestall disclosure of the personation."

"And what of Booth?"

"Harbored by Dr. Richard Stewart of King George County, Virginia. I presume the Doctor nursed him back to health and aided his escape after the hunt had been called off, but where he may have fled afterward, I have not yet learned."

"Dr. Stewart, you say?" exclaimed Mr. Stanton.

"I think you may have heard the name before," I said. "I wish that you had shared it with me, for it would have saved some time."

"I know no Dr. Stewart," said the Secretary.

"Then you will find him in the files of your Department," I said, "along with a Captain Cox, a Thomas Jones, a Mrs. Quesenberry . . ."

"Stay!" exclaimed the Secretary. He turned to the pair of attending officers and ordered them to leave us and wait downstairs in the parlor. When we were alone he regarded me in silence for a long moment.

"How do you know these names?" he finally asked.

"It is my business to know them," I replied. "They are landmarks along the trail of the man you have set me to find. It is not remarkable that I should know them, for, as you have reminded me, I have followed that trail for most of a week. If there is something to be remarked upon here it is that I did not know their names when I departed your office on Monday."

The Secretary turned away before replying to this.

"Mr. Cosgrove, I have misjudged you twice over. I must apologize. I withheld these names from you because I misprized your discretion. And because I also misprized your acumen. I failed to anticipate that you would find them out for yourself. I will tell you now, in candor, that the persons you have named were involved in a matter that could cause me surpassing embarrassment, were it to become known. Although I wish to speak no more of it to you, I fear now your acumen may eventually reveal to you that which I prefer you do not learn. I can only hope that your discretion exceeds even your admirable astuteness. May I rely upon that?"

"Let us speak plainly," I replied. "I have uttered some names you were not pleased to hear. You need not hear them again, save one. Unless you wish me to abandon the trail of John Wilkes Booth, I must, perforce, pursue my inquiries with Dr. Stewart."

"Then do so," said Mr. Stanton, with a gesture of dismissal, "for Dr. Stewart's is a name that causes no discomfort. It is the other names I wish you to forget."

"The other names are no longer of any consequence to my inquiries," I said. "I am content to forget them."

I was, in fact, anxious to forget them, or, at least, to discuss them no further with the Secretary. Were I compelled to disclose the means through which I learned them, I should have to reveal that they came to me, not by virtue of my acumen, but my good fortune, in the persons of Edward Murphy and Vinnie Ream. I had no wish to disclose

Mr. Murphy's meddling to Secretary Stanton, and I was obliged to conceal Miss Ream's role as an agent of Mr. Pinkerton's. I recalled my chief's specific admonition that our client was to learn nothing of any other matter of concern to the Chain of Agencies. Whatever Miss Ream's assignment, it surely was something of which Mr. Pinkerton wished Mr. Stanton to remain ignorant. And finally, there was Mr. William Bryant, whose name I had not uttered, but whom, I presumed, belonged to the company of persons the Secretary of War wished, for reasons best known to himself, to forget. I should have been loathe to remind Mr. Stanton of the saintly old man who had aided the assassin's escape. Thus, I shared my client's pleasure with the bargain we had struck, although, as later discoveries were destined to reveal, Mr. Stanton's reasons for striking it were infinitely superior to mine own.

"So, it was Dr. Stewart that engineered Booth's escape," mused Mr. Stanton. "How do you propose to follow his trail from there?"

"The Doctor must know something of that," I replied, "but I do not think it will be an easy task to prize the information from him."

"I think not," agreed the Secretary. "You surely will not succeed through guile, for the man had wit enough to evade suspicion at the time, when the cells of the Old Capitol were filled with those of even the most casual acquaintanceship with the assassin."

But not Cox, Jones or the others, I reflected. Mr Stanton's Forbidden Fruit tempted my curiosity, but I did not voice the obvious question.

"I do not think the truth can be forced from the man, either," continued the Secretary. "He is a tough nut to crack. Twice during the War, Baker threw him into the Old Capitol on suspicion of aiding the Rebels, but he learned nothing from him."

"I made some inquiries regarding the doctor at King George," I said. "He owns two homes in the country, one on the banks of the Potomac, and the other some miles inland, near King George Court House. He seems to be possessed of a large household, requiring many servants. It may be I can go there in the guise of an itinerant laborer and find some species of casual employment. Perhaps I can learn what we wish to know from one of his retainers."

"Perhaps," reflected Mr. Stanton, "but that is by no means certain. And the effort might cost considerable time. Booth's lead is too long as it is. We must employ swifter methods."

It transpired that the Secretary had a specific plan in mind, for he summoned his officers and dispatched one from the house on some errand. I did not fully overhear the man's instructions, but the final few words were audible. He was to fetch some person and bring him to Mr. Stanton at the Sixth Street Pier.

"Come, Cosgrove," said the Secretary, returning his attention to me. "I think it would be well if you joined us in this night's excursion. I promise you shall find it fascinating, for you shall learn something of your own craft I'll warrant you do not already know."

I inquired as to the name of our destination.

"King George County," replied Mr. Stanton, "to interview Dr. Stewart. I think I know how he can be made to part with his secrets. Where my force or your guile may fail, there is another thing that shall succeed."

"What might that be?"

"Science, Cosgrove," replied Mr. Stanton. "And most appropriately in this instance, the Science of Medicine. We shall introduce the Doctor to one of his colleagues, a physician who specializes in curing lockjaw."

·21·

A Medicament for Mendacity

·•—◆—•·

I must now recount an episode which I should prefer to omit entirely. My predilection to dispense with it derives not from a single motive, but from a pair of them, two distinct considerations, each providing its own excellent grounds for excising the incident from this report of my inquiries regarding John Wilkes Booth. These considerations are propriety and credibility.

There are matters a gentleman may speak of in private (although never in the presence of the gentler sex), but would not dream of committing to paper, and certainly not a paper to be handed to a typesetter. Yet there are other matters (one, at least) which a gentleman might judge so shameful as to be denied voice as well as ink, and would stickle at speaking of them, even to one of his own gender. However, it is just such stuff I must now incorporate into this account if I am to report that which we learned of Booth and Herold from Dr. Stewart.

Were this a tale I invented of my own imagination, I should not be ready to defend the inclusion of this sort of theme, nor would I need to, for I am not possessed of a fancy that would give birth to such monsters. Yet in recounting that which we were told by Dr. Stewart, I risk being adjudged its author, and not its reporter. It is not that the Doctor's scandalous revelation is, itself, improbable (physicians, secret detectives and other men of the world will doubtless not be astonished by it); it is the means used by Secretary Stanton to prize the information from the Doctor's lips that will affront the reader's credence, and cause him to suspect I made it up. Thus I hesitate, and would let the matter pass unrecorded, were it not essential to the account of my inquiries.

But I forget my readers! I write for those yet unborn, or, at least, now in their nonage. These words are for a different world, one yet hidden in the womb of Time. This infant century already promises great and unforseeable prodigies in both science and public morals. That which would inspire outrage and disbelief today may prompt nothing more than a casual shrug when the crisp white sheets bearing this story have yellowed and gathered sufficient dust. Dust is my refuge in any event, for I shall long since have taken my departure when these pages are read. If, at that distant date, my reader is scandalized, let me apologize to him now, for I shall be unable to do so then. Old bones cannot blush. Onward, then, with the tale.

When Secretary Stanton and I departed the house on K Street, in the company of the remaining officer, we three got aboard his carriage and removed to the Sixth Street Pier, where we boarded a large tug. (I do not recall the name of the vessel, nor did I make any note of it at the time, for, at this juncture, I had not slept for close upon two days.) Shortly we were joined by a small squad of perhaps a half-dozen cavalrymen and their sergeant, each with his mount and full field kit. A little while later the officer Mr. Stanton had sent off arrived in the company of a gentleman who was introduced to me as Dr. Cady. We then got underway and headed downriver, and I found myself embarked upon my third Potomac voyage within twenty-four hours. I went below and, finding a suitable place, lay down and was immediately asleep.

I do not know exactly how long I slept, but it must have been a span of many hours, for I awoke refreshed, and I think I should soon have wakened of my own accord had not one of Mr. Stanton's officers been sent below to fetch me. The tug's engine was silent, and as I climbed on deck I saw we were anchored in the river. Darkness hid the banks, but a cluster of lights seemed to mark some place on a shore not far off. I found Mr. Stanton at the rail, his gaze directed toward these beacons.

"Ah, Cosgrove, here you are," he said. "Our guest will soon be aboard, unless I am mistaken. Those lights, I believe, mark the home of Dr. Stewart, and they were not lit when we lay to, some forty minutes ago."

Dr. Stewart, as I have noted, lived in two houses. One, which was called Cleydael, was located in a woods several miles inland, about a half-mile from the main road leading to Port Conway. The other, the name of which I do not know (if, indeed, it had a name), was situated immediately upon the river. Curiously, the Doctor wintered on the river and spent his summers at Cleydael, which is the opposite of what I might have supposed. I do not know his reasons for this unusual pattern of habitation,† but, at all events, this was where Dr. Stewart was to be found in the early morning hours on Sunday, March 29th, 1868, when Mr. Stanton's troopers hammered upon his door.

It transpired that, while I slept, the tug had steamed downriver to King George County, and the cavalry squad was sent ashore to arrest the Doctor and bring him aboard. The troopers' mounts had been left aboard the tug; they were not needed, as the pilot knew the precise location of Dr. Stewart's house, and lay to directly abeam of it. A small boat had been used to take the soldiers ashore, and, as Mr. Stanton and I watched from the rail, it emerged from the darkness.

The scull lay alongside the tug, and a pair of the troopers climbed aboard, accompanied by the gentleman who had been introduced as Dr. Cady. A litter bearing an apparently unconscious man was then hoisted aboard by the soldiers, under the direction of Dr. Cady. The man on the stretcher was a thin, elderly fellow, who appeared to be dressed in a nightshirt. He had been wrapped in a blanket to protect him from the cold, damp night. When the stretcher had been set upon the deck, his eyelids began to flicker and he moved his head a little.

"Take him inside," ordered Dr. Cady.

The troopers carried the man aft and into a cabin, there transferring him from the litter onto a bunk. Then they departed, leaving him with Dr. Cady, Mr. Stanton and myself. Dr. Cady adjusted a

---

† Dr. Stewart spent his summers inland to avoid the mosquitoes and malaria of Mathias Point, where his riverfront home was located. During the Civil War, the Doctor lived year round at Cleydael, avoiding the Federal gunboats on the river, as well. It was for this reason Booth found him there in April, 1865.—M.C.

lantern so that the face of his charge was bathed in bright illumination, while the Secretary and I remained hidden in deep shadow. The old man was possessed of a fine, patrician countenance, and a shock of snow-white hair fell across his brow. He opened his eyes and made as if to sit up.

"Where . . . what . . . ," he whispered.

Dr. Cady gently pressed the fellow against the pillows. He produced a small bottle of some fluid and soaked a bandage with it, then put the cloth over the old man's nose and mouth. The man lapsed back into insensibility, and the air in the cabin was presently filled with the smell of chloroform. Cady opened a window near the bunk and the fumes were soon attenuated by the damp river air.

"This is Dr. Stewart," said Mr. Stanton.

I replied that I had gathered this much, but wondered why he was anesthetized.

"You may explain it to Mr. Cosgrove," said the Secretary to Dr. Cady.

"It is a technique discovered during the War," said Dr. Cady, "and one which proved most efficacious in procuring information from captured Rebels. It happens that, when partially under the influence of pure, unadulterated chloroform, a man's ability to resist interrogation is greatly weakened, so much so that it is impossible for him to dissemble, or even to refuse to answer questions put to him. Thus, chloroform, in addition to its other benefits, is a drug that can be used to procure truth."†

---

† When I first encountered this episode in the Cosgrove narrative I was convinced it was proof that the entire manuscript was a hoax perpetrated by or on Lawson. It happens that I've had quite a bit of professional experience with the various techniques of interrogation and lie detection, including what is properly called narco-analysis, and popularly known as "truth serum." It was my impression that this method was unknown until the twentieth century, and I had never heard of chloroform being employed in the technique. Sodium amytal, sodium pentothal, and a variety of more exotic substances and techniques are used by modern intelligence services and criminal investigators as a means of this kind of interrogation, but none of these items was known until the middle of this century. O'Toole, who has written extensively on several methods of lie detection, wrote in a recent popular piece ("The Pinocchio Machines," by George O'Toole in *Murder Ink,* edited by Dilys

I expressed wonderment at this news, but privately reflected that it was the sort of wonder I should have to be shown before I would believe in it. In the event, it was only a matter of minutes before Dr. Cady had proved his claim. The old man presently overcame the effects of the chloroform and commenced to regain consciousness.

"You may begin, sir," said Dr. Cady to the Secretary.

Mr. Stanton leaned forward, but remained beyond the lantern's ambit.

"Booth," he said. "John Wilkes Booth. Where has he gone?"

Dr. Stewart's eyes opened. He blinked, then squinted in the lamp's glare, searching for the owner of the voice from the darkness beyond. An expression of confusion possessed his countenance.

"Who is that?" His voice was faint, near a whisper.

"Where is Booth?" repeated the Secretary.

The old man shook his head.

"I don't know," he croaked.

Dr. Cady leaned toward Mr. Stanton.

"It may be better if you approach the matter in a more gradual way, sir," he suggested. The Secretary nodded and was silent for a moment. Then he resumed.

"You are a loyal Confederate, are you not, Dr. Stewart?"

The old man nodded.

Winn; Workman, 1977) that scopolamine has been used for this purpose since the early 1920s. I called O'Toole and asked him about this report of the use of chloroform for narcoanalysis during the Civil War, and he said he'd never heard of such a thing and suspected my leg was being pulled. He was later as astonished as I to find out it is true.

In the records of the Bureau of Military Affairs, which can be found among the Lincoln assassination records in the National Archives, there is a letter dated April 22, 1865, from Dr. Charles E. Cady, Surgeon, Headquarters 138th Pennsylvania Volunteers, 3rd Division, VI Army Corps. It is addressed to General Christopher C. Auger, commander of the Washington Military Department (the wartime entity that included the District of Columbia), and details the use of chloroform as a means of interrogation (essentially, through narcoanalysis), suggesting it be employed on the "supposed implicated parties now in custody" in connection with the Lincoln assassination. While there is no evidence his suggestion was followed in that instance, Cosgrove's account reveals that Secretary Stanton took note of Dr. Cady and his technique and made subsequent use of both.—M.C.

"You have often sheltered Confederate soldiers on secret missions?"

"Yes," replied the old man, nodding again.

"You remember the two men who came in the night, one on crutches?"

"Booth," said Dr. Stewart.

"Yes, Booth," Mr. Stanton agreed.

"Murderer!" the old man uttered.

"But you harbored him. You nursed him."

Dr. Stewart shook his head.

"Yes, you did," insisted the Secretary. "You took him in and nursed him."

The old man continued to shake his head. Finally he spoke.

"Scum! He was scum!"

"He was a Confederate soldier," insisted Mr. Stanton. "You sheltered him. You doctored him."

"Not a soldier!" insisted the old man. "Scum, unnatural scum! Who are you?" He tried feebly to raise himself with his elbows. Dr. Cady silenced the Secretary with a gesture and pressed the old man back against the pillows. He held the soaky bandage to the captive's mouth for a moment. Dr. Stewart's eyelids flickered and he fell back with a sigh.

"He was scum," Dr. Cady offered. "Booth was scum."

Dr. Stewart nodded.

"Why was he scum?" asked Cady. "Was he scum because he murdered President Lincoln?"

Dr. Stewart shook his head.

"Why was he scum?" Cady repeated.

"He and the other one. Both scum," croaked the old man.

"Because they were murderers? Assassins?"

The old man's eyes flew open and he struggled to his elbows.

"Because they were sodomites!" he hissed.

All three of us—Mr. Stanton, Dr. Cady and I—were stunned into momentary silence by this sudden, shocking charge. Dr. Stewart blinked angrily in the lantern's glare for a few instants, then sank wearily back onto the bunk. His eyes drooped shut.

"Booth and Herold were sodomites," repeated Dr. Cady.

Dr. Stewart nodded. His eyes remained shut, but an expression of distaste now twisted his visage.

"Yet you sheltered them," persisted Dr. Cady.

The old man nodded.

"Booth," he said. "Not the other. I sheltered only Booth."

"Herold left with another, someone who impersonated Booth?" asked Mr. Stanton.

Dr. Stewart nodded.

"A good man," he whispered. "A good man, who lost his life for scum."

"And what of Booth?"

"He made himself into a woman," croaked Dr. Stewart, his eyes flickering open. "He was neither man nor woman. He was unnatural scum."

"He became a woman?" demanded Mr. Stanton. "You mean he dressed in woman's clothes?"

The old man shook his head.

"More," he gasped. "You could not tell otherwise. He *became* a woman. I think he was a devil."

Dr. Stewart made his confession piecemeal. It needed the better part of an hour, repeated applications of the chloroform, and a multitude of questions, some of which had to be asked several times before eliciting a useful response. Some considerable mental labor was required to assemble the pieces of this dissected puzzle† into a coherent picture of the events which followed the arrival of Booth and Herold at the Doctor's home on the night of April 23, 1865. I shall spare the reader a detailed account of this tedious process, and, instead, present him with a summary of the facts released from the durance of Dr. Stewart's innermost secrets through the miracle of the "truth drug."

When the assassin and his helper arrived at Cleydael that Sunday night, it was not by prearrangement. The actor and the physician knew

---

† Jigsaw puzzle (a term which did not come into use until after 1900, although such puzzles had been first invented in the eighteenth century and were quite familiar in the nineteenth) .—M.C.

each other, for Booth had found shelter at Dr. Stewart's home while engaged in other Confederate missions that brought him through King George County, but of the murder plans, the Doctor was entirely innocent. Quite contrary to having had a hand in the assassination, Dr. Stewart lamented it when word of the killing reached him, for he regarded it as both base and futile. Thus it was that the appearance of the crime's perpetrator and his accomplice on the physician's doorstep presented a harsh dilemma to the ardent Secessionist. His conscience made him loathe to welcome them, but his loyalties kept him from turning them away.

It happened that, on the night of Booth's arrival, Dr. Stewart's manse was filled to overflowing with humanity. The household was comprised, to a great part, of the Doctor's children, children-in-law, and a few of their friends. All the young men were recently home from the War, in which, it need hardly be said, each wore Gray. While likely none of the young bloods surpassed Dr. Stewart in courage, at least a few fell far short of matching his wisdom or moral sense, for they looked upon Booth and saw, not a murderer, but a hero. One, Sid Carton by name,† offered to take Booth's crutch and depart with Herold, in order to lead the Federal pursuers away, while the assassin remained in Dr. Stewart's care.

Dr. Stewart sought to forestall this plan by objecting that, were the ruse to fail to draw the Federals away from his door, the lives of all beneath his roof would be in terrible jeopardy. At this, Booth begged the Doctor's leave to take his ease in private for a few hours before resuming his flight, and Dr. Stewart agreed to this in the hope it would prove a compromise agreeable to all, and a swift means of being rid of the assassin and his accomplice.

However, absent from the Doctor's presence, the actor seems to have procured the aid of others in the household in obtaining a variety of toilet articles, makeup, and feminine attire. One of the young ladies of the house sacrificed a generous portion of her locks for the

---

† The impersonator is not named in Cosgrove's notebook covering this portion of his investigation, but seems to have been added when the manuscript was written many years later.—M.C.

fabrication of a wig. When the actor's preparations were completed, Dr. Stewart was summoned to witness the result. To his children's amusement, the old gentleman gallantly begged them to introduce him to the lovely young stranger he discovered in his parlor. Booth's personation of a member of the fair sex was of such consummate perfection the Doctor refused to believe the "woman" was, in fact, the actor, until he heard that averment from the assassin's own rouged lips.†

Booth's *fait accompli* seemed to leave Dr. Stewart no room for further maneuvers, and he believed he had no choice but to consent to Carton's plan. Thus, Carton departed Cleydael with Booth's crutch and accomplice, while the assassin remained securely concealed in his disguise in the Doctor's household. It was during this leavetaking that Dr. Stewart witnessed that which convinced him his unwelcome guest, as well as the assassin's whilom companion, were a pair of sodomites.

Carton had already departed the house and was waiting with William Bryant and the horses at some remove from the building. Booth, limping, followed his comrade a few steps into the darkness to bid him farewell. Dr. Stewart believed the pair thought themselves

---

† John Wilkes Booth was, in fact, a highly accomplished female impersonator, although Cosgrove would not have know that fact, as it was only revealed by Booth's sister, Asia Clarke Booth, in her memoir of John Wilkes, *The Unlocked Book,* which was not published until 1938. In it she writes:

> On several occasions he dressed himself in a petticoat and draped a shawl around him for a toga; then he put on my long-trained dress and walked before the long glass, declaring that he would succeed as Lady Macbeth in the sleep-walking scene. He secretly "got himself up" after Charlotte Cushman as Meg Merrilees, and terrified me and all the darkies, who shrieked—"Ondress Mars Johnnie, ondress him!" . . . dressed in my skirts, with a little scarf held over his shoulders, he walked the room before the mirror, becoming more and more charmed with himself.
>
> He said merrily, "I'll walk across the field yonder, to see if the darkies can discover me."
>
> He put on the tiny bonnet then in fashion, and went out across the fields. The men took off their hats, as they paused in their work to salute him; he passed on to the barn, where he was greeted in the same respectful manner, and came back to the house delighted with his success, which he attributed to his "elegant deportment."—M.C.

unobserved, although the physician was watching from a window. Herold and the actor kissed, he said, and it was not the comradely sort of kiss that is customarily exchanged by natural men in some European lands. Rather, the Doctor insisted, it was a distinctly carnal and lascivious kiss of the sort a man might bestow upon a maid, and then only as a token of the most intimate sort of affection. This, then, is what the Doctor believed he saw, and it is the proof he claimed to support his accusation against Booth. Whether or not the charge is true, I cannot say, but I do not think the Doctor would have made it had he been familiar with the actor's many conquests among the fair sex.†

Before Carton departed Cleydael to assume his personation of Booth, the actor presented his understudy with an assortment of his

---

† There is no evidence that John Wilkes Booth was homosexual, although he may have been a transvestite; the two are confused even in this day when sexual preferences and practices are discussed more openly, so it is not surprising that Booth's cross-dressing should have predisposed Dr. Stewart to place this interpretation on whatever he witnessed between Booth and Herold (assuming, as seems likely, it was a factor). If Booth's relationship with Herold was sexual, then Booth was bisexual, because there is ample record of his heterosexual affairs.

However, it is entirely plausible that Herold's affection for Booth was sexual in nature, regardless of whether their physical relationship was homosexual. Most historians have portrayed David Herold as a dull-witted, immature young man who became involved with Booth out of hero worship, was too stupid to extricate himself from the situation when it became obviously dangerous, and so went to the gallows. But those few who have taken the trouble to read the transcript of Herold's interrogation after his capture by the Federal authorities (available in the National Archives) know better. He was by far the shrewdest of Booth's immediate circle of co-conspirators, and was cool-headed, resourceful and loyal under pressure that would have cracked the average person. He told the authorities little, and almost nothing they didn't already know. In recounting his twelve-day flight with Booth, he did not utter the names of Dr. Mudd, Charles Cox, Thomas Jones, William Bryant, or even Dr. Stewart.

Herold's motives for involving himself in the assassination are a mystery. He alone among the accused conspirators had no demonstrable record of Confederate sympathies. The historians who believe he was drawn into the plot because he was impressed by Booth's celebrity may be right, but this explanation cannot account for his persistent involvement with the assassin after Booth's broken leg made capture appear certain. Herold could have abandoned Booth at any point during the flight from Washington to Port Royal and made good his own escape, as John Surratt did. No one knows why he chose not to, but Dr. Stewart's theory, as it regards Herold, is as good an explanation as any other.—M.C.

personal possessions—letters, papers, photographs and the like—in order to make the brave young man's mimicry of himself as thorough as possible. Among these items was the actor's now famous notebook, and Dr. Stewart recalled that Booth tore a handful of pages from the book before presenting it to Carton. Thus, the Doctor's revelations finally solved the mystery of the missing pages, and exonerated Mr. Stanton of the accusation made against him by General Baker.†

Booth was not insensible to the jeopardy in which his presence placed the occupants of the house, and he bent every effort to lessen those dangers. He knew that William Bryant might unwittingly send his pursuers there, and even were he not recognized, the simple fact that his path had touched Dr. Stewart's home might be adjudged sufficient grounds to arrest the physician and all who dwelt beneath his roof. Thus, even before Carton and Herold had departed, Booth hit upon the clever device of the insulting note, which he quickly penned, insisting that Carton take it along with him and later send it back to the Doctor by the hand of someone who could subsequently confirm the episode to the authorities.‡ In the event, the note failed to forestall the Doctor's arrest, but was instrumental in procuring his immediate release. None of the others dwelling at Cleydael were molested. Booth's feminine disguise was never put to the test, however, for he was gone from the place long before his pursuers reached it.

Dr. Stewart treated the assassin's injured leg, first by bathing it in a solution of salts to reduce the swelling, and then setting the fracture with a proper splint, all the while keeping Booth from using the

---

† Dr. Stewart's disclosure clears Stanton of Baker's implication that it was the Secretary of War who tore the pages from the notebook, but it does not explain why Stanton kept the very existence of the notebook a secret when it contained among the remaining pages, evidence that might have saved Mrs. Surratt from the gallows, viz., Booth's implied statement that his plans to kidnap Lincoln were abandoned in favor of murdering the President shortly before the assassination. Neither does it explain why Stanton continued to suppress word of the diary's existence until Baker revealed it in his memoirs in 1867.—M.C.

‡ The note was delivered to Dr. Stewart by William Lucas, a black man who lived in a shack a short distance from Cleydael. Herold and his companion spent the night in the shack and, the following day, hired Lucas to take them to Port Conway. The ploy worked, and Lucas, who had no idea of what Booth looked like, gave his story to investigators from the Bureau of Military Justice on May 6, 1865.—M.C.

broken limb. The Doctor recommended confinement in bed for a few days, but Booth declined this suggestion, reasoning that a bed-ridden patient might evoke suspicion, and that his feminine imposture might be more convincing in the attire of the parlor, rather than the bedchamber. The Doctor's repairs to his leg would be concealed by the actor's petticoats and the prerogatives custom affords women would permit him to remain seated even were General Grant to enter the room.

In this manner Dr. Stewart's unwelcome patient spent the next several days in convalescence at Cleydael. Then, quite abruptly, he insisted on being removed to the Doctor's winter quarters on the banks of the Potomac. The Doctor was more than pleased to oblige him in this, for the assassin found secreted in the disused house would be colorably less an indictment of him and his than were Booth to be discovered in the midst of his household. By the time this transfer was undertaken, news of Sid Carton's tragic death at Garrett's Farm had reached Cleydael, and the youngsters of the house, while prizing the actor's act no less, suspected that this strangely plumed falcon with whom they shared their nest might transpire to be a bird of ill-omen. (They might have held Booth in a wholly different regard had they known it was the assassin's accomplice, and not a Union sergeant, who slew Carton, but this intelligence seems no more to have been abroad in King George County than anywhere else.) In any case, none objected to Booth's proposal, and several of the sons and sons-in-law of the household transported the assassin to the river house and stayed to care for him there.

Late on the second night of their stay in the disused winter house, a party of men came to the door. Immediately it was thought by Booth's guardians that the Federals had found them out, and they made ready to do battle with the visitors. But it quickly transpired the men were not foes, but friends of the assassin, sent to complete his escape. They had come ashore in a skiff, and into this craft they carried the actor, and rowed to a lugger lying some distance out in the river. When Booth and his rescuers had boarded the ship, it set sail downriver and was soon lost from sight. This, then, was the last that any of Dr. Stewart's household ever saw of John Wilkes Booth.

When the chloroform and questioning had prized this much of the tale from Dr. Stewart's lips, it was clear to Mr. Stanton and myself that a bit more of the story remained untold, to wit: the means the assassin's accomplices employed to know where he could be found. The Doctor, it seemed, did not know the answer, but had reached his own conclusion regarding the matter, and this he eventually disclosed.

Before their tender leave-taking in the darkness, Booth had given his erstwhile companion a pair of messages to take along with him and forward at the first opportunity. Booth had known of the Doctor's winter house from his earlier connivances with him, and would have seen in the riverside manse a perfect place to rendezvous with those who would deliver him from the vicinage of Maryland and Virginia, perhaps to escape across the ocean to Europe, or to some land to the south. Dr. Stewart believed Booth had extemporized this plan on arriving at Cleydael, and summoned his confederates by means of the messages he entrusted to Herold. I thought the Doctor likely correct in his diagnosis.

"What manner of message were they?" demanded Mr. Stanton.

"I did not try to read them," replied Dr. Stewart. "I do not know."

"Were they to be posted, or sent by telegraph?" pursued the Secretary.

"I think one of them was for posting," croaked the captive. "Booth begged an envelope and other materials for the writing of it."

"And the other? What of the other?"

"A telegram, I think," breathed the Doctor. "He scratched it on a page from his pocketbook. He folded it and wrote a name on the back."

"What name? Did you see it?"

Dr. Stewart closed his eyes and sighed, but did not reply. The Secretary turned to Dr. Cady and indicated with a gesture that his services were needed. Cady shook his head.

"I cannot help you," he said. "Further application of the drug will do no good, for we have almost killed him with it. He will sleep now, but any more of the chloroform, and he will take his secrets to the grave."

Secretary Stanton turned back to the captive, now deeply drowsing in the lantern's glare. He struck the old man a sharp blow across the face with his open hand. Dr. Stewart's eyes flickered. Another blow, and they were half-open.

"The name, man! What name did Booth write on the page?"

With great effort, Dr. Stewart turned his head toward Mr. Stanton.

"The name of the President of the United States," he gasped.

"What, Lincoln? Booth wrote Lincoln's name?"

The old man shook his head.

"Johnson," he replied. "'To A. Johnson.'"

So saying, Dr. Stewart fell back against the pillow, shut his eyes and was deep in a deathlike slumber.

PART FIVE

The Twelfth Article of Impeachment: Assassination

· 22 ·

High Crimes, Misdemeanors and Murder

·⎯⎯◈⎯⎯·

Dead men tell no tales.

Whatever Booth had written on that leaf torn from his pocket-book, it had been read by David Herold. But David Herold lay buried in the yard of the Old Arsenal, and there was no profit in digging up his box to see if he was truly in it, for the matter could not be in dispute. Herold had been hanged, thoroughly and professionally, in the company of three other felons in that yard three years before. The ceremony was recorded for the edification of generations yet unborn by a photographer, and I had seen the pictures. If Herold was not in that grave, he was in some other, and all his secrets with him.

Dr. Cady had gone ashore with the cavalry to return his drugged colleague to the care of the Stewart clan. Mr. Stanton had repaired to his own cabin without a word, leaving me to reflect upon our astonishing discovery. I climbed to the pilot house and there found a map of the nearby counties of Virginia. I traced the route Herold and the decoy followed when they departed Cleydael.

Port Conway was little more than a bunch of warehouses and a ferry ship; there was no telegraph there. Port Royal, across the Rappahannock, was somewhat more of a town, but I thought it unlikely it boasted a telegraph office. My finger traced the pair's route southward from there, to the point where Garrett's Farm must be. No mark on the map signified any kind of civilized oasis wherein a telegraph key might be found. Perhaps the letter Booth entrusted to his acolyte was posted in Port Royal, but the telegram must have remained unsent when Herold was taken. Then I remembered my Pitman.

The record of the Conspiracy Trial contained the testimony of one of the three Confederates who guided Herold and his companion from Port Royal to Garrett's.† I remembered it because there was something wanting in it, and as I studied the map, I recalled what that had been.

The Rebel had testified that he and his comrades had left only Booth at Garrett's; Herold, he said, had gone with another of the trio on to Bowling Green, there to spend the night with some woman.‡ *It was only on the following night that Herold rejoined "Booth" at Garrett's Farm.* I remembered then why I had found this curious.

No reason had been given why Herold had not stayed with his companion when first they arrived and were taken in by Garrett. Yet more remarkable was the fact that Herold, having gotten as far as Bowling Green, did not continue his flight southward, but, instead, retraced his steps northward to Garrett's on the following night, to rejoin "Booth," for in that fateful move, he surrendered his last chance to escape the noose. But now that I had Dr. Stewart's information, I could make sense of the matter.

Was there a telegraph office in Bowling Green? Perhaps, but if there was not, then surely there were places nearby from which a dispatch could be transmitted. The railroad line between Richmond and Fredericksburg passed a scant few miles to the west of Bowling Green, and there were station stops at Guineas', Milford and Penola, all within a dozen miles of Bowling Green. (Milford looked to be little more than a short walk west of the town.)§ Wherever the rails went, there also went the telegraph lines, and if the sending of travelers' telegrams was not part of the station-master's duties, then a few coins could purchase his cooperation.

---

† The Confederate soldier was Willie S. Jett. His testimony is on pp. 90–91 of Pitman.—M.C.

‡ According to testimony given at the Conspiracy Trial (Pitman, p. 91), Herold and one of the Confederates spent the night "at Mrs. Clark's." Mrs. Clark is not otherwise identified in the testimony. She probably was the proprietor of a local rooming house where Herold and his companion spent the night.—M.C.

§ Milford is two miles southwest of Bowling Green.—M.C.

I had the answer to my Pitman puzzle: Herold had left Garrett's to find a place where he could end Booth's dispatch "To A. Johnson." And then he returned to Garrett's to see to it that his hero's understudy did not lose his nerve and melt into the nearby woods.

As I studied the maps, Mr. Stanton joined me in the pilot house and I apprised him of my conclusions.

"It is a satisfying discovery," I said, when I'd finished, "but not a very profitable one, I'm afraid. Even if my theory is correct, there is likely no copy of Booth's dispatch to be found among these little railroad stops, and yet less chance of finding some local bumpkin who can recite its text. I think it will be more useful to see what can be discovered of the lugger Booth made off in."

I unfurled a chart of the lower Potomac River, which showed, as well, the southern reaches of Chesapeake Bay.

"The vessel doubtless carried him past Point Lookout. From there, it may have sailed up the Bay to Baltimore, but I think not. A man with a handsome price on his head, whose name and face were sent to even the tiniest hamlet in the land, would likely waste no time before fleeing the country. I think we can depend on that lugger having shipped its dangerous cargo aboard an ocean-going vessel at the earliest opportunity. And such opportunity seems most likely to have been found in the lower Bay, perhaps in the form of a ship out of Norfolk. It may be that if I go there and work the waterfront as a stevedore or some other species of casual laborer, I shall hear talk of a vessel that carried a mysterious passenger some years ago."

Mr. Stanton did not reply, except by way of his countenance, which revealed scant interest in my words.

"It's pretty slim," I admitted, "but I can offer no better course. Even a hound loses the scent when the prey takes to the water."

"No, Cosgrove," said the Secretary, "I have no doubt you are right, for you have proved you know your craft. You have done your job so well, in fact, that it needs no further doing. I set you to find the assassin's whereabouts; you have done better than that. You have found the name of his master."

"With all respect, Mr. Secretary," I said, "that may be true, but I think it premature to say so."

"You heard Dr. Stewart's words," said Mr. Stanton. "The assassin sent his message to the President."

"Those were his words," I agreed, "but not the words he read on Booth's paper. *Those* words were nothing more than 'To A. Johnson.' Were you to send your troopers ashore at any place along this river and instruct them to fetch the first hundred people they met, I'll warrant you'd find a half-dozen Johnsons among them, and likely one, at least, whose Christian name begins with the letter 'A.' Let us pray Dr. Stewart takes more time in treatment than he does in diagnosis. Show him a kiss and he sees sodomy, show him a Johnson and he sees a President. Take care not to cough in his presence, else he'll dose you with some medicament for consumption."

"Well said, Cosgrove," declared the Secretary, "but do not think that I have borrowed the Doctor's diagnosis without first examining it carefully. I readily grant you that, were there nothing more to support this charge against Andrew Johnson, Dr. Stewart's disclosure would offer small justification for making it. But what the Doctor revealed to us is but the clincher pin in the case that Andrew Johnson achieved his office by procuring the murder of his predecessor. You may not know it, but this telegram of Booth's is not the only instance we know of in which the assassin made to communicate with Johnson. Scant hours before he fired the shot in Ford's Theater, the actor was at the Kirkwood House, doubtless seeking final instructions from his employer."

"Yes," I said, "I recall hearing that."

"I could not believe it at the time. I knew the Rebel leaders—Davis and all the others—were behind the murder, and so the Military Commission found. But Andy Johnson had us fooled. He played the part of the pre-eminent Rebel-hater all during the War, and even after, for a time. I knew of Booth's visit to the Kirkwood House, but I dismissed it as of no significance, for I could not put Johnson in the company of Davis and the others.

"But once in the Presidency, Johnson showed his true colors. That which the Union had won on the battlefield, he surrendered back to the Enemy when he gained the White House. At heart, he is as black a Secessionist as any who spent the War in Richmond."

"Mr. Stanton," I replied, "the law is your profession, and I know you are the best of all those who practice it, so I ask you to forgive the ignorance of a layman. But, if Jefferson Davis had a hand in Lincoln's murder, none has been able to bring him to Justice. I cannot see, then, how, with nothing more than the evidence of which we have spoken, you can hope to punish Andrew Johnson for the crime."

"You're right, Cosgrove," said Mr. Stanton. "There is not sufficient evidence to prosecute him. Not yet. But that is a situation you shall remedy."

"I, sir?"

"Cosgrove, you are the best of secret detectives. You have given me ample proof of that. I assigned you to an impossible task, and you have succeeded beyond my most optimistic expectations."

"I have not caught Booth, sir," I said.

"You are well on your way to doing it," replied the Secretary, "and I have no doubt that you should accomplish it, given more time. But I have more important work for you, instead."

"And what is that, sir?"

"We know that Andy Johnson was behind the assassination of President Lincoln, but, as you say, we lack the means to prove it. You must get me that proof, Cosgrove. Let Booth go, he was only the hireling. Take whatever you need, whomever you need, spare nothing. But bring me the proof that Justice demands. I no longer care about catching Booth. The man I want to see on the gallows is President Andrew Johnson."

"I shall convey your wishes to Mr. Pinkerton immediately upon our return to Washington City," I replied. "If the evidence you desire can be found, I have no doubt Mr. Pinkerton's Chain of Agencies can find it for you."

"Do not waste precious time on such formalities," commanded the Secretary. "I shall see to whatever arrangements Mr. Pinkerton requires. But you must begin your work at once."

"With all respect, Mr. Secretary, I fear that is impossible."

"Impossible, Cosgrove? How is it impossible?"

"It is impossible, sir," I replied, "because as of this noon I shall have resigned from the employ of Pinkerton's National Detective Agency."

·23·

The Gentleman from Kansas

···•——◆——•···

"Resign, Nicholas?" exclaimed Mr. Pinkerton. "Surely you are not serious!"

He was seated at the escritoire in the parlor of the house on K Street, which was where I unexpectedly discovered him on my return from Mr. Stanton's Potomac expedition. It seemed my dispatches had persuaded him matters in Washington City must needs take precedence once more over the pursuit of the Reno Gang.

"I am serious, sir," I assured him, "and sad, as well. It is not my heart's desire to leave the Chain of Agencies, but it is something I think I must do in the interest of the firm."

"Pray, explain yourself," he said.

I quickly recounted the events that had transpired since my last dispatch to him, finishing with a report of my recent discourse with Mr. Stanton aboard the tug, in which the Secretary had stated his new requirements.

"So," remarked Mr. Pinkerton, "the Secretary of War now accuses Johnson of ordering the murder."

"He is free to hold his opinion," I said, "but it is nothing more than that. Yet he has presented it to me as certain truth, and ordered me to fetch whatever is needed to make it stick. He begins with a conclusion and sets out to search for the evidence to prove it. That is work for a lawyer, not a detective. A detective, as I should not presume to tell you, of all men, travels a route opposite to the one Mr. Stanton would set me on. It is only in that direction one is likely to overtake Truth."

"I cannot dispute that," replied Mr. Pinkerton. "Did you suggest such a course to Mr. Stanton as an alternative to the one he proposed?"

"No, sir, I did not, for it is clear to me the Secretary conceals some guilty secret of his own which he knows would likely be exposed by a proper investigation of the entire affair."

I then recounted to my chief the matter of the relevant War Department files I had not been shown, and Mr. Stanton's candid admissions regarding them, made only after I had confronted him.

"And is this, then, the reason you gave the Secretary for withdrawing from the case?" asked Mr. Pinkerton.

"No, sir. Mr. Stanton is a prominent and powerful man, and he is your client. I do not know how you may be disposed to deal with him, but that is your business, and it is not my own to prejudice matters by angering your patron."

"So you lied to him?"

"I did. With craft, imagination, and delight. I told him this business of Booth was to be my last assignment, and one I had hoped to conclude forthwith. I said I was chafing to join my elder brother, Orion, who had struck gold near Virginia City, and wanted some assistance in digging it up. This project of establishing Mr. Johnson's guilt, I said, promised to be the sort of thing that might take some time. I told Mr. Stanton you would likely put several men on the task."

Mr. Pinkerton gazed at me for a moment, then erupted in laughter.

"A bonnie tale, Nicholas. Tell me, have you an older brother?"

"No sir. I was an only child."

"Then, how did you strike on a name so unlikely as Orion?"

"Well, as you know, I once visited Virginia City.† While I was there I met a witty fellow who claimed to have an older brother of that name, who was forever engaged in one impossible adventure or another. Whether or not it was so I cannot say, but the name was singular and it stayed with me."

"I think you are entitled to borrow it as your own, if I recall my classics correctly. But what will you do now?"

---

† Cosgrove is obviously referring to Virginia City, Nevada, the site of the famous Comstock Lode.—M.C.

I shrugged at the question.

"I've scarcely had time to give the matter any consideration. I suppose the plan I told Mr. Stanton will answer as well as another. Perhaps I shall, in fact, go prospecting in Virginia City. It may be I can find this fellow's brother, adopt him as my own, and take him on as a partner. If I can thus rescue my soul from the toils of prevarication by transforming a lie into the truth, Providence may reward me with a rich strike."

"None deserves it more," laughed Mr. Pinkerton, "but it is customary for a man to tender some notice when he takes leave of his employer. Am I to be denied this?"

"You shall have all the notice you wish," I replied, "but since the object of my departure is to spare you embarrassment, I thought the more abruptly it were done the safer would be your interests."

"You are a loyal fellow, Nicholas," sighed Mr. Pinkerton. "May I impose once more on that loyalty and ask a favor?"

"Anything."

"There is a gentleman in Washington City named Ross. He is, in fact, a United States Senator from Kansas. Senator Ross has sought our services, but, for reasons I cannot explain, it is not possible for me to accommodate him. I should very much appreciate it, Nicholas, if you would handle the matter after you have left my employ."

"I shall be pleased to do so," I said. "Where might I find the Senator?"

"He lives on Capitol Hill at 325 North B Street. It is a rooming house, and I believe you are acquainted with the landlord's daughter, Miss Ream."

"I am," I replied, and reflected that, even having left Mr. Pinkerton's employ, it seemed I was not to be entirely quit of his admirable intrigues.

"This will be a private matter between yourself and Senator Ross," said the detective chief, almost as though he had read my mind, "but both you and your client may rely on the goodwill of the Chain of Agencies. I shall put it to you plainly, Nicholas: If you find yourself in need of any help whatsoever, you need only ask me for it."

I thanked him, and after he had penned a note introducing me to the Senator, warmly shook his hand before taking my leave.

The rooming house wherein dwelt Senator Edmund G. Ross, the Junior Senator from Kansas (and, like the Senior Senator from that state, a Republican), offered little to distinguish it from the many similar Capitol Hill establishments that provided accommodations for Congressmen during those months of the year when Congress was in session. To that observation I must make the very considerable amendment that this hostelry was uniquely graced by the vivacious presence of the landlord's daughter, the comely Vinnie Ream. My initial visit to the house was blessed by a genial augury, for it was Miss Ream who answered my ring.

"You have come about the papers," she declared, without any other word of greeting.

"Papers?"

"Mr. Murphy insisted on having them back," she said. "He has found a journalist who has taken an interest in the matter. The papers are Mr. Murphy's property, so I had no choice but to return them."

"Oh," I remarked, "those papers. He's welcome to the wretched things. No, I am not here in search of them. I didn't know they were missing, but I shouldn't have journeyed all the way to Capitol Hill over them, even had I known. Still, they would be a welcome occasion to visit your door, had I no other."

"But you have another?" she inquired.

"Regrettably, I do," I replied. "It seems I am ever on business. I am here to see Senator Ross."

Unfortunately, this announcement seemed more to startle Miss Ream than disappoint her.

"I see," she said, ushering me into the foyer. "Please wait here while I announce you."

Senator Edmund G. Ross was not possessed of an imposing physical stature; nonetheless, he somehow managed to radiate a certain significance. He was a small, slight man of about forty years. His face, constructed along fine, classical lines, was not totally obscured by his

full, black beard, and bespoke a soul blessed by God with great forti-
tude and intelligence. He'd likely not be the first to seize your attention if you encountered him in a crowded chamber, yet, had you a
trace of wit, he'd be the last you'd forget when you'd departed. But
he was by himself when I was introduced to him in a small sitting
room at the back of the Ream rooming house, and, as events transpired, I incline to doubt I shall ever forget him.

After he had read Mr. Pinkerton's letter, he put it aside and turned
to me.

"You come to me with the highest recommendations, Mr.
Cosgrove," he said. "The task I have for you deserves one such as
yourself, but I am not at all certain my purse is equally appropriate
to the matter. I am a United States Senator today, but I was a simple
printer yesterday.† In short, I am not a wealthy man. May I be blunt
and ask you to name the fee you will require?"

"I shall require no fee," I replied.

"No fee?"

"Mr. Pinkerton has asked me to serve you as a favor to him, and
that is why I am here. I do not charge fees to do favors. Of course,

---

† Edmund G. Ross was a printer in 1866 when he was appointed by the Governor of Kansas to fill out the term of Senator James H. Lane, who had shot himself.
According to some historians, Lane killed himself because of the abuse he received
from many, including Ross, after defending President Andrew Johnson in the Senate against the attacks of the Radical Republicans; others attribute the suicide to ill
health. A third theory has Lane taking his own life for the same reason that Preston
King, another Johnson crony, had, shortly before, tied a weight around his neck
and jumped into the Hudson River: remorse over the role both had played in the
death of Madame Surratt. On the morning of the hanging, Annie Surratt, the unfortunate landlady's daughter, went to the White House to plead in person with
President Johnson for her mother's life. She did not get to see the President; her
way was blocked by Lane and King. Within little more than a year after the execution of Mrs. Surratt, the two men had both died by their own hands.

Edmund Ross had fought in the Union Army during the Civil War; he enlisted
as a private and was discharged a major. As he told Cosgrove, he was a printer by
trade, and certainly not wealthy. In Kansas, he had been among Andrew Johnson's
harshest critics. That the death of one of Johnson's closest friends was the proximate cause of his membership in he Senate is considered one of history's ironies. If
Mrs. Surratt's death was the ultimate cause of his appointment to Washington, then,
as we shall see, his role as Cosgrove's client is an even greater irony.—M.C.

should your task, whatever it may be, involve extraordinary expenses, it may not be within the resources of my own pocket to bear them, for, like you, I am not a wealthy man. Were I, I should not mention the matter."

"Of course," said Senator Ross. "I certainly would not ask you to pay your own expenses. You are more than generous in waiving your fee."

Then the Senator smiled, as if at some private joke.

"You know," he said, "the bargain you have struck has a venerable precedent. It is the same arrangement General Washington made with the Continental Congress: no salary, but all expenses."

"It is flattering to be in such august company," I replied, "but for the sake of both your purse and my labors, I hope the task you have for me is somewhat easier than General Washington's. It needed several years and many fortunes to persuade the British to depart."

The Senator was abruptly somber.

"No, Mr. Cosgrove, I shall not ask you to lead an army. I shall only ask that you lead one man, myself, through a most devious and perplexing labyrinth. The job is surely smaller than the one given General Washington, but whether it is of much less import, I cannot say. I think it may prove to be quite as vital to the survival of the Republic. But before I tell you the substance of the case, there is a matter of procedure I wish to make clear. I assume it is your practice, when making any investigation, to furnish regular reports of your progress?"

"It is. Of course, sometimes, when I am working under cover of a disguise, or my inquiries take me to some distant territory or land, or some other circumstance intervenes, it is not possible for me to do so. But you have my assurance that I shall make every effort to supply you with regular and frequent apprises of my progress in your behalf."

Senator Ross shook his head.

"No," he said. "In this matter it is the very opposite that I wish. In fact, I must insist on it."

"You wish no reports?" I asked, with puzzlement.

"None, until either your inquiries are complete, or I have instructed you to terminate them. I do not know how much time this matter will require, nor how much time is available for its pursuit. Certainly it need be concluded, one way or the other, in a few weeks, but I cannot say with more precision than that. At all events, I wish no report save your final one. It may be that I shall have no choice but to summon you here at some juncture when your work is still incomplete, instructing you to terminate your inquiries and report all you have discovered as of that moment. I hope that does not happen, but it may, as I have no voice in the question of how much time can be allowed for your investigation. And so, while I want no reports of your progress, I must know exactly where you can be found at all times, in case I need call you back. For several reasons it is not advisable that you communicate with me directly, so I ask that you report your whereabouts and itinerary to the young woman who left us a few minutes ago. Her name is Vinnie Ream. She is the daughter of the landlord of this house, and a thoroughly reliable person."

"I am sure she is," I said, omitting to remark that Mr. Pinkerton employs no unreliable secret detectives. "I shall do as you have instructed. And now I must confess you have inspired a deal of curiosity in me regarding the nature of your project, which promises to be quite a singular sort of thing."

"Of course," said Senator Ross, who then lapsed into silence for some moments to marshal his thoughts.

"Mr. Cosgrove," he began, "you are doubtless aware of the dispute which now divides the Congress, even as it divides the Nation itself."

"I am," I admitted, "but I do not claim to comprehend it. It seems a lawyerly sort of dispute, and so beyond the powers and experience of one such as myself."

"It is that," he said, "but it is also much more. On the surface, it seems a simple matter, hardly worth the protracted deliberations of the lawmaking body of a great Nation. Mr. Johnson has discharged Mr. Stanton, or, at least, attempted to do so. His authority to have done it is in dispute. Some say his action is grounds for removing him from office. Others disagree. It seems a mere bagatelle, something one should think a civilized country could settle in an hour's time and then move on to matters of real import."

"I should have thought so," I agreed.

"Yet, instead, this seemingly trifling matter has thrown the United States of America into a national crisis. There is good reason for that, Mr. Nichols, for there are more momentous questions in this affair than the minor issue of whether the head of a government may fire one of his cabinet ministers. These questions pertain to the powers of the various branches of our Government, and the respective limits of those powers. We are not debating the case of *Johnson versus Stanton,* we are trying to mark out a boundary line in a region less explored than the Dark Continent of Africa. We are attempting to define the place where the power of the President ends and that of the Congress begins."

"With all respect, Senator," I remarked, "I did not understand the dispute to be thus. I have not read the Constitution lately, but I seem to recall, from the last time I looked at it, that it is very clear in awarding the House power to impeach the President, and the Senate that needed to remove him from office. I thought the only question you gentlemen were trying to settle is whether or not to go ahead and do it."

"How I wish it were that simple!" replied the Senator, who then considered matters in silence for a moment before continuing.

"As you know, I have been sent to the Senate by the State of Kansas. Have you been to Kansas, Mr. Cosgrove?"

I said that I had.

"You may know that during much of the year in Kansas," said Senator Ross, "we are continually threatened by a species of violent storm we call a 'twister,' which arrives with little warning and brings with it winds of such fury as to level everything in its path."

"I know. I once saw one of the things," I recalled with a shudder.

"Well," continued the Senator, "most Kansas folk protect themselves against the twisters by digging cellars beneath the ground, under their houses or somewhere nearby. When the storms threaten, they take to the cellars. If a twister strikes a house, it is demolished, but the occupants survive to rebuild their homes.

"Some years back there was a fellow in Kansas who had survived three twisters this way. Each time he rebuilt his house, only to see it demolished again within a year or two. But the last time he reconstructed his house, he set out to build it to withstand even the mighty forces of a twister. He made the walls three feet thick, and used stone and mortar, instead of wood. He equipped the windows with shutters of iron plate that can be locked in place when a storm threatens. The wood out of which he manufactured the roof is of several times the normal strength and thickness, and pinned down with nails as large as railroad spikes and, in number, many times that commonly employed for the same purpose. The house is a virtual fortress and, by far, the sturdiest in Kansas. When he completed it, he called in a noted mathematician and a civil engineer to study it, and they pronounced it proof against any windstorm, even a Kansas twister."

"And were they correct?" I asked.

"We do not know," Senator Ross replied, "for the house has not yet been put to the test. It has never been struck by a twister. The man who lives in it says he takes great peace of mind from its sturdiness, but he had not filled in his storm cellar when I recently visited him."

"I see," I said. "But considering the fractious history of Kansas weather, especially the weather in the vicinage of this gentleman's abode, sooner or later his fortress will be put to the test, and it will be assailed by that very species of storm for which its designer has made such estimable preparations."

"'Better later than sooner,' he says," replied Senator Ross. "He is content to wait, and will not be discouraged should a twister never arrive. In fact, he would prefer that, for his curiosity regarding the strength of his house is far exceeded by his hope never again to see it wrecked."

"That seems only prudent," I said, "but it strikes me he has little control over the matter. An engineer may assure him his house is sturdy, but I know of no profession that can promise a storm will not strike it. It is surely beyond the capacity of a secret detective to discourage twisters."

"Nor impeachments," agreed Senator Ross. "No, Mr. Cosgrove, that is a storm the Nation seems destined to endure. We can only pray to God that, should there be no choice but to remove Mr. Johnson from the Presidency, the Constitution will function as its engineers planned, and, when the storm has passed, we shall yet have a Union, not the sorry wreckage of a demolished Government."

"Then what message should I seek in your parable?"

"I'm sorry," he said, "I did not set out to speak in riddles. But I will risk working my little homily to death by giving it an added bit of duty. Thackeray wrote, 'There is a skeleton in every house.'"

"A skeleton of the sort sometimes said to repose in cupboards?"

"And sit at feasts," he agreed. "An unwelcome presence at any time, but especially this one."

"The wind makes the bones rattle," I offered.

"It is a melancholy sound which has been heard throughout the house."

"And the Senate, as well."

"Exactly," said Senator Ross. "The noise distracts us from our deliberations at a critical moment."

"We are speaking of the murder of President Lincoln," I said, "and the sundry rumors that still surround it."

"We are," confirmed the Senator, "as has all of Washington City for most of two years. Lay that ghost for me, if you can, Mr. Cosgrove, and you will have served your country as few have done before."

"Even if such exorcism unmasks a devil in high office?"

"Yes, even that, for one ugly truth is less hurtful than a host of ugly suspicions."

"Very well," I said. "I shall begin at once. I promise you nothing, except that whatever I present you when the time comes to report, it shall be the truth."

"The truth is all I ask," replied Senator Ross. "It is said to set men free."

·24·

Cosgrove Confesses

·····──────◆──────·····

I must now confess a felony. To omit it would be to blemish this otherwise complete account of my inquiries with a lacuna, a mysterious gap that would leave my reader to puzzle over the means I employed to acquire certain necessary intelligence. Of course, I might prevaricate, and write that Mr. Murphy's papers, whose value in my private market had once again soared, had been returned to my hand by the phonographer, and were the rich source of information upon which I drew as I advanced my assassination inquiries, now in the service of Senator Ross. Alas, that would be a lie, and I have resolved to tell the truth.

Mr. Murphy, it transpired, had no sooner taken the documents back from Miss Ream than he bestowed them upon one Mr. Ben Green, proprietor of an obscure publication called, I think, *The People's Weekly*. It was, of course, impossible to approach Mr. Green to request he share Mr. Murphy's present with me, without also I risk reading in the next issue of his weekly that a secret detective, recently in the employ of Allan Pinkerton, was hot on the trail of persons unknown who may have had a hand in the President's exitus. Thus, it seemed that were I to regain the opportunity I had so recently and casually dismissed, I must needs resort to a felony, to wit: burglary.

I have not troubled to consult my attorney before setting down this confession. I believe any crime, short of murder or treason, that is near four decades old has likely expired, and I am long since beyond the reach of human law. If not, I soon shall be, for none will read this confession until I have made good my Final Escape. Post-humous candor seems the least painful variety. I'll get on with the confession.

When I decided on burglary as the most expedient solution to my immediate paucity of information regarding those matters which pertained to the assassination and had been suppressed by Mr. Stanton, I at first thought to make the journalist, Mr. Green, my victim, for the very obvious reason that it was in his custody Mr. Murphy's unauthorized copies of the War Department's files were to be found. But I decided against this course.

Mr. Green had come by the copies honestly, even if Mr. Murphy hadn't, and it seemed a shame to invade the premises of a man charity demands I presume to be honest, his professions (journalist and publisher) notwithstanding. But if my candor is to be total, I must offer the true reason I decided against sacking the offices of *The People's Weekly:* Mr. Murphy's documents were only copies. They might contain errors; they might not be complete. If I were to commit a felony, I should demand richer loot than this. Nothing less than a look at the original papers would answer. Thus it was that I settled on my plan to burglarize the offices of the Secretary of War in the War Department.

The reader may wonder what means I might have used to burglarize Mr. Stanton's offices at a time when it was his habit to occupy them at all hours of the day and night, and when a battalion of soldiers surrounded the War Department building to fend off intruders, around the clock. Were I simply to report that I accomplished this intrusion, and omit any word of how it was done, I should court the skepticism of some readers, and cast doubt upon the veracity of the entire report. Thus I offer the details to those interested in reading them. If, in thus preserving my credibility, I risk being thought a braggart, so be it. I admit there may be some merit in the charge.

It was a Sunday, this day which had begun upon a tug in the Potomac and seen me quit the employ of one man and join that of another. I'd scarcely noted what day it was, so relentlessly had events progressed since the inception of this matter. I had missed Mass, but no matter. The Lord forgives such omissions when the excuse is necessary and honest employment. My labors were necessary, and they remained beyond reproach during church-going hours. I had not begun to entertain the idea of burglary until fully an hour after the last Catholic church in Washington City had closed its doors for the day.

The vernal day was waning when I departed the Ream rooming house. I returned to the house on K Street, having not yet made other arrangements for a place to hang my hat. Mr. Pinkerton was absent on some business, but his offer of assistance was fresh and, I had no doubt, authentic, so I did not hesitate to enlist the aid of Patch and one of the household carriages in my scheme. While the lad went to fetch the coach, I sat down before a mirror with my makeup kit and made some necessary preparations.

The sun had set when we drew up to the curb across Pennsylvania Avenue from the War Department building, and the gathering darkness shielded our conspicuous presence from the curiosity of the infantrymen standing watch about the place. The building, too, was much in darkness, and lights were to be seen only in those windows of the second floor, eastern wing, wherein were located the offices of Secretary Stanton; his loyal secretary, Major Johnson; and the telegraphers. At length, the light in the Major's window was extinguished, and some moments later I spotted the clerkish figure of its occupant as he departed the front portico of the building and walked into the night. I had rehearsed my plan with Patch, so he needed no word from me to recognize this development as the signal for him to go into action. We both departed the carriage, he in the direction of the War Department, and I on a course that brought me into brief apposition with the Major as he strode up 17th Street.

Major Johnson did not see me as I passed him; I was invisible to him, as were all mortals below the rank of Brigadier General. For my part, I inspected him closely (but covertly) as he strode through the auriole of light beneath a street lamp. I was completely satisfied with what I saw. My memory of Major Johnson, his taste in (civilian) garb, the luxuriance of his graying whiskers, his pince-nez, and the other tiny details of his person, had been accurate. It was fortunate that I was invisible to Major Johnson; had he deigned to glance at me as we passed, he would have seen his own identical twin.

I stopped on the corner of the Avenue and waited. After a moment, Patch came running from the direction of the War Department. Still under cover of the darkness, he passed an envelope to me, and wordlessly departed back toward the carriage. I tore open the thing, removed the paper it contained and, unfolding it, strode briskly across the boulevard.

As I approached the ring of troops standing at parade rest about the War Department, the pair of fellows nearest my path snapped to attention and saluted smartly. I strode past them unchallenged. The gesture was repeated by the sentries standing guard on the main portico, and, a moment later, I was facing the captain of the guard, who arose from behind his desk as I entered the building.

"Good evening, once again, sir," he said, glancing at the envelope and paper in my hand. "I see the lad overtook you."

I nodded, but did not reply, stopping for a moment, instead, to glance at the paper I carried. Then, with a petulant shake of my head, I walked past him and ascended the main stairs to the second floor. I was inside.

Very well. It may not need it, but I shall explain.

I had, as I have intimated, gotten myself up to pass as Major Johnson. This was not difficult, for whatever the Major may possess by way of facial lineaments to distinguish himself from other men he conceals behind a luxuriant growth of whiskers, remarkable only in their grizzle. The uniform he wears is that of a chief clerk, which is a costume more easily assembled than, say, General Baker's full-dress Army uniform. I have said I became his identical twin, and, so, have said too much. I became a simulacrum of Major Johnson, but one that would deceive only an eye already predisposed to an expectation of seeing Major Johnson. And that expectation had been created by the estimable Patch.

The lad, attired in a livened uniform that bespoke service in some august household, had presented himself breathless to the captain of the guard and claimed the envelope he carried bore an urgent message for Major Johnson. He was, of course, informed that the officer he sought had just that moment departed the War Department building, and could be overhauled if pursued without delay. Thus, Patch, envelope in hand, ran off into the night, and, in the privacy of its umbrage, passed the envelope into my hand. The reader knows the rest. It was the sort of thing Professor Haselmayer would call an "illusion."

The War Department building of a Sunday night in peacetime was not a busy place. Indeed, it was, I think, deserted, but for the guard at the door, and the occupants of the second floor, east wing. Across the corridor opposite the stairs was the telegraph office, and within, I suppose, drowsed some lonely telegrapher, who watched throughout the night, lest some urgent dispatch be received or need sending. Next door was the Cipher Room, wherein I had read Dr. May's deposition, and next to that the now vacant office of Major Johnson. The last room in the suite, the one in the corner of the building, was Secretary Stanton's chamber. I thought it near certain the Secretary was within, and as I paused outside his door, the sound I heard confirmed this. The Secretary of War was snoring.

It cannot be said, least of all by me, that Mr. Stanton was sleeping the sleep of the Just, for I know better. But I do not think the Secretary had sought repose, as I had, aboard the tug, on either its voyage downriver or the return trip. Thus it is likely he had not slumbered at all since Saturday morning, and it was, as I stood before his door and listened to his exhalations, Sunday evening. No, Mr. Stanton did not sleep the sleep of the Just; he slept the deeper sleep of the utterly exhausted. And this was reassuring to my plan, for, in the circumstances, the Secretary of War's fatigue promised to be more reliable than his righteousness. I returned to the door of the Cipher Room, and after some fumbling, located a skeleton key that conquered its lock.

I entered and, according to good professional practice, relocked the door so as not to be surprised by an unexpected visitor from the corridor. I was pleased to discover that the door to my left, which led to the telegraph office, was closed and locked; thus interruption of my labors from that quarter seemed unlikely. The door to my right, which opened into Major Johnson's office, was also locked, but I immediately remedied that situation of affairs, for his chamber would have to serve as my refuge, if one were needed. There was no question of exiting through a window, as it should have been beyond the resources of my guile to convince a battalion of soldiers I had dropped from Heaven. These preparations completed, I turned my attention to the safe, which reposed beside a desk between the two windows.

As noted in the account of my earlier visit to the Cipher Room, the peter was of an especially sturdy species, manufactured by the New Haven firm of Thompson & Co. I assailed the thing with skill, rather than force, for I had no wish to rob Mr. Stanton of his slumber, nor interrupt the telegrapher's dreams. Neither did I wish to leave behind evidence of my visit. Still, I should not have proceeded differently had I labored in the middle of the Sahara. It is a matter of professional pride.

The safe, as I have said, was of excellent design, and so resisted me for most of an hour. Then it yielded. As the door swung free I took out my watch and noted that hour. It was just past eight o'clock.

The box was bursting with papers. Every dispatch that had been received or sent from this office during the preceding six years seemed contained within it, and there were other sorts of papers, and even photographs, as well. Major Johnson, as might be expected, proved an orderly fellow, and all that pertained to the matter that had brought me there was together. I removed the bundle from the safe and took it to the famous desk nearby. I labored, not by the light of some furtive candle, but in the full illumination of the gas lamps. This I did, not out of recklessness, but of prudence, for the guard believed Major Johnson on duty, and darkness in the windows of both his office and the Cipher Room should have evoked suspicion.

For eight hours I read the secrets of the man who slept two rooms away. Sometime after four o'clock in the morning, I finished my work. I knew that which I had been intended never to learn. I returned the sheaf to the box and re-locked it. The heavy door escaped my hand and swung closed with a crash, shattering the nocturnal stillness. I stood frozen as the noise echoed in the empty corridor without. Several long moments passed, and there was no further sound, save that of my own quickened respiration. I had nearly counted the incident unnoticed when I heard a door open in Major Johnson's office.

"Albert?"

It was the Secretary.

"Major Johnson, are you about?"

I heard the sound of footsteps and Mr. Stanton crossed his secretary's office to the door that separated it from the Cipher Room, that same portal I had been at some pains to unlock upon my arrival. Quickly I extinguished the lamp, then stood stock-still. The door to the Major's office opened and Secretary Stanton stood silhouetted in the rectangle of light. He thrust his head into the darkened Cipher Room. I weighed my choices.

If I acted without delay, I could be across the room and at Mr. Stanton's side before he discerned my presence. A swift and well-aimed blow could render him insensible without inflicting serious injury. Before he recovered I should be gone. The identity of the intruder would remain unknown to him. Yet the fact that there had been an intrusion would be obvious. Presently he would discover the intruder had impersonated Major Johnson and spent many hours of the night in the Cipher Room. I did not misprize the Secretary's powers of deduction; likely he would guess the name of the nocturnal visitor. I surely could not rely that he would fail to do it. Thus I remained motionless. An eternity elapsed.

At last Mr. Stanton shrugged and turned away, closing the door as he withdrew. After a moment I heard another door shut, as the Secretary returned to his office, to resume, I prayed, his interrupted slumber. I remained immobile for some half-dozen minutes, then took my leave. The drowsy guards saluted as I exited the building, and the faithful Patch was waiting where he had kept his lonely vigil in the carriage. We departed.

And that, for the benefit of the curious and the skeptical, is how it was done.

· 25 ·

Saddles, Steamboats and Shank's Mare

My narrative thus far covers an interval of ten successive days, from the morning of Saturday, March 21, 1868, until the early hours of Monday, March 30 of the same *anno Domini*. The events that transpired during this period were remarkable, in that they revealed astonishing and unsuspected intelligence material to the most momentous event of the Century, the assassination of President Abraham Lincoln. But they are remarkable in yet another regard: the singular absence of any pause whatsoever in the unfolding of events. Scarcely an hour, and certainly never a day, passed that did not bring with it some new discovery. Some steps I took in pursuit of my inquiries came, at times, perilously near to failure, even disaster! Yet none was futile. None failed to advance my search for the fugacious assassin.

The reader knows that my successes in the matter owe as much to good fortune as good sense, for I have been candid. I shall not abandon that candor now, and so must inform him that, on the Monday morning where I have momentarily suspended this account, the unusual pace of events abruptly changed. Doubtless this remarkable run of successes would soon have ended of its own accord, as a gambler's lucky streak at the gaming tables, but I believe the proximate cause of my change of fortune was my change of client, and the consequent change in the object of my inquiries.

Mr. Stanton set me to find Booth. Those, at least, were his instructions during the nine days I served him. Senator Ross had a different sort of job for me: Find the assassin's accomplices, if indeed he'd had any. Of course, there had been accomplices; four were buried in the yard of the Old Arsenal, and four more languished in the dungeons of Fort Jefferson. These were not my quarry. The Senator required to know if any others, men of higher station, had a hand in the crime, and, if so, their names. Thus I was removed from the trail of one man, who had been thought dead, was not, but whose name I knew. And I was set on the trails of several men, who may never have lived in the first instance, but, had they, I must needs find their names for myself. Small wonder, then, no little time was needed before further developments worthy of inclusion in this account transpired.

My nocturnal visit to the War Department Cipher Room had yielded intelligence of inestimable value to my new inquiries. But the loot from that raid was a budget of questions, not the answers my client sought. Still, it served to point the direction in which those answers lay. There were, in fact, many directions in which to search, for the questions that next needed answering could not all be asked within the limits of Washington City nor its vicinage. There was to be a deal of travel in my immediate future, and scarcely a point on the compass rose which would be neglected.

Garrulousness is a weakness of age, and I am tempted to deliver unto my reader a detailed recounting of the many days and weeks that followed; but I will hold firm instead, and deliver him from it. I shall not ask him to share with me those long hours passed in railroad stations, or aboard trains of cars, stages, saddles, steamboats and, of course, shank's mare; nor the disguises, pretexts, subterfuges and other such guile I employed; nor the interviews with hosts of witnesses located only at great cost of time and effort, who, it often transpired, had nothing to say worth the investment. In short, I shall eschew the construction of a true account of the secret detective's trade as it was practiced in those days (and, I suspect, remains little changed today), and cleave instead to those particulars bearing directly upon that matter which was the occasion of my invitation to the reader in the first instance, to wit: the substance of my inquiries into the circumstances of the assassination of President Lincoln.

The infant Spring, that was scarcely quit of its wintery womb, burgeoned toward Summer maturity while I wandered the land in my quest. Dutifully, I reported each stop along my path with a telegram to Miss Ream, sent by way of the house on K Street, a measure which saved Senator Ross's door from the notice a parade of Western Union messengers might earn it. I had no word in return from Washington City while I pursued my peregrinations, but, as it was clear the time allotted to me to complete my task was rationed by the events transpiring in the Senate, I endeavored to follow the progress of the Impeachment Trial as reported by whatever newspapers came to hand along the way. This proved a dreary duty, except once, in late April, when one Senator† betrayed a little wit and proposed the matter be settled through the passage of a new law prohibiting the President of the United States, on penalty of a fine of $10,000 and ten years in prison, from saying anything displeasing to Congress, using any phrase deemed unintelligible, misquoting sacred Scripture, or employing bad grammar. His colleagues omitted to avail themselves of this excellent avenue of escape from their deliberations, and I do not think the suggestion was put to a vote.

The same daily brought word that Mr. Charles Dickens had embarked for London from New York City. I hoped he had not chanced to meet General Baker and discuss the subject of impresarios with him.

I also passed my time between trains and such by keeping a sharp eye out for *The People's Weekly*, for I was curious to know what its publisher might make of Mr. Murphy's documents. The publication was scarcely in evidence, however, for, although its proprietor had tossed the gauntlet at the feet of *Harper's* and *Leslie's* weeklies, and promised to flood the land with copies of this new periodic sensation, he had failed to carry out his threat, at least in those purlieus to which my inquiries summoned me. But I did succeed in procuring the May 2nd number of *The People's Weekly*, which happened to be the one which first made mention of Mr. Murphy's documents.

The editor, Mr. Ben Green, wrote that he had been latterly approached by a phonographer who had taken testimony in regard to the Conspiracy Trial and who had supplied him evidence identifying

---

† It was on April 25, and the speaker to whom Cosgrove refers was not a Senator, but William S. Goesbeck of Cincinnati, one of President Johnson's defense attorneys.—M.C.

"The Real Instigators of the Assassination of Lincoln." (The phonographer was not named or otherwise identified.) At first, wrote Mr. Green, he thought the claim a wild vagary, but "subsequent developments" persuaded him otherwise. "The Real Instigators" of the crime were Edwin M. Stanton, Joseph Holt,† and Lafayette C. Baker. Mr. Green wrote he had not "time or space in this number to continue this subject," but he promised his readers to do so in the next. Whether or not he made good his promise I cannot say, for I never saw the next number of *The People's Weekly*.‡

About the middle of the first week in May I received a dispatch from Miss Ream suggesting I make ready to present myself in Washington City within a few days. As I was, at that time, at some considerable remove from the Nation's capital, I immediately set about to conclude my inquiries and set out for Washington City. On Thursday, May 7, I received word from Miss Ream that my presence should be required no later than the evening of Sunday, May 10. I wired back that this would not be possible, but that I was en route by the swiftest means available. As it transpired, my journey to Washington City was plagued by several misadventures, which, according to my earlier resolution, I shall eschew recounting, except to say they resulted in serious delays. I did not reach Baltimore until the early evening of

---

† The Army's Judge Advocate General and chief of the Bureau of Military Justice, who directed the prosecution at the Conspiracy Trial.—M.C.

‡ Nor, apparently, has anyone alive today. The existence of *The People's Weekly* had all but vanished from historical record until 1948, when a copy of the same issue Cosgrove describes (May 2, 1868) was discovered in Baltimore, Maryland, in the most romantic circumstances. A local resident was exploring the living room of an old house on West St. Paul Street when a mirror on the wall suddenly shattered, revealing a hiding place behind it. Inside the secret compartment, he discovered a handgun, and resting beneath the weapon, was a yellowing and brittle copy of the periodical. The magazine found its way into the hands of the noted historian Otto Eisenschiml, whose works on the Lincoln assassination have proved so useful to my investigation of the Cosgrove manuscript. Eisenschiml tried mightily, but was never able to locate the following (May 9) issue of *The People's Weekly*, in which Ben Green had promised to continue his revelations. Eisenschiml did manage to turn up much interesting information regarding Green, his magazine, and his other ventures, but unfortunately nothing in the way of evidence material to Cosgrove's story. Those who are interested in the matter can find it in Eisenschiml's *O. E., Historian Without an Armchair* (Indianapolis: Bobbs-Merrill, 1963), pp. 173–177.—M.C.

Friday, May 15. There I found awaiting me a dispatch from Miss Ream informing that an extension had been procured through some unspecified means,† but that I must, at all costs, present myself to my client in the Capitol Crypt (her studio) next Friday night. "Next Friday" was that very day, so I boarded the next train of cars for Washington City, arriving there at 9:50 P.M., local time.

I wasted no time, but betook myself directly to the Capitol from the railroad station, which was situated at the foot of Capitol Hill, and thus but a few mintues' walk from my destination. As on the occasion of my last nocturnal visit, the Capitol was deserted and silent save for the sibilance of the gas jets that lighted its facade. I made my way to the darkened entrance below the Inaugural Steps and entered the Crypt. Miss Ream had not neglected her labors while I pursued my own, and I saw by the light of an oil lantern that the plaster likeness of Abraham Lincoln seemed near completion. He stood atop a pedestal, appropriately, and at his feet stood another, a man of flesh and blood, and nerve. It was Senator Edmund Ross.

"Here you are, at last, Cosgrove," he said. "I had begun to fear you'd disappoint me."

"I hope I have not," I replied. "Please stay your verdict until you have heard my report. Meantime, you have my apology for keeping you waiting. I was far from Washington City when I received your summons."

"But close to the Truth, I hope," he said.

"I share your hope, but I do not promise that. I have done what I promised when we struck our bargain. I have done my best in the

---

† On May 7 the Senate adjourned after setting Monday, May 11, as the date for its next meeting. It seemed possible the impeachment vote would be taken then. However, on Monday it was agreed the vote would be taken the following day when, apparently, Cosgrove was still somewhere en route. On Tuesday, May 12, however, the vote was again postponed until the following Saturday, May 16, because Senator Jacob M. Howard of Michigan had been taken suddenly ill, was delirious, and could not be present. Howard was expected to vote against Johnson, and he did, having recovered by Saturday. The nature of his brief illness is not in the record. Whether he contracted it on his own or had help is something that can only be a matter of speculation. In any case, his sudden indisposition provided the extra time Cosgrove needed to make it back to Washington.—M.C.

time permitted me. I bring you a deal of facts. I have been at some pains to collect them, and some more to verify them. What I shall report is, to the best of my knowledge, true. I can only pray that you will find in this intelligence the Truth."

"Truth!" exclaimed a voice from the circumambient darkness. "You expect truth from this man? I can tell you he is a liar! Is this the reason you've called me here, to hear this brigand?"

The voice was familiar to me, as was the face, when their owner stepped into the light. It was the Secretary of War, Edwin Stanton.

"It is," replied Senator Ross, "and the invitation was extended as a courtesy, since you have been so recently accused in the press of complicity in the matter I have engaged Mr. Cosgrove to investigate. I refer, of course, to the assassination of our late President."

"And how is it that you have taken such a fancy to *that* matter?" demanded Mr. Stanton. "I should think that another, more immediate issue would command your full attention at this moment, and you would have no time to waste in pursuit of scurrilous rumors."

"If you mean the trial in the Senate when you speak of 'more immediate' issues, I reply to you that this question of the assassination has never been separate from it," said Senator Ross.

"What?" exclaimed the Secretary. "There are eleven Articles of Impeachment to be decided. I recall none that mentions Lincoln's murder."

"No," replied the Senator, "that is the Twelfth Article, the unspoken one. Unspoken in the formal charges against President Johnson as drafted by the House, but spoken of constantly elsewhere, first in whispers, then in shouts. There is not a man in the Senate who has not heard the accusation that the President stole the office he now holds by shedding the blood of his predecessor. They have heard all of the rumors and insinuations. I have heard them, too. Now I will hear the facts. You are welcome to stay and hear them with me, or not, as you wish."

Mr. Stanton regarded the Senator with wordless displeasure for a long moment before making his reply.

"Very well, I shall listen," he said. "But I know this man Cosgrove, or whatever name he now goes by, and he is a liar. I hope I shall not hear him repeat the slanders I have so recently suffered regarding this matter of the assassination."

"Well, if that's what you hear, Stanton," spoke yet another voice from the darkness, "I can promise it won't kill you. I've been hearing the same thing said of me for years, and it never has proved fatal. After a while you get used to it. Being slandered, you see, is like doing hard manual work; it builds up calluses, so you don't feel it after a while. But I don't expect you'd know about such things.

"Anyway, we ought to hear whatever this fellow has to say about the matter, since we've heard the opinion of just about everyone else in Washington City on the subject."

The voice was not familiar to me, but it seemed it could belong to only one man. Yet I could not believe it was he.

"You!" exclaimed Mr. Stanton. "Senator Ross, you did not inform me *he* would be here in your message. I find this outrageous!"

"I regret that, sir," replied Senator Ross, "but if anyone is entitled to hear this, it is President Johnson."

The man stepped into the circle of light, arms folded, head defiantly thrown back. Incredibly, it was none other than the President of the United States.

"Gentlemen," said Senator Ross to his pair of august guests, "forgive me if I presume too much, but what I do, I do with great reluctance, and only because it has fallen to me to decide the issue that now divides the Nation. That is not an easy burden. I did not ask for it, but I bear it, nonetheless. I have been put in an extraordinary predicament, one without precedent in the history of the Republic. If I have resorted to extraordinary measures, I ask your indulgence and understanding."†

---

† Two-thirds of the Senate, thirty-six votes, were needed to convict Johnson and remove him from office. Most of the members of the Senate had made their intentions known during the trial, and on the eve of the impeachment vote, there were thirty-five who could be relied upon to vote against the President. Senator Ross had long been among Johnson's harshest critics, and he was originally counted on as a certain pro-conviction vote. However, since the beginning of the Senate trial, he had made it clear he was holding his judgment until he had heard all of the arguments, and so, on the eve of the vote, he was the only member of the Senate whose verdict remained in serious doubt, and thus he held the outcome in his hands.

"I suppose you must be indulged," said Mr. Stanton, "since you have denied me any choice in that, but you do not have my understanding. Indeed, I do not understand your motives in staging this midnight farce. The duty God and Country demand of you must be done upstairs in the Senate Chamber in tomorrow's daylight. I do not understand why you think it can be aided by skulking about the Capitol's cellars in the dark of night."

"Both the time and place are appropriate to the matter that summons us here, Mr. Stanton," replied the Senator, "for there is a dark question hidden beneath the issues that are daily debated on the floor above this place. Mr. Cosgrove has agreed to bring whatever light he can find to illuminate the mystery, and he has labored at doing it for many weeks, and without any payment. I have no inkling of that which he will shortly tell us, for I have forbidden him to make any sort of report until now.

"I regret, Mr. Stanton, that you object to Mr. Johnson's presence, but he has more right to be here than do you, sir, for he has oftener been the object of accusations in this matter. And I am sorry you dislike the place I have chosen to hear Mr. Cosgrove's report, but it has several advantages; for one, we shall not likely be interrupted here; for another, all of the interested parties are present."

Saying this, Senator Ross turned and glanced briefly at the statue Miss Ream had constructed. Then he looked toward me.

"Very well, then. If there are no further objections, Mr. Cosgrove, please let us have your report."

Pro-impeachment forces had sought to influence him with an outrageous barrage of threats and attempted bribes, and Ross knew he had nothing to gain and everything to lose by voting for acquittal. (His dilemma was eloquently recalled by President Kennedy in his book *Profiles in Courage*.) On the night of May 15 the Radical Republicans sent General Dan Sickles to see Ross at his rooming house and convince him to vote for conviction. History records that Sickles did not reach Ross's rooms because the General was kept at bay by Vinnie Ream, who placed herself in his path and refused to let him past the parlor. Sickles maintained his siege until four in the morning, at which time he gave up and went home. Now we know, from Cosgrove's account, that, had Sickles gotten past Vinnie Ream, he would have found Ross's room vacant, and we can presume he might have guessed his quarry was to be found in the sculptor's studio in the Capitol Crypt, and gone there to interrupt the meeting between Ross, Stanton, Johnson and Cosgrove.—M.C.

PART SIX

Nicholas Cosgrove's Report

· 26 ·

Some Remarkable Disclosures

···──◆──···

Three important pairs of eyes turned toward me. I undid my portfolio and busied myself shuffling the papers within for some moments.
There was no genuine need for it (I had studied the sheets so often I
think I could recite them today), but it offered a pause in which I
was able to marshal my thoughts and consider how best to begin.

"Gentlemen," I finally said, "I hope you will forgive me if I indulge in a personal comment regarding myself before getting down
to cases. I ask this, not from any illusion of my own importance, but
of an appreciation of yours. It has been said of me that I lack sufficient respect for authority. To whatever extent this is so, I thank God,
for had he equipped me with a full measure of that virtue, I should
flee this chamber without uttering a word, and not rest until I had
crossed the frontier of another country.

"Senator Ross has implied I am his agent. It was generous of him
to do so, but I ask you to disregard this averment, for the Senator has
burden enough on his shoulders without adding to it the weight I
have brought here tonight. Neither should Mr. Allan Pinkerton be
held in any way responsible for what I am about to say, for I quit his
employ many weeks ago. As the Senator has told you, I have worked
without pay. Thus, I have worked, not for him, but for myself, and
no other should be held responsible for that which I shall shortly
deliver here.

"I find myself addressing the three most powerful men in Washington City, nay in the United States of America; the President, his
most puissant adversary, and the man who holds in his hands the fates

of the other two. Senator Ross's duty awaits him tomorrow in the chamber above, and when the sun next sets, he will have made an enemy of an important man. My duty presents itself here and now, and, for the moment, it is even less enviable than that of the Senator, for long before that same sun has risen, I shall have made enemies of *two* important men. I have many unpleasant truths which I am bound to assert. Not the least of them is the melancholy fact that you, Mr. President, and you Mr. Secretary, have both stained your hands with innocent blood."

"Scoundrel!" exclaimed Mr. Stanton. "I might have known you planned slander!"

"Simmer down, Stanton," admonished President Johnson. "Let the man explain himself. If you've got a clean conscience, you'll have an answer for him."

"And what of yourself, Mr. President?" demanded the Secretary. "Is your own conscience so pure you can hear this sort of thing with equanimity?"

"I don't know," Mr. Johnson admitted. "I haven't heard the charges read yet. But I generally don't get to hear them, for they're usually made behind my back. I think I may enjoy the novelty of hearing them said to my face, and I'm certain I'll take pleasure in having a partner such as yourself to share the guilt. Please get on with it, Mr. Cosgrove. Tell us whose innocent blood is on our hands."

"That of a woman," I replied, "and I think you already know her name: Mary Surratt."

"You say she was not guilty?" inquired the President.

"Not of murder, the crime for which she was hanged," I said. "Nor are the four who languish in Fort Jefferson guilty of it, although some of them can be blamed for another offense, and it may be Mrs. Surratt had a share in that crime, but I do not know."

"What crime is that?" asked Senator Ross.

"A conspiracy against President Lincoln, but one aimed at his abduction, not his murder."

"Is this a sample of the truths you have labored so diligently to un-earth, Cosgrove?" Mr. Stanton demanded. "For if it is, I fear you have wasted your own time and now promise to waste ours. This business of Booth and his accomplices having planned President Lincoln's kidnapping is well known to everyone. We have known it for most of three years, since it was disclosed during the trial of the conspirators."

"Yes," I replied, "but it was known to yourself somewhat longer, sir. In fact, Mr. Stanton, you were well aware of the plot even before the plotting was complete and the attempts to abduct the President were made."

"That is an absurd and slanderous accusation!" exclaimed the Secretary.

"Perhaps," I allowed, "but there are many other than myself who make it. They include the very people who informed you of the plot at the time."

"Does Weichmannt† claim this?" demanded Mr. Stanton.

"No, Weichmann has little to say of any of these matters today, but those few words he will offer are not much different from the ones he swore to at the trial. He worked too hard at keeping his neck out of a noose then to stick it so recklessly in one now. If one presses him regarding such questions today, they are directed to read his words in Pitman. I have done that.

"Mr. Weichmann testified he voiced his supicions that Booth and his cohorts were planning some outrage against the President to one Major Gleason,‡ then a fellow worker in the War Department. According to Weichmann, Gleason dismissed the matter as some sort of joke. It's a pity the Military Commission did not call Major Gleason as a witness, for he would have told a different story, and his words might have been more highly prized than Mr. Weichmann's, for the Major's neck was not in jeopardy of a noose."

---

† Louis J. Weichmann, who worked as a clerk in the War Department and lived in Mrs. Surratt's boardinghouse at the time of the assassination and for some months before. He was initially arrested as a conspirator, but was not charged as such. He became one of the Government's chief witnesses during the Conspiracy Trial, and his testimony was crucial to the conviction of Mrs. Surratt.—M.C.

† Major D. H. L. Gleason, while recovering from battle wounds in January, 1865, took a job in the War Department's Commissary General of Prisoners, which had offices in a building at 20th and F Streets, N.W. There he met and befriended his co-worker, Louis J. Weichmann.—M.C.

"You questioned Major Gleason?" asked Senator Ross.

"I did," I replied, "and received most enlightening intelligence from him."

"Major Gleason reports that Mr. Weichmann did indeed come to him, on or about the 20th of February, nearly two full months before the assassination, with information that John Wilkes Booth was a frequent visitor to the boardinghouse in which he stayed, and that Booth, John Surratt (the landlady's son) and several others, including some who boarded there, were planning to abduct the President and spirit him into Rebel territory, where he was to be used to ransom Confederate prisoners held by the North. The kidnappers planned to strike on Inauguration Day, March 4th. Contrary to Weichmann's testimony, Major Gleason says he took the report to be a gravely serious matter, and conveyed it to his associate, Lieutenant Joshua W. Sharp, who was then an Assistant Provost Marshal on the staff of General Auger. Sharp, he reports, was skeptical at first, but soon shared his concern that the conspirators were in earnest. Lieutenant Sharp assured Major Gleason he would see that the intelligence was brought to the attention of Secretary Stanton, forthwith."†

"If that be so," declared Mr. Stanton, "and I doubt it, then this Lieutenant Sharp did not make good his promise, for I know no one of that name."

"Perhaps the information was conveyed to you by Sharp's superior, General Auger, or some other officer," Senator Ross suggested.

"There were ever vague reports of some such threat to the persons of the President and others," Mr. Stanton allowed, "but I certainly was never apprised of anything regarding John Wilkes Booth, or Surratt, or any plan so specific as the one Cosgrove claims. Certainly, had I been notified a kidnapping was planned during the Inaugural, I should not likely have forgotten it. And, in fact, no such attempt was made, as we well know. It is not the sort of thing likely to escape public notice."

---

† All of this agrees with Gleason's own account, which he did not publish until February, 1911.—M.C.

"On the contrary," I replied, "I have evidence the attempt came within an ace of execution. When President Lincoln stood on the Capitol steps, scant yards from the place we now stand, and delivered his Inaugural Address, there lurked before him in the crowd John Surratt, David Herold, George Atzerodt, Edward Spangler and Lewis Paine. And on the balcony behind him, but a few feet away, stood John Wilkes Booth, himself."

"Indeed!" exclaimed the Secretary. "That must be a singular species of evidence. Pray tell us what form it takes. A divine vision, perhaps?"

"A vision," I replied, "but one of mortal origin. The plotters' attempt did escape public notice, for it was abandoned at the last moment, owing to some motive I have not learned, but can guess. But the attempt did not escape the eye of a camera brought to record the Inauguration by Mr. Alexander Gardner. I have had a copy of the photograph made for your inspection."

I withdrew the photograph from my portfolio and presented it to Senator Ross, who strained to examine it in the dim lantern light.

"By misadventure the President's likeness was spoiled," I said. "We are fortunate Mr. Gardner kept it nonetheless. It is an imperfect portrait of the Inaugural, but it is a priceless record of another momentous event, one that did not happen.† You will find the persons I have named among the throng."

As a convenience to the eye, I had marked their places in the photograph.

"I have seen none of these men in the flesh," said Senator Ross, "but I have often seen their photographs, and the faces in those pictures do

---

† From Cosgrove's description of the smudged photograph, it seems certainly the same one I found among the photos Lawson included with the manuscript. Lawson's notes on the back of the picture suggested it had been forgotten among Gardner's files from the time it was taken until it was rediscovered in recent years, when close examination revealed the presence of Booth and the others in the picture. Alexander Gardner had left Washington in 1867 to go West and photograph the Union Pacific Railroad, but he probably left the contents of his gallery in the care of someone in Washington, perhaps his old friend and former employer, Mathew Brady. In any case, Cosgrove seems to have managed somehow in 1868 to find, not only the historic photograph, but the historic faces in the crowd.—M.C.

closely resemble the men you have pointed out in this picture. What say you, gentlemen?"

He presented the photograph to President Johnson, who studied it and returned it to the Senator without comment. The Secretary next inspected the Inaugural view.

"I cannot say," he rejoined, after some moments. "The light is dim here and my eyes are poor. I'll grant you Booth is likely somewhere in the picture, for we know he boasted of being there, close enough to Lincoln to have murdered him then.† And I'll readily grant the others may have been there, as well, for, as this photograph proves, if it proves nothing else, half of Washington City seems to have been present. But if that band of cut-throats was there to abduct or murder the President, I certainly had no knowledge of the matter. I knew nothing of such things until after the bloody deed was done in April."

I withdrew another sheet from my portfolio.

"Mr. Secretary, this paper is an exact copy of a dispatch you sent during the tragic hours following the assassination. It bears as its place of origin Number 458 10th Street (which is the house to which President Lincoln was taken), and the time of its composition as 4:10 A.M., April 15, 1865. It is addressed to Major-General Dix in New York, and it apprises him of the situation of affairs at that moment. Do you recall inditing it?"

"How did you obtain that?" demanded Mr. Stanton.

"By the methods of a secret detective," I replied. "The dispatch includes the following passage: 'It appears from a letter found in Booth's trunk that the murder was planned before the 4th of March, but fell through then, because the accomplice backed out until "Richmond could be heard from."' Do you recall writing those words?"

"Perhaps," Mr. Stanton allowed. "What if I do?"

"I think the words suited your purpose then, when you hoped to lay blame for the murder at the feet of the Rebel leaders. But I think they may prove an embarrassment for you now."

"If they do, I fail to see it," he replied.

---

† Booth's fellow-actor, Samuel Knapp Chester, reported Booth's boast in his testimony at the Conspiracy Trial. (See Pitman, p. 45.)—M.C.

"Then permit me to explain the problem they pose. Within a few hours after the assassination, one Mr. William Eaton, acting on authority of the War Department, went to Booth's room in the National Hotel and took charge of the assassin's papers and other possessions. These he turned over to Lieutenant William H. Terry of Colonel Ingraham's office. I have consulted with both Mr. Eaton and Lieutenant Terry, and they inform me that no such statement regarding the 4th of March was contained in any letter found among Booth's papers.†

"Thus, Mr. Secretary, it seems you did know something of some plan of Booth's that was to have been carried out by the March 4th Inaugural. Yet you say you did not have such prior intelligence from Mr. Weichmann. And it transpires you could not have learned of the March 4th date from Booth's trunk, as you claimed in your dispatch. We must inquire of you, then, how did you come by such information?"

"What say you to that, Mr. Secretary?" the Senator inquired.

"What say I? I say I have been euchred to this place in the midst of the night to be made a defendant against the most heinous and outrageous accusations, made by one lacking integrity, before a court lacking authority, and without any word of notice in advance that might permit me to prepare a defense, should I incline to dignify this travesty with such. That, sir, is what I say!"

"You're not a defendant, Stanton," said the President. "There's only one defendant down here tonight, and that's me. As you say, this isn't a court of any legal jurisdiction. You have been asked a question which,

---

† Cosgrove has quoted accurately from Stanton's dispatch to General Dix, which may be found in the National Archives. Eaton's and Terry's testimony, and the text of one of the letters they found is contained in Pitman, pp. 41, 236 and 237, respectively. That letter, which was to Booth from Samuel Arnold, is dated March 27, 1865, and does not refer to March 4, although it does imply involvement of the Confederate leaders. At least some of the other papers found in Booth's trunk were in cipher (Pitman, p. 41), and, whatever they said, it seems unlikely they had been deciphered in time to inform Stanton of the March 4th date by 4:10 the following morning. Whether or not some other clear text message supporting Stanton's claim was discovered in the trunk is not stated in the Conspiracy Trial testimony.—M.C.

I'll allow, is embarrassing. Do you have an answer for it that is any less embarrassing?"

"My reply is no embarrassment at all, to myself," huffed Mr. Stanton, "although it will surely embarrass you. You have my humblest apologies, gentlemen," he continued in a tone that seemed far from apologetic, "if I cannot, *ex tempore,* deliver a full and complete accounting of some dispatch I sent in the line of duty nearly three years bygone. I fear I should be unable to do it without reference to my records even were the dispatch occasioned by the usual course of business in the War Department. But the dispatch regarding which you interrogate me was but one of many it was my melancholy duty to compose during the small hours of that lamentable morning, *while others slept, or were otherwise engaged in more pressing matters.*"

Here he turned and fixed the President with a gaze so fiercely censorious it stripped every shred of ambiguity from his words.

"President Lincoln was dying, you see," he continued, "and thus could no longer govern. Now, the Constitution provides for such exigency by furnishing us with a Vice-President, who has little else to do but collect his pay and stand ready to succeed the President in the event he is removed from office by death. Or other means.

"But, curiously, on the night in question, the Vice-President was, it appears, not ready. Some say he was not even standing, and that his powers were dimmed by the same cloud under which they labored on that very Inaugural Day that has been recalled by Mr. Cosgrove.†

"And where was our esteemed Vice-President at this grave moment in the history of our Nation? He seems to have retired early that evening, or was otherwise preoccupied abed, for it needed a half-hour's

---

† Andrew Johnson disgraced himself on March 4, 1865, by delivering his Inaugural Address in the Senate, almost literally from the floor of the chamber. He was thoroughly drunk, and he barely managed to stumble over an incoherent series of unconnected sentences, and then follow outgoing Vice-President Hamlin through the oath of office. Johnson's detractors claimed the performance was further evidence of the charge he was a drunkard. His apologists deny this, and blame the incident on his very abstemiousness; they say he was such a stranger to booze, the several pre-Inaugural cups he took had a disproportionate result on his faculties. A third, and much smaller, school of thought says there was something in the drinks besides whiskey. Cosgrove does not address the question.—M.C.

hammering on his door to bring him to it, and several hours to fetch him to the bedside of his dying chief. And he'd scarcely arrived before he was gone again, presumably to the resumption of whatever matter of greater import had been so rudely interrupted by this tiresome business of President Lincoln having been assassinated. Thus it fell to me to do, not only my own duty, but Mr. Johnson's. Otherwise the Ship of State would have remained as the Vice-President left it: adrift, without any man's hand on the tiller.

"Thus it was I found myself somewhat heavily preoccupied during the night in question, and so do not recall with absolute precision every dispatch I sent or received while so engaged. Among other duties, I was directing the pursuit of the assassins. Had I had time to reflect on the curious behavior of the man who profited most from the assassination, I might have perceived that the ultimate perpetrator of the crime was no farther away than his rooms in the Kirkwood House.

"And that, gentlemen, is my reply."

Senator Ross turned to Mr. Johnson.

"Mr. President, do you have a comment of your own to offer here?"

"It needs more than a comment," replied the President. "Unfortunately, I don't share Stanton's gift of the gab. He exhibits a singular economy in laying down a barrage of words. He rarely fires one off that doesn't inflict a deal of damage. I'm afraid I'm not equipped with any corresponding talent, and I may run short of breath before I've completed the repairs."

"You shall have my attention, sir, for as long as you require it," offered Senator Ross.

"Maybe I won't need all that much time to answer," President Johnson said. "As I reflect on the matter, I've had plenty of practice answering these charges, because I've heard them all before. But I've always heard them made singly. Stanton has contributed his own touch by making them in combination.

"It has been suggested before, you see, that I was tardy in answering the door and getting myself to the President's side because I was drunk. Another theory puts the delay down to my entertaining a lady who was not my wife. I confess I like the second theory better than the first for two reasons: first, it can also be used to explain why, having reached Lincoln's deathbed late, I was so early in leaving it to return to my rooms. It explains more of the facts, you see, so it must be more scientific; and second . . . well, gentlemen, let me put it this way: any old fool of my years can get himself drunk.

"Now, the third theory, also previously and frequently advanced, is one I must admit I don't care for at all. That slanderous mirage has me tarrying in my rooms, not out of bibulousness or lust, but owing to guilt. It would make me the ultimate author of the assassination, you see, but authors of assassinations are unlike authors of books and plays, in that they are not eager to see their work in public form. And so, by this theory, I was late in going to Lincoln's side and eager to leave it for the same reason Cain wished to change the subject when the Lord broached the question of Abel's whereabouts. Now, I admit this theory is more interesting to hear than either of the other two, and I further admit I might enjoy it better than the others, except I happen to be its subject, so consequently I like it the least.

"But Stanton does not lack originality in repeating these oft-told tales, for in combining the three of them into one, he has created his own singular version, which is much more diverting, if less believable. According to the revised Stanton version of Ugly Writ, I saw to the arrangements I needed to steal the White House through the murder of its occupant, then went back to my rooms where I held a little victory celebration in my bed with a bottle and a wench. Why, gentlemen, I say that story is positively Homeric in its design. And, like Homer's tales, Stanton's is completely mythological.

"I dislike to spoil a good story, but I fear the truth of the matter is much more pallid than the myth. It is not so widely known as the myth, as it hasn't been repeated near as often, but it is not my exclusive property, and may be had by anyone taking the trouble to discuss the event with those who were present in the Kirkwood House that night, especially Governor Farwell. It was Farwell, you see, who brought me the sorry news, and it was Farwell who remained with me that night.

"It is true that I retired early that night, but my reasons are much less interesting than those heard amongst the theories. I had recently recovered from a case of typhoid fever, which, as is well known, I had suffered while in Nashville. The illness left me weakened for several months, during which time it was often my habit to take to my bed early, when the day's events had exhausted my strength. I needed no bottle to put me to bed, and had there been a woman beneath the linen, I should have been unable to do anything about it but snore at her.

"Governor Farwell came to my door and awakened me. He has said it needed ten minutes, not thirty, but if 'a half-hour's hammering' lends color to Stanton's tale, I'll let it stand. I don't know how long Farwell was at it, as I was asleep. I incline to believe Farwell over Stanton. I think I would do so even if Stanton had been doing the knocking and Farwell doing the telling, rather than the other way about, but, as I say, I'll let it pass.

"I believe Farwell says he found me alone when I finally opened the door and let him inside. After I heard the unhappy news I busied myself putting on my clothing, so I can't say if Farwell searched in the cupboards and under the bed for any sign of a bottle or a wench, but I doubt that he did, for Farwell is not Stanton. In any case, Farwell says he found me sober and alone.

"It is true, as Stanton says, I did not come to the house where President Lincoln lay dying until some hours after Farwell's arrival at my rooms. It was my wish to go there immediately, but Farwell counseled otherwise. He had chanced to be in Ford's Theater when the shot was fired, and, on learning its meaning, came immediately to alert me, for he feared the murder was part of a larger plot, and that I might be another intended victim. As the Military Commission concluded, he was right, and I was saved from sharing Lincoln's fate when the assassin Atzerodt lost his nerve.

"To his credit, Mr. Stanton had the same concern, and he sent Major O'Beirne to the Kirkwood House to see to matters there. At length I resolved that O'Beirne and Farwell were guard enough, and, in their company, I betook myself to the place where the President reposed. There I found Stanton and several of his assistants in the parlor interviewing witnesses, taking testimony, and otherwise engaged in locking up the barn after the horse had gotten out. In a back bedroom, I found the President, insensible, and in the hands of more physicians than I would have believed could be found in Washington City. They seemed unanimous in their prognosis that the President would neither regain his awareness nor survive the night.

"I began my bedside vigil, but was shortly informed that there was one who found my presence in the house odious. I should not have taken the news to heart, except that the one who objected to me was Mrs. Lincoln (who had made it known on other occasions she was not to be found among the meager ranks of my admirers). I did not wish to add my presence to her grief, and so I departed immediately.

"If there were foreign emissaries about, waiting to present their credentials to the Head of Government, I did not see them. If there were messengers from Congress with bills needing a presidential signature before sunrise, they did not approach me. Indeed, the only official business needing immediate attention were matters that were included in the Secretary of War's responsibilities. He was responsible for preventing the assassination of government officials, for example, but he hadn't distinguished himself in that regard as of the moment in question. There remained the business of catching the assassins, and he seemed to have busied himself with it. For my part, I saw that in a few hours I would be required to assume the presidency of a Union already torn apart by war, and one whose chief executive had just been murdered. It seemed at the time that I could make myself most useful by removing myself from underfoot and going back to the Kirkwood House to get some sleep, and that is what I did.

"Mr. Stanton says I left the Government of the United States of America in his hands, and, as I look back on the event now, I must admit this was, in effect, what I did. I turned the Republic over to the exclusive control of Edwin Stanton, and even though it was only for a few hours, I am compelled to describe *that* as a 'high crime and misdemeanor.' Should the radicals add it to their Articles of Impeachment, I suppose I'll have no choice but to plead 'Guilty' and step down."

At this juncture Senator Ross was abruptly, but briefly, seized by a fit of coughing; but it seemed the President was done speaking for the moment.

"Mr. Cosgrove," inquired the Senator, "have you explored any particulars of this incident?"

"Yes, sir. I have spoken to Governor Farwell, Major O'Beirne and others present at either the Kirkwood House or President Lincoln's bedside. All the facts the President has just now stated were confirmed by them."†

"Then, unless the President or the Secretary wish to add anything to what has been thus far said, you may continue with your report."

Mr. Stanton, who had turned his back on us during the President's remarks, made no sound. Mr. Johnson shrugged and shook his head. I looked once again to my portfolio.

"There is yet another matter that demands some remark," I said, "although I fear I've found more questions regarding it than answers to match them. I refer to the protection of the person of the President, a responsibility that seems to have been that of the Secretary of War."

At this Mr. Stanton wheeled about.

"Yes!" he exclaimed, "that was my responsibility, and I have no apologies to make for the manner in which I discharged it. I protected the President from all enemies save the worst one!"

"Do you mean Booth, sir?" asked Senator Ross.

"No, sir! I mean Lincoln, himself, for he was his own worst enemy. I would have surrounded him with guards, but he would not permit it. He was reckless in his disregard for his own safety, and he ignored my frequent warnings, and forbade me to take the measures I saw his safety needed. Had he done otherwise, he would yet be alive."

"I have ample evidence to confirm what the Secretary says," I offered. "President Lincoln showed little interest in the matter of his

---

† Leonard J. Farwell, former Governor of Wisconsin, testified at the Conspiracy Trial (Pitman, pp. 151–152), that he went to Johnson's room sometime between 10:00 and 10:30 P.M., and that the Vice-President did not immediately answer his knock, but he was eventually admitted to the room. He is not specific as to how long he knocked, or who else, if anyone besides Johnson, was in the room. Farwell gave a more detailed account of the incident and the events of that night to Senator J. R. Doolittle of Wisconsin, on March 12, 1866, which generally confirms what Cosgrove reports President Johnson as having said.

Moorfield Storey, private secretary to Senator Charles Sumner of Massachusetts, confirmed, in an entry in his diary, that Johnson left Lincoln's bedside in deference to Mrs. Lincoln's feelings. (*Atlantic Monthly*, April 1930, pp. 463–465.)—M.C.

personal security, and made difficulties for Mr. Stanton and others who tried to see to his protection. Yet on the very day of his death, he seemed to alter his disposition in this regard. He made some attempt to have his guard augmented for his attendance at Ford's Theater that evening."

"That is extraordinary!" Senator Ross remarked. "Do you say he had some warning of the plot?"

"President Lincoln was often warned by many of his associates, including Secretary Stanton, that he was in physical danger. If he had some special warning on that day, I have not discerned it. I think not, however, at least not the sort of warning you mean. President Lincoln was much given to premonitions, often of a melancholy species. It is said that, shortly before his murder, he dreamt of his own death. It may be that on the day of the assassination his mood was afflicted by the memory of some such prescient vision. Mr. Crook, who guarded the President that day, recalls Mr. Lincoln remarking that there were men who would try to kill him, and they'd likely succeed."†

"This is shocking, Mr. Cosgrove!" Senator Ross exclaimed. "And you see no proof in it that the President had nothing more by way of warning than some dismal dream?"

"I do not," I replied. "I have said Mr. Lincoln requested some extra guarding for his theater visit that evening. It was denied him. Had he more substantial reasons to fear for his life, I should think he'd have insisted on having it."

"Denied him? By whom?" demanded the Senator.

"By the Secretary of War," I replied.

"That is a damnable lie!" cried Mr. Stanton.

"Perhaps, but if it is, I am not its author. I have the story from one Mr. David Bates, now of the Western Union Telegraph Company,

---

† William Crook, who was one of the four Washington Metropolitan Police officers assigned to protect Lincoln. Crook published his memoirs in 1907, in which he recalled Lincoln saying on the afternoon of April 14, 1865: "Crook, do you know, I believe there are men who want to take my life. And I have no doubt they will do it . . . Other men have been assassinated . . . I have perfect confidence in those who are around me. In every one of you men. I know no one could do it and escape alive. But if it is to be done, it is impossible to prevent it."—M.C.

but on the date in question, a War Department telegrapher. Mr. Bates recalls that during President Lincoln's visit to the telegraph office he encountered Mr. Stanton there, and asked the Secretary to assign Major Eckert to accompany him to the theater that night, making specific mention of the Major's remarkable strength, and suggesting that it would provide an added measure of safety to the outing."

"And this request was not granted?" asked the Senator.

"According to Mr. Bates, the Secretary refused it, claiming he planned some work that evening which would require Major Eckert's assistance."

"If Bates says that, he is either a liar or a lunatic!" exclaimed the Secretary.

"That is useful to know," I replied, "for he also says you urged Mr. Lincoln to forgo the theater that night because you feared it might be dangerous to his person."

"That . . . that is so," stammered the Secretary in unaccustomed confusion. "I did fear for him, and for Grant as well. I urged them both not to go there. But as to the other matter, regarding Major Eckert, I mean, I do not recall it, and I think Mr. Bates is mistaken, if that is what he, in fact, has said."†

"Perhaps a lapse of memory is the cause of the contradiction," offered Senator Ross. "It may be, Mr. Secretary, you have forgotten that detail of the incident, or perhaps Mr. Bates has in mind a thing that actually happened on some other date. Did you and Major Eckert, in fact, have work to do in the War Department that evening?"

"No," replied Mr. Stanton. "I positively recall otherwise. I spent that evening with Secretary Seward at his home, where he was recovering from his misadventure.‡ Of course, I had departed before the heinous attempt to murder him was made. I do not recall assigning

---

† David Homer Bates recounted both the Eckert matter and Stanton's admonition to Lincoln and Grant in his memoirs (pp. 366–367). Stanton's warning to Lincoln and Grant to avoid the theater was confirmed by Captain Samuel H. Beckwith (New York *Sun,* April 27, 1913), who also was present on the occasion. However, Captain Beckwith makes no mention of Lincoln's request for Eckert's protection.—M.C.

‡ A carriage accident.—M.C.

any extra work to Major Eckert, and I do not think he worked late that night, but I cannot say with certainty."

I knew that what the Secretary said of his whereabouts and that of Major Eckert was so, but this intelligence rendered Mr. Bates' report just so much more damning, if it could be relied upon. I reflected that Mr. Stanton should have removed himself from any suspicion of complicity (and, perhaps, from this world, as well) had he tarried longer at Mr. Seward's house and been present when Lewis Paine came to the door armed with knife and pistol. But such speculations were doubtless obvious to Senator Ross, and added nothing to our knowledge of the issues, in any case, hence I denied them my voice.

"Very well," said the Senator. "But what of the President's protection at the theater? Surely he did not go there unguarded."

"He did not," I said. "He was guarded at Ford's Theater by a constable of the Washington Police, armed with a .38 Colt's revolver."

"Indeed," remarked the Senator. "And was this fellow overwhelmed by the assassin?"

"No, there was no need of it. The guard was absent from his post when Booth entered the President's box. Where he may have been, I do not know. He was seen some time earlier taking a drink in the saloon next to the theater."

"Yes," said the Senator, "I remember hearing of it, now. It was a disgraceful dereliction, but I had forgotten it. The tragedy itself eclipsed my recollection."

"Then you've likely never heard the particulars of the matter," I suggested. "They are remarkable and may bear some significance to the issues we consider. You see, the guard, John F. Parker by name, had, long before the assassination, proven himself unsuited to the position of constable, let alone the responsibility of guarding the President of the United States.

"Parker joined the Metropolitan Police in 1862. From thence, until the time of the tragedy, he had been brought before the Police Board some half-dozen times on such charges as conduct unbecoming an officer, insubordination, sleeping while on duty, and using insulting language to a lady, among other things. He was twice reprimanded."

"But, that is deplorable!" exclaimed Senator Ross. "How was it such a man was entrusted with so grave a responsibility?"

"I do not know," I replied. "There seems to be something of a mystery about it. Curiously, he was borrowed from the ranks of the constabulary and sent to guard at the White House less than a month before the assassination."

"That seems passing strange," remarked the Senator. "Was he questioned to learn if he was in league with Booth?"

"He was not," I said.

"That is lamentable," observed Senator Ross. "Now we shall not know. Tell me, was he hanged, or was he shot?"

"He was not hanged," I replied. "If he was shot, he seems to have recovered fully from the wound, for he yet serves today as a constable in the Washington Police Department."

· 27 ·

Secretary Stanton in the Dock

····———◆———····

"The guard who deserted his post in Ford's Theater and so permitted the assassination of President Lincoln was not punished in any way?" demanded Senator Ross.

"He was brought up before the Police Board on charges of neglecting his duty by Superintendent Richards, himself. However, the complaint was somehow dismissed. Constable Parker seems to lead a charmed life, for he was brought up again that same year on a lesser infraction, yet he has never been discharged from the Police Department, much less punished for his neglect of the President's safety."

"And what has Superintendent Richards to say of his man Parker?" inquired the Senator.

"Very little," I replied. "He declines to discuss the matter with me, except to say Parker shall be discharged presently."

"'Presently'?" repeated Senator Ross. "He is not more specific than that?"

I withdrew a sheet from my portfolio and quoted from it:

"'Constable Parker shall be discharged after Secretary Stanton has been fully and finally removed from the War Department.' That is all Superintendent Richards will offer regarding the subject."†

---

† This is more than Richards has offered history. In fact, he seems never to have addressed the matter for historical record. However, the records of the Washington Metropolitan Police show that Richards had Parker brought up on the charge, which was dismissed for unspecified reasons on May 3, 1865. Eisenschiml speculated that Parker was protected by Stanton or some other high official, but didn't prove it.—M.C.

Senator Ross turned to Mr. Stanton.

"Mr. Secretary," he demanded, "is this man Parker under your protection?"

"He is not!" replied the Secretary indignantly. "I know nothing of the matter."

The Senator regarded Mr. Stanton in silence for a long moment.

"Would there were time enough to bring both of them, Parker and Richards, before the Senate," he finally said. "I'd see to it we'd get a better answer than the one Mr. Cosgrove has been given. Regrettably, the only answers of any use to me are those that can be had tonight.†

"In candor," added the Senator, "I must confess Mr. Richards disappoints me. I had thought better of the man than to expect him to obscure so important a matter."

---

† Constable John Parker's involvement in the conspiracy must remain an open question. His disgraceful career with the Washington Police is a matter of historical record. It was examined at length by Eisenschiml, who discovered a remarkable document bearing on the matter during his research in the 1930s. It was a letter, apparently assigning Parker to the White House guard, and dated April 3, 1865, just eleven days before the assassination. *It was signed by Mrs. Lincoln!* Thus, a generation of historians has believed the guard whose dereliction of duty cost Lincoln his life was put in the position to do so by none other than the President's wife. Some have read exquisite irony in this, while others have found darker meanings. However, it happens to be untrue, and we must thank the diligent research of James O. Hall for setting the record straight.

Hall discovered evidence that Parker had been assigned to the White House in March, and that Mrs. Lincoln's letter of April 3rd was intended only to keep him from being drafted back into the Army (in which he had originally enlisted in 1861) and sent into combat. Hall takes most of the same information Eisenschiml had, adds some interesting additional data discovered in his own research, and presents a plausible, if speculative, defense of Parker (The Maryland *Independent,* July 19 and July 26, 1978).

Eisenschiml says Parker was eventually discharged for "gross neglect of duty," and cites Washington Metropolitan Police Department records. Hall reports he has been unable to find record of the dismissal, but that he did locate another record which shows that Parker went A.W.O.L. from the police department and, apparently, did not return to it. The A.W.O.L. report bears the same date as the dismissal report Eisenschiml mentions: August 13, 1868. So, whether Officer Parker quit or was fired, it happened, as Superintendent Richards predicted to Cosgrove, shortly after Edwin Stanton finally departed the War Department on May 26, 1868.—M.C.

"Superintendent Richards is close-mouthed only in the matter of Parker," I offered. "In sundry other issues of interest to us he has been much forthcoming."

"Oh? Then please share his advice with us," said Senator Ross.

"Mr. Richards chanced to be among the audience at Ford's Theater that night," I said. "He saw the assassin leap to the stage, and recognized him to be John Wilkes Booth. He went immediately to the police station and within the hour had interviewed sixteen witnesses who confirmed that it was Booth."

"Well, it was hardly a secret," interjected the President. "Word that it was Booth who had done the deed reached the Kirkwood House almost on the heels of Governor Farwell. I do not recall now, but Farwell may have brought the news with him. At all events, it was known there before eleven o'clock, so I imagine Booth's name was abroad in every part of Washington City by midnight."

"One might so imagine," I agreed. "Yet there was a place in Washington City where, to judge from some appearances, one might have thought it a secret. I mean the room in the house across from Ford's where the Secretary of War directed the assassins' pursuit."

"What is this, now?" demanded Mr. Stanton.

I resorted once again to my portfolio, withdrawing another paper from it.

"Here is a *verbatim* copy of another dispatch sent by the Secretary to General Dix on the night in question. It was sent before the one I have recently quoted. In anticipation of your question, Mr. Secretary, it was obtained through the same means used to fetch the other one."

"No doubt it contains something darkly suspicious," observed Mr. Stanton dryly.

"No, sir. There is nothing suspicious in it. It contains only your initial notice to the General of the attacks on President Lincoln and Secretary Seward, and a summary of the situation of affairs as of the moment you penned it, which is noted on the message as 1:30 A.M. The remarkable thing is not what is contained in the message, but what has been omitted. The only significant particular you failed to include was the name of the assassin. You will not find the name of John Wilkes Booth in the dispatch."

"Well, then, it was an oversight," the Secretary said. "I knew very well it was Booth by half-past one that morning. I must have omitted mention of it in my haste to get on with other matters. Gentlemen, you must understand I was occupied with a hundred things at that moment."

"Yes," I agreed, "such as the taking of testimony from witnesses. Corporal Tanner told me he recorded enough evidence within fifteen minutes of his arrival in the room to hang Booth several times over."†

"Well, there you have it," Mr. Stanton said. "I knew very well it was Booth, as did Tanner, and all others about the place. I made no secret of it."

"Then," I inquired, "as of 1:30 in the morning, there was no doubt in your mind Booth was the assassin?"

"No, no, of course not!" Mr. Stanton replied. "No doubt whatever about it."

"Then permit me to read from yet a third of your dispatches to General Dix, this one written at three o'clock that morning:

"'Investigation strongly indicates J. Wilkes Booth as the assassin of the President.'

"Now, Mr. Secretary," I said, "I beg your pardon if I misconstrue the meaning of your words, but the phrase 'strongly indicates' suggest to me something less than utter certainty that Booth was the assassin. Can you explain why you put it quite that way?"

"I suppose I put it that way," Mr. Stanton replied, "out of professional habit. As you gentlemen very well know, I am, by training and experience, a lawyer. In law, a man is presumed to be innocent unless and until he has been proved otherwise in a court of law."

---

† Corporal James Tanner lost both of his legs at the Second Battle of Bull Run, and thereafter became a stenographer in the War Department's Ordinance Bureau (he managed to walk on artificial legs). At the time of the assassination he was living in the Peterson rooming house, the house across the street from Ford's Theater to which the dying President was taken, and where Stanton set up his temporary command post that night. Thus, he happened to be available to assist Stanton in recording interviews with witnesses, and other clerical duties. Tanner's statement quoted by Cosgrove is substantially the same as one he made in a letter written shortly after the assassination, and is well known to students of the assassination.—M.C.

"But, Mr. Secretary," objected Senator Ross, "you were not pronouncing a sentence; you were merely constructing one. I confess I share Mr. Cosgrove's puzzlement at the tentativeness of your tone."

"There is nothing puzzling about it," replied the Secretary. "The tentativeness suited the occasion. Very well, there were sundry persons who had been at Ford's and said they recognized the assassin to be Booth. Yet, for all I knew at that moment, there were twice the number waiting to tell me they too had seen the killer, and he was not Booth, but some other person. Gentlemen, I have been in far too many courtrooms to place an absolute reliance on the eyes of one witness, or even a score of them. No, my words were appropriate. There were strong indications the assassin was Booth. To have said more at that hour would have been to say too much."

"But 'that hour' was near five hours after the shot was fired," I said. "Granted, a throng of theatergoers might have been mistaken in their belief they had seen a famous actor leap from the President's box, proclaim his crime to the house from before the footlights, and flee the scene. Granted even that they could all have made the same mistake and shared a unanimity of error. Granted that the Superintendent of Police of Washington City could have mistaken some other one for Booth. Yet among the sixteen witnesses who came to the Superintendent within an hour and confirmed that the crime was done by John Wilkes Booth was the same actor who shared the stage with the assassin for that terrible moment, an actor who had oft trod the same boards as Booth in happier performances.† He stood on Ford's stage no farther from the assassin than I stand here from yourself, and he knew Booth's countenance with a greater familiarity than even the most ardent patron of the theater. He went immediately to Superintendent Richards, and Mr. Richards had soon conveyed the assassin's identity to General Auger, and Gen-

---

† The actor was Harry Hawk, who, in the role of "Asa Trenchard" in *Our American Cousin,* was alone on the stage delivering a monologue when Booth shot Lincoln. There were many others offstage who recognized the assassin as John Wilkes Booth, and they promptly made that fact known to the authorities.—M.C.

eral Auger, I surely need not remind you, was at your side at least a dozen times between the hours of midnight and three o'clock."

"As were a score of others," rejoined Mr. Stanton. "If General Auger conveyed this matter of the actor having named Booth, it escapes my recollection now as it likely escaped my attention then. I stand by what I have said: There were strong indications the murderer was Booth at the hour I sent the dispatch; if there was proof beyond doubt, it was not known to me."

"I can't let that go by," interjected President Johnson. "Stanton, just two or three minutes ago you told us there was no doubt whatever in your mind that night the assassin was John Wilkes Booth. But now you've changed your story and claim there was room for some doubt about it. Well, which way do you want to have it? Or do you want to have it both ways?"

"You know very well the intent of my words, sir!" retorted the Secretary, his fists now rapidly closing and opening as he spoke. "Even the most ignorant of scoundrels discovers the legal meaning of *reasonable doubt* when he finds himself in the dock, and the guiltier he is, the better he grasps the idea. It cannot have escaped your own attention, granted your present circumstances."

"I beg your pardon, Mr. Secretary," I offered in a conciliatory way. "It is surely a credit to your fairness of spirit that you did not fail to remember Booth's legal presumption of innocence at that late hour, when all about you had already judged the man."

"I do not require your approval, Cosgrove," snapped Mr. Stanton. "But whether you offer your comment honestly or in some spirit of Irish irony, I am proud to say you happen, in this instance, to be correct."

"Oh, sir," I said, "I assure you my admiration for your equitable disposition on that hectic occasion is as sincere as you claim to have enjoyed it. But I assume that sometime between three o'clock of that melancholy morning and this present moment you became absolutely convinced beyond peradventure of a doubt (even a reasonable one) that the assassin was, in fact, John Wilkes Booth. I wonder if you might tell us just when it was you were so persuaded, and share with us whatever item of intelligence was at the base of your conviction."

Mr. Stanton did not reply to this, but, instead, transfixed me for a long moment with a stony and lethal glare. Then he turned to Senator Ross and addressed him.

"Sir, it seems I am to be examined and cross-examined regarding every word I have ever uttered or written. Your Mr. Cosgrove's portfolio looks to be fairly bursting with purloined papers and other miscellaneous items, all doubtlessly intended to trap me into some sort of contradiction. I fail to comprehend the great significance that seems to attach to the matter of when and why I concluded John Wilkes Booth was the assassin. But, granting that it may hold some significance in Mr. Cosgrove's mind, I assure you I can answer his question. Yet I am equally certain he will then reach into his portfolio and we shall spend some further time examining some other minute particle, and after we had done with *that,* he will have another, and yet another, until the sun has not only risen, but crossed the sky and set beyond the Potomac."

"Mr. Cosgrove?" inquired the Senator.

"I fear the Secretary is correct," I replied. "I was summoned from my inquiries before they were complete, and so, alas, have returned to you with more questions than answers."

Senator Ross took his watch from his frock coat and consulted it.

"It is near to midnight," he said "Even were the Secretary willing to indulge us, I am afraid I could not avail myself of his generosity. It would be unseemly to answer with a snore when my name is called in the Senate chamber during tomorrow's voting. You say you have brought me both answers and questions unanswered, Mr. Cosgrove. I think there will not be time enough tonight for you to make a detailed recountment of your inquiries. Can you, instead, in the way of a summation, tell us more generally that which you have learned and that which remains mysterious?"

"I can promise to attempt it," I responded, "but I should not be surprised if one of your distinguished guests (perhaps both of them) demands frequent halts in the recitation to enter his answers to some questions which are, perforce, implied in my report, whether or not they are particularly framed."

"Mr President, Mr. Secretary," said Senator Ross, "may I ask your indulgence to permit Mr. Cosgrove to complete his report uninterrupted, in consideration of the hour? Of course, when he has finished I should welcome whatever responses you wish to make."

"I'm content with that," declared the President.

"I suppose I must tolerate whatever promises to bring this wretched and outrageous business to a speedy conclusion," said the Secretary.

"Thank you, gentlemen," said the Senator. "Mr. Cosgrove, please tell us what you have learned."

"Very well," I said. "The Secretary wonders why so much importance attaches to the omission of the assassin's name from his dispatches during the five hours that followed the crime, and to the tentative manner in which Booth's name was sent abroad even at that late hour. It is important because a telegraphic dispatch travels more swiftly than the swiftest mount, and it is yet faster than a ball from a rifle or a cannon. A murderer fleeing the scene of his crime may hope to outpace his pursuers if he is on the back of a faster horse. Given a lead of a minute or two, he may also hope to betake himself beyond the range of his pursuers' firearms. But there is no animal so fleet it can outdistance a telegraphic dispatch. The fugitive can only rely that, through luck or design, no dispatch is sent until sufficient time has passed for him to put many miles between himself and those places where the telegraph lines go. Booth seems to have enjoyed such advantage, at least to the extent that the Secretary of War omitted his name from any telegraphic dispatch while he galloped off through the Maryland countryside. It may have been nothing more than a piece of luck, but, if that is so, it was but a solitary example of a wonderful series of lucky strokes, all of which together insured the assassin would make good his escape.

"Had the Secretary composed a dispatch naming Booth as the assassin immediately after the crime, it would not have gone abroad until after midnight, for, by another strange whim of Fortune favoring the assassin, all telegraphic lines leading from Washington City ceased functioning for some several hours after the murder, after which time they resumed service in an equally mysterious fashion, which none has since been able to explain.†

"But Dame Fortune did not then retire for the night," I continued. "No, she had yet more favors to bestow upon the handsome fugitive."

I withdrew from my portfolio a map of those parts of Maryland and Virginia which touch upon the District of Columbia, and rolled it out atop one of Miss Ream's work tables, where the lantern light permitted its principal features to be discerned.

"Consider, if you will, gentlemen, the formidable task which faced the Secretary and his Department during the frantic hours of that long night when the President lay dying. The murderer, and the man who assaulted Mr. Seward, together with whatever accomplices they employed, should not be expected to tarry near the place of the crime, or to betake themselves from it at a leisurely pace.

---

† One contemporary writer has it that "at precisely ten minutes past ten there were twenty-two wires leading from the War Office in different directions, and connecting with the fortifications and outposts cut. These wires having been cut at a considerable distance from each other, together with the simultaneousness of this work, shows very plainly that a number of men were engaged in it . . ." (Hawley, p. 63). However, Major Thomas T. Eckert, Stanton's chief telegrapher (of whom more later), told the House impeachment investigation that only the commercial telegraph lines between Washington and Baltimore were interrupted, and that the War Department lines remained functioning (*Impeachment Investigation,* p. 673). A note in the official records made by assistant adjutant General R. Williams puts the time of interruption at 11:45 P.M., about thirty minutes after the assassination. Present-day researcher James O. Hall has confirmed that the War Department lines were working, and Booth's name was sent to the military outposts surrounding Washington. Thus Cosgrove seems to have overstated the situation. Nonetheless, the fact remains that, during a period of an hour or more immediately following the assassination, no one outside of the War Department was in a position to telegraph word of the assassination, let alone the identity of the assassin, to any point north of Washington. Exactly how much this interruption might have aided Booth's escape, if at all, is a matter of conjecture. However, in his testimony before the House Impeachment Investigation Committee, Major Eckert claimed he didn't know the cause of this mysterious malfunction, and admitted he hadn't taken the trouble to investigate it and try to learn whether it was deliberate sabotage carried out by the assassination conspirators. In view of the irrelevant minutia which were dug up and examined by the War Department in buiding its case for the Conspiracy Trial, *that* omission now seems more significant than the telegraphic interruption itself.—M.C.

Rather, one would know that guilt and a full conception of the monstrous work they had accomplished would rowel them into flight from Washington City and its vicinage, not to rest until many miles separated them from the scene of their actions. But in which quarter of the compass rose might they be sought? While the Government gathered its wits together and dealt with such misadventures as broken telegraph lines, the murderers had ample time to make good their escape, whatever the directions they chose. Let us examine the manner in which the War Department arose to that occasion. It is a marvelous thing to regard, for I believe it must have been the greatest manhunt in all History, and, but for one small lapse, it offers no cause for rebuke.

"Before 11:30, little more than an hour after the shot was fired, Colonel Thompson at Darnestown had three squads abroad, scouring the roads leading to Tenellytown, Barnesville and Frederick. Thus, all avenues of escape into Maryland northwest of Washington City had been blocked.

"By midnight, General Slough in Alexandria had taken measures that none could leave that city, and the stationmaster there had been alerted that the assassins might be headed toward his premises. Shortly thereafter, General Gamble had dispatched his troops to search the roads from Washington City to Leesburg, and Major Waite of the Eighth Illinois Cavalry at Fairfax Court House had his instructions to arrest anyone who attempted to pass his lines. Thus, escape across the Potomac into Virginia had been rendered impossible, and the alarum had been sounded at such distant points as Winchester, Cumberland and Harper's Ferry.

"By 3:00 A.M. General Morris had posted guards at every avenue leading to Baltimore, and would permit no trains or ships to leave that city. Three trains of cars were halted at Relay† and were not permitted to pass until they had been searched. For some days thereafter all trains leaving Washington for Baltimore carried a contingent of one officer and ten men, who searched the cars after every stop along the way.

---

† A railroad junction just south of Baltimore.—M.C.

"Had the murderers taken to the water? It would have done them no good. Before midnight Commander Parker had received his orders at Saint Inigoes, and no ship could pass down the Potomac. Word had also been sent to Point Lookout to stop all ships and hold their passengers, and no vessel could leave the port of Annapolis. Presently, the whole of the Atlantic coast from Baltimore to Hampton Roads had been blockaded.†

"Now, gentlemen, you may find such efficiency to be amazing, for, as you can see, it was no simple task to wrap this enormous region in so tight a net, even granted the resources of the Army and the Navy, and we should not be astonished if, through some momentary oversight, a tiny opening were left in it. But you may find it astonishing that this insignificant rent in the otherwise perfect surroundry of the city chanced to be the very one and the same to which infatuated Fortune guided the fugitives' feet.

"Here it is, the Navy Yard Bridge. Booth crossed it within minutes after his departure from Ford's, and made his way into southeastern Maryland along the road to Surrattsville. Some moments later he was followed by his accomplice, David Herold. Both were passed by the soldiers guarding the span who, it can be understood, had heard nothing of the murder at that early hour. Did none pursue them? One man did, but he, like the bridge guards, knew nothing of what had taken place at Ford's. He was a hosteller, in charge of the mount Herold was riding, and gave chase to capture the animal, not the fellow on its back. But the sentries at the bridge seemed to judge enough traffic had crossed that night, and the stableman, one John Fletcher, was turned back. Doubtless the hand of Fortune once more, and none who know the capricious ways of noncommissioned officers will read anything sinister in *that* stroke of luck.

"No, the curious thing about this incident is not what took place, but what failed to take place. When, after many hours had elapsed, some person in the War Department remembered the Navy Yard Bridge and the hundreds of square miles of southeastern Maryland

---

† All of the precautions Cosgrove describes are supported by the Official Records of the War Department.—M.C.

that could be found on its farther end, and a squad of troopers was dispatched in that direction, they did not pause to inquire of the span's guardians whether any who might resemble those they sought had preceded them. Sergeant Cobb,† who was doubtless by that hour snoozing in his barracks, might have been some use to them in this, for he had asked the first of the travelers who passed to give his name. And the assassin must have known Fortune was riding with him, for he did not offer a "Smith" or a "Jones," but informed the Sergeant in clear and even tones that his name was Booth.

"Now, I'll grant you not every officer would have the courage to awaken a sergeant at four o'clock in the morning and annoy him with questions regarding the assassination of the President of the United States, and I'll further admit that the officer in charge of this squad was a mere lieutenant. Still, he might have been judged capable of such affront, for he was not an ordinary lieutenant; he chanced to be the younger brother of Mr. Charles A. Dana, who was then Mr. Stanton's able Assistant Secretary of War. But Fortune made him too humble to recall that relationship, and so Lieutenant Dana led his squad into the Maryland countryside unaware that he was hot on the trail of John Wilkes Booth. In fact, Lieutenant Dana believed he left Booth behind him in Washington City, for this is what he told one prominent citizen of Bryantown on Saturday morning, a citizen by the name of Dr. Mudd."

"Dr. Samuel Mudd?" exclaimed Senator Ross.

"No, his cousin, Dr. George Mudd," I replied, "who was well known and unpopular in the region for his Union sympathies. I might note that Dr. Samuel Mudd, who was accused and convicted of taking part in the conspiracy by reason of his bandaging Booth's broken leg, conveyed the fact that he had been visited by a pair who might be Booth and Herold to Lieutenant Dana through the intermediary of his cousin, but, as I say, Lieutenant Dana was convinced Booth was yet in Washington City and so did not act on the intelligence he had been given for some days. It is a puzzlement to me why Dr. Samuel

---

† Silas T. Cobb, who commanded the guards at the Navy Yard Bridge on the evening of April 14, 1865.—M.C.

Mudd is in a prison cell today, while Lieutenant Dana is not, but that is one of the lesser prodigies of the affair I shall eschew, as I promised, in consideration of the hour.†

"Permit me, instead, to return to John Fletcher, the hosteller, for it is in his career after being refused the Navy Yard Bridge that we may read more of the gifts Dame Fortune bestowed upon her favorite that night.

"Mr. Fletcher was the foreman of T. Nailor's Stables on E Street, where David Herold and another conspirator, George Atzerodt, took their custom. On the afternoon of the day of the assassination, Herold hired a horse from Fletcher, with the stipulation he would return it to the stable no later than nine o'clock that night. But that hour came and went without bringing Herold and the mount back to the stable.

"The hosteller went abroad in the city in search of his employer's animal and his perfidious patron. At twenty-five minutes past ten o'clock, he sighted man and horse on Pennsylvania Avenue, near Willard's Hotel. When Mr. Fletcher hailed Herold, demanding the return of the mount, the young man spurred the animal and galloped off northward along 14th Street. The hosteller, who was afoot, returned to the stables, which were nearby, close upon 13½ Street, and drew a mount of his own to carry him in pursuit. He questioned a passerby and discovered that Herold and the horse were last seen making haste in the direction of the Navy Yard Bridge. Fletcher went there, and, as I said, was turned back by the sentries.

"Now all this was given by Mr. Fletcher at the Conspiracy Trial and may be found in Pitman's excellent record of those proceedings.‡ But, curiously, Mr. Pitman truncated Fletcher's testimony, and so omitted some of its most interesting particulars. These may be found in the full transcript of the trial.§ Foremost among these obscured details is the fact that, after returning to the stables from the Navy Yard Bridge and then learning of the assassination, Mr. Fletcher be-

---

† Cosgrove's references to Sergeant Cobb, the scene at the Navy Yard Bridge, and the Cousins Mudd are supported by testimony of Cobb and George Mudd given at the Conspiracy Trial. (Pitman, pp. 84–85, 206)—M.C.

‡ Pitman, pp. 83–84.—M.C.

§ Poore, Vol. I, pp. 326–341.—M.C.

thought himself that Herold might be murderer as well as horse-thief, and promptly took his suspicions to the Police Headquarters. From there he was escorted by a city detective to General Auger, to whom Mr. Fletcher recounted the incident again, including such particulars as Herold's name, and a detailed description of both horse and rider.

"Now as to why Mr. Pitman chose to excise these matters from his estimable book, I cannot say.† They can be found, as I said, in the trial transcript by any who cares to read it, and they can be verified by Superintendent Richards. Mr. Richards recalls the incident with great clarity, you see, for, although General Auger seems to have failed to perceive the meaning of Mr. Fletcher's report, the Superintendent of Police read it correctly. In fact, Superintendent Richards immediately applied to General Auger for horses to mount his constables in pursuit across the Navy Yard Bridge. Unaccountably, the request was not granted.‡ Once again, Booth was in debt to Fortune.

"But Superintendent Richards was not the only one to propose leading a squad across the Navy Yard Bridge that night. Major Gleason was yet another. The Major, you will recall, was the associate to whom Mr. Weichmann confided his knowledge of Booth's plans to kidnap President Lincoln some months earlier. This confidence included such

---

† Cosgrove must have had his suspicions. The suppression of the important segment of Fletcher's testimony is only one instance in which Pitman omitted, or even altered, details in the Conspiracy Trial testimony that would have proved an embarrassment to the War Department, which had commissioned his book. Eisenschiml examines Pitman's cosmetic touches at some length in both *Why Was Lincoln Murdered?*, and *In the Shadow of Lincoln's Death.* That Cosgrove did not pursue Pitman may seem strange to the reader who has no experience with the mechanics of a classic government cover-up. Pitman probably had no real knowledge of the true extent of the assassination conspiracy, and lacked any interest in acquiring such. He probably knew little more than on which side his bread was buttered, and was disinclined to be curious about such things. Pitman's species possesses powerful survival characteristics, and many examples of it can be found today, especially in and around Washington, D.C., and other camps of the federal government.—M.C.

‡ There is no official record of Richards' request, but the incident is recounted in Oldroyd, p. 64. Oldroyd, who is not a revisionist historian, wrote one of the accepted standard works on the Lincoln assassination, based, in part, on interviews with many of the surviving witnesses.—M.C.

details as the route the abductors planned to follow, which was, in its general outline, the same route Booth and Herold followed when they crossed into Maryland that night.

"Shortly after the assassination, Major Gleason went to General Auger and proposed to lead a mounted troop to Surrattsville, informing the General of his reasons for believing Booth could be found there, which, indeed, at that very moment, was where he was. But, strangely, the Major's plan was also refused, and the murderer and his accomplice rode unmolested to the Surratt Tavern and beyond.†

"We see then, that, although a single tiny gap had been left in the otherwise airtight seal constructed with such alacrity by the War Department, General Auger, and one might presume Secretary Stanton, as well, had been twice reminded at an early hour that such a gap existed, and it seems passing curious they refused to venture a few troopers to go to that southeastern quarter and insure the murderers had not made use of it in their flight. And the gap itself becomes more remarkable when we recall that it coincided with the planned abduction route, which had been discovered some months before by Mr. Weichmann and conveyed by Major Gleason to some senior officers in the War Department, if not to the Secretary himself. But, gentlemen, the omission becomes positively astounding when viewed in light of the fact that the assassin's escape route was one frequently employed by Confederate agents, *and known to the War Department at least three months before the assassination.* I can scarcely believe it, myself, and would not ask you gentlemen to do so, had I not proof in the form of a copy of a secret dispatch sent to Washington in January, 1865, by the United States counsel at Toronto, who, it appears, had learned of this "underground railroad" which was then in use by Rebel couriers between Richmond and Canada.‡ I have the copy here for your inspection. The original can be found locked away in a safe in the War Department building.

---

† D. H. L. Gleason confirmed what he had apparently confided to Cosgrove in his February, 1911, memoir.—M.C.

‡ The dispatch of which Cosgrove speaks can be found in the War Department records, and a portion of its text appears in Eisenschiml, *Why Was Lincoln Murdered?*, p. 99.—M.C.

"So, there, gentlemen, are some of the favors Dame Fortune showered upon Booth and his cohort that night. I have omitted pressing a full list upon you, for it would take even longer, but what I have told you, I think, serves to demonstrate her affection for the murderers."

"Let us speak plainly, Mr. Cosgrove," said Senator Ross. "It is clear these things did not happen by chance, and your argument is not against Fortune, but is an accusation that Secretary Stanton wished Booth to make good his escape."

"No, sir," I replied, "I do not make that accusation. In fact, I believe quite the contrary."

"How can that be?" exclaimed the Senator. "Everything you have told me seems to implicate either Mr. Stanton or his closest lieutenants in the War Department in a conspiracy to aid Booth in getting away scot-free."

"I have no doubt," I replied carefully, "that such was not Mr. Stanton's desire, and, in fact, were Booth alive today, the Secretary would make a genuine effort to see he was tracked down. I would state my reasons for thinking so, but I am bound to silence by a professional confidence."

"I release you from it," proclaimed Secretary Stanton.

"Thank you, sir," I replied. "Senator, what I have just now said, I have said with certainty, for I have recently labored on behalf of the Secretary in this very matter. You see, it happens that Booth *is* alive, and he is still at large."

The Senator was thunderstruck.

"Alive? Still at large, you say? Where is he hiding?"

"That I do not know, nor does the Secretary, although he engaged Pinkerton's to learn the answer, and I labored in equal earnest to discover it. Booth was harbored by a Rebel in King George County, and was last seen carried down the Potomac on a lugger some days after the crime. Where he ventured from there, I did not learn."

"Speak the whole truth, Cosgrove!" demanded the Secretary. "Stay! I shall do it for you: Our secret detective has omitted mention of what he learned regarding the means Booth used to procure this vessel. It was sent by the assassin's accomplice in response to a message from the assassin. And we learned the name of that accomplice. It is the name of this same criminal who stands here in our company at this very instant!"

"I presume I'm the intended beneficiary of that encomium," remarked President Johnson, dryly.

"Booth entrusted two messages to Herold's hand when they parted," I admitted. "One of them seems to have been a telegram addressed to 'A. Johnson.' I have been unable to discover more of that matter, but I need not point out that the President shares his surname with likely tens of thousands of our countrymen. I have no evidence that the dispatch was intended for him."

"Except," insisted the Secretary, "that the assassin was in communication with Mr. Johnson on the afternoon of the very day of his crime."

"That is another riddle I have as yet been unable to solve," I allowed.

"Really?" exclaimed the President. "You surprise me, Mr. Cosgrove. I should have thought you'd have long since learned the truth behind that famous slander. Booth was never in communication with me at any time. What is more, there is no reason even to suppose he tried to see me, on the day of the assassination, or at any other time."

"No," sneered the Secretary. "Not a thing, besides sworn testimony and the assassin's own handwriting."

"Go and read that sworn testimony!" demanded President Johnson.

"Gentlemen, please!" implored Senator Ross. "I scarcely have time to consider the new disclosures that have been brought to my attention, so I beg you to hold your peace of such familiar stuff as Booth's visit to the Kirkwood House.

"Mr. Cosgrove, you are as good as your word. You promised me more new questions than answers to old ones, and none can say you defaulted. But you know the one great question that is foremost in my mind tonight. Willy-nilly, I must take some sort of answer to it along with me when I go to the Senate Chamber tomorrow. Have you nothing to offer that might abet me in the hazardous task of making my own conclusion?"

"I do not know," I replied. "My own conclusions are, at this moment, of only the most general and tentative nature."

"I would hear them, nonetheless," said the Senator.

"Very well. Both of these distinguished gentlemen have been accused of instigating the murder of President Lincoln. If either is guilty, it seems likely the other must needs be innocent, for their interests appear to be in direct opposition. They are improbable accomplices.

"Let us begin with Motive. Which had reason to want President Lincoln dead? Mr. Johnson clearly profited by the tragedy, in the ascendancy of his political fortunes. But Mr. Stanton benefited nearly as much, perhaps even more, for the murder of Mr. Lincoln removed what, at that time, was the only obstacle to the harsh policies he proposed in dealing with the defeated Rebels. No, I fear Motive is no key to Truth when a President or a King is murdered, for the number who will profit from the crime are legion, and not all can be guilty.

"Then let us consider Opportunity. Which of these two gentlemen was able to arrange the assassination? Again, we find no key, for either could have hired Booth or some other one to murder Mr. Lincoln. Indeed, there were more who had opportunity to carry out the deed than even the number who profited by it, and for this we can blame none but the victim himself. If the absence of the guard, John Parker, seems mysterious and suspicious, I must point out to you that his presence would have been equally remarkable, for it was President Lincoln's habit to disdain his personal safety and often go about unguarded. He was ever offering the opportunity for his murder to whoever wished to do it. It is entirely plausible that Booth knew nothing of a guard, and should have been surprised had he encountered Parker or any other person assigned to protect Mr. Lincoln. No, sir. Motive and Opportunity, the two most important considerations in the investigation of most crimes, do not answer in the slightest way in this case, so we must look elsewhere for the Truth."

"Perhaps we should look to neither the White House nor the War Department to find those who may have had a hand in the crime," Senator Ross offered hopefully. "For if you can assure me no blame is to be found in either of those houses, then you will have given me all the answers I require for tomorrow's business.

"I wish I could offer you such assurance," I replied, "but I cannot. Indeed, I must counsel otherwise, for while I cannot tell you particularly what it may be, I am convinced Secretary Stanton harbors some species of guilty secret bearing on the matter, and, strange as it seems, there is reason to suspect it is a secret President Johnson has helped him keep."

I had expected the Secretary to bridle at those words, but he remained silent, instead. Likewise, the President held his peace.

"What leads you to believe such things?" inquired the Senator.

"A multitude of facts," I replied, "most of which bear on the so-called Conspiracy Trial. It was called a trial, though it was nearer a court martial. Yet it was not even that. I am no lawyer, sir, but I have served as both Army officer and secret detective, and so have some experience with courts of both military and civilian authority. I do not pretend to great knowledge of such matters, but I know that the manifest purpose of any trial is the establishment of Truth. Yet it is impossible to believe this was the object of the trial of Booth's accomplices. It was not a search for Truth, but a ceremony of silence that seemed devised to obscure the Truth."

"It was an affront to Justice," agreed Senator Ross. "There are few who would dispute that, save those who cannot deny having a hand in it."

The Senator glanced at his two distinguished guests, both of whom eschewed this tacit invitation to argue the matter.

"Indeed," continued the Senator, "that the trial of the conspirators was an obscene blight upon American justice is one of the few issues on which a man can find anything like a consensus in the Congress."

"Then I shall not belabor what is widely known," I said. "Please permit me, instead, to present some particulars that are less familiar.

"If you read Mr. Pitman's book, or even the full, unexpurgated text of the trial, you will find a curious omission: of the pages and pages of testimony taken from scores of witnesses, there is not one word from any of the eight defendants. The trial began on the 10th of May and lasted into early July, and every day the accused sat in the courtroom in shackles and chains from ten o'clock in the morning until six o'clock in the evening, and not once was even one of them permitted to speak a single word in his own behalf.

"Now, this fact is no secret, for, as I said, it may be discerned by anyone troubling himself to read the proceedings, but it is obscure, nonetheless, for we now view it as an injustice, and, as such, it must compete for our indignation with a host of worse injustices that were perpetrated by those who staged this travesty of a court. The outrage is eclipsed by other outrages which are even more stunning.

"But, upon reflection, I do not think the silence enforced upon the defendants was an expedient to deny them justice, for they had no hope of finding justice in that courtroom, even had they been permitted to cry out for it. The accused were *never* permitted to speak, you see. They were mute in court, but they were mute in their cells, as well. Indeed, from the moment they were put in custody until the day four were led to the scaffold and four more were put aboard a ship bound for the most distant and inaccessible dungeon owned by the Government, the eight defendants were as dumb as though their tongues had been cut out of their heads."

"How could that be?" asked Senator Ross.

"It was accomplished through means near as cruel and hideous as the knife," I answered. "The prisoners were no sooner ironed in the anchor well of the *Saugus* when the order came to place over each of their heads a canvas bag, which was to be tied about the neck, and designed to permit breathing and eating, but to prevent vision. This was done, as I said, immediately upon their capture. Later, when time permitted elaboration of the fiendish devices, the first hoods were replaced by more ingenious models, which fitted the head more tightly, and incorporated cotton pads which pressed into the eyes and ears. These things were worn by the prisoners at all times, day and night, except in the courtroom, where they could have been an embarrassment to the Government. They were removed each morning before the prisoners were led to court, but they were replaced in the evening, immediately upon their return to their cells.

"Dr. Porter objected to these devilish things, and warned they might drive the defendants insane. His judgment was confirmed by a famous alienist, but their warning was to no avail; the hoods remained.†

"By whose orders were these devices employed?" demanded the Senator. "What reason was given for such measures?"

"By order of Secretary Stanton, on April 23, 1865," I replied, reading from a sheet I had withdrawn from my portfolio. "Their purpose was to ensure 'better security against conversation.'"‡

"The hoods were the cruelest, but not the only measure taken to prevent conversation among the defendants. No visitors were permitted them while in the Arsenal. Each was locked in a cell between two empty cells to keep him at some remove from his neighbor,§ and the sentries guarding the prisoners were assigned according to a scheme of rotation which insured the same soldier never guarded the same prisoner twice. Thus were the accused conspirators kept isolated, and blind, deaf, and consequently, dumb, during every hour of their durance."

"But that is appalling!" exclaimed Senator Ross. "Then these wretches were never permitted even one word, in or out of court, to offer in their own defense?"

"I do not think these measures were designed to prevent them from uttering words of defense," I replied. "I think they were to forestall words of accusation."

---

† The "alienist," as physicians specializing in treatment of mental disorders were then called, was Dr. John P. Gray, director of the Utica (N.Y.) Infirmary, and often an expert witness in trials in which insanity was offered as a defense. The "Dr. Porter" Cosgrove refers to is Dr. George L. Porter, who was the attending physician at the Arsenal Penitentiary and the same man Cosgrove interviewed at the Arsenal regarding the burial of the body assumed to be that of John Wilkes Booth. According to Dr. Porter's 1911 memoir, Stanton agreed to the removal of the hoods after Drs. Porter and Gray made their objections known to him, although Dr. Porter recalled that he was the only person permitted to converse with any of the prisoners without the presence of witnesses (presumably from the War Department). But according to Samuel Arnold, one of the defendants who was sentenced to prison and eventually pardoned, the hoods were *not* removed after the physicians' objections (Arnold, "The Lincoln Plot," Baltimore *American,* 1902).—M.C.

‡ The text of Stanton's order is cited in deWitt, p. 13, and was apparently based on some official record.—M.C.

§ Described in Dr. Porter's 1911 memoir.—M.C.

"Against Mr. Stanton?"

"Mr. Stanton was the inventor of the canvas head bags, and it was on his authority that the prisoners were held incommunicado. He picked the Military Commission that judged the accused, and the prosecutors were also his trusted lieutenants.† Thus, he seems to have acted as stage manager of this travesty of a trial, which had as its effect, if not its sole objective, the silencing of the eight accused, first with canvas hoods, then, for some, the soil of the Arsenal yard, and for the others, the walls of distant dungeons. Yes, I think it fair to conclude the words thus stifled were words the Secretary did not want heard. But those words could never have been stifled without the consent, nay, the active cooperation of another: President Andrew Johnson.

"It was the President, you will recall, who ordered the trial by Military Commission in the first instance, and it was the President who approved the findings of the Commission when it had finished its dirty work. And it was President Johnson who hanged Mrs. Surratt, for he had more to do with that killing than even the soldiers who put the noose about her neck and sprung the trap from beneath her feet."

"But it was the Military Commission that said she must hang," said the Senator.

"Yes, but the Commission played the role of Pontius Pilate in that matter," I replied. "It sentenced her to hang, but at the same time, it recommended her life be spared.

"Mary Surratt alone among the eight defendants was spared the head bag, yet she was as silent as the others in the dock. None thought she would be sent to the gallows, least of all the lady herself, and so she kept her peace during the trial. Indeed, on the very morning of the hanging neither she nor her jailers could believe it was to happen. The woman's daughter, Annie, had gone to the White House to beg for

---

† The government's case was presented by the Army's Judge Advocate General Joseph Holt, assisted by Colonel Henry L. Burnett and John A. Bingham, a Congressman from Ohio. All were either friends or faithful servants of Edwin Stanton.—M.C.

her mother's life, and the Army was so confident the request would not be denied that a chain of soldiers stood along the route between the presidential mansion and the prison yard, so that, if the order to spare her did not come until the eleventh hour, it would be passed in a timely way to the place of execution. But the eleventh hour brought no such word, nor did the twelfth, and when the commander of the Arsenal had delayed matters as long as he could, there was nothing left for him to do but follow the order signed by the Military Commission and endorsed by President Johnson. Mr. Johnson may yet fail to earn the dubious distinction of becoming the first President of the United States forced from office through impeachment, but he has already achieved another: he is the first to have hanged a woman, and he chanced to pick an innocent one for the occasion."

"But if she was innocent," the Senator inquired, "what dangerous knowledge did she possess?"

"That I do not know," I answered. "Perhaps it was the same knowledge possessed by others who were more guilty than she but were not hanged, nor even put in the dock."

"What is this you say?" demanded Senator Ross.

"Cosgrove!" interjected the Secretary. "Need I remind you you are under an obligation of professional confidence to me?"

"Need I remind you, sir, that you released me from that obligation only some minutes ago?" I replied.

"I did not give you the authority to tell all!" insisted Mr. Stanton.

"I beg your pardon," said President Johnson, "but I think you did. As I recall your very words, they were 'Speak the whole truth!' That is what you said, Stanton, and that is what Mr. Cosgrove must now do."

"I think the President is correct," offered Senator Ross.

Secretary Stanton glowered at each of us in turn.

"Mr. Cosgrove does not *know* the whole truth," he finally proclaimed, "and I know him to be a liar, as well. I do not propose to stand here and listen to any more of his falsehoods, half-truths and distortions. If you wish to do so, Senator Ross, that is your business. But you shall do it without me standing by."

So saying, the Secretary of War turned on his heel and strode from the Crypt.

· 28 ·

President Johnson Explains

.··⊷⟐⊷··.

"Mr. President," inquired Senator Ross, after the Secretary was gone, "will you consent to stay?"

"Consent? I insist on it, sir," replied Mr. Johnson. "I find Mr. Cosgrove's revelations most interesting, even if they are occasionally painful to me. And I have not had my turn to reply yet. Stanton may well wish to waive his own turn, for I doubt he has much to say to improve his case, but I want to have my say, feeble as it may be, when Mr. Cosgrove is finished."

"Thank you, sir," said the Senator. "Mr. Cosgrove, please resume and explain the meaning of your reference to persons guilty but not prosecuted."

This I did, recounting that there were some half-dozen or so residents of nearby counties of Maryland and Virginia, to the south of Washington City, who had sheltered, fed and otherwise aided Booth and his companion during their flight; that the names of these people were known to the War Department, and especially to Mr. Stanton; that they had been questioned by military detectives, and the facts of their actions had been learned, which, according to Mr. Stanton's own edict sent abroad some days after the assassination, entitled them to the gallows; but that they had not been put in the dock, much less on the gallows, and, instead, had been turned loose without any kind of punishment. I named some of those so involved, but I may have forgotten the name of one of them.

"And you say the Secretary knows all this?" asked the Senator.

"He is trying to forget the matter, and instructed me to do the same," I replied. "I think it is an embarrassment to him. But the records that prove the War Department knew every particular of the aid these people furnished Booth well before the Conspiracy Trial commenced are in a safe no more than a dozen yards from Mr. Stanton's desk in the War Department. Or, they were some weeks ago, when I saw them myself."

"They are likely destined for Stanton's fireplace now," suggested the President.

"I think not," I said. "They have escaped the flames too long to be sent up the chimney at this late date. There are too many men alive who can attest to them, for the Secretary did not personally conduct the investigation or write these reports. In any case, you can obtain a verbatim copy of the lot by applying to Mr. Ben Green, who publishes *The People's Weekly.*"

"Oh? And how does he chance to have them?" inquired the Senator.

"That would seem a question more properly put to Mr. Green," I replied.

"And can he tell us, as well, why these persons who partook in planning President Lincoln's murder have gone unpunished?" asked the Senator.

"I cannot say what Mr. Green has made of them," I replied, "but, speaking for myself, I do not think these people had any hand in planning the assassination, or even knew it was to be done. I have, as I said, read their statements carefully, and I visited some of them in various guises calculated to disarm their caution. All of them served as station masters along the Rebels' 'underground railroad,' which was used for the passage of Confederate agents during the War. I think some were witting of the plot to kidnap Mr. Lincoln, and were ready to take a hand in it. But none knew of the murder until after it was done. Indeed, they could hardly have known of it, for, as Booth's diary revealed, the assassin had not resolved to do the deed until just one day before he fired the shot."†

---

† The diary entry to which Cosgrove refers is probably this:

April 13, 14 Friday, the Ides
Until today nothing was ever thought of sacrificing to our country's wrongs.
For six months we have worked to capture. But our cause being almost lost,

"But," said the Senator, "as you have already observed, Mr. Stanton decreed that any who might aid the assassins in their flight would be punished by death. Yet he omitted to punish these persons at all."

"Yes," I agreed, "and that is another puzzle I have not solved. I think it may be the heart of the whole mystery that confronts us."

"Have you delivered your full budget of puzzles, then?" asked Senator Ross.

"No," I replied. "There are puzzles enough to last a night and a day, as I have told you. But I shall burden you this night with but one more. It is among the most puzzling, and concerns John Surratt, the son of the lady who was hanged. He lent Booth a hand in his efforts to kidnap President Lincoln, and the Government says that same hand was bloodied in the assassination. Surratt claims he was in Elmira, New York, on the night of the murder, and was not witting it was to take place; the Government says he was here in Washington City on the night in question, and shared in the crime. I do not know which is right, but his whereabouts on April 14th is not part of my puzzle.

---

something decisive and great must be done. But its failure was owing to others who did not strike for their country with a heart. I struck boldly, and not as the papers say . . .

Booth's words leave room for interpretations other than the one Cosgrove seems to have placed on them. Whatever they were intended to mean, they obviously were written after the assassination, certainly not before Sunday, April 16, and probably a few days after that, since the only newspaper accounts of the assassination Booth could have seen were those furnished him by Thomas Jones while that Maryland farmer was sheltering the two fugitives in a swamp near his home. Exactly when Booth abandoned the kidnap plan and replaced it with an assassination scheme is not known with precision, but most historians agree it was no more than a matter of days prior to the act. Booth *could* have informed everyone prepared to aid in the kidnapping of this change in plans, but it seems unlikely he did, since there was no reason to do so and ample reason not to. Obviously Booth did not anticipate breaking his leg during his escape, so he could not have foreseen his need for help from people like Dr. Mudd, Colonel Cox, Thomas Jones or William Bryant. Thus he would have had no reason to inform them in advance of the assassination, and probably realized that doing so would have been needlessly borrowing trouble, since he could not rely that everyone who approved of kidnapping Lincoln to ransom Confederate prisoners of war would likewise condone murdering the President, which might have seemed a dubious victory for the South.—M.C.

"John Surratt's whereabouts begin to seem curious only after April 18th, or thereabouts, when he slipped past the detectives sent to watch for him along our northern frontier and made his way to Montreal. But that, of itself, is not remarkable, nor is his murky career during the months immediately thereafter. He was sheltered in Canada by Confederate agents and, it pains me to recount, some priests of the Roman Catholic Church, but even that fact is more shameful than surprising. No, Surratt did not become a puzzle until some six months after the murder of President Lincoln. Then it was that he was flushed from Canada and flew to Europe, but he did so with such disdain for secrecy that I, a practiced tracker of men, find it near impossible to believe he was not returned to this city until sixteen more months had passed."

"Perhaps he would have been captured sooner had you been set upon his trail," suggested the Senator.

"A blind man on crutches could have caught him as swiftly as I," I replied, "for his whereabouts were rarely unknown, and none seem to have harbored him. Indeed, there were sundry persons of authority who tried to make a present of him to our Government, but he was a present that was often refused."

"Refused?"

"That is the word I should use to describe the matter," I said. "But I'll relate the particulars, and perhaps you will know a better one.

"Surratt took leave of Canada in September, 1865, sailing to Liverpool aboard the *Peruvian*. Enroute he disclosed his identity to the ship's surgeon, who promptly advised the American Consul when the vessel reached its destination. The Consul notified his superiors here in Washington City immediately, but even after repeated dispatches, he received no official representations which would have caused Her Majesty's Government to arrest the fugitive and return him.

"On the *Peruvian*'s return to Canada, the surgeon raised the matter with our Consul in Montreal, who also notified the authorities here without effect. In fact, shortly afterward, Secretary Stanton ordered the $25,000 reward for Surratt be revoked.

"Meanwhile, Surratt had continued his flight and arrived in Rome, where he enlisted in the Papal Zouaves under an assumed name.

However, he soon chanced to encounter a former acquaintance, who recognized him and informed the American Minister in Rome. The Minister reported the discovery to Washington City, but again no authorization for an arrest was forthcoming. But the Papal authorities, who were also told of Surratt's true identity, bethought themselves that a man said to have had a hand in slaying a President was not a proper sentry to guard the person of a Pope. They retired him from their service and put him in a cell to await American Justice.

"Surratt doubtless understood that this amounted to a life sentence, so he deserted the Papal hospitality at the first opportunity and fled, first to Naples, and then to Egypt. But the American Consul in Alexandria, who soon learned of Surratt's presence there, did not wait for instructions from his superiors. He arrested Surratt on his own authority and then informed our Department of State of the matter. Thus, an American corvette was reluctantly dispatched to Egypt, returning to this city with its unwanted prize in January, 1867, more than a year after word of his whereabouts had first been sent from Liverpool.

"Now, I must beg your pardon if I have rehearsed this matter with unseemly amusement, for it might be imagined that, hidden beneath this farce, were the dark and serious motives of persons in the Government who had good reason to fear that Surratt in captivity would name them as his accomplices in the assassination. However, such has hardly transpired.

"John Surratt was brought to trial, as you gentlemen doubtless know, and, while he was unable to persuade a full jury of his innocence, neither was the Government able to convince all of them of his guilt, and so he is a free man.† Did he name some person in high office as a partner in his crimes? He did not, although Mr. Stanton's friends encouraged him to say President Johnson was such a one. Thus, Surratt has proved himself no danger to Mr. Johnson and, for a time, seems to

---

† Since Surratt's trial ended with a hung jury, the Government attempted to try him again, in June, 1868, just a month after the date of the occasion on which Cosgrove met with Ross, Stanton and Johnson in the Capitol Crypt. However, Stanton was gone from the War Department by that date, and the prosecution was only half-hearted. On November 5, 1868, the second trial of John Surratt ended, when the case was dismissed.

have been regarded as a possible ally by Mr. Stanton. And so the Government's disregard of this fugitive is a riddle most profound, which lies beyond the bourne of any theory I can devise which might assume the guilt of either the President or the Secretary of War.†

"Now, gentlemen, I shall trespass no further on your patience. I have imposed too much already, and I could not blame you had you long since followed Secretary Stanton's vexed footsteps from this place.

"Senator, I promised to present you with my conclusions, rough and unfinished as they may be. Very well, here they are:

"I think Secretary Stanton had foreknowledge of Booth's plans to kidnap President Lincoln, yet failed to take the action such knowledge demanded. I think he abetted Booth's escape, although I cannot comprehend his motive. I think these facts bespeak a guilty secret harbored by Mr. Stanton, and one he has been at pains to conceal, including the cruel and ruthless measure of hanging and imprisoning those who might know something of it. I do not know what this secret may be, but I am near certain I know what it is not. I do not think Secretary Stanton had any hand in the murder of Abraham Lincoln."

Senator Ross gazed at me for a moment before commenting on this.

"You have certainly presented a deal of evidence that seems to suggest the opposite."

"I have," I agreed, "yet I have also presented some powerful arguments to set against the evidence. If Mr. Stanton wanted President

---

Surratt was tried both times in civilian courts because, after the Conspiracy Trial, the United States Supreme Court, in considering the appeal of another case (*United States* vs. *Milligan*) decided that such military trials of civilians were unconstitutional. Historical champions of Mrs. Surratt point out that the defense which saved her son from the gallows was little different from the one advanced in her behalf at the Conspiracy Trial, and, had she been tried by a civilian court, she too would have escaped the noose.—M.C.

† Stanton may have feared Surratt knew the War Department had advance information on the plans to abduct President Lincoln and would disclose this, if captured. In fact, Surratt may well have had such knowledge; in 1870 he delivered a lecture in Rockville, Maryland, in which he recalled, "Upon one occasion, I remember, we (Booth and the others) had called a meeting in Washington for the purpose of discussing matters in general, as we had understood that the government had received information that there was a plot of some kind on hand."—M.C.

Lincoln dead, he had good reason to hope his wishes might be realized without his lifting a hand, for, as I have told you, the President fairly courted the assassin's stroke. But did the Secretary sit by complacent and hope that some Rebel would do that which he could do himself only at grave risk? He did not. He was ever cautioning Mr. Lincoln to look to the safety of his person. And on the very day of the murder, Stanton warned the President that he should not go to the theater, for the risk was too great. Could he have done this and hired Booth, as well?"

"But you have revealed to us he knew of Booth," protested the Senator, "and yet took no action against him."

"That is so, but all he knew of Booth, I think, concerned the plan to kidnap, not the one to kill. I think the Secretary may well have hoped for *that*. I think he would have welcomed news that the Rebels had kidnapped the President, or had tried to do it. Perhaps he was so disposed in February when he learned of the plan, or in March, when it was to be consummated. But, regardless of his disposition in April, he must have thought a kidnapping unlikely then, and in the event, the kidnapping plan, as we know, had been abandoned. But I cannot believe he knew assassination had taken its place, for he would have been a strange sort of accomplice to premonish the intended victim from going to the place designated for the slaughter. No, there were at least two witnesses who heard him beg Lincoln to avoid Ford's Theater. Edwin Stanton cannot have been an assassin."

"Very well, then," said Senator Ross. "Can Andrew Johnson have been such a one?"

This question was asked with such consummate insouciance a blind bystander would never have guessed its subject stood in our presence.

"He could have been," I replied, "but there is hardly a particle of evidence to suggest he was.

"Those who charge the President was the architect of his own succession can recite sundry rumors and hearsays, but, when closely pressed, the only fact with any flesh on its bones is Booth's visit to the Kirkwood House on the afternoon of the tragic day. Now, I do not know why Booth chanced to go to the Kirkwood House that day, but I am certain I know what could not have been his reason: to confer with his accomplice, presumably Mr. Johnson."

"How can you be that certain?" asked the Senator.

"Because, like Booth, I have some experience with clandestine affairs," I replied. "Booth was a secret agent of the Confederacy, and had been seasoned in the craft through many clandestine missions from Richmond to Canada. He was neither stupid nor naive. Why then would he visit Mr. Johnson scant hours before he was to do the murder if Mr. Johnson had been his patron in the crime? Suppose he had found the Vice-President at home. Would the two have then repaired to the public room to order a brace of drinks and haggle over the price of the murder? Would Booth have demanded a bonus for the dispatching of General Grant, as well, who then was expected to share the President's theater box? No, sir. One does not purchase an assassination as one might buy a horse. Such bargains are not struck at noon in a stylish hostelry on Pennsylvania Avenue. That sort of business is done in dark and lonely places, away from the eyes and ears of any who might later bear witness to it.

"We may never learn the reason for the incident unless Booth is taken and chooses to tell it. Otherwise, it seems likely to remain a riddle forever. But the answer to that riddle cannot be that the assassin wished to visit his patron, for that is an absurdity."

"Yes," agreed the Senator, "I see that now. It is a wonder I failed to see it long ago. And have you found nothing else that might cast blame upon President Johnson?"

"Oh, there is a deal of matters to blame on him," I said. "Mr. Stanton, as I have told you, harbors some guilty secret. But it is a secret which he could not have kept without Mr. Johnson's abetment, whether it was witting or otherwise. Today Mr. Stanton is the President's unwelcome servant. Mr. Johnson would be rid of the man, a situation of affairs that is famous and the ground of the difficulty in which the President is now ensnared. So, for that which Mr. Stanton may do today, we cannot demand the President answer. Yet such was not always the case, and I think it not unfair to require President Johnson to answer for some of his subordinate's past actions, most especially those in which he, himself, took a hand.

"Mr. Stanton hampered the pursuit of Booth. Very well, Mr. Johnson was in no position to perceive the treachery, for it must be allowed that any man who awakens to the unexpected news he has become President of the United States will require some interval to digest that development.

"But next Mr. Stanton orchestrated the simulacrum of a military trial, the purpose of which seems to have been the hanging of all who might know some part of whatever guilty secret the Secretary harbored. But from whence did the Secretary of War receive the authority to try eight civilian citizens of the United States of America before an Army court-martial? From an order instituting the Military Commission signed by President Johnson on May 1, on which date he'd been Chief Executive for two weeks and might have been expected to accommodate to the idea.

"But, the Military Commission could not have been completely satisfactory to Mr. Stanton, for it condemned only half of the defendants to the gallows, and even suggested one of them might be spared in consideration of her gender. But President Johnson did not prove similarly disappointing to the Secretary, for he endorsed all the death sentences, including Mrs. Surratt's, and was deaf to all pleas that her life be spared.

"Next, there was the problem of those who had cheated the gallows. The Commission said they were to spend the remainder of their days in prison, but that could have offered only meager comfort to Secretary Stanton, if he feared they might have something to say which could embarrass him. The four were destined for the prison at Albany, New York, by the President's order of July 5, 1865. But Albany is not very far from Washington City, and is even closer to the City of New York. It would not take long for the gentlemen of the press to take the cars for the short ride to Albany to hear whatever they thought might interest their readers, directly from the lips of the convicts, or, failing that, at second hand from their jailers.

"Clearly, Albany was not an acceptable substitute for the gallows as a measure to insure nothing more was heard from the survivors of the Conspiracy Trial. How Mr. Stanton must have rejoiced, then, when ten days later, on July 15, the President changed his mind and directed the convicts spend their remaining days in Fort Jefferson, instead of Albany. Could a newspaper reporter interview the prisoners there? Indeed, any reporter could, if he were willing to journey to Key West, the remotest island of the State of Florida, and from there cross some fifty miles of water to the Dry Tortugas, and there persuade the commandant of Fort Jefferson to let him speak with his celebrated charges. He might even find one of them still alive, not yet having succumbed to tropical fever,† and the reporter himself might survive the expedition and return to his desk to write the story he'd been told. But, as a means of insuring silence, Fort Jefferson must be adjudged to be surpassed only by a noose or a canvas head bag. And, as I have said, the order consigning the four to Fort Jefferson was written and signed by the hand of President Johnson.

"Finally, there is the comic-opera odyssey of John Surratt, and the Government's curious reluctance to see him returned to its custody. I have already recounted the matter to you, and have told you I am unable to devise any theory to explain it, so I shall only add this point: The affair promised to involve the governments of Great Britain, the Vatican, and sundry other states, and I cannot believe it was the sole responsibility of the Secretaries of State and War, and a thing that completely evaded the attention of their only superior in the Government.

"Thus, Senator Ross, I cannot say that no act of the President's is without blame, or even that all of his actions are comprehensible, yet in none of them do I read evidence of guilt in the murder of his predecessor.

"Now you have my conclusions. They fall far short of satisfying me, but they may answer your own present needs. There is a deal of mystery about the death of President Lincoln, and I think neither the President nor the Secretary of War has told all he knows of the matter, but I trust you may go to the Senate to cast your vote confident

---

† The prison at Fort Jefferson had been the scene of an outbreak of yellow fever, and one of the four, Michael O'Laughlin, had died of the disease on September 23, 1867. Samuel Arnold, Edward Spangler and Dr. Mudd survived, however, and were pardoned and released by President Johnson shortly before he left office in 1869. —M.C.

of this much: neither Andrew Johnson or Edwin Stanton is guilty of the murder of Abraham Lincoln."

A silence fully appropriate to the place followed my words as they echoed in the dark and distant reaches of the Crypt. The lantern having near exhausted its store of oil, now smoked and guttered, throwing shivering shadows against the ring of columns and the vaulted ceiling. The snowy visage of Mr. Lincoln looked down upon us from the pedestal on which he stood. The President and Senator Ross followed my glance, and we three, the living, stood for a moment, as though to give him who had by far the strongest claim to it, his turn at being heard. But Mr. Lincoln stayed silent as the Sphinx and left us to solve his riddle.

"He cannot speak," Senator Ross reflected, as though he had read my thought. "Do you wish to do so, Mr. President?"

"I don't know," replied President Johnson. "Mr. Lincoln was a fine lawyer, and a practical man, as well. I think, if he could advise me now, he'd say, 'Andy, you seem to have been acquitted of the charge. Now, don't go and make any new trouble for yourself. Keep your mouth shut and get out of the courtroom. Go home, and maybe stop in a church on the way to thank the Lord for your deliverance.' But I'm a fool, and good advice is wasted on me, so I'll speak my piece, anyway. And I'm a double fool, for what I have to say is not by way of defense, but confession.

"No, I shall not confess to murder, as Mr. Cosgrove is right. I had no hand in it, and I don't know who might have. But Mr. Cosgrove is also on the right track in the questions he's asked. I can't give you an answer to every one of them, because I don't know that much. But you've been fair with me, and I'll tell you all I do know of the matters you've raised.

"First, I can clear up my part in the question of John Surratt. Stanton's already owned up to that one,† but I must allow that I too

---

† Stanton admitted to the House Impeachment Investigation Committee that he withdrew the reward for Surratt on his own authority, but the reason he gave them is far from clear: ". . . many months had elapsed without accomplishing the arrest of (Surratt)."—M.C.

hoped we'd never see that young man again. My reason was simple: I expected the Radicals would try to get him to lie and accuse me in exchange for his life. I was right. They did give him a try, but I misjudged his character. I didn't know he'd have the spunk to stick to the truth.

"Now as for the rest of it, the trial and Mrs. Surratt. Mr. Cosgrove has likened the Commission to Pontius Pilate. Well, he may be right, but he'd have been closer to the truth if he called me Pilate, for that was the role I played. Oh, I could blame it all on Stanton, could say I was acting on his advice,† but that doesn't change the fact that I was, I am, the President. In the long run, it was my responsibility, and I can't push Mrs. Surratt and the others off my own conscience and onto Stanton's or anyone else. But I can offer you some information I think you've neglected, and it may help you solve some of your puzzles.

"First, I have to remind you that I was one of the fiercest Rebel-haters around, up until recently. I don't make that claim with any special pride, but just to put things straight, as I've lately come to be viewed as Jeff Davis' twin brother. Well, that's just not so.

"Now I'll allow there are some pretty powerful Rebel-haters in the Congress. But they're men from places like Massachusetts and Ohio. I'm from Tennessee, as you know, and while there's generally a deal of spite when neighbors fall out, it's nothing to the bile you're like to see when a man and his brother take to hating one another. Which is not to say I was brother to the likes of Jefferson Davis and the other aristocrats who ran things in the Confederacy. No, I was a man who worked for his bread with his hands, a tailor. Maybe that had something to do with it, I can't say. But, when the Union split, I was the only man in Congress from any Secessionist state that didn't go back home and join the Rebels. I stayed in Washington City and cast my lot with the North. And if I had no love for the Confederates at Sumpter, I hadn't found any in my heart by Appomattox. When it

---

† According to Johnson's Secretary of the Navy, Gideon Welles, Stanton suggested the prisoners be sent to Fort Jefferson, instead of Albany. (Welles, Vol. II, p. 334).—M.C.

came to hating the Rebels, I'd yield to no man, not Sumner, not Butler, not even Stevens.† But that was before I woke up one morning and found myself President—President, not of the North, but the Union, *the United States of America.*

"I can't say exactly what it may be, but there's something about this job that changes the man who holds it. Maybe it's the Grace of God, or maybe it's just the awe a man feels when he sees the hand he's been dealt. But, whatever, the job changes the man. It might even have changed Stevens. Maybe if he'd stepped into Lincoln's boots, instead of me, Stevens would be in the dock today on the same charges. I don't know. I guess I can't ask you to understand that; you haven't spent any time looking at these things through the windows of the White House, from the inside.

"Well, that's neither here nor there, I suppose. I've taken the long way 'round to arrive at a simple point: On that sorrowful morning when I was sworn into the Presidency, I was still 'Johnson the Rebel-hater.' I had yet to travel my own road to Damascus.

"Now, Mr. Cosgrove may be right in his belief that Stanton wished to hang Mrs. Surratt and the others for his own guilty purposes, but he was out to hang some others, such as Jefferson Davis, and Benjamin, and Thompson, and the rest of them,‡ *and I was ready to help him do it.* Now, that was the reason for the Military Commission, at least so far as I was concerned.§ Well, it didn't work, thank God, but we accomplished some appalling injustice with the thing, nonetheless.

"Now I've said it often, that I never saw the Commission's recommendation for clemency for the Surratt woman, and that's true

---

† Senator Charles Sumner of Massachusetts, Congressman Benjamin F. Butler of Massachusetts, and Congressman Thaddeus Stevens of Pennsylvania, three of the most vigorous foes of the South and Johnson's mild Reconstruction policies, and the most outspoken proponents of impeachment.—M.C.

‡ Judah P. Benjamin served, first as Attorney General of the Confederacy, then as its Secretary of War, and finally as its Secretary of State; Jacob Thompson was head of the Confederate underground in Canada.—M.C.

§ Much of the Conspiracy Trial was occupied with the Government's efforts to show that the leaders of the Confederacy had been behind the assassination, and so provide another excuse to hang them. In the event, however, none of the Confederate leaders was hanged.—M.C.

enough.† But it's no excuse. I didn't need nine of Stanton's Army officers to teach me right from wrong, and that's just as well, for I don't think those gentlemen are especially qualified for such a task.

"The fact of the matter is I was at no great pains to review the record of the trial and make sure Justice had been served. I didn't know how much of a hand the defendants may have taken in Lincoln's murder, nor did I especially care. I was satisfied they were all Rebels, which they were, and to my mind, at that time, that was cause enough to hang them. The Commission said to hang four of them, and that's what I did; if it'd said to hang the lot, then I'd have done that, instead. I reckoned Stanton was of a similar disposition, and that was his reason for being so keen to string them up. I never thought he might have any other reason, because I never took enough trouble over the matter to reflect on it.

"Mr. Cosgrove says I've got innocent blood on my hands. Well, he's right. The four of them that're in Fort Jefferson, I can yet do them some good, and I'll see they're turned loose before I leave this office and the power to do it. But I can't bring back the Surratt woman, so I'll have the stain of her blood on my hands when they lay me in my grave.

"Well, Senator, you've let me speak my piece, and I'm done. I thank you for the consideration and I've tried to speak as honestly of these matters as I know how. I don't think I can add any more to what has been said here tonight, so, if you'll excuse me, I'll be on my way."

The President waited for a moment, but when neither the Senator nor I seemed to have anything to say, he departed. The Senator gazed in that direction long after Mr. Johnson had disappeared into the darkness and was gone from the chamber. Finally he turned to me.

"Our conference seems to have ended," he finally said. "Mr. Cosgrove, you have done more than any could have asked of you."

"I have left the job half-done," I said.

---

† Andrew Johnson claimed he had not been shown the Commission's recommendation for clemency for Mrs. Surratt when he was given the verdicts and sentences to approve and sign.—M.C.

"The work I needed done you have completed," the Senator replied, "and I have not words enough to thank you for it. You have done your job superbly. Now it remains for me to do mine."

So saying, Senator Ross departed.

The night was nearly gone. I had little strength and no appetite for a stroll across the city to the house on K Street. And the place where I stood was near the place I would betake myself on the morrow, for I had resolved to be in the Senate Gallery when the Impeachment vote was taken. So I gathered up some of Miss Ream's tarpaulins and made a bed for myself on that very spot.

Thus it was that I took my repose for what remained of that night in a place that had been built to shelter the Father of Our Country in his Final Slumber. He had never rested in the Crypt, so I did not think he would make any objection if I used it. General Washington and I, after all, had something in common: We had labored for the Republic without pay, and only claimed our expenses.

I put out the guttering lantern and was soon asleep.

·29·

A Verdict of a Single Vote

General Washington's ghost did not disturb my slumber that night, yet I did not rest unmolested. But it was not a revenant from beyond the grave who troubled my repose; it was the phantasm of a living man, albeit a sorcerer. It was Professor Haselmayer who came to me in the Crypt, borne there aboard a dream I'd dreamt once before.

I sat alone in the empty opera house, while the magician stood beside a pine coffin which had been trussed in chains and padlocked. The Professor once again made his mocking invitation to undo the bonds that secured the box.

"Come, Cosgrove, unlock this thing. You have the key. It is in your pocket."

But my wrists were shackled by the magician's irons, and I could not get to my pocket.

"Come, Mr. Nichols, unlock it," taunted the sorcerer.

I knew there was a trick to the Professor's shackles, and if I could but guess it, I'd be free of them, free to retrieve the key and unlock the coffin. I stared at the irons. What was the trick?

"Come, Mr. Nichols."

It was a woman's voice. The sorcerer had transmogrified himself into a woman, and a pretty one, at that. Why, he had made himself over in the delightful image of Vinnie Ream, who was standing over me, the lantern in her hand.

"Come, Mr. Nichols, you must not sleep all day. You shall miss the voting."

I arose, but could not comprehend at that instant where I might be, or why Miss Ream had awakened me in the midst of the night. But as I gazed about in wonderment, I perceived where I was and recalled that I had sought repose in a place where it was never ought but the midst of the night. I greeted the young lady with as much gallantry as I could free from the cobwebs of sleep that encumbered my tongue. A glance at my watch revealed the hour to be near eleven o'clock, and as I reflected momentarily on my visitor's words, I perceived that it must be morning, rather than night.

"Come, Mr. Nichols," repeated Miss Ream. "I have a pair of tickets from Mr. Ross to admit us to the Senate Gallery. One of them is for you."

The lovely sculptress showed me where to find such humble comforts that equipped her gloomy studio, and which might be of some use in preparing my morning toilet. Days of constant travel, and a night spent enshrouded in her dusty tarpaulins had bestowed upon me the singular disguise of the plaster likeness of a beggar. A mirror, a basin, a brush and a comb aided me in the personation of a living man, and, at that, a fellow who might even be supposed by the doorkeeper of the Senate Gallery to be one who could have come by his ticket honestly.

Emerging from the entrance beneath the Capitol steps, I found that I had slept away all but the last minutes of a warm and beauteous Spring morn.

I followed Miss Ream into the Capitol's gloom. Outside the Senate Chamber I glimpsed Mr. Ross amid the throng. He was halted and looked to be inspecting the floor, while a pair of his colleagues spoke urgent importunaties into his ears. I did not stop, but was carried on by the human flow and ascended to the corridor above, where the doors to the galleries were to be found.

Those embankments above the Senate Chamber were near filled with the human tide that had risen there, and Miss Ream and I found two of the last remaining seats. The gentler sex was well represented in the galleries, and the combined fluttering of their fans filled the upper reaches of the chamber with a gentle zephyr. By contrast, the room below was near vacant, for scarcely a dozen Senators were at their desks, although it was then close to half past the hour.

We found ourselves seated beside Mr. William Crook, the young constable of the White House guard I had interviewed in the course of my inquiries. I greeted him and introduced him to my charming companion. In return, he served as guide to the proceedings, in which he seemed well versed. Indeed, he had brought a tablet and pencil along to keep his own tally when the voting commenced.

At 11:30 sharp, Senator Wade rapped his gavel and the Chamber immediately began to fill, as his colleagues took their places expectantly. Wade had a special claim to their attention on this occasion; he was President of the Senate, but, if during the next hour that body should find Andrew Johnson guilty as charged, Mr. Benjamin F. Wade would then, by succession, become President of the United States. Senator Wade had already made known his own plans regarding the coming vote. He would eschew the duty of a gentleman to abstain from casting a vote in a matter of great personal interest to himself, and, instead, would cast his "Guilty" vote, so as not to deny his Ohio constituents their voice in demanding the Great Criminal's expulsion. It was a reassurance to know that, should Mr. Johnson be convicted, he would leave the Nation in the hands of a man of such legendary unselfishness.

I chanced to turn about and look up over my shoulder, as a pair of the last of the spectators was admitted to the gallery. I saw two men. One had a familiar face, but the other, whom I did not recognize, was a remarkable-looking fellow, a man of middle years, who nonetheless looked as strong as an ox, and, I might add, as shrewd as a fox.

"Who is that fellow?" I inquired of Mr. Crook.

"Do you mean the Major?" asked the constable.

"No, I know the Major. But who is the giant he's brought with him?"

"That is General Eckert," replied Mr. Crook.

Here, then, was the famous Eckert, former chief telegrapher to Secretary Stanton, and now, so I understood, chief of all the eastern lines of the Western Union Company. I had often heard his name during the past months, but I had never seen him.

My attention was recaptured by events on the floor below. A murmur passed through the galleries as a chair was borne into the

Chamber by a pair of the stalwarts who seemed all about the place, their presence to insure order. In the chair sat a corpse, or a creditable imitation of one. It was Mr. Thaddeus Stevens of Pennsylvania, and I knew that, even were he as dead as he looked, he would arise when his name was called to rattle out his "Guilty," for of all men there, he alone could claim the title of "Father of the Impeachment."

But Senator Stevens was not the only Radical who refused to let illness keep him from the Chamber on this historic day of days. Mr. Howard of Michigan, whose indisposition on the previous Tuesday had stayed the vote until this day, was helped to his desk by a pair of friends.

On the stroke of noon, Senator Wade announced to his assembled colleagues that he would then yield the rostrum to the Chief Justice of the United States, who, according to ceremony, would conduct the poll. Chief Justice Salmon P. Chase then made his entrance, his black judicial robes flowing in his wake as he ascended the rostrum, seated himself, and admonished the galleries to absolute silence and decorum, on pain of immediate arrest. These words seemed to have had some effect on a gentleman on the Senate floor (I think it was General Sickles), who had followed Senator Ross to his desk and was there whispering to the Senator with great vehemence, but without any kind of response. The man broke off and departed.

The first item on the agendum, so Mr. Crook informed me, was the reading of the eleven Articles of Impeachment; but before this could commence, Senator Williams of Oregon rose to his feet and moved that the Senate rescind its rule to ballot on the articles in their numerical order. This motion was quickly approved by a voice vote of those assembled, and Mr. Williams then immediately made a second motion, to wit: that the Eleventh Article of Impeachment be voted upon first, and then the remaining ten in succession. This, too, was passed by a count of thirty-four "yeas," against nineteen "nays." The significance of all this parliamentary maneuvering had escaped me, but not apparently Mr. Crook, whose countenance registered grave concern. I begged him to elucidate the thing.

It was a trick of the Radicals, Mr. Crook explained. Of all the Eleven Articles of Impeachment, the last held the best promise of passage, for it was a catch-all charge, and, in effect, a summary of the other ten. Thus, while some Senators could be relied upon to find the President guilty of the charges contained in the First Article, but perhaps not those of the Second, and yet others would agree with the Second after having dismissed the First, and so on, and so forth; all who would vote "Guilty" on any one of the first ten, must, perforce, also vote "Guilty" on the Eleventh Article. Thus, of the lot, the Eleventh Article stood the best chance of winning the approval of two-thirds of the Senators there assembled, some of whom might waver in the direction of acquittal if the first ten failed. The Radicals, Mr. Crook lamented, had won an important victory.

Before voting on the notorious Eleventh Article could commence, however, Senator Fessenden of Maine was on his feet to move that the voting be deferred for some thirty minutes to give the ailing Senator Grimes of Iowa sufficient time to take his seat. The proposal evoked general displeasure among the pro-Impeachment Senators, because, as Mr. Crook explained, should the ailing Senator Grimes cast his vote, it would surely be for acquittal. Before the motion could be put to a vote, however, Senator Reverdy Johnson of Maryland (Lord, how full of Johnsons is the land!) announced that the indisposed Mr. Grimes was in the building and would be at his desk forthwith. The deed followed immediately upon the heels of the word, and a pair of guards carried a litter into the Chamber, upon which reposed Mr. Grimes, his face ashen and his eyes shut. He was borne to his desk and his helpers got him into his chair. A murmur of wonderment moved across the Chamber and rose throughout the galleries.

The Eleventh Article was then read by the Senate clerk, and the polling began. The vote was to be taken in the alphabetical order of the Senators' surnames, and the first called by the clerk was that of Senator Anthony of Rhode Island.

"Mr. Senator Anthony, how say you?" intoned the Chief Justice. "Is the respondent, Andrew Johnson, President of the United States, guilty or not guilty of a high misdemeanor, as charged in this article?"

"Guilty," replied Senator Anthony, which, Mr. Crook informed me, was no surprise, as he was among the Senators whose vote against the President had already been declared. There were to be no surprises, in fact, until the turn came to Senator Fessenden of Maine, the first of the Senators who had not already made known his disposition regarding the Impeachment. The Senator got to his feet when he heard his name and proclaimed, "Not Guilty." Mr. Crook joined the other friends of President Johnson in an audible sign of relief. It was a good omen.

The next member whose vote remained unknown was Mr. Fowler of the President's own Tennessee. But when his turn came, Mr. Fowler's voice seemed to betray him, and the Chief Justice required him to repeat his vote.

"Not Guilty," cried Mr. Fowler in a strong and steady voice. Yet there are some who heard his first whisper, and say he voted for Impeachment, changing his mind in the instant Fate had granted him to reconsider. I was at too great a remove to hear the earlier utterance, and so I cannot say if they may be right.

When the name of the feeble Senator from Iowa, who had been carried to his place, was called, Chief Justice Chase announced, "Mr. Grimes need not rise." But the stricken man climbed to his feet, nonetheless, to deliver his vote for acquittal. Even the President's foes (some of them, at least) applauded this gallant gesture.

Mr. Henderson of Missouri was the next on the roll whose disposition was not already known. When he arose and called his "Not Guilty," Mr. Crook became ebullient.

"By my count," he explained, "of those who have voted, and those remaining whose vote is already known, the Radicals have thirty-four, or thirty-five votes, at most. But they require thirty-six to impeach Mr. Johnson, and there remains only one Senator whose vote is in doubt."

"And who might he be?" I inquired.

"Senator Ross of Kansas," replied Mr. Crook.

The polling moved on relentlessly. I looked toward Senator Ross, who sat as a man in some species of trance, the unabated shredding of a sheet of paper being the only visible sign of anxiety or animation. Presently his name was called. He got to his feet.

"Not Guilty," said the Senator, in the most matter-of-fact fashion, and then resumed his seat.

"It is over! We have won!" proclaimed Mr. Crook joyously. He made as though to rise, but dropped back into his seat to hear the remaining votes read, although he said he knew what they would be. He fidgeted and seemed eager to be off (to the White House, I suppose, although the votes were known there almost as they were cast, by virtue of a telegraph wire strung from the Capitol to Willard's Hotel and a small force of messengers), yet would not go, as if to do so might tempt Fate. But when the final vote was cast, and no doubt could remain, Mr. Crook was vanished from my side so abruptly one might have thought it an illusion arranged by Professor Haselmayer.

The Radicals next proposed and carried a motion to adjourn the Senate at that hour, and convene again in ten days to vote upon the remaining ten Articles of Impeachment. It was a maneuver aimed at purchasing the time required to turn some more Senators to their side, but all there knew it was in vain. If the Eleventh Article had not succeeded, the other ten would surely fail as well. The Radicals had lost, not only the battle, but the war.

The Chamber and galleries emptied, and I was presently sitting alone and reflecting on what had transpired. President Johnson kept his office by virtue of a single vote, that of Senator Ross. Mr. Ross's responsibility was an awesome one, but, I saw, it was a responsibility I must needs share with him, for, while many men spoke to him during the past twenty-four hours, I think I may have been the only one to whom he listened.

I sat in the Senate gallery in silent prayer. I had done a job of work for Mr. Ross. I prayed I had done it well.

I was thus deeply engaged in my meditations when I felt a hand upon my shoulder. I looked up. It was Mr. Pinkerton.

"Good work, Nicholas," he said.

"I hope so," I replied.

"I have no doubt of it," he answered. "Are you ready for a new assignment?"

"But, sir," I replied, "I have resigned from your employ."

"It was but a leave of absence," he said. "Remind me not to neglect the back pay you are owed."

My face spoke my astonishment.

"There was no other way," he said. "I have been walking a tight-rope since that day Edwin Stanton came to me with his request. I could not refuse without I also reveal to him I had as my client his own hated adversary."

"You have been serving the President?" I asked.

Mr. Pinkerton nodded.

"For many months. I have been spying on the Radicals for him. When Stanton came to me with this business of Booth, I found myself and the Chain of Agencies in a most delicate and unenviable position. Your own instinctive discretion saved us, however, Nicholas. I hope you will not hesitate to return."†

"I shall gladly return," I said. "What assignment do you have for me?"

"Why, to finish the work you began, Nicholas. I want you to find John Wilkes Booth."

"I see," I said. "And the client?"

"This time I am to be your client," replied Mr. Pinkerton. "Do you think it possible to trace the man?"

"It may be," I said, "for I have acquired a new piece of information. I believe I know the identity of Booth's 'A. Johnson.'"

"Indeed?" Mr. Pinkerton remarked. "And do you know, as well, where this man might be found?"

"I do," I said, "but I think it shall not be necessary that I seek him out, for unless I am greatly mistaken, A. Johnson will call on me very soon."

In the event, my expectation was fulfilled quite promptly. When I returned with Mr. Pinkerton to the house on K Street, I found a

---

† According to Milton (pp. 411, 732), Pinkerton later told Henry S. Monroe, a Chicago Democratic attorney, that "he had a pretty girl make up to the Committee's stenographer (they were male in those days) and she quickly began furnishing verbatim reports of the hearings." Milton cites as his source a communication from one "Miss Harriet Monroe," of Chicago (presumably kin to Mr. Henry S. Monroe), dated October 23, 1928. The Committee in question was the House Impeachment Investigation Committee.

The identity of the "pretty girl" is not disclosed, but in light of Cosgrove's report one is tempted to suspect it was Vinnie Ream. But that is only conjecture.—M.C.

message addressed to my name, which had been delivered there by the hand of a messenger scarcely an hour earlier. It read:

> My Dear Mr. Cosgrove:
>   There is a matter of great mutual interest to us which I would discuss with you at the earliest possible moment. If it is convenient for you, please come to Washington's Monument at 7:15 this evening.
>
>   A. Johnson

PART SEVEN

The End of the Game

· 30 ·

A Major Disclosure

The abandoned obelisk that had been designated as the place of our rendezvous stood on the marshy western end of the Island, a desolate quarter of a desolate place. The pillar rose but a hundred feet above the derelict shanties grouped about its base, in which were stored the stones that had never been lifted into place. They provided a haven for the thieves and vagabonds that made the Island a hazard for any who visited it by day, and a wilderness by night. It was a sorry memento to the Father of Our Country, and better served, in its deserted and unfinished state, as a monument to those noble aspirations of our Forefathers, which division and war had made us forget. Johnson could not have chosen a more appropriate place.†

Had I gone to this lonesome place to view the sunset, I should have taken along a Colt's revolver to insure my safe return. But, in con-

---

† "The Island" was the common designation of that sparsely inhabited part of Washington south of the Washington Canal. Apart from the Smithsonian building farther to the east, the unfinished Washington Monument was the only notable structure on the Island, which was indeed a likely place to find muggers and vagrants. The cornerstone of the Monument had been laid on July 4, 1848, according to a design of the famous Washington architect Robert Mills, who envisioned a 600-foot obelisk rising above a colonnaded temple of some hundred feet in height. Stones had been donated by many foreign countries desiring representation in this proposed memorial to President Washington. However, lack of funds brought work to a halt at the 184-foot level, and the Civil War caused the structure to be all but forgotten, even though it was visible from most parts of the city. Work was not resumed on the Monument until the 1880s, and it was completed (555 feet, 5½ inches) and opened to the public on October 9, 1888.—M.C.

sideration of the person who had asked me to meet him there, I took along a brace of Colts and a Bowie knife, as well. I did not fear "A. Johnson," himself, but I suspected he was given to bad company. In the event, he arrived alone aboard a barouche. He reined up the team, and I stepped from the shadow of a shed. I climbed into the buggy and seated myself beside him without waiting for an invitation. If there were a sharpshooter somewhere off in the trees, he would have to risk dispatching his patron. Indeed, the scene was already blood-red in the waning light of the sun, now hidden behind the distant hills of Arlington Heights.

"Good evening, Major Johnson," I greeted.

"Hello, Mr. Cosgrove. Thank you for coming."

"It would certainly be my pleasure, in any case," I replied, "but I confess to some curiosity regarding what sort of matter might be to our 'great mutual interest.'"

"I think you know the matter very well," he said.

"Were I to guess, I should say it concerned a telegram. One sent some years ago to one A. Johnson, who was none other than Major Albert E. H. Johnson, Custodian of Military Telegrams in the Department of War, and private secretary to Mr. Edwin Stanton."

"You have guessed that much correctly," allowed Major Johnson. "Were I confident you could guess all of the matter with the same accuracy, I should not have troubled you to meet me here."

"I prefer not to guess when a surer knowledge is at hand."

"Then please permit me to inform you of the affair. What I shall say I mean for your ears and no other's. I cannot expect you to agree to a confidence, and that is why I have chosen this place for our meeting. It is imperative that you know certain things, yet it is equally imperative you remain unable to prove them."

"Yet I shall remain free to try," I said.

"Agreed. Very well then, I shall tell you of the matter of Booth's dispatch, but I shan't begin with it, for the telegram marked the end of the story, and I must begin it by recounting some events of an earlier date."

"A date in February, 1865?" I asked.

Major Johnson stared at me a moment before replying.

"Yes. You know, then, that this affair began when we learned of Booth's plot to abduct President Lincoln."

"Secretary Stanton knew of that matter, then?"

"Of course. None would dare withhold such intelligence from him. When he learned of it, he immediately moved to arrest Booth and everyone connected with him. But I counseled otherwise."

"You wished Lincoln kidnapped?" I demanded.

"No. Not then, at least. But there was little chance of Booth succeeding then. Had he seemed likely to succeed, I should have wanted him arrested. At ground, Booth's plan was to ransom the Rebels captured in battle to replenish the dwindling ranks of the Confederacy. Victory for the Union was in sight, but, had Booth succeeded, he would have added another year to the War. No, I did not wish President Lincoln kidnapped. That is why I proposed that Baker be set to watch Booth and the others, and that is what the Secretary did."

"I fail to understand your reasons," I said.

"My reasons were simple. The War was nearly ended, but we knew, the Secretary and I, that its conclusion would not also bring an end to all other difficulties. Another conflict, the same that reached so lamentable a climax today, had already begun. There were those among us who were strong in war, but who were too weak for victory. Mr. Lincoln was such a one."

"I think I see, now," I said. "President Lincoln was too soft-hearted toward the Rebels. You thought some experience of Confederate hospitality might harden that heart."

"Precisely," agreed the Major.

"Well, I think you were mistaken," I said. "President Lincoln wasn't a soft-hearted man; he was a good man. But I don't think you know the difference."

"I know it well," said Major Johnson, "and you may be right. So much the worse, if you are."

"There is a riddle," I commented.

"A man who wishes to make a profession of goodness in everything must necessarily come to grief among so many who are not good. He who abandons what is done for what ought to be done will bring about his own ruin. A wholly good man has no business being President. A leader must learn how not to be good, and either use the knowledge or not, according to the necessity of the case."

Major Johnson recited this in a manner that suggested he was quoting someone, if only himself.

"That seems a lesson you and your chief have mastered. I think it comes to you naturally," I observed.

"Your words might be taken as irony," said Major Johnson, "if they did not come from the lips of a professional spy and secret detective."

I made no answer to this; I fear there was none to make.

"What was your plan, then?" I inquired. "To wait until victory was assured, and then let the kidnappers have their way?"

"That was it," Major Johnson agreed. "Yet it was not that simple. It was essential, you see, that the conspirators act on our initiative, and not their own. Otherwise, the attempt might be made too early, and we should have no alternative but to thwart it. Thus it was necessary that General Baker assume to connive with Booth, revealing the fact that the Secretary knew of his plans and suggesting he would countenance them for his own selfish purposes. As it transpired, this was not a prudent step."

"Because Booth disclosed Secretary Stanton's complicity to others to gain their support?"

"We think he may have," Major Johnson agreed.

"Oh, you merely suspected it, then? But you took no chances, and tried to hang all whom you even suspected shared his secret."

"None were hanged who had not earned that punishment," he answered. "Treason is a capital crime."

"Is it a crime that robs those charged with it of their right to a trial?" I asked.

"Answer your own question, *Colonel* Cosgrove. How many traitors have *you* slain without benefit of trial?"

"None, save during war."

"Very nice, but I do not think Booth or his accomplices planned to sign a peace treaty. But let it go. I have not asked you here to apologize to you for any of our actions, but to inform you of them.

"Booth was a fool. Nothing would satisfy him but that the abduction be executed as if it were one of his melodramas. Thus he settled on the Inaugural as the stage on which he would perform, and Baker could not dissuade him from it. It was madness, of course. Booth could not have taken the President from the midst of the Inaugural if he'd had Moseby and all his men to help. But we had no choice, so we made as though to go along with the plan. Immediately before the ceremony, Baker arranged that an informer tell the police an attempt would be made on Lincoln's life. Thus, the guard was doubled, and even Booth could see the thing was hopeless. He gave up his plan for that day and never suspected what had happened. I believe Baker went so far as to find some drunkard the police could arrest to lend credence to the maneuver, and so stifle any suspicion Booth might have.†

"Booth's next plan was somewhat more practicable. About the middle of March the President was to attend an entertainment put on for wounded soldiers in a hospital. As you well know, it was Lincoln's habit to go about the city on such errands without any guard at all, and Booth counted on intercepting his carriage en route, and thus make good the abduction. But, in the event, the President found at the last minute he could not attend, and he sent another in his place. Booth and his men nearly abducted the substitute before they saw it was not Lincoln.

"After the failure of the second attempt, the Secretary would have no more of the affair. He ordered Baker to see that no further efforts were made to abduct Mr. Lincoln."

"He did not arrest Booth," I observed.

"He could not very well do that," said the Major. "He could not risk Booth's accusations, or the witness of those in whom Booth may have confided."

"He didn't want word of his treachery to get out," I agreed. "I can understand that."

---

† This may have been one Thomas Clemens of Alexandria, Virginia, who was arrested a few days after the Inauguration on a charge of having declared his intention of murdering President Lincoln. (See the Washington *Daily Morning Chronicle* of March 6 and 7, 1865.) In any case, Major Johnson's story explains the remarkable gathering of Booth and his accomplices revealed in the Gardner photograph of the Second Inauguration.—M.C.

"Call it what you will," said the Major. "What I ask you to believe, what I swear on my oath to be the truth, is that, from that day forward, Mr. Stanton knew nothing of Booth or his plans. Would that I could say as much of myself."

"Major Johnson," I inquired incredulously, "do you confess to taking a hand in President Lincoln's murder?"

"Yes, in effect, that is what I say. I had a hand in it, a foolish, unwitting hand, but a hand, nonetheless. I was deceived by Baker, and became an instrument of his treachery. Thus I brought unjust suspicion down upon Mr. Stanton, who is entirely innocent. That is the reason I have asked to meet with you: to tell you this."

"But for what reason?"

"Because I know Andrew Johnson. He has won his case, but I know he will not now be content to see Mr. Stanton gone from the Cabinet. He will pursue this matter of the assassination with a vengeance. I should not be surprised if you had already received your instructions to assemble the case against Mr. Stanton."

"I am no lawyer, Major," I replied. "I do not 'assemble cases,' I investigate them. I refused to do this dirty work *for* Mr. Stanton; why should he think I would do it *against* him?"

"Mr. Stanton knows nothing of this meeting. I come at my own initiative."

"Very well, but I have received no instructions from President Johnson; he is not my client. Do you wish to continue, in view of that?"

"Yes, if I may, for I do not think you have abandoned your inquiries, even if you do not pursue them on the President's behalf.

"As I told you, the abduction plans were abandoned in mid-March, and the Secretary instructed General Baker to watch Booth and the others, and insure no further attempt was made. I heard nothing more of the matter until sometime during the first week in April, when Baker came to me with his treacherous scheme.

"General Baker asked to speak with me in private regarding a matter he described as needing the utmost confidentiality. I agreed to see him in a place where our words could not be overheard. There he made his proposal.

"He admitted Booth had proved inadequate to the complexities of so vast an orchestration as the abduction of the President. He further acknowledged that the time for such a thing had passed, since the Rebels had been driven too far from Washington City to offer a proximate haven for the kidnappers. But he proposed a way in which Booth might be employed in a different scheme that would produce the same result we desired, an improved appreciation in Mr. Lincoln's mind of the true degree of treachery and danger of the Confederates. The thing he claimed to have in mind was an *attempt* at assassination. As he further unfolded his plan, he showed me how such an attempt might be instigated without serious risk to Mr. Lincoln's person.

"Booth would be procured to do the deed, and he would be told the killing was to be in earnest. But he would be instructed to come to the designated place unarmed, against the risk of a personal search. His weapon would be handed to him immediately before the act. But, unknown to Booth, the pistol would contain but a single charge of powder and no ball. Thus, all would think the assassin had missed his mark, and the President was in hazard of nothing worse than some superficial burns, which, should he suffer them, would make him yet less likely to forget the lesson.

"Booth would be guaranteed that none should bar his way to the President, nor the route he would use to make good his escape. It was the same route that had been planned for the abduction, and it ended in the same place, a certain farmhouse near Richmond, where President Lincoln was to have been held captive. But now the house would shelter Booth, he was told. In fact, Baker planned to station some of his men there to greet the assassin, silence his lips forever, and produce his remains in that vicinage as proof the Confederate leaders had inspired the outrage."

"A tidy plan," I remarked. "But what reason did he offer for bringing it to you? Surely not for your approval."

"No. Baker said the Secretary had ordered him to New York City, which, indeed, he had. Thus, he claimed, another must see to the particulars of the affair, most especially the disposal of the guard and the furnishing of the pistol. He said these matters were of such moment he would entrust them to none but myself. Alas, I agreed, and he handed me the derringer. I hardly need tell you the rest of the story."

"You did not inspect the weapon to assure yourself it held no ball?" I asked.

The Major made a mirthless laugh.

"No, I placed it most gingerly in my desk until the night it was needed. Then I took it out as one might pick up a sleeping cobra and put it in my pocket. When I handed it to Booth in the darkness at Ford's, I held it between thumb and forefinger, for I feared I might discharge the thing by mischance. You see, while I enjoy a military rank, I am far from being any sort of soldier. I have never worn a uniform, and, until Baker gave me the pistol, I had never held a gun in my hand. Even had I overcome my timorousness and taken a good look at the thing, I should never have been able to see there was a ball in it. I should not even have known where to look."

I did not find this difficult to believe.

"And the guard, Parker?" I asked.

"I sent him away on an errand."

"What of Booth's dagger? He slashed Major Rathbone† and an actor with it. He surely would have stabbed the President had the pistol not done its work."

"I knew nothing of it," declared the Major. "Baker said Booth was to come to the place unarmed."

"What did Mr. Stanton know of all these things?"

"Nothing!" exclaimed Major Johnson. "On my oath, sir, I never told him of the plan. It was a thing I saw needed doing, but what I did, I did on my own responsibility. Thank God, I did not involve him in it."

"Would God you had," I said. "He'd likely have counseled against it. No, he should have forbidden it."

---

† Major Henry R. Rathbone, who, with his fiancé, Miss Clara Harris, accompanied the Lincolns to Ford's Theater and shared their box. Major Rathbone tried to capture Booth and was slightly cut by the assassin during the skirmish.—M.C.

"You are right."

"When did he learn of the matter, then?" I asked. "After Booth had fled into Maryland?"

"Mr. Cosgrove, may God strike me down on this spot if I am lying, but Mr. Stanton has never heard what I have told you!"

"But, sir! You cannot ask me to believe he took no hand to insure Booth's escape."

"Of course he did, for when he learned the name of the assassin, he saw how gravely compromised his own position had become. Suppose Booth had been taken. Even if he went no further than the truth, as he believed it, of the abduction scheme, who would fail to conclude the Secretary had also taken a hand in the murder?"

"None," I admitted. "Even Booth, himself, must have suspected as much, owing to your own involvement."

"That is probably so," said the Major, unhappily.

"It seems his broken leg pained others even worse than it did Booth," I observed.

"Oh, but for that damnable thing all would have been well!" lamented Major Johnson.

"Yes, Booth would have been dead, Stanton secure in his ignorance, and Baker would have enjoyed the protection of the silence I am confident you would have steadfastly kept. Of course, President Lincoln would have been no less dead, but I cannot fancy the fulsome lot of you saw that as anything worse than a mixed blessing. And I give you that much only as a consideration of Charity."

"I do not apologize, Mr. Cosgrove, I only explain."

"So you've said. I don't think you're done."

"No, there is the matter of the telegram. It was a ruse, but I have only recently discovered that, as a consequence of your investigation."

"What did it contain? Why send it to you?"

"It was sent to me, but it was meant for Baker. Booth did not know where Baker might be found, but he knew I would be at my desk in the War Department. It was a coded message, signed with a pseudonym, and it informed of Booth's location and begged assistance in furthering his escape. It was actually intended to lead us to his impostor, and it succeeded in that effect. Booth was more clever than we imagined, and he divined our plans for him. He assessed Baker's cupidity, as well, and foresaw the hunt would end when his substitute was slain. He relied on Baker to conceal the imposture so to collect the reward, and the General did not disappoint him."

"So you conveyed to Baker the word that Booth could be found at Garrett's Farm, and that is the secret of the General's remarkable feat of deduction."

"That is so," Major Johnson allowed, "and until your own discoveries, neither the Secretary nor I suspected the man killed near Port Royal and buried beneath the Arsenal was other than the assassin."

"That cannot be entirely so, sir," I observed. "For I should not have undertaken to make my discoveries had Mr. Stanton no clew that the dead man might not be Booth."

The Major seemed perplexed.

"You must be right, Mr. Cosgrove, but I do not know the cause of Mr. Stanton's doubts. I am only certain it cannot be the fruit of guilty knowledge, for, as I have sworn to you, the Secretary knows nothing, even to this day, of the matters I have disclosed to you."

I stepped out of the Major's buggy and turned to him.

"I believe you, Major Johnson. Another might not, for you seem to share Mr. Stanton's confidence in every other thing. Yet I believe you, for the Secretary of War likely knows you better than does any other man. He has looked into your soul and seen some reflection of himself. Thus he knows he cannot trust you completely.

"Good evening to you, sir."

I turned and walked away.

·31·

The Letter of the Truth

·⋅•⋅━━◈━━•⋅⋅·

I strolled through the soft Spring evening and took stock of the state of my inquiries. There were fresh entries in the ledger, not a few of which could be put in the column marked "Mysteries Solved."

I had learned Edwin Stanton's secret, the guilty thing that had spurred him into worse crimes, greater guilt and more dismal secrets. And with this knowledge came comprehension of the Secretary's true motive in hiring me to search for Booth. I was to have been the hound that would flush the prey into the hunter's sights. Stanton would murder the murderer, and silence forever one more who might accuse him.

I knew the meaning of Booth's telegram and the identity of "A. Johnson." That acquisition brought with it the answer to the riddle of General Baker's feat of perspicacity. Now I knew what had guided his hand when he drew the circle about Port Conway on the map of Virginia. A circle! He could have drawn a cross, had he known with precision the location of Garrett's Farm. But he could credit a circle to sheer deduction; a cross would require he claim Divine Inspiration!

And I knew now it had been Baker's bloody hand that had held the strings of the murderous marionette, yet there was a new riddle. Lafayette Baker was a creature of diabolical cunning and ruthlessness, but he was, at heart, nothing more than a grossly venal scoundrel. Here was no secret Rebel, no Radical fanatic. He was a murderer, but he served no cause other than his own, of that I was certain. He might kill out of hate or for profit. Why had he killed President Lincoln? A fresh entry under "Mysteries Remaining." But an older entry in that column was my concern: Where to find John Wilkes Booth?

When I departed the house on K Street that evening to keep my rendezvous with the Major, I had high hopes of some progress toward answering that question. But Booth's telegram had a different purpose than the one I imagined. It was sent to betray the brave man who had traded places with him, and through this treachery, insure his own deliverance. *There* was a deed as black and foul as the assassination itself, but to know of it was to know nothing more of where its author might be found. It was not the telegram, but the letter Booth had given Herold, which summoned the lugger to rescue him from Dr. Stewart's Potomac house. Would that the Doctor had glimpsed the name on the letter, instead of the one on the dispatch. But Fate deemed otherwise, and so I returned that evening to the house on K Street no closer than when I departed to the trail of John Wilkes Booth.

What next, then? Or had I truly lost the scent forever? Enough! I would grapple no more with the riddle that day, which had yielded more than its share of surprises. I resolved to think no more of the matter until I had slept one night in a proper bed, a thing I had not done in near two weeks.

My slumber was restful and dreamless, until the hour before dawn, when Professor Haselmayer arrived to proffer his familiar advice that the key to unlock his coffin could be found in my own pockets. I arose and went to the wardrobe, and there searched through my clothes. I found my pocketbook, my watch and some coins, but no key of any sort. I returned to my bed and resumed my sleep. When next I awoke, sunlight streamed through the windowpane, and the only problem that preoccupied my mind concerned the swiftest means of procuring my breakfast. That riddle I easily solved.

I dined alone, for Mr. Pinkerton was already abroad in the city on business. In the midst of my meal the maid brought to the table a letter that had arrived with the morning mail and was addressed to me. It bore the postmark of San Francisco.

It was from Major Bierce, and was in reply to my inquiry of several weeks past regarding General Baker's California days. I had quite forgotten the matter, but I opened the letter immediately and read it in the midst of my repast. When I reached the end of Bierce's epistle, I had no more thought of breakfast. I quickly withdrew my pocketbook and consulted an item contained therein. The Professor Haselmayer of my dreams had not lied; the key to the mystery I sought to solve was there, as it had been for weeks, right in my own pocket.

I leapt from the table and within minutes was on my way to the railroad station. The 7:45 train for New York had not yet departed. When it did, I was aboard.

·32·

The Player's Palace

It was past five o'clock when the ferryboat delivered me to the Cortlandt Street slip. From the river, I had observed the haphazard procession of families promenading along the riverside walks of Battery Park, for it was a Sunday afternoon, and one of the most congenial of such that grace New York City in the midst of May.

I went directly to my rooms at the Astor House to refresh myself after a day spent aboard the cars, although such discomfort had ceased to be a novelty. It seemed I had spent most of the past two months aboard the cars.

I bathed, dressed and dined, for my abrupt departure from the breakfast table in Washington City had been prompted by enthusiasm, and not any desperate urgency. The one I sought could be found tomorrow as easily as today, for he was no fugitive or transient, but one of New York's most prominent citizens. The theatrical season was over, and I was confident he could be found at his home. I had no difficulty learning his address from the desk clerk at the Astor House, for there were few such observers of the city's notables who did not know the place of residence of Edwin Booth.

The assassin's elder brother lived in a house on East 19th Street, a fashionable neighborhood about midway between Union and Madison Squares. He had survived the smirch Wilkes had cast upon the Booth family escutcheon, and went on to obscure that black mark with festoons of fresh laurels earned by his most estimable ability to enchant the boards he trod and the lines he spoke. He had forsworn the theater after his brother's crime, but the public held him blameless and demanded he return to the stage. This he did, about a year after the tragedy, although he kept his resolve never to play again in Washington City.

Edwin Booth's resumption of the stage scandalized the parsons of the press, but, when they were done scribbling their reprehensions for tomorrow's editorial, they were off to elbow their way into the theater tonight, to see Richard, or Henry, or Romeo, or whomever this superlative player had chosen to bring to life. That his brother had slain Lincoln was considered remarkable, but the fact was quickly forgotten; there was so much about Edwin Booth that was so greatly more remarkable.

The Astor's clerk told me Booth was building a new theater. The Winter Garden, in which he was interested, had burned down,† and now Edwin Booth and his family were constructing a replacement on the southeast corner of Sixth Avenue and 23rd Street, which, when completed, was to be the greatest and most elegant hall in America. It was to stand among other theaters as its builder stood among other players. If evidence was wanted that the name of Booth was not anathema, here it was: This superlative house was to be called "Booth's Theater."

Mr. Booth was not in when I arrived at his door. Thus I was informed by a freckled Irish maid, from whom a bit of pleasant coaxing produced the intelligence that Mr. Booth was truly not in his house, but had taken a post-prandial stroll, and likely could be found a few blocks away admiring the construction of his new theater. I thanked her and betook myself there.

It was yet nothing more than the shell of a building, but what a magnificent shell!‡ It was a sumptuous and elegant shell, and looked more to be meant to contain an imperial palace than a place where men played king for but a few hours. A ticket-taker would be the last of the furniture to be installed, so there was none to bar my way as I stepped within the newly raised walls.

---

† The Winter Garden Theater on Broadway, which Edwin Booth owned at the time, burned down on March 23, 1867.—M.C.

‡ The cornerstone had been laid only a few weeks earlier, on April 8, 1868. However, progress in the construction must have been rapid, since the theater opened only ten months later (its first production was *Romeo and Juliet*) on February 3, 1869.—M.C.

The exterior walls seemed complete; there were four of them surrounding a vast, dark abyss of a basement, although enough unfinished flooring had been put down to permit a visitor to journey from
one side of the place to the other without climbing down among
the foundations. There was no roof yet, but the distant tops of the
walls had been bridged by a latticework of beams beneath the
evening sky. Some twilight filtered partway down, but a growing
dimness filled the bottom of the shell in which I stood. The shadows had been driven away from a place near the far wall by the flickering glow of a torch. The light betrayed the distant figure who held
it aloft. Silently I crossed the void that separated us. When I had
gotten near I called to him.

"What, a rehearsal? So early?"

Edwin Booth turned and strained to see into the blackness.

"Who is that?" he demanded.

"Tell me what line you practice," I said. "Is it this one: 'The evil
that men do lives after them; The good is oft interred with their
bones?'"

The player raised his torch and came nearer until I was encompassed by the ambit of its glare.

"Who are you, sir? What business have you here?"

"I am called Nichols, Mr. Booth," I replied. "My business? It is
the evil that men do, that is my business. But sometimes I also deal
in bones."

"You deal in riddles, sir."

"That is so. A riddle is what brings me here. Shall I recite it?"

He made no answer.

"'They buried a box containing some bones, but one dug it up
and found only stones.' There, that is my riddle. Can you solve it?"

The actor came closer until he could see my eyes.

"Are you Baker's man?"

"I am no baker's man," I said. "But *there* is another riddle: 'When
is a baker a butcher?' But you have not puzzled the first one yet."

"No, you could not be from Baker," he mused.

"For Baker knows ought of stones," I agreed.

"But you do. And I can name only two who might have told you of them."

"That is not the answer to the riddle. It was I who dug up the box. There is your answer."

"What do you want of me? Is it money?"

"I hope you do not propose to sell those bones," I replied. "They belonged to a brave and honorable man, and he was not your brother."

"What! You say you want the remains?"

"No, sir. I want your brother."

Edwin Booth turned away.

"I fear I do not understand your meaning, Mr. . . . is it 'Nichols'?"

"It is not, but that is what I told you. Let it stand. Perhaps you do not understand what I said because I was not specific. You have, after all, several brothers. The brother I have in mind is the one who murdered Mr. Lincoln. I'm afraid none of the others will do, you see, for I mean to hang him, and only John Wilkes will answer that requirement."

"Wilkes is dead!"

"You know better. It could not have escaped your recollection, but, if it had, there is your bank account to remind you. 'Your lies have drawn your teeth. Do your worst, if you will. We have no fear. Not another cent.'"

I had read from the onionskin sheet that had reposed these many weeks in my pocketbook.

"You have a distinctive hand, Mr. Booth. You need not put your signature to your notes."

"Baker learned I had claimed Wilkes' body. He threatened to embarrass General Grant and myself if I did not pay. Then his lies became so famous he could no longer blackmail me with the truth. That is all that paper means."

"But Baker knows ought of stones," I repeated. "No sir. Baker knew nothing of your claiming the body, and he would scarcely have believed you had, if he'd been told. For he knew what you knew: The body brought back from Garrett's Farm was not your brother's. But what Baker did not know was that he'd broken the wrong leg of the corpse before delivering it aboard the *Montauk*. Had he broken the proper

one, you could have let it lie beneath the Arsenal, secure from the fear
that someone might dig it up, see the problem, and sound the alarum.
Tell me, how did you learn the wrong leg was broken?"

Edwin Booth made no answer.

"I imagine the news came from Dr. May, by one route or another.
I think he enjoys the distinction of having put a name to the nameless wretch, and is given to chat about it. He is not particularly respectful of truth, but he has such a memory for scars, he cannot have
forgotten which leg was broken. If ever he learns it was the wrong
one, it will discourage his reminiscence, I think."

"I do not know who you may be, Mr. Nichols. And see no reason
to discuss any of these things with you."

"Perhaps you should not discuss them. I would know whatever
you could tell me of your brother's whereabouts, but I'll allow that
would be tantamount to confessing you aided his escape. But I suspect you may have darker secrets than that. I think you may have had
a hand in his crime."

"What! The assassination? Well, sir, you may have learned a deal
about this matter, but that remark proves there is a deal more of which
you remain ignorant. There are certainly many other persons as guilty
as Wilkes, even more so, but I am far from being one of them."

"Is General Baker such a one?"

"He is."

"Then, Mr. Booth, not only have you a brother who is an assassin, but an old friend who is one, as well."

"Baker is no friend of mine."

"Comrade, then, or whatever term of fellowship was used among
members of San Francisco's Vigilante Committee some dozen years
ago."

"I was not a member of the Committee; my brother Junius was.
But it is true we both knew Baker during our California days, before
the War. Yet I do not call him my friend, or my comrade, or anything other than treacherous murderer."

"What does Wilkes call him?"

"You seem to be some species of secret detective. What name do
you call your chief?"

"Wilkes was one of Baker's agents?"

"I am sad to say he was, and sadder still to say *there* was a thing for which I must bear some guilt, for I introduced the two of them beneath my own roof in this city early in the War, when Wilkes was scarcely more than a lad."†

---

† Surprisingly, neither Eisenschiml nor any other analyst of the Lincoln assassination makes reference to the association between Lafayette Baker and John Wilkes Booth's elder brothers, Edwin and Junius Brutus Booth, Jr. The brothers, together with their famous father, Junius Brutus Booth, Sr., went to California in July, 1852, to seek new audiences. The elder Booth departed for home the following September, but died of an illness en route. Edwin and Junius Brutus, Jr. stayed on in San Francisco for several years. Junius prospered and became a respected resident of Telegraph Hill (although he had left a wife and family behind in Maryland and started a new household with an actress in California), while Edwin's fortunes were not as happy. He was drinking heavily during these years, spent most of one of them on an extended tour of Australia and Hawaii, and returned to the East in 1856. His brother remained in California until 1864. But, according to Lafayette Baker's biographer (Mogelever, p. 34), both Baker and Junius Brutus Booth, Jr. joined the San Francisco Vigilante Committee in May, 1856. Kimmel (pp. 81–82, 269–270) reports that the two men became good friends as a consequence of their membership in the Vigilantes. Neither Mogelever nor Kimmel cites the source of his information. However, this much seems well established from a variety of sources: Junius Brutus Booth, Jr. lived in San Francisco from 1852 until 1864; Lafayette Baker lived in San Francisco and Sacramento from 1856 until 1862; both men joined the Vigilante Committee in 1856; both men were prominent members of the community. Therefore, although there were several thousand Vigilantes at the time, it is likely Junius Booth and Lafayette Baker were acquainted with each other, if not fast friends.

Regarding the claim that John Wilkes Booth worked for Baker as a Union spy, this is exactly contrary to every other account of the actor-assassin, which depicts him in roles ranging from a simple Confederate sympathizer, to a highly accomplished and active Confederate agent, with most of the evidence favoring the latter end of the spectrum. He was ostentatious in his public embrace of the Confederate cause, and he certainly served the Confederate secret service in some capacity, if nothing more than as an occasional courier. However, if Baker recruited him to penetrate the Confederate intelligence apparatus, John Wilkes Booth would not have been the first nor the last instance of a double agent in the history of espionage. There are a few clues that suggest Booth *was* a Union agent, and several of them were offered by his sister, Asia, who, herself, believed him to be a Confederate spy. In her memoir of Booth, Mrs. Clarke recalls Booth admitting to her that he was able to travel to Texas, Kansas and other places by virtue of a pass signed by General Grant (Clarke, p. 117), and she quotes him as describing the Abolitionist hero, John Brown (whose execution he happened to witness), as "a man inspired, the grandest character of this century!" (p. 124). If Booth was an ardent Secessionist and actually held John Brown in this regard, he was unique.—M.C.

"If that be so, sir," I replied, "then you are right. There is a deal I do not know about this matter. Yet I hope to learn it. Perhaps I shall hear it from your brother, when I find him."

"If you knew it now, you might not be so keen to drag him to the gallows. There are sundry others who deserve it better."

"Such as General Baker?"

"Yes."

"And Edwin Stanton?"

"Is he a wealthy man?"

"I don't think he is particularly wealthy."

"Then he is likely not one of the plotters," said Edwin Booth. "Wilkes, you see, acted from some deranged sense of duty. But all the others were in it for gold, fortunes in gold."

"Baker is no Croesus."

"He got his pay, I hear, but he gambled it all away. That is why he sells his silence. But the others kept their bloody profits."

"Name them."

"I do not know their names; I do not wish to know them."

"Then how do you come to know *of* them?"

Edwin Booth did not reply. Instead he regarded me for a moment.

"Mr. Nichols, I do not know who you could possibly be. And I can think of no good reason to answer you."

"As you have surmised," I said, "I am a secret detective. I am in private employment. While making some inquiries recently, I discovered that your brother, John Wilkes, is still at large, and I learned sundry other particulars of the matter. Now I serve a private patron who would learn the whole of it. In candor, I must tell you I've been sent to find John Wilkes Booth. I can also say I shall very likely succeed."

"Then you will do so without my assistance. Do you think I wish to help you hang my own brother? No matter. I could not help you even if I would. I do not have the slightest inkling of his whereabouts."

"Yet you know of others you say deserve the noose more than he. Perhaps if I knew as much, I should see they received it. But, as matters stand, Wilkes is destined to hang alone, and, after he has, the matter will be considered closed."

The actor stared at me for a while. Presently he turned, and I thought he was making to leave, but he walked slowly toward the nearby masonry, his torch held before him and his eyes cast down, as if he were searching the unfinished floor for some missing thing. When he reached the wall, he turned and paced back in the same fashion. Thus he paced to and fro for a time, and I think he must have walked a half-mile before he abruptly stopped before me and looked up.

"Very well. I see no wrong in it. I think there may be some right in it. What I shall give you was given me by Wilkes to do with as I saw fit. I do not think there is any clew in it that could lead you to him. Yes, you shall have it, but, as to where you obtained it, that is something you must content yourself to forget, for I shall deny giving it to you.

"Now, should you have any questions as to the means by which Wilkes made good his escape, keep them to yourself. I shall not answer them, for I do not admit to having had any hand in it. Is that understood?"

"It is. But what, then, do you propose to give me?"

"The pages Wilkes tore from his notebook."

"You have them?"

Edwin Booth shook his head.

"No, but I know where they are hidden. During his flight Wilkes used them to chronicle a true history of his involvement in the abominable affair. He named all the others who had a hand in it, or all whose names he knew. And he included with the names, places, dates and other particulars. These pages he later concealed in a place not very far from where we stand, against the chance he would be taken and not live to tell his tale. Still later he wrote to me and asked that I fetch them and see to their publication, so that the public understand the true reasons for his act, and know the names of the others who held a larger share of the guilt. This I did not do. I let them stay where he hid them, for the matter has brought grief enough to my family. Let the dead stay buried, I thought. But you, damn you, whoever you are, Mr. Nichols, have opened a grave, and I see you have robbed me of any choice in the matter. What you say is so.

"You know Wilkes lives. Others, then, must know as much. The hunt is on once more, and, should you fail in your quest, there will be another following in your footsteps, and, if he fails, yet another. Perhaps you'll all fail, every cursed one of you, but even if you never learn where Wilkes hides, you have already discovered the only secret I wished to keep.

"Yes, Wilkes is still at large. Damn him! Damn you! Damn you all who never let me forget, me or mine, but eternally worry this thing like a pack of terriers.

"God, let me be done with this thing, once and for all! Yes, Mr. Nichols, I'll give you those pages. Take them and hang those they name. Hang them all. Have a carnival of hangings. Hold it here, in this place, Booth's Theater. Is there another more fitting? It will seat two thousand. Two thousand, Mr. Nichols! You can invite the press, General Grant, the crowned heads of Europe, the august from every place on the Great Globe. We shall illuminate the scene with lime-lights, and the photographers can make a panorama of it, so that those we cannot pack within these walls will not be cheated of the spectacle. And after we are done, we'll cut them down and bury them in the cellar, then raze the building, leaving not one stone atop another. For there can be no comedy nor tragedy, not even from the pen of the Bard himself, that would be sequel enough to that magnificent occasion."

He dashed the torch to the floor, and we were thus abruptly wrapped in the twilight dimness of the place. The tragedian stood gasping for a minute. Finally he spoke again, this time in a different voice. "Do you know the ferry slip at the foot of Whitehall Street?"

"I do."

"Then be there at midnight. Bring a lantern and a compass. Do not bring another. We shall go to Wilkes' secret place without a witness."

·33·

A Secret Place

···———◆———···

A thick and encroaching fog had rolled in from the sea to cloak the harbor and those streets close to the waterfront. Only a handful of travelers waited in the ferry house on Whitehall Street, doubtless some of them printers, their hands stained with the ink of Monday morning's news, and a few other Sunday visitors to New York, who had stayed late, and now were bound for their Brooklyn homes.

I had spent the hours that intervened since my meeting with Edwin Booth composing a detailed report of the situation of affairs and transcribing it into telegraphic cipher. This I had dispatched to Mr. Pinkerton from the Western Union station, which is one of the conveniences of the Astor House. The desk clerk was able to provide me with a map of the streets of Brooklyn, for I thought this likely to be my night's destination. Two ferries left from the foot of Whitehall Street, and both crossed the river to points in the City of Brooklyn. One landed at the Atlantic Dock, that vast waterfront works near Red Hook Point. The other crossed to Atlantic Street.† Thus I knew I should require a map. New York was the city of my birth and early life, and I knew it as well as any knows his home. But the City of Brooklyn‡ was a foreign port to me, and I was more intimate with the streets and avenues of San Francisco and London than with those to be found in Brooklyn.

---

† Now Atlantic Avenue.—M.C.

‡ Brooklyn was not incorporated as a borough of New York City until 1898.—M.C.

I entered the ferry building a few minutes before midnight. Mr. Booth was there before me, but he emerged from his place of concealment only after he saw that I had come alone, as I had promised.

"Have you a lantern and compass?" he inquired.

I had them with me in a poke. I followed the actor aboard the ferryboat, the one bound for Atlantic Street. We remained on deck throughout the brief voyage through the fog, for Edwin Booth's face was a famous one in these parts, and though it was partly obscured by a slouch hat and a scarf, he did not wish to risk the curious attention of our fellow passengers. But we stood near a window of the cabin so he could employ the light from within to show me a paper he carried.

"I do not have Wilkes' letter, of course," he said. "I burned it after I'd read it, but not before making this transcription of his instructions. Now you must make your own copy or commit it to memory, for I cannot give it to you, as it is in my own hand."

"Then keep it in your hand while you guide me," I replied.

"No. I shall not go with you to the place. I shall leave you at the slip and return on this same boat. You must follow these instructions by yourself."

I took the paper from him and read it by the light from the cabin, making a copy within my head. When I'd finished I comprehended why the lantern was indispensable, and saw that the compass was to be put to an unusual and ingenious use. I returned the paper to Mr. Booth.

"You have no wish to see the place?" I inquired.

The player shook his head.

"The underground is not my district. I leave it to the likes of Wilkes and yourself. And to the dead."

I left Edwin Booth at the ferry slip at the foot of Atlantic Street, and went some short way along the waterfront to a pier, which seemed to be the same the assassin had designated. Following his instructions, I walked a few steps into the fog and found, as Wilkes had promised, a ladder leading down to the water. I lit the candle lantern and descended.

Just above the level of the river, I saw some planks that had been nailed in place to form a walkway which led among the pilings and back toward the riverbank. The wood was damp and rotten, and I stepped gingerly as I made my way beneath the wharf. When I reached the base of the pier, I saw the entrance described in the instructions. It was a pipe that emerged from the earthen bank, and was some five feet or so in diameter, large enough for a man to walk through at a crouch. The level of the tide had risen above the floor of the massive tube, and near a foot of water stood in it. I stuffed the ends of my trousers into the tops of my boots and waded into the thing, my lantern held before me. The lapping of wavelets filled the pipe with hollow echoes, but the sound of claws scampering over stone proved that drier regions lay ahead, and were enjoyed by a multitude of the small gray denizens of the waterfront.

Presently I entered a larger chamber, in length and width approximating the dimensions of a prison cell, but of indeterminate height, for the ceiling was beyond the range of my little lantern. Against the wall opposite the entrance from the river, I saw a makeshift wooden ladder, which rose into the blackness above. I waded across to it, and carefully ascended the thing.

The ladder rose some twenty feet, and the top of it rested against what looked to be a ledge. On this I placed my lantern and then my feet. Then taking the light up once more, I held it before me and saw a most remarkable sight.

I stood in the mouth of a cavern, but one of human manufacture. It looked to be some dozen feet in height and perhaps twenty in width, and the floor, walls and ceiling were not hewn from rock, but constructed of masonry. It was the tunnel Wilkes had promised in his instructions. I could not see the end of it, nor should I have expected to, for the assassin had told his brother to advance "one thousand paces" into the thing, so I knew that much of the brickwork cavern lay before me. I went forward, counting off my steps as I advanced.

There was not a curve nor corner in the subterranean passage. It had been dug along a perfectly straight line, which, so my compass and map suggested, lay directly beneath Atlantic Street. There was not a thing in the tunnel which might reveal the intent of its builders. Nought but dust lay upon the bricks on which I trod. From time to time I glimpsed some small, dark shapes scurrying ahead to escape the advancing ambit of my lantern. These were the only residents of the place. Thank God, they were not pleased to welcome me.

When I had walked a thousand paces I halted. I had not yet reached the end of the passageway, and in the darkness ahead, it might have extended for miles. I never learned the full extent of the tunnel, for the place I had stopped was my destination.

The assassin's instructions said to approach the wall to my left, and this I did. Next, following Wilkes' guidance, I raised the compass to shoulder height and, holding it close to the brickwork of the wall, moved ahead. The needle pointed obliquely toward the wall, for the tunnel had been dug along a southeasterly line. But after I had gone on some paces, the needle abruptly swung about and pointed directly away from the wall. I had found the spot.

The brick at the place where the needle turned looked no different from any of its neighbors, but when I put the lantern on the floor and thrust my fingers into the tight crevasses surrounding it, I found it could be worked loose, as Wilkes had promised. I removed it from the wall and set it down, then, raising my lantern, I looked into the aperture thus formed. Within I saw the bar of magnetic iron that had spun the compass needle, and a small metal box. Quickly I snatched the latter from the hiding place, and setting the lantern again upon the floor, I squatted down and held the box in its light.

It was a curious object, a rectangular brass case a few inches in length and width, but scarcely a quarter-inch thick. It was highly polished, and the edges were ornamented with wire beading. I lifted the lid.

It was empty.

So the assassin had become impatient, it seemed. When his brother failed to retrieve the pages, and see to their publication, John Wilkes Booth had come back to this place and fetched them himself. That seemed the only explanation. Yet, if it were the right one, why had he replaced the empty box in its hiding place and concealed it again within the block? I turned the little box over in my hands, opened it again, but it was as empty as before. I went back to the hole in the wall and held the lantern to it. There was nothing left within but the bar. I took that out and inspected it closely. It was a foot long, but of solid iron. The pages were not inside it.

Thus far in this recountment of my subterranean exploration, I have had little to say of one unpleasant topic: the rats. Indeed, I have avoided recollecting them now as I tried to drive them from my thoughts even as I heard them scattering and chirping beyond the range of my lamp in that black and lonely place. I do not care for the creatures, which is not remarkable in itself, nor near as remarkable as some examples of their species I've seen along the Thames in the Limehouse district of London, or on the Marseilles waterfront. I have seen rats that have never troubled the worst bad dreams of most men. I have seen large ones, although I cannot say how large, for never have I inclined to measure or weigh one of them. But I have seen rats that could surely destroy a man if they chose to attack in concert, and I have seen a few of them who might accomplish the same in single combat.

Had it not been my deepest desire to avoid reflecting on the creatures whose home I had disturbed, I might have taken more notice that their loathsome little sounds issued, not only from the dark reaches ahead of me, but from the equally Stygian region through which I'd come. I was, in fact, surrounded by the rats, and deep within me a vexatious appreciation of this situation of affairs commanded my senses to dull themselves, lest a keener apprehension of the sounds reaching my ears might rowel me into panic. In the event, this nearly proved fatal.

But I could no longer ignore the rats, for one rushed out of the dark expanse of tunnel behind me, from the thousand paces of blackness that separated me from the entrance to this cavern. He was followed by another, and then two more. They ran past the lantern, past my boots and on into the unexplored darkness on the other side of the lantern's range. It was not an attack, and I thanked God for that, but I may have taken too long at it, for only when I had completed my prayer did I think to wonder what might lurk beyond in the darkness that had frightened the rats into flight. It was no longer necessary to wonder about the thing, for now I could see what had stampeded the rats. It was a pair of men, and one of them held a pistol.

They had followed me in stealth, but I could not have failed to hear some sound of their passage had my mind not plugged my ears against the din of the rodents. Yet such wisdom arrived too late. I was unarmed (even my knife I'd carelessly left behind in my rooms at the Astor House), and the fellow with the gun was pointing it at me.

"Put it down, sir," said the other, "and back off."

He had not been specific, but I put everything I held onto the floor of the tunnel; the lantern, Booth's empty box, and the magnetic bar. I backed away. They advanced into the light as I withdrew, and then I saw them clearly and recognized them.

The man holding the pistol bore a familiar visage, but it took me a moment to recall where I'd seen it before. Then I knew: He was one of the pair who had waited before the clockmaker's shop opposite Mr. Brady's Gallery. He was the lad who dared trail Baker, and who had found me at Willard's. When last I saw that face, it bore an expression of astonishment and chagrin, for its owner was aboard the Alexandria ferry, and I was not. But now it was my turn for astonishment and chagrin.

The other fellow was easier to place. I had seen him scarcely a day earlier, and he was not such as might easily be forgotten, for he was a giant. It was General Thomas T. Eckert, the man I'd seen in the Senate gallery in the company of Major Johnson, the man Mr. Crook had identified for me. The Senate gallery on Saturday noon, and a deserted tunnel beneath the streets of Brooklyn in the small hours of Monday morning. General Eckert was a large man in a small world. He bent and retrieved the box, opened it, and turned it over in his hands.

"Very well, sir," he said. "Hand them over."

"I do not have them," I answered.

He turned to his companion.

"Fetch them," he commanded. "Kill him first," he added, almost as an afterthought.

The fellow raised his pistol. I stared into the muzzle in horror. I was to be given no chance; I could not outrun a bullet. I charged toward him, confident I was a dead man unless the weapon misfired. Then *he* would be a dead man.

Before I could cross the yards that separated us, before he could squeeze the trigger, a look of sudden dismay seized his countenance. He opened his mouth, but no sound issued forth. He raised onto the tips of his toes, as some ballet dancer, then crashed to the floor, knocking over the candle lantern and plunging the fearsome tableau into blackness.

There were some sounds of scuffling from the direction of the pair, and I heard Eckert shout an oath. I ran toward the place I'd seen the man fall and felt about on the floor to retrieve his pistol. I did not find it, but I grasped the magnetic iron bar, which lay where I had placed it. It had the mass and length to serve as an estimable truncheon.

I had a tin box of matches in my pocket, but I left it there. If Eckert held the pistol, lighting a match would certainly be fatal. But after long moments passed and the darkness remained, I concluded Eckert had not located the pistol. Or else he had no matches.

There is a special craft of combat in total darkness. It is little known in America or Europe, for it is an Oriental skill. I learned it from a Chinese detective who works for Mr. Pinkerton in San Francisco. Curiously, it has little to do with conquering one's opponent, and much to do with conquering one's self.

We fear the dark. That is a natural thing, and the more sudden the darkness (the less expected it is), the greater the fear. If, in such circumstances, we are confronted by a dangerous foe, our fear is infinitely larger, for we fear for our lives. I know such fear. It is said to raise the hair upon one's head, although I do not think this is so. But it freezes one's insides, and it makes a desert of one's mouth. But most important of all, it quickens one's breath. In the darkness a frightened man will gasp as one who has run a mile. This then is the Oriental craft: It is a simple trick of respiration, whereby one silences his own breath, so that he cannot be heard, but may hear the breathing of his foe. To one who has learned this trick, darkness becomes an ally.

I had no wish to wrestle with Eckert. His strength was legendary. It is said he once broke five iron pokers over his arm. I do not know if this is so, but none who had seen the man would deny it might have happened. Whether or not he could break iron pokers, I knew he could wring my neck were he to get his hands on it. Eckert unarmed was near as lethal as when he carried a gun, and I was grateful for the darkness and the trick I'd learned in San Francisco.

Someone was moving near me, and he was puffing like a locomotive. My own breath was almost stopped and I could hear the other's respirations above the chatter and scamperings of those tunnel dwellers we'd disturbed. I flattened myself against the wall, and he passed scant inches from me. When he crept by, I turned my own head to gauge that point in the blackness where the head of the other seemed to be. And then I swung the iron bar. It was halted in mid-career by some obstacle, and I felt a satisfying thump transmitted to my hand. Next there was the sound of a large body striking the floor. I waited for some moments before lighting a match.

Eckert and his companion were down. No other seemed about. I found the candle lantern and lighted it, then retrieved the pistol. Next I examined General Eckert. He was breathing, but the blow had caught him on the back of his head, and, had it been the skull of an ordinary man, he would have been dead. As it was, the General was due for a prolonged snooze.

His partner was destined for a much longer sleep. The lantern light revealed the hilt of a dagger protruding from between his shoulder blades. I searched the dead man's pockets and found some credentials identifying him as one Richard Harley, a private constable of the Erie Railroad Company's police. I put them in my pocket, for they might contain some unseen clew, and Mr. Harley would have no further use for them, such papers carrying no authority in Hell.

I heard a new sound, footfalls far off in the distance, retreating toward the tunnel entrance. I took up the lantern and the empty metal box and made off in the same direction. Eckert and his dead companion I was pleased to leave in the company of their brother rodents.

I covered the thousand paces and the trip down the ladder, through the pipe and up into the world of men in a deal less time than I had spent on it before. But I failed to overtake the one who had gone ahead of me, and I think he may have been aboard the ferryboat I saw sailing into the fog as I hurried from the pier toward the Atlantic Street slip. I would, of course, have known who he was, and I wished to thank him for my deliverance. I did not know it as I waited that night at the wharf for the next boat back to New York, but both of these things were destined to be consummated very shortly. I passed the time between ferries by gazing at the fog-enshrouded City of Brooklyn, and wondering how far beneath it had the mysterious tunnel been burrowed, and what other subterranean boulevards might be hidden beneath the streets of the city.†

---

†At my request, O'Toole made informal inquiries of some friends, an artist and a pair of filmmakers, who live in the Cobble Hill section of Brooklyn, which is bounded on the north by Atlantic Avenue. He says his friends had taken an interest in the rich history of the area in which they live, and were well steeped in its lore, but had never heard of a tunnel having been built beneath Atlantic Avenue. Such a tunnel seemed unlikely, since, even in Manhattan, no subways were constructed until many years after the date of Cosgrove's reported adventures. The Brooklyn waterfront near Atlantic Avenue is, of course, completely changed since 1868, and there was no point in looking for Cosgrove's tunnel entrance. Thus, for a time, it looked like Cosgrove's tunnel (or, I should say Booth's tunnel) would have to remain an open question. But it did not.

There *was* such a tunnel beneath Atlantic Avenue in 1868, and, so far as I can determine, it is still there. It is seventeen feet high, twenty-one feet wide, and runs along beneath Atlantic Avenue for about a half-mile. It has a curious history, altogether appropriate to Cosgrove's adventures.

The tunnel was built during the 1840s and completed in 1850. Its purpose was to carry the Long Island Railroad along that segment of Atlantic Avenue, which was then a beautiful, tree-lined boulevard, whose residents planned to keep it that way. Thus, if the railroad was to pass along Atlantic Avenue, it would do so out of sight; hence the tunnel. For reasons too complex to recount here, the railroad tunnel was taken out of use and the last train passed through it in 1858. It was sealed up in 1861, and has been put to no legitimate use since then. It is said that, during the Civil War, it was used by smugglers to transfer their goods from the river to warehouses farther inland. It is said it was used for the manufacture and storage of illegal spirits during Prohibition. It is reported that, in 1936, the tunnel was suspected to contain the body of a famous and missing gangster, and it was opened and searched (the gangster actually reposed in a barrel of cement in Buffalo). It is further reported that a team of WPA laborers opened the tunnel and inspected it in 1941 to insure its structural soundness, and that the traffic on busy Atlantic Avenue would not someday come crashing through its roof. It is further reported that J. Edgar Hoover sent some of his men into the place during the Second World War in search of German spies. None was found. (Neither has there been any report of the remains of Constable Harley of the Erie Railroad Police, but a century has passed, and there have been countless generations of rats.) Apparently the tunnel has remained unvisited during the past three decades.

At this point the reader may understand why I didn't go to the trouble to explore the tunnel myself. Presently, when he has read a few more pages, he will change his mind and find that fact astonishing. But when he has finished all of this book, I think he (or she) will understand once again.

Those who wish to learn more of the tunnel (and of many other wonders to be found beneath the sidewalks of New York) are directed to a fascinating book by Robert Daley, *The World Beneath the City,* Lippincott, 1959. The matter of the Atlantic Avenue tunnel can be found on pages 210 through 213.—M.C.

· 34 ·

The Magic Box

·‥•──◆──•‥·

I returned to my rooms at the Astor House, but I did not sleep. I was too astonished at finding myself alive. When dawn came, it discovered me still awake, puzzling over the mysteries the night's exertions had yielded.

Had Edwin Booth betrayed me? I thought not. There were too many byways in the city in which murder might be arranged without I be sent to so strange a place as the tunnel in Brooklyn. And, had he hired some men to murder me, would he have given that job of work to a former Assistant Secretary of War, now Chief of all Eastern Lines of the Western Union Company?

The Western Union Company! Why, it was to Western Union I had entrusted my dispatch to Mr. Pinkerton last night, wherein I had recounted in many particulars my discourse with Edwin Booth and my appointment with him at the Whitehall Street ferry house. And it was Western Union that had carried every single dispatch I had sent Mr. Pinkerton in report of my progress since the inception of my inquiries. Yet, I had sent them in cipher. But now I saw it: That cipher had been defeated. And if General Thomas T. Eckert had come in person to see to that dirty business in the tunnel, there could be no other conclusion than it was he who had broken the cipher, and his name was among those John Wilkes Booth had written in the pages of the diary.†

---

† Thomas T. Eckert was accomplished in both the construction and the defeat of secret ciphers, having spent much of the Civil War engaged in that very activity.

Now I understood many other things. The counterfeit telegram I sent over Baker's name to summon Dr. May to Washington City, I had sent by Western Union. It brought May, but it also brought the railroad policeman who now lay with a knife in his back beneath the streets of Brooklyn. And that man might carry the credentials of the Erie Railroad Company, but he clearly had been in the employ of Eckert. And it was the dead man's partner who had trailed Mr. Murphy from Brady's Gallery, and likely the same who burglarized Murphy's rooms for the conversation they supposed Dr. May had with General Baker. So they had followed Dr. May to Washington City, and to Brady's Gallery, and that led them to follow Mr. Murphy and myself. Like Stanton, Eckert suspected Booth was still at large, and when he learned I'd been set on the assassin's trail, he strove to put his detectives on my own trail, hoping I would lead him to the man who knew of his bloody hand in the assassination of President Lincoln. There was no doubt that Eckert's name was writ on one of those missing pages.

But the pages stayed missing, and there was yet another riddle. For the hundredth time I took the strange little case in my hand and opened it. Empty. Why had the assassin replaced it in its hiding place? Why hide an empty box? The box, itself, might be the answer, if I could guess the meaning of its curious design.

I knew of one man who was an expert in such things, a police detective with whom I had served during my days with the New York Department. His name was Patrick Flynn, and, although he was not an old man, he had lived a long time, and had a vast knowledge of the odds and ends of the world. I inquired at the local district station house, and was told that Officer Flynn could be found at the Commissioner's Office on Mulberry Street. With the mysterious case in my pocket, I betook myself there.

"Aha, Nicholas Cosgrove! Well, the Millennium is surely upon us," declared Mr. Flynn by way of greeting. "Here, help me sort through these reports, so I can finish early and be safe in church when Gabriel arrives."

For a full account of the cryptographic and cryptoanalytic work of Eckert and others during the Civil War, see David Kahn, *The Codebreakers,* Macmillan, 1967, Chapter 7.—M.C.

I was as glad to see him, and I said so.

"Has Mr. Pinkerton sent you to hire Mr. Kennedy† for him, or have you come to pay a social call?"

"Neither one," I replied. "It is a professional visit, but it's yourself I've come to see, in hope you might share with me one small fragment of your encyclopedic knowledge of mankind."

"Oh, is that all you want," remarked Mr. Flynn with delight. "Well, I think I may be able to spare ye a moment or two, as one officer of the law to another."

"Excellent!" I exclaimed, taking the metal case from my pocket and presenting it to him. "Might you be telling me what this is?"

Mr. Flynn turned the thing over in his hands, then cast a sly glance at me.

"You don't know what this is, Nicholas?"

"I do not."

"Are you sure?"

"Would I be here if I were not?"

"Well, I'm very glad to hear that, lad. I wouldn't like to think you'd taken to a life of crime. At least not petty crime, like bamboozling gents in saloons or aboard trains."

"What is it, then?"

"What is it? Why, it's a card box. And what is that? Why, it's a tool of petty swindlers. It's used to separate the gullible from their gold. Here, I'll demonstrate with this streetcar ticket. (A playing card is what's generally used, but there's none of them about.) Observe."

Mr. Flynn opened the box and placed the ticket inside it. Then he closed the cover and held the case out before me. He opened it again. The ticket was gone, and in its place there was a tiny scrap of paper, which fluttered out onto the detective's desk.

"What's this? There's not supposed to be anything at all. Well, you see the idea. The ticket has disappeared."

He shut the box, then quickly reopened it. The ticket was back.

---

† John A. Kennedy, who was a member of the New York Police Board of Commissioners and the Department's General Superintendent.—M.C.

"Here's the trick," explained Mr. Flynn, withdrawing a long needle from the end of the box. When it was removed, a part of the box in which the ticket had been placed swung free, revealing a second compartment which had enclosed the first, but, although minutely larger so as to encompass the other compartment, was in every other respect, identical to it. There was, in other words, a box within the box, and the needle was the key that locked or released it. The ticket had seemed to vanish because the compartment that held it had become part of the cover, and the second compartment had been empty.

But the second compartment had not been entirely empty. I picked up the scrap that had fallen onto Mr. Flynn's desk. It looked to be the corner of a page.

A page from a notebook, or a diary.

I turned the fragment over carefully and placed it in my palm.

"Is *that* what you were after, Nicholas?" Mr. Flynn inquired.

"It's a tiny part of it," I replied. "I think it may have gotten torn off by someone who was in a great rush and working in the dark, as well."

"In the dark, was it? I've never heard of a swindler using one of these things in the dark."

"And none but swindlers use such devices?" I asked.

"It's for card tricks, Nicholas. If the man who owned it was not a swindler, there is only one honest trade he might have pursued."

"What trade is that?"

"Why, think about it, Nicholas. Who, besides a swindler, takes his card trickery so serious as to buy one of these things?"

"A stage magician!"

· 35 ·

Pursuit Above the Clouds

It was a curious coincidence, observed Officer Flynn, that I should have come to his office that day and speak of stage magicians. It was a coincidence, he explained, for it was a matter involving a stage magician that was the reason I found Mr. Flynn at his desk in the Commissioners' Office. Superintendent Kennedy had left him to take charge of the place while he went off on a lark at the beseechment of one such member of the conjuring fraternity.

The fellow was to launch his appearance at an uptown theater on the following night, but he had devised a scheme to put himself on the front page of tomorrow's papers. The magician, it was to be understood, was especially expert in the art of escaping, and he proposed to exhibit a free sample of his tricks to the public during the dinner hour today, and he'd hit upon a way to insure the presence of the gentlemen from the press, to wit: he would do some of his escaping, from the embrace of a pair of police bracelets, while drifting above the city in a free balloon. The magician had provided a second balloon for some daring representatives of the press, who would follow along in it, and observe and photograph the conjurer free of his shackles a mile above the spires of the town. To prove to one and all that he was well and truly shackled, he had invited Superintendent Kennedy to apply the irons.

And that, explained Officer Flynn, was the reason I was so fortunate as to find him at his desk, for he had hoped to be off witnessing that same spectacle himself. The spectacle, he informed me, was to begin in Battery Park.

And the magician's name?

Professor Haselmayer.

Mr. Flynn had scarcely uttered the name when the bells of a nearby church began to toll out the arrival of the noon hour. I shouted my thanks at the man over my shoulder as I dashed downstairs, ran into the street, and halted a passing cab by grabbing the bridle of the frightened animal in front of it. I opened the door and hauled out the startled passenger, excusing this act with a bark that it was police business I was about. I silenced the protesting hack man with a handful of cash, and promised him as much again if he could deliver me to the Battery Park within five minutes. The money accelerated his perception of the situation of affairs, and he'd lashed his horse to a gallop before I was entirely aboard the vehicle. I managed to secure the door before some defect in the pavement over which we sped might toss me out.

I think the man earned his bonus, but I am not certain, for the trip seemed to require an hour, yet from the pitching and leaping of the cab, the clatter of the horse's hoofs and the chorus of curses and exclamations that marked our way, I incline to think the cabman beat my five minutes with a couple to spare. At all events, I did not worry the matter, but thrust the cash into his open palm after I'd leapt out onto State Street. I dashed into the park. There, down near the water, I saw two giant balloons tethered above the heads of the crowd. I pressed my way through the throng and presently arrived at the platform the magician had provided for his exhibition.

Professor Haselmayer and Superintendent Kennedy were already out on this makeshift stage, as were the Professor's company of Zouaves, who were seeing to the pair of airships. Close by was a camera atop a tripod, and some fellow crouching behind it, a black mantle draped over his head and shoulders, and the dorsal section of his instrument. He was surrounded by a contingent of reporters, their pencils and notebooks at the ready, and several further equipped with pint bottles bulging their pockets. At some small remove was the park bandstand, with a band aboard, and a brisk military march enlivened the air.

The weather of this mid-May noon was a delight, and the Park would, in any case, have been the noontime destination of many, who went there on such days to eat a box lunch upon the green commons and stroll along the promenade to inhale the salty air. But the pair of gaudy marvels that towered above the park had drawn many times the number that might otherwise be expected, and there was no room for any to sit near the Professor's platform, so most who had brought their lunches ate them while standing and gazing at the spectacle. A freshening offshore breeze tilted the balloons and sent the Zouaves to see to their lines.

Professor Haselmayer looked to be in fine form, his hairless head glistening beneath the noonday sun. He was attired in tights for his performance, and he'd added a monocle to his costume, his only facial adornment apart from his luxuriant and well-barbered imperial. He was already encumbered with his stage shackles when I reached the platform, and he turned and signaled for the band to suspend its march, that he might address those assembled.

He stepped forward and recited his now familiar explanation of the difficult and apparently impossible feat he proposed to accomplish in the basket of the airship high above the city, and then he introduced Superintendent Kennedy, and explained the role he would play in the ceremony. When he had finished he turned to Mr. Kennedy and held out his arms for the police irons. I climbed onto the platform.

"A moment, if you please, gentlemen!" I cried.

Superintendent Kennedy turned and gazed at me with astonishment.

"Why, Mr. Cosgrove! What is the meaning of this?"

"A bit of advice, if you have no objection," I replied. "Do not put the shackles about the gentleman's elbows, or they will fall away after he has rid himself of his trick bracelets. See if you can find some room to put them about his wrists."

Superintendent Kennedy turned and looked in bafflement at the Professor's irons.

"What is this, then?" asked the magician in his heavy Germanic accents. "Am I under arrest?" he inquired in a merry manner.

"You are, sir," I answered, placing a hand upon his shoulder.

"John Wilkes Booth, I arrest you for the murder of President Abraham Lincoln!"

A stunned silence struck the crowd, broken only by a few titters and some embarrassed applause. The onlookers thought the interruption to be some curious elaboration of the performance. The Superintendent thought I had taken leave of my senses. Only the magician perceived the meaning of my words. He spun from my grasp, scattering his stage shackles across the platform, and seized a saber from the belt of one of his Zouaves. He swung the blade in a great arc, and I heard it cleave the air before my face as I leapt back. My only weapon was the Bowie knife in my belt, too short a length of steel with which to counter a sword. I turned to another of the Professor's helpers and swiftly borrowed that fellow's saber. Mr. Kennedy, the photographer and the reporters, and all others aboard the platform backed away. Thus Booth and I stood alone, facing each other across a pair of blades. The assassin struck a fencing stance and advanced.

John Wilkes Booth was an accomplished swordsman. Audiences that cared nothing for Shakespeare came to see Booth's Richard, and his Henry and his Anthony, not to hear him recite the Bard's immortal words, but to enjoy the actor's swordplay. Booth groomed his arm quite as much as he did his voice, and he studied with diligence under the best fencing masters he could hire. The man holding the saber before me knew what to do with it.

He thrusted; I parried.

I was no stranger to the blade, myself, yet I had never been taught by a fencing master. My teachers had been sergeants of the Union cavalry, and what I had learned I had been taught, not in the gymnasium, but in the saddle.

I slashed, he retreated a step.

Booth was an artist, a dancer as much as an actor. He was agile and skillful, and his arm was well educated.

He struck my blade aside and made another thrust. The saber tip ripped through my coat and stung my shoulder. I jumped back.

Booth was a fencer and I was not. But the saber was not made for fencing. That is better done with lighter blades, the foil or épée. The saber is too heavy for it. It is not for artful fencing, but for bloody mayhem. It was not Booth's weapon, but it was mine. He was an actor, but I was a soldier. I charged.

He had no chance for thrusting, for he was fully occupied in parrying. His ability was considerable, but he had trained to use the blade in skilled avoidance of damaging his fellow actors. All I knew of the saber was how to kill with one. I proceeded with this objective.

Booth retreated before the onslaught. Twice he made to hold his ground and even to regain some he had lost. But he could not. He had nearly backed to the end of the platform when he abandoned the contest. He circled to my right and ran.

"Turn loose the lines!" he shouted to the astonished Zouaves, who, as all others looking on, could not decide the meaning of our swordplay. Could it be in earnest? It must be part of the clever magician's performance. The men let go the ropes depending from the balloons, and both craft abruptly tilted to the lee, each constrained to the earth by a single line. The actor, sword in hand, leapt from the platform and grabbed one of the lines. He raised his blade, then brought it down, slicing through the rope at a point below his feet. The craft leapt into the air and drifted over the heads of the throng, while the actor dangled beneath it.

Booth dropped his saber among them and climbed the line. As the airship passed over State Street, he had achieved the basket and was secure inside it. Immediately one of the sandbags draped around the side of the car fell away to burst on the pavement below. The airship soared into the blue May sky. A second bag was loosed as the balloon drifted near the towering steeples of Trinity Church, and the craft accelerated its ascent, clearing the structure by many safe yards.

All of us stood there gazing after the rapidly retreating prodigy. Then the Superintendent turned to me.

"Mr. Cosgrove, what can all this mean?"

"It would need several hours to explain and several months to persuade your belief," I replied. "I must leave that task until my return."

So saying, I followed the actor's example, leaping to the line beneath the remaining airship, and parting it with my saber. I climbed to the basket and, immediately upon clearing the crowd, loosed a pair of sandbags. The ground fell rapidly away beneath me, and soon I was treated to a breathtaking vista few human eyes had enjoyed.

The City of New York was spread out before me, spanning the two rivers that bounded it to the East and West. The busy commercial district was directly below, but I could see the residential districts uptown, and the farms and shanties that dotted the landscape north of 50th Street. Even the sparkling ponds that decorated Central Park were visible from my elevated vantage.

The city was surrounded by hundreds of vessels, most moored along the waterfront and forming the likeness of a prodigious family of piglets, all suckling at the multitudinous teats of some gargantuan sow. Other craft plied the rivers and the harbor behind me, and I made out several ferryboats in the midst of their endless voyages, shuttling between the city and its neighbors. Jersey was to my left and Brooklyn to my right. But all these proud works of man had shrunk, and become perfect miniatures of themselves. It was as if I gazed upon the toys that equipped the playroom of some princeling.

Yet I had not ascended in the airship to contemplate the city and its environs, and so that object to which I turned my gaze was the other balloon, with its criminal cargo.

The airship was not difficult to discern, for it was a gaudy, striped thing, with alternate bars of orange and blue running between the north and south poles of its spherical envelope. It was covered with a vast rope netting, from which depended the wicker car in which its passenger rode. My own airship was its twin.

To my dismay, Booth's craft had drifted eastward, beyond the City of Brooklyn, and was rapidly lengthening the expanse of thin air that separated us. It had dwindled and become nothing more than a painted ball. But soon I perceived the reason for this development, and saw it was to be a temporary advantage.

Booth had achieved a greater altitude than had I, and had caught some invisible river of wind that blew him away to the east. But, when my craft had ascended to an equivalent height, it was swept into the same current and acquired the same speed and direction as that of my prey. Thus I saw the means I must needs employ to keep Booth's ship in sight: I must see to it that I kept a common altitude with it, for if it were to rise above mine, or fall below it, it might find a different stream, which would bear it off on some course other than my own. The sky was filled with a multitude of winds, I discovered, but, if Booth and I rode the same wind, he could not leave me behind.

A balloon is a captive of the wind and cannot be steered; it must answer the zephyr's whim. But, to some extent, its elevation may be controlled, and this is accomplished through the simplest procedure imaginable. To ascend, one casts away part of the ballast, the sandbags fastened about the car; to descend, one releases a portion of the buoyant gases that fill the envelope above, by working a valve at the base of the bag, which is opened by tugging a line that depends into the car. There is no more to it than that.

The fugitive craft was not done ascending, so I drew my knife and dispatched a small sack of sand, to follow him to his airy refuge. Soon the earth had retreated to a distance I judged to be more than a mile, perhaps even two miles. We were above Long Island Sound, and the ships that sailed its waters were tiny fly-specks, invisible but for their foamy wakes. Soon nothing of the earth could be seen, for we had drifted over a vast snowy plain. The clouds that hid the sky from those beneath us, hid the earth from our eyes.

Thus we remained for many hours, a pair of gaudy balls adrift in the sky, with no clew as to whither the winds bore us. I neither gained upon the other ship, nor lost it. The assassin and I remained suspended in space, some miles between us, and miles above any of our fellow mortals. We were in Limbo.

Presently I saw a change in the billowy cloudscape beneath us. It had lost its smoothness, and now had become a rugged place of ridges, valleys and deep ravines. Off in the distance, there were some mountains, but none that stood upon the earth. They were towering peaks of cloud that rose far above our fragile craft. The Himalayas could be nothing more than hillocks beside these things, and I could not guess at the height of their summits, nor, had I, could I have believed my reckoning.

And there was yet another change, one that was not unexpected but was unwelcome, nonetheless. The sun had dropped down behind us. It turned the snowy vistas beneath us to sundry hues of pink and red. It was, by far, the most beautiful of Nature's exhibits I had ever beheld. It was also the most disagreeable, in the present circumstances. Soon Booth's distant craft would be hidden by the cloak of night, and I should no longer be able to mimic its risings and fallings. Then, I was certain, it would drift into some oblique current of atmosphere, and, when the sun again visited the sky, it would be gone.

Soon my fear was realized, when the sun had dipped below the distant rim of the cloudy plateau, and the last light of the day was gone. The other balloon had faded against the darkening mountains of cloud, and finally disappeared from view. Long after it had become invisible I stared at the place where it had been, but strain as I might, I could no longer discern it. Finally I resigned myself to Booth's escape, and vowed I should find him again, if it wanted the rest of my days to pick up his trail once more.

I must return to earth, but I saw the hazards of attempting such a maneuver at that moment. There were clouds beneath me; I knew not what lay beneath them. Whatever it might be, land or water, forest, mountain or plain, it was obscured not only by the clouds, but by the dark of night. It seemed more prudent to wait until dawn before I started my descent. I settled myself down in the car and was soon gently rocked to sleep.

Near dawn I was awakened. I had been roused by the keening of the wind in the craft's rigging, but there was another sound: the roar of the sea. Before I could open my eyes, my face was doused with a spray of icy droplets. I stood up and peered over the rim of the wicker basket in which I rode. It was a sight to freeze the soul.

I was over water, and apparently far at sea, for I could find no sight of land in any quarter. I was, as I have said, over water, but not high over it. I know now that the buoyant gases in the balloon must have cooled when the sun's warmth was gone, and the envelope shrunk as the volume of gases it held was thus reduced. Throughout the long night, while I slept happily in my ignorance, the craft had descended. It had descended over a vast expanse of water, and one which, at that moment, was wracked by the throes of the fiercest storm I have ever seen sweep across the surface of any ocean.

And that surface was no more than a score of feet beneath the car. As I gazed in horror, a sea at least as tall rolled toward my fragile craft. I was rescued by a gust from the storm, which lifted the balloon slightly, so that all but the foamy crest of the wave passed beneath the car. The car was swept along for a short distance, and the water broke about the sides of the basket and surged through the interstices of the wicker walls. This added weight burdened the craft, and it began to sink toward the furious maelstrom below. I looked up to see the sequel of the wave that had passed.

It was bearing down upon me.

·36·

High Risk

·····➤◆◄·····

Swiftly I drew my Bowie knife and began slashing the lines that held the ballast bags to the car. I had sawed through three of the ropes before risking a glance at the awful hill of watery devastation that was advancing upon me. The craft had ceased its descent. It seemed to have begun to rise. The wall of water was at hand. But it passed some feet below the floor of the car, and only some flecks of spume struck the wicker sides. I did not pause to say a prayer of thanks until I was done cutting loose the remaining bags of sand. Then, as the craft climbed into the gray and turbulent sky, I knelt in the car and offered two prayers, one of thanksgiving, the other a supplication for my further deliverance. During the hour that followed, I had need to repeat the second of these orisons many times over.

The craft ascended into the dismal clouds, and the raging waters below were soon lost from sight. But if I had left some species of watery Hell beneath me, Heaven proved to be at a considerable remove overhead. The storm seized my craft and dragged it about, while the tiny wicker basket I inhabited swung crazily, like a pendulum in a clock gone wild. A gray darkness enveloped the ship, and its mists were so thick I could not see the gaudy envelope above my head. The dimness was broken, from time to time, by flashes of lightning, and the thunder that closely followed seemed louder than ten batteries of cannon discharged in concert. The violence of the storm promised to tear my craft to shreds and drop me into the churning waters below, but there was nothing I could do but cling to the lines and pray. This I did for an eternity.

But, despite all evidence to the contrary, Eternity was not my destination that morning, for, after a very long while, the violence of the storm abated, the mists about me brightened, and at long last, I ascended through the roof of the storm into the cold, thin air and sunlight that lay above it.

A miracle had delivered my craft from the waters. A second miracle had held it together when the raging storm tried to tear it to ribbons. Now I witnessed a third miracle: Here, high above the clouds and not a quarter-mile off, was the striped ball of Booth's balloon.

I could see the car beneath the craft quite clearly, and, like mine, it was devoid of any bag of ballast, at least on the side presented toward me. But the basket looked to be empty. If its passenger was within, he sat below the rim of the car. I was powerless to discover any more. The craft might as well have been a thousand miles from that place, for I could no more cross that quarter-mile of thin air than I could swim the ocean far beneath us.

There was another unhappy truth. Even could I cross the intervening space to that other car, what, then, should I do? There would be no advantage to it, unless drowning in famous company can be counted as such. For this seemed our Fate, both the assassin's and mine. We had drifted far out over the Atlantic, and abandoned all our ballast. Now we both ascended slowly into the highest regions of the atmosphere. Already a faint dimness fought for possession of my senses, and I had no doubt it should conquer them unless I tugged on the valve rope and released some gases from the envelope. But then, would I descend once again into the tempest below? If not now, then after the sun had set some dozen hours hence, for what the craft had done last night, it would surely repeat tonight. Might we have been carried safely to Europe by that hour? We might, if the wind that bore us blew three thousand miles in a day! No, there seemed no escape. Before the sun had risen again, Booth and I would lie on the bottom of the sea.

But Death seemed impatient. It could not wait for another dawn, but fluttered about the car like some black bird of prey. Its dark wings covered my eyes at times, and when I could see at all, it was a blurred vision, as if through some frosty glass.

Frost! It caked the wicker car and the lines that supported it. I tried to raise my head to see if it covered the envelope above me, but my muscles would not answer my command. None of them would. I sat there, sensible, yet paralyzed. And then, I think, I became insensible, and remained thus for a time, until some unnamed grace roused me, and I pulled myself to the rim of the car.

My vision seemed to have returned, for I could discern the table of clouds below. I had risen far above that exalted level. Yet was I seeing truly, or merely dreaming? I looked toward every quarter, yet could not find Booth's craft. Then I saw it.

It was drifting slowly by, perhaps a dozen yards below. Now it was directly beneath me, and all of it I could see was the gaudy striped disk of its envelope. Why was it there? Out of all these miles of empty sky about me, why had his craft been placed thus, directly beneath mine own? I could imagine no earthly reason for it, but we were far from earth, and in several ways, closer to Heaven. There seemed but one purpose for this singular conjunction, and I had no time to consider the question, for the craft was drifting by and should soon have passed. Neither had I very much to lose if events should prove I'd acted in haste. Thus, I acted.

I lifted one leg over the rim of the car, and then the other. I hung thus for a moment, gazing down at the balloon some yards beneath my feet, and the clouds a mile, or more, below.

I released my hold on the car and plummeted into space.

As I fell, I turned upon my back and saw my own craft retreating above me. Thus I landed atop the envelope as one might fall backward onto a bed. Indeed, to my dimming senses, it seemed for a moment that I had jumped into a most delightful featherbed, so soft and yielding was the envelope of buoyant gases. I thank God, now, that I did not come down on the thing with my boots, for I should likely have pierced the envelope and exploded it. But I did not, and I lay there for how long I do not know, in some dreamy stupor, watching my own little craft shrink to a gaudy dot in the blue-black sky above me.

Eventually I roused myself, and taking some grasp of the fantastic situation of affairs, I also grasped the netting which covered the envelope, and from which Booth's car depended. Like some clumsy spider, I climbed across the top of the balloon and down the web of its netting. Soon I could see the car, and the prostrate form of its passenger. I climbed down the ropes and joined him in the basket.

We both were cold as corpses, and my hands were too numb to feel for his pulse. Thus I could not tell if he were living or dead. But death would soon take us both, for the air man was meant to breathe lay far below us, and we should soon expire if we could not betake ourselves down to those regions. I tugged at the valve cord. There was no effect; the valve was frozen shut.

I climbed back up to the ring where the suspension ropes culminated, and standing on it, tried to free the valve. This I could not do, for it was sealed with ice. There was only one means remaining to me to free the gases from the envelope and bring about our descent. It was the Bowie knife in my belt, but once I had used it, there would be no other means to terminate our descent. We would continue downward until we reached the earth. Or the sea. But there was no choice to be made. That which would likely follow our return to the surface would certainly overtake us shortly if we remained so far above it. I climbed partway up the side of the balloon and pressed the point of my blade into the envelope, and then withdrew it. Dimly I perceived the sibilant evidence of the escaping gases. I climbed down again to the car and looked for some sign of our descent. I think the clouds looked closer, but I could not be certain. I was thus engaged in considering the matter when consciousness deserted me.

I cannot say how long I remained thus, but some considerable time seems to have elapsed, for when I regained my senses, the first of these was hearing, and the sound I heard was that of the sea. But it was not the violent sounds of the ocean storm that had so dangerously battered my craft when last I visited the planet. It was the gentler sound of waves rolling onto a shore. The car was stationary; it was neither swinging below its envelope, nor floating on the surface of the water. I pulled myself to its rim and looked about. I do not think I had ever glimpsed a happier sight, nor one less expected. The wicker car rested on a sandy beach, and its envelope, now empty, drifted at the ends of its tethers among the tiny waves that broke upon the beach.

Booth lay beside me, and he was alive. I cut some lengths of rope from the wrecked rigging of our craft and tightly trussed him hand and foot. He remained unconscious.

Next I climbed from the car and dragged it farther up the beach, first severing the remaining lines so a change of tide would not cause the envelope to drag the basket back into the water. Then I started along the beach, choosing one direction rather than the other purely by whim, since neither promised any sign of human habitation.

Presently I espied a man some mile or so ahead along the beach. I quickened my pace and, after perhaps a half-hour, I was within hailing distance of the fellow. He looked up when I called, for he had not seen me approach, as he was diligently occupied in digging up some clams from those regions temporarily quit by the tide. He made no response, so I resumed my progress toward him, and when I had reached him I asked him that question which was uppermost in my mind.

"I beg your pardon, sir," I began, feeling rather foolish, "but would you kindly tell me where I might be?"

I was astounded by his reply. I did not understand it, but that was the cause of my astonishment. No, I could not comprehend the man's words, but I recognized the language to which they belonged.

It was French.

The wind that had borne our craft, it seemed, *had* blown three thousand miles in a single day!

·37·

The Prisoner's Tale

．···━◆━···．

So it seemed. Yet, in the event, such was not the case.

I spoke some French, and the clamdigger had some acquaintance with the English tongue, and thus we achieved some limited intercourse. Our conversation created astonishment in the stranger, but it diminished my own wonder.

We had not crossed the broad Atlantic, Booth and I, and landed in France. We had been carried northeastward by the wind, and thus drifted along a course that was, in its general form, parallel to the coastline of New England. Whether we passed over the pleasant countryside of Connecticut and Massachusetts, I do not know, but I think now it was at a point not very many miles off the coast of Maine, or perhaps within the Bay of Fundy, where my craft made its dawn descent and came near to drowning me. We had drifted along a more northerly route after that, and crossed, not the Atlantic, but either the State of Maine or the Canadian Province of New Brunswick. Then we had crossed the Gaspé Peninsula, and it was on the bank of the Great St. Lawrence River (which is some thirty miles or more in breadth in those parts) we had landed, in the Canadian Province of Quebec, wherein French is the common tongue.

Through our labored discourse, I learned from the clamdigger that we were on the northern bank of the river, not very far from the mouth of the Outardes (which was a tributary), but not very close to much else. There was a fishing village a bit farther along the beach, and the stranger explained that his profession was not limited to the exhumation of clams, but encompassed fishing the

St. Lawrence and the broader waters beyond its mouth, and that, for such pursuits, he was equipped with some species of seaworthy vessel. I asked if he might be persuaded to carry me in his boat as far up the river as Quebec City, which was more than a hundred miles distant. The gentleman seemed to have some familiarity with the denominations of American currency, for when I exhibited a generous handful of cash to hire his services for such a voyage, he promptly assented.

The fisherman then concluded his digging and, picking up his pail of clams, set off in my company in the direction of his village. We came to the little place late in the day, and enjoyed a meal of the fisher's morning find before proceeding to the place where his craft was beached.

It transpired to be a sturdy-looking yawl of some thirty feet, and with the aid of some of his fellows, we put the craft into the river and raised the sails. I explained to the man that I had left a companion some distance below the point of our meeting, and thus it was necessary that we should first go there and fetch him before starting our journey up the river. We reached the wreckage of the airship presently, and I waded ashore and found my prisoner where I'd left him, still trussed securely, but now conscious. As I peered in over the rim of the car, he opened his eyes and glanced at me.

"Well, Mr. Cosgrove," he said, "you seem to have caught me. I cannot fathom how you accomplished it, but you seem to have done it, nonetheless. Or are we both dead, and is that the Styx I hear flowing past?"

"We are alive, by the Grace of God," I replied, "and it is the St. Lawrence. We are in Canada, but we shall presently be in the United States of America."

"I see. Then, it would seem, the Styx is my destination, in any event."

"Perhaps. I have been hired only to bring you to Washington City. You will have to arrange your own itinerary beyond that point."

"Doubtless there will be no scarcity of persons eager to arrange it for me. I imagine my vehicle will be equipped with some steps and a rope."

I made no reply to this, but undid the bonds about his ankles and helped him to his feet. He required assistance, for he had been lying there for some hours, and the ropes had interfered with the circulation of blood in his feet. I did not remove the bonds from his wrists, for I remembered that my prisoner was famous, not only as an assassin, but as a master of the art of escape.

The fisherman remarked on the bonds, but when I explained I was an American policeman, and that this man was my prisoner, he made no objection, but helped me get Booth into the yawl. We placed him in the bottom of the boat near the bow, and I remained with my charge while the fisherman went aft to handle the tiller. We were soon under sail again, now bound for Quebec City, far to the southeast. We proceeded a mile or more offshore to obtain the benefit of the brisker winds that blew out there, but even at that remove, I could not see the other bank of the river, which was more than twenty miles to the south of us. Presently we turned onto a southwesterly heading, and thus made our way upriver toward the battlements of Quebec City.

The sky was leaden with remnants of the vast storm through which our crafts had been carried. To pass the time, I recounted to Booth my experience of that dreadful dawn (Booth had had a similar adventure, and, as I, had escaped by discharging all his ballast) and the remarkable circumstances that enabled me to join him in his craft and bring it safely to earth.

"Well, then," he remarked when I had finished, "I suppose I owe you my life, even though you mean to collect that debt presently."

"I owe you my own," I replied, "for had you not skewered that fellow in the tunnel, I should still be down there, and never would have had an opportunity to rescue us both from asphyxiation in the airship."

"I cannot claim to have taken his life to save yours," he said. "It was the pages from my notebook I rescued, and I should have murdered the three of you, had I come equipped for the task. But, as it was, I thought it best to leave you and Eckert to each other, and pray that no more than one of you survived. Did you kill him?"

"No, but not for want of trying," I replied. "Whatever the reasons for your intervention, it saved my life. How came you to be there at that propitious moment? Were you alerted by Edwin to my inquiries?"

"I have not spoken to Edwin for a long while. It was not you who led me to the tunnel, but Eckert. You see I've had it in mind for some time to sell him those very papers, since my brother has declined to make them public. His is among the names written on them, and his fortunes have lately prospered. I thought he might be willing to share his wealth as the price of the evidence that could send him to the gallows. I chanced to see him in Washington City some days ago and followed him to New York while I considered the best means to broach the matter with him. I was watching his house when he departed with his lackey, who I think he had sent to watch Edwin in the hope I might pay my brother a visit someday. Thus Eckert and his man trailed you and Edwin, while I, in turn, followed them. I was dismayed to discover that it was my little hiding place that was the parade's destination."

"And you rescued your pages from us all. Why did you leave your trick box behind?"

"Had I taken it, would you have failed to guess it had not been empty? And if you had seen there was a trick to the box, mightn't you have realized its owner was a stage magician?"

"I should have," I agreed. "In fact, I did. And when I learned the 'Professor Haselmayer' I'd seen twice in Washington City, and once more in Rockville, was in New York, I thought our paths had crossed once too often to blame on chance. I must agree: removing the box might well have betrayed your identity to me, but leaving had the same result. Unmasking you seems to have been my destiny."

"Then I must regret failing to kill you."

"If Destiny heeded our regrets I think there would be things better to regret."

Booth laughed.

"Well said. I should certainly regret not killing Baker and Eckert."

"You shall have another chance at that when you reveal the hand they took in the assassination."

"If anyone believes me."

"I can provide some confirmation of the charge."

"Would you enjoy hearing the tale?"

"I should be delighted to hear it, if you wish to tell it."

"Very well," he said, and as we sailed along through the evening, he recounted to me the full circumstances of his crime.

As his brother, Edwin, had told me, John Wilkes Booth had been one of General Baker's secret detectives. Baker had recruited him in 1862, and assigned to the young man a single, but essential, mission: to insinuate himself into the Confederate Secret Service, and so spy upon Richmond's own spies. Booth had no experience with such things, but his natural qualifications were perfect: an excellent physical specimen, an athlete, an accomplished horseman, a talent with fire-arms, and an occupation that gave him an unquestioned pretext to travel. But beyond all these things, Booth was possessed of a special quality which, in the young, may be called fearlessness, and if preserved past maturity, deserves the name "courage." Given these things, the craft of the secret detective was a thing that could be learned, and Booth proved himself an able and enthusiastic student. Within but a few months he had accomplished that most difficult and dangerous of all the works of the professional espion: He had beguiled his way into the ranks of the enemy's secret service. He was a double spy!

Before the War, Booth had taken little interest in politics. All of his brothers were ardent Abolitionists and champions of the Union. He did not share their ardor, but neither did he dispute them. The fanatical Secessionist was a role he learned and played with the same consummate skill he brought to his other roles, those he played on theater boards. It was but another costume, but one calculated to invite Confederate overtures, for any man who volunteers to spy is met with the closest scrutiny and suspicion. These Booth artfully avoided, and only after repeated entreaties by the Rebels did he agree to work in their service.

Thus, while he had yet to see his twenty-fifth birthday, John Wilkes Booth was a success, and he had succeeded twice over. He had risen to the very top of the theatrical profession, and his renown as an actor had spread from one end of the land to the other. He was not simply another Booth who had distinguished himself upon the stage, he was *John Wilkes Booth,* a tragedian famous in his own right, and not merely by virtue of a common family name. He earned twenty thousand dollars in one year of acting, and if there were yet more worlds to conquer, they lay on the other side of the proscenium arch.

One such world was the shadowy realm in which he traveled for Baker. If it was a world necessarily devoid of fame, it was not lacking in honors. Here, too, Booth was an early and spectacular success, and he reported directly to the man who commanded all of the North's agents, an officer who was daily in the company of the Secretary of War and even the President. It was not an achievement he could boast of, for that was precluded by the very essence of the vocation, but it was something to be savored.

Yet whatever glories Booth enjoyed in his career as spy, they were transient things, destined to end when that same victory for which he labored was consummated. What then? Not the stage, Booth resolved, for the stage could offer no new triumphs. Indeed, he longed for some species of future glory that would not merely surpass those he'd earned upon the stage, but would eclipse them. He would be pleased if his theatrical triumphs were not only surpassed in some other calling, but were completely forgotten.

Much of what the actor said was not spoken in his words, but hidden behind them. The meaning, nonetheless, was clear. The theater was a splendid place, and it was a grand thing to be judged the best of actors, yet that distinction lacked one quality. It was a thing that cannot be had in the theater, but it was a thing Booth keenly desired: respectability.

Theater-folk inhabit a special kind of demimonde, and the great majority of them are held by the world in little more regard than that claimed by gypsies, tramps, or thieves. Even the actor who rises to the top of the pile, the one who plays before crowned heads or Presidents, who earns several fortunes at his craft, cannot claim the same respect that society bestows upon a moderately prosperous dry-goods merchant. That which John Wilkes Booth wanted more than any other thing, he could never have in the theater. Thus the theater did not figure in his post-War plans.

Public office seemed to answer, and Booth had every reason to believe the successes he had achieved upon the stage and on the secret battlefields of espionage he could repeat in the world of politics. He was famous, he was rich, and, when the War had been won, credit for his secret braveries could not but aid his quest for public office. And if these things were not sufficient assurance that Booth would be admitted to the world of Congressmen, Governors, Senators and Presidents, Booth had an additional recourse: He could marry into it, as he might into some patrician family. Indeed, he was engaged to marry the daughter of a United States Senator.†

This, then, was the disposition of the actor-spy as the War approached its end and Baker and Eckert came to him with their heinous plan. Sometime in December, 1864, the pair approached Booth, and, after swearing him to the utmost secrecy, and threatening dire vengeance should he betray them, they informed him that they, together with sundry other persons, including many Senators and Congressmen, and the Secretary of War, were dissatisfied with Mr. Lincoln's post-War plans for the South, and so proposed to seize the government in a coup d'état.

They justified such desperate measures by claiming that Lincoln himself intended to extend his own powers beyond those granted him by the Constitution, and would already have done so had the vote gone against him in the election of the previous month. Such a thing was not beyond the actor's belief, he said, for these were bloody and troubled times, and while Lincoln had striven to hold the Union together, he had often put the Constitution aside during the War to accomplish that end. Power corrupts, and Booth was prepared to believe it had corrupted Lincoln.‡

---

† Lucy Lambert Hale, daughter of former Senator John Parker Hale of New Hampshire, who had been appointed Ambassador to Spain by President Lincoln. The engagement was secret, and the secret was kept by the Government and only disclosed by Eisenschiml. Shortly after the assassination, Miss Hale joined her father in Spain, and later married William Eaton Chandler, a U.S. Senator from New Hampshire (1887–1901) and Secretary of the Navy (1881–1885).—M.C.

† According to Booth's sister, Asia, John Wilkes Booth already believed something of this sort even before the presidential election of 1864. In her memoirs she recalls him saying of Lincoln, "He is a Bonaparte in one great move, that is, by overturning this blind Republic and making himself a king. This man's re-election which will follow his success, I tell you—will be a reign!" (Clarke, p. 124.)—M.C.

At the date of this discussion, Booth had already learned of plans then being discussed by the Confederate leaders in Richmond to kidnap Lincoln and use him to ransom back those Rebel soldiers held in prison in the North. On his own initiative, Booth had proposed to those who believed he served them that he should take charge of the matter and arrange for the abduction. They agreed to this, and Booth promptly returned to Washington City and reported the matter to Baker. Booth had, in fact, made a brilliant move, for he could be in no better position to know of the Rebels' plans against the person of the President than by making himself the secret agent responsible for carrying them out.

Baker and Eckert saw something else in the development: an opportunity to further a scheme they were already hatching. It is likely they saw that an abduction could become an assassination by the mere pressing of a trigger, but neither of those things suited their timetable at that moment; what they would have happen must not take place until victory over the South was achieved. Therefore, Baker instructed Booth to proceed with the Confederate plot, and do everything demanded, but to insure that no kidnapping was carried out at that time. And this he did. When the proper moment arrived, he was told, the abduction would provide the signal for the coup.

Quite by accident Secretary Stanton learned of Booth's abduction plans in February, and, ignorant that Booth was one of Baker's detectives, thought them genuine. With Major Johnson's guidance, Stanton (like Baker and Eckert) saw how the thing could be put to his own private use, and so he connived to let it take place, unwitting that it could not take place until Baker and Eckert gave the order. Thus time passed and no kidnapping occurred, and, finally, Stanton thought better of the plan and abandoned it. Not so Baker and Eckert. They bided their time and waited for Appomattox. When it came, they met with Booth in a secret place.

There could be no abduction, they explained. A harsher duty must fall to Booth, but one for which the reward would be commensurate. When the truth of Lincoln's coronation plans was known, a grateful nation would hail the assassin's act. And Secretary Stanton, who would take charge *ad interim,* would reward the heroic savior of the Republic with appointment to high office, the military governor-ship of the conquered South.

"It was a sell, pure and simple," said Booth, "but I was taken in by it. I did not guess the truth until I saw the newspapers. I hoped to see my name written in glory. Instead, it had become anathema. There had been no coup, and my reward was to be the gallows. But there was nothing for me to do about it, except bend every effort to get away with my life. And that I did, for I knew a few tricks, myself."

"And the world thought you dead, so you were free to become 'Professor Haselmayer.'"

"The stage seemed my destiny," the actor admitted, "although I dared not take up my career as an actor. I settled on the role of con-jurer, a magician who made a specialty of escapes. You must admit I'd shown some talent in that direction."

"I do," I agreed. "I should have had great difficulty in tracing you beyond Dr. Stewart's home."

"I boarded a ship bound for Europe, the *Amazon,* a brigantine fly-ing the English flag. In Europe I studied under Houdin, who was the father of stage illusions. When I had mastered the role, I returned to these shores."

"And master it you did, indeed," I said. "Will you tell me how you managed to ascend in that balloon near Rockville, and then reappear before your tent?"

"It's a simple trick," laughed Booth. "I will explain it to you, but not tonight. I shall tell you how it was done on the day I go to the gallows. Thus I can depend on having some visitor to share my final hours. I'll trade you the secret for a quart of brandy."

"Done!" I agreed. "But there are some things I would learn now. Stanton believed you dead; what made him suspect you lived?"

"I think it was Baker who told him. Poverty had made him reck-less and vengeful. He knew I had escaped, and he believed it had been done with the aid of my brother, Edwin. I will not tell you if he was right. At all events, he blackmailed Edwin and my other brothers, threatening to tell the world I lived. When I discovered what he was about, I wrote Edwin and told him where he could find that which might be used to blackmail Baker in return. In the event it proved unnecessary, for Baker had taken up a career of lying, and none would have believed anything he said."

"Yet you think Stanton gave it some weight?"

"I do not think he could afford to do otherwise."

While I was thus absorbed in this discourse with my prisoner, I had failed to observe the worsening condition of the weather. The wind had grown in intensity, and we were running before some heavy seas. Flashes of lightning illuminated the water, and a dangerous storm seemed to have arisen on the river. But the yawl now moved so violently I could no longer ignore this development. I went aft and consulted with the fisherman, who I found struggling with the tiller. It was but a passing thunderstorm, he explained, not uncommon in these parts in the Spring, but he proposed to sail closer to the shore and lay to in the first safe harbor until the violent weather had passed. I asked if I could be of any assistance, but he assured me he had matters well in hand. Thus I went forward and rejoined Booth.

"You have left one thing unexplained," I said, "and I think it may be the most important part of your tale. You've told me that Baker and Eckert connived to have you murder Mr. Lincoln. Very well, but what was their motive? Was it simple malice?"

"It was simple greed," Booth replied, "as I have since discovered. Both were well paid for their deeds. Baker took his pay in cash, and lost it all in some unwise venture. Eckert received his in favors, and he continues to profit from it."

"And who provided these payments?" I inquired.

"A very rich man. A man who became rich during the War, has gotten richer since, and, I am confident, will someday be the richest man in America, if not the world. I could tell you his name, but you do not know it, for, although he is wealthy, he is not famous. But I trust he will be, someday. He thought to profit from a harsher Reconstruction of the South than what Lincoln planned. He has not fared as well as he hoped with Johnson, but I think he will do better with Grant. I have written his name, along with Eckert's and Baker's, and a few others in those pages you did not know you held in your hand when you found my little trick box in its tunnel hiding place."

"And where are those pages now?"

"Why, they're still in the tunnel, but they're hidden behind a different stone, and there is no magnet there to guide a compass. I dared not take the things with me when I fled, for, had Eckert overtaken me, they should have been my only life insurance. You won't find them without my guiding you to the place, unless you propose to demolish the tunnel one brick at a time."

"Will you lead me to them?"

"Perhaps. I shall have to discover what the things are worth, first. I shan't know that until I've met those who would hang me. You see, those pages are all I have left to me to strike a bargain."

Before I could press him further, a blast of lightning struck the yawl. I turned and saw that the aft mast had been shattered. I climbed over the wreckage and found the fisherman slumped and insensible in the bottom of the boat. The tiller swung wildly and the craft was coming about. I struggled to regain our heading, but could not do it, and presently we stood athwart the pursuing seas. As I clung to the tiller, a wave washed over the gunwales and swamped us. The storm seemed to increase in its fury, and the little boat began to flounder. How near or far the shore might lie I could not see, for the night was black, and rain now fell in heavy sheets. When I looked again to the bottom of the boat the fisherman was gone. He had been swept away.

I clambered forward and found my prisoner still aboard.

"Here, cut these bonds!" he shouted. "I cannot swim while bound!"

He turned his back and thrust his wrists toward me. I took my knife and made to cut him free. Then I paused.

"The name!" I demanded.

"What name? Cut these bonds!"

"The name of the wealthy man!"

"Gould!" he cried, and I cut him free. A towering sea washed over the boat, and carried us into the water.

· 38 ·

In Quest of Myself

❖

There is little more for me to tell. Of that storm, of the boat, of what may have become of John Wilkes Booth, I cannot say, for I have no recollection. Indeed, my very name was beyond my recall for many weeks after that dreadful night. What little I know of it was told me by the old man and his wife who found me half-drowned and washed up upon the riverbank the following morning.

These kindly people spoke only French and, in my delirium I raved in English, and thus whatever I may have uttered during those days, when my life had been despaired of, I have no knowledge. A village priest was called to give me the Last Rites of the Church, and the aged couple could do no more than keep a vigil and see to my comforts while they awaited my expiration. But it did not come.

For many days I struggled in that middle land between Life and Death, or so I am told. Then my fever abated, and with June came the promise I would recover my life, if not my mind. Summer was nearly gone before I regained my feet and a disposition to believe I was called "Cosgrove," or else "Nichols." Autumn came, and each falling leaf seemed to mark some fleeting fragment of my recollection, which would creep timorously into my mind, and then flee when I made to grasp it.

I'd been given many a puzzle to solve in my days, but none was more difficult than that with which I struggled as I stared into my rescuers' fire and tried to piece together the fragments of my shattered senses.

Who was I?

Cosgrove, or else Nichols. But it was Cosgrove, I thought. At times I was certain. Who was Cosgrove?

My hosts had discerned from the clothing I wore when they found me, the condition of my hands, and other clews, that I was neither fisherman nor farmer, but more likely a denizen of some town or city. As I spoke English much better than French, they thought I likely hailed from some such place as Toronto or Ottawa, although they allowed I might be from Montreal. None of these places seemed right, but I could think of no other, for, like them, I presumed myself to be Canadian, and did not think to search my mind for any recollection of places south of the international frontier.

The Winter passed and became Spring, and then another Summer arrived. Late in August the old grandfather with whom I lived returned from the nearby village with a newspaper. It was in French and came from Montreal, and I believe it was several months old. I could read only the most elementary French, and rarely perused the occasional newspaper that found its way to the old couple's cottage. But there was something about this newspaper that caught my eye, the portrait of a bearded man large upon its front page. I asked my friends who this gentleman might be, and they took up the paper and read it for me, then conveyed the information in their language which I had learned to speak passing well. The gentleman depicted was the new President of the United States of America, Ulysses S. Grant. General Grant. I took the paper and studied the portrait, reciting that name over and over again. It was then that my memory returned.

It was as if every recollection of my past life lay together to form some vast river, a river whose flow had been stemmed by a dam, and I was left to wander in the arid valley beyond. But now that dam had burst, and all these pictures, these sights, sounds, smells, textures, tastes, all suddenly flooded upon me. I leapt from the place I sat with such a cry I fear I frightened the kindly pair who sheltered me into the belief that my last remaining shreds of reason had finally flown away to follow my memory, and they were left with a raging madman as their charge. But, when I had calmed myself, I calmed them as well, and we spent the night in prayerful thanks-givings and celebrations, and a detailed recountment of the minute particulars of my former existence, to answer the curiosity they had concerning this stranger who had stayed so long beneath their roof.

When dawn came I was up and eager to be on my way, but not before I took a long and tender leave of this sainted pair to whom I owed so great a debt and of whom I'd grown so fond. I promised to repay their kindness in more tangible ways, and that is a promise I later kept.

I completed my interrupted journey to Quebec City, arriving there on the following day. I immediately betook myself to the largest bank I could find, and there arranged that the necessary communications be made with that bank in New York City wherein I kept my finan-cial reserves. Next, I went to a hotel, and there obtained a room, de-spite the visible doubts harbored by the clerk at the front desk. I would next have dispatched a telegraphic message to Mr. Pinkerton, but ignorant of where matters might stand, and mindful of the dangers I had discovered lurking in the telegraph office, I eschewed doing this, and reflected that more than a year had gone by since my last com-munication to him, and so a few days more were not likely to have very much effect.

Quebec is a beautiful and historic place, but it was as a prison to me, and I chafed at the delay which must needs intervene before funds should arrive that might permit me to continue on my journey which had been interrupted for so long. But at last the money came, and I settled with the hotel and took the cars for Montreal, proceeding from there to Toronto and Detroit. At last I had crossed the frontier and was again within my native land.

When I arrived in Chicago, I went directly to the Headquarters Office of the Chain of Agencies. My face, of course, was unknown there, and I did not give my name, but simply asked where I might find Mr. Allan Pinkerton. My question elicited a strangely evasive response, so I departed and immediately consulted with a local news-paperman, who was my trusted friend. He advised me he'd heard reports that Mr. Pinkerton had suddenly been taken ill, perhaps with a shock† and was convalescing at "the Larches," his home some distance south of the city.

I went there, but was refused admission to the presence of my chief by Mrs. Pinkerton, who, of course, had never seen me before. I disclosed my identity to her, and she then permitted me entrance to the sick room, but cautioned me that her husband's faculties had been greatly damaged by his illness. When at last I was led into his presence, I perceived the tragic truth of her words.

Mr. Pinkerton looked to have aged a quarter century in the year and some months since last I had seen him. I had left him in Washington City, a robust and busy man of affairs. Now I found him confined abed, gray and shrunken. But I had yet to discover the worst.

Mr. Pinkerton could no longer speak. What little he managed to communicate to those attending him he did by means of a shaky, near-illegible scrawl. And what he scribbled on his pad that day were some of the saddest words I have ever read.

He did not know who I might be, and had never heard of one called Nicholas Cosgrove.‡

Thus I left my chief amid the peace of his country home, and returned to New York City. I felt like the ghost of one long dead and forgotten. Had I made to resume my career with the Chain of Agencies, I should have had a difficult task. None of the firm knew my face, and its chief had forgotten even my name.

But I had no wish to pick up at the place I'd left off. Indeed, to have done so would have been a kind of imposture, for the Nicholas Cosgrove who had served as secret detective in Pinkerton's was no more. I remembered him as one might a close friend who had passed away. I had become another man.

---

† A stroke.—M.C.

‡ According to his biographer (Horan, pp. 180–182) Allan Pinkerton was thus incapacitated by a stroke in the late summer of 1869. Horan notes that during the latter part of 1868 and early 1869, Pinkerton became "slightly paranoiac about the mysterious 'powers' that were fighting the Agency," and quotes a letter Pinkerton wrote to a subordinate in which he declared, "The year 1868 has been marked by a determined fight against us . . ." Horan reports that Pinkerton overcame his paralysis and regained most of his health in 1871.—M.C.

I did pursue some inquiries to learn of the aftermath of my last assignment. General Baker was dead more than a year.† He had passed on abruptly, but his death was attributed to natural causes.

General Eckert had fared better. He seemed to have recovered fully from the blow I struck him, and was still in his powerful position with the Western Union Company. Indeed, he holds that position to this very day, having become president of the company some ten years ago, and, recently, chairman of its board of directors.‡ He is undoubtedly a man of formidable talents, but I doubt that any would deny his advancement in the telegraph company is owed in part to his close friendship with one of its principal stockholders. That man's name was Jay Gould.§

For my part, I chose to seek my fortune in other pursuits, and I cannot say the world has treated me badly. It was a fortunate choice, and not one taken in any spirit of disappointment. But I could no longer pursue the craft of the secret detective, for like Booth, and Alexander before him, I had no more worlds to conquer.

---

† Lafayette C. Baker died on July 3, 1868. The cause of his death was listed as spinal meningitis. Some newspaper obituaries reported he died possessing "considerable property." Other newspaper accounts denied this, and implied he died a pauper.—M.C.

‡ Eckert became president of Western Union in 1892 and chairman of its executive committee in 1902. He died on October 20, 1910.—M.C.

§ Jay Gould's association with Thomas Eckert seems to have begun during the Civil War, when the millionaire was building his fortune through stock speculations based on advance information he received of Union victories and defeats from some source in the War Department's Military Telegraph Bureau, of which Major Eckert was then chief. Gould's name was unknown to the public until March, 1868, when he became a director of the Erie Railroad Company. In 1874 Eckert was instrumental in helping Gould acquire a message multiplexing system developed for Western Union by the then young and unknown Thomas Edison. Eckert, who was at that time an executive of Western Union, escorted Edison through the service entrance of Gould's Fifth Avenue home, and sat by while Gould bought the valuable invention for his own Atlantic & Pacific Telegraph Company, a competitor of Western Union. Shortly thereafter Eckert left Western Union to assume the presidency of Atlantic & Pacific, taking with him David Homer Bates and others of his former subordinates from the War Department. Atlantic & Pacific, under Gould and Eckert, then proceeded to swallow all of its competitors, and, in 1881, forced a merger with Western Union. Eckert became Western Union's vice-president and general manager, and a member of the board of directors. (O'Connor, Chapter 8.) Gould died on December 2, 1892.—M.C.

Mr. Pinkerton had sent me to find the Greatest Criminal of the Nineteenth Century. My prey was one skilled not only in the guile of the secret agent, but a man of a hundred faces, and a master of escape. Nonetheless, I found him and took him captive. I cannot believe Fate set him free.

I do not think John Wilkes Booth is still at large. I believe he lies beneath the broad St. Lawrence, or somewhere on the bottom of the vast ocean beyond it. Yet I shall not be certain of that until the Final Day, when Gabriel blows his trumpet, and earth and ocean yield up those who lie beneath.

Even a hound loses the scent when his prey takes to the water.

Afterword

BY MICHAEL CROFT

··•––––◆––––•··

"Now then, that is the tale. Some of it is true."
—Mark Twain: *Autobiography*

How much of it is true? Is any of it true, or is it all a mischievous hoax concocted by a wealthy old fellow with plenty of time on his hands, who received his inspiration from the then freshly published memoirs of those other old fellows, who did have some direct experience of the circumstances surrounding Lincoln's death? Or is Cosgrove's manuscript the fantasy of an old man who had daydreamed his story so often he had come to believe it was true? Those are the questions I was hired to answer, and this is the place where I'll try to earn my fee. In the terms of Raymond Lawson's posthumous assignment, I've given the job my best efforts. Lawson arranged with O'Toole that, whatever I found, it would be published along with the manuscript.

So here it is.

I'll begin with two basic questions that have to be answered first: Who was Nicholas Cosgrove? And, was he assigned by Pinkerton to trail Booth and investigate the Lincoln assassination?

Who was Nicholas Cosgrove?

I thought this was going to be the easiest to answer; it didn't turn out that way. Lawson said his grandfather was born in New York City in 1835. I checked with the Bureau of Records and Statistics at New York's Department of Health, and found its birth records only go back to 1866.

According to Lawson, Cosgrove served in the New York City Police Department from 1855 through 1859. Not surprisingly, the Department doesn't keep records going back that far. There are some old Police Department records in the New York Public Library's Municipal Archives. But the fact that Cosgrove isn't listed in them doesn't prove he never served as a New York cop.

Lawson says Cosgrove was recruited by Pinkerton in 1859 and was with the detective agency until 1869. In his manuscript, Cosgrove tells us he served in a special capacity, reporting directly to Pinkerton and virtually unknown to anyone else in the firm. Even so, there should have been some record of his employment in the company's files. I checked with the firm, now simply known as Pinkerton's, Inc., and learned that virtually all of the company records from the Civil War period and immediately thereafter were destroyed when the company's headquarters were gutted in the Chicago Fire of 1871.

There are plenty of records of Cosgrove's post-1870 period, however: the deed of his estate in Newport, his marriage license, his daughter's birth certificate and his death certificate—these last two on file in the Rhode Island Division of Vital Statistics in Providence. Having pretty much struck out in the public record department, I decided to see if Nicholas Cosgrove left any private records which might shed some light on his early life.

James Marsh, Esq., the proper young executor of Raymond Lawson's estate, admitted that some of Grandfather Nicholas' papers had been found among the late attorney's personal files. These, per the late attorney's instructions, were being held pending a suitable proposal from a university library to receive, index and preserve them. At the moment they were reposing in a Providence warehouse, and it took some considerable arm-twisting before Marsh would authorize me access to them.

I spent a long afternoon breathing dust and straining my eyes in the dim light of a naked electric light in one of the warehouse's bins, and for a while I thought it wasn't going to be worth the trouble. I was hoping to find the original handwritten manuscript from which the typescript was made. It wasn't there, and the closest I came to it were the invoices from the secretarial service Cosgrove hired to do the typing. There were also voluminous records of the millionaire's financial transactions—bankbooks, stock certificates, etc. These revealed one interesting fact: Cosgrove did not amass his wealth over a period of years; he got rich very fast in 1870 and he stayed that way for the rest of his life. Apparently the millionaire was as camera-shy as the detective; there is no extant photograph of him in either role.

The only pre-1870 records I found were a set of twenty-four leather-bound diaries covering the period from 1861 to 1869. The dates were embossed on the leather covers. The pages inside were filled with printing in some sort of cipher. It seemed to be a variation of Cosgrove's telegraph code. Like many nineteenth-century spies, Cosgrove had an amateur's knowledge of cryptology and no knowledge at all of cryptoanalysis. In other words, he invented and used his own cipher system, blissfully unaware of how simply it could be cracked, until he discovered, to his dismay, that someone had done it.

As a favor, an old friend in the National Security Agency had several pages of the first diary transcribed to computer tape and processed. It took one of NSA's IBM 370s exactly twenty-seven seconds to break the cipher and print out Cosgrove's key. Armed with the page of print-out paper, I set about the laborious chore of deciphering the diaries.

The diaries were the day-to-day record of Cosgrove's missions during the Civil War, and his post-War cases. Each volume covered a period of only a few months, so that several diaries were needed to fill out a full year. Obviously for security reasons, the detective took along a fresh diary on each adventure; then if he were captured and forced to disclose the cipher key, the information compromised would be limited to his current assignment.

I have not deciphered all, or even most, of Cosgrove's diaries. To do so would be a big job, and one best done through the extensive use of some pretty expensive computers. However, I did decipher enough to support the story that Cosgrove was a Pinkerton's detective who served as a Union spy during the Civil War, and that he later served in a special capacity reporting directly to Allan Pinkerton. The last two volumes contain all of the essential details presented in the Cosgrove manuscript, from his trip to Washington in March, 1868, up to the point at which he returned from his adventures in the tunnel beneath Atlantic Avenue. Apparently, when he returned to New York in 1869, he did not update his records of the intervening period.

If necessary, the paper and ink used in the diaries can be tested to verify that they are from the Civil War period, and weren't manufactured at some much later period. However, I don't doubt that the diaries are authentic; if they were fraudulent it would mean someone took incredible pains against the remote possibility the journals would be discovered and deciphered, all to bolster a rather pointless hoax.

Thus, the diaries answer my first question. Based on the information they contain, and in the absence of any contrary evidence, I am satisfied that Nicholas Cosgrove was exactly who he said he was—a detective who served with the Pinkerton Agency during the Civil War and immediately thereafter. The diaries also settle the second question; Cosgrove was assigned to pursue Booth and investigate the assassination of President Lincoln.

Granting that much, then, the next question is this: Was Cosgrove right?

One thing that is apparent from the Cosgrove manuscript is that the Pinkerton's agent was dealing with some very cute customers during his "inquiries." It seems there were as many devious characters per capita in the Washington of 1868 as there are today or in recent years. Did Cosgrove really get to the bottom of the mystery of the Lincoln assassination, or was he simply sold a bill of goods by people who were a bit cleverer than he, and who knew how to manipulate him? Since Eisenschiml, the few historians who have challenged the traditional, history-book version of the assassination have put the blame on Stanton. There is, as Cosgrove, and later Eisenschiml, discovered, a pretty good circumstantial case to be made against Edwin Stanton as the mastermind behind the assassination. Could it possibly be that Stanton *was* the guilty party, and the entire Cosgrove episode was contrived by the Secretary of War to prove he was innocent? Or was Andrew Johnson the real culprit, as so many people, apparently including Stanton, seemed to think at the time? Allan Pinkerton, after all, *was* working for Johnson, and Cosgrove for Pinkerton. Could Johnson have been the *eminence grise* working through Pinkerton to stage a charade starring Cosgrove which would finally exonerate the President?

I think it may be impossible to come up with any final and absolutely conclusive answers to these questions, although, as I promised, I did my best. As I promised, I have not been bashful about sticking footnotes throughout the text, and I apologize to the reader if they've been a distraction. They were necessary, however. Anyone who has gone to the trouble of reading all these notes will have seen that there is plenty of "solid" collateral evidence to support most of Cosgrove's discoveries, but I have to caution the reader against leaping to the conclusion that, therefore, Cosgrove must have been right. I have put quotation marks around the word "solid," because, when it comes to the Lincoln assassination, there isn't much evidence of any kind, traditional or revisionist, which deserves that adjective. The most commonly accepted details of the case, the most basic and innocent "facts," often seem to fade away under closer scrutiny.

Enough books bearing directly or indirectly on Lincoln's assassination have been written during the last hundred years to fill a small library. Some, like Eisenschiml, are revisionist; most are not. But, to me, the most astonishing discovery I made in the course of checking out Cosgrove's story does not consist of his evidence that Booth escaped, or that General Baker, Eckert, Gould and others were involved in a conspiracy. To me, the mind-boggling news is this:

In the century that has passed since one of the most important single events in American history, not a single book written about it, traditional or revisionist, can be relied upon to be accurate, even as to details that should not be controversial, and which don't seem to have any sinister meaning. In the case of Lincoln's assassination, no writer, to my knowledge, has yet really done his homework!

I could prove my point by citing scores of instances in which the accepted accounts fail to stand up under close examination, but I won't, because it would be tiresome. Instead I'll offer the most colossal example of the phenomenon. I discovered it almost by accident, and after I thought I was finished checking out Cosgrove's report. I had sent the manuscript plus my footnotes to George O'Toole, and asked if he could suggest any means I might have overlooked that might further establish the truth or falsity of Cosgrove's story. He wrote back and suggested I visit him at his home in Danbury, Connecticut. I did.

When I arrived, O'Toole showed me a list he had compiled of present-day researchers who had looked into the Lincoln assassination. Some were professional historians, but most were amateurs. It was not a long list, and I had spoken to a few of them, and had found some of them very helpful. I told O'Toole as much, and asked if there was anyone on the list he especially wanted me to contact. He pointed out one name, a Mr. L. B. Barton.

"He's not really a Lincoln assassination expert," O'Toole said. "He calls himself a 'trivialist.' But I know he's done a lot of reading about the Lincoln assassination, and he lives right here in Danbury, so we might as well get his opinion. I sent him a copy of the manuscript and your notes when I received them a week or so ago, but I haven't heard from him. Would you like to meet him?"

I said I would, and O'Toole telephoned the man and arranged for us to go over to his place that afternoon.

"He lives in the last house on Fermat's Hill," O'Toole remarked, as he turned off Route 6 and started up a steep, winding road. At the top was an old farmhouse and a wide spot in the drive. O'Toole pulled into this and parked.

After repeated knocking (there was no bell) the door was opened by a tall, cadaverous old man, with a luxuriant and snowy mane, and a long, matching beard. This, said O'Toole, by way of introduction, was L. B. Barton. The specter said nothing, but motioned us to enter. He was a retired government worker, long a resident of Washington, but almost as long one of Connecticut's more eccentric citizens. He lived alone with a collection of clocks and other rubbish, but O'Toole assured me the man was quite sane and had a broad knowledge of many subjects, including the Lincoln assassination. Since he seemed disinclined to speak, I opened the conversation by asking what he thought of Cosgrove's manuscript and my notes. He stared at me for a full minute before answering.

"I think you are wasting your time," he said.

Period.

"Oh?"

"Yes."

It seemed that was to be all he had to say on the matter, but after a few moments he turned toward me and demanded, "Have you ever heard that President Millard Fillmore introduced the first bathtub into the White House?"

I said I had not. The answer seemed to startle him.

"That's just as well," he snapped. "There's not a word of truth to it."

Barton reflected for a moment, then disappeared into another room and returned with a book. I recognized it as a volume of Poore's verbatim transcript of the Conspiracy Trial.

"How many books do you suppose have been written about the impeachment of Andrew Johnson?" he asked.

"Scores, I imagine."

"Wrong! Hundreds! Thousands, perhaps. I haven't checked. How many of them do you suppose make reference to the mysterious visit of John Wilkes Booth to Andrew Johnson at the Kirkwood House just hours before the assassination?"

"I suppose most of them do. At least the ones that deal with the earlier moves to impeach Johnson in 1867."

"I think you are probably right," L. B. Barton agreed. "Now, that mysterious visit was never explained by your Mr. Cosgrove. He said it was a riddle he hadn't been able to solve. Am I right?"

"You are."

"And Johnson told him to read the testimony regarding the matter. Am I right?"

"I think you are."

"And did he?"

"I don't think he says."

"Did *you?*"

"No," I confessed.

"Then read it now," said Mr. Barton. "Read the sworn testimony of the room clerk, Robert Jones, who is the only witness who had anything to say of the matter."

He handed me the book. I took it from him and read aloud the lines he designated with his finger:

> *Q:* Do you know anything about J. Wilkes Booth having called that day, and inquired the number of Vice-President Johnson's room?
>
> *A:* I do not know that he inquired about the room. I gave a card of J. Wilkes Booth to Colonel Browning, Mr. Johnson's secretary: it was put in the box. I gave him that card, and it was left for Colonel Browning.

Q: Did you receive it yourself from Booth?

A: I have no positive recollection of having received it, although I may have done so.

Q: Would you know J. Wilkes Booth?

A: I do not think I should. I saw him at the house some time before the occurrence; but I do not think I should recollect him.

"Now," said Mr. Barton, "that is all you will find in any record of this famous incident. It is all there is. You, so I understand, are a detective. What do you conclude from the room clerk's testimony?"

I reread the passages. I couldn't believe it.

"I can only conclude that Robert Jones is saying he doesn't recall receiving the card, in the first place; that he found it in Colonel Browning's box, and not Johnson's, so it seems it was intended for Browning in the second place; and that Jones couldn't tell us if it was Booth who left the card even if he remembered the incident, since he doesn't remember what Booth looked like."

"Very good!" said Mr. Barton. "That's what I think. And if you look at the card, as I have, you'll see that, although it was Booth's calling card, it does not bear his signature, nor any salutation, so there's no reason to suppose it was intended for Browning, except that it was said to have been found in his box. And there isn't a shred of evidence even to imply it was intended for Johnson. Furthermore, to my knowledge, the only person who has ever identified the handwriting of the message on the card as that of John Wilkes Booth was another room clerk, from the National Hotel. Not that I'd give much weight to a so-called handwriting expert, for they always seem to be wrong.

"Now do you see my point?" Barton asked.

"I think I do. There wasn't any evidence at all against Johnson."

"No! I mean, that is correct, but it is not my point."

"What is your point, then?" O'Toole asked.

Barton turned toward him, then back to me and leaned foward.

"My point, gentlemen, is this: You will not find truth in history books. You will not find truth in newspapers. You will not find it in long-lost manuscripts. What you will find in those things are either lies or inaccuracies, or goddamned blunders!"

"Well, where do you suggest we look for the truth?" asked O'Toole.

"The truth, if it is to be found at all, can be found in the middens and trash piles and junkyards of a civilization. If you can't find it there, give it up! You won't find it anywhere else!"

"You have formed no general impression about the manuscript, then?" asked O'Toole. "I mean, in general, whether or not it seems genuine."

"No, I *have* formed such an impression."

"Well, would you tell us what it is?"

"I would prefer not to," said L. B. Barton.

And that was all. The old gentleman turned away from us as though he'd forgotten we were there and began to fiddle with a clock he'd taken apart on a kitchen table in the middle of his living room.

O'Toole thanked his strange friend and ushered me out of the house.

"Barton's a peculiar old guy," he ventured as we drove away.

"He certainly is. You say he used to work for the government. Was it the Smithsonian?"

O'Toole shook his head.

"National Archives?"

"He worked for the Post Office."

"A postal inspector?"

"No," O'Toole replied, as he dropped me at the railroad station in Danbury. "The Dead Letter Office."

In the end, I found the answer—I should say part of the answer—to the mysteries posed by Cosgrove's manuscript in exactly the sort of place L. B. Barton would have looked for it. But I'm getting ahead of myself.

There is one remaining question regarding the manuscript which I have not yet addressed:

Were any significant facts altered or omitted from the Cosgrove manuscript?

The answer is yes. There were several alterations and one serious omission. The most significant falsehood appears on the first page where the author is named, for the so-called Cosgrove manuscript was not written by Nicholas Cosgrove, even though his notebooks were used as its basis.

I'm not sure when I began to suspect this. It started with a vague feeling that the assignment Lawson gave me just didn't make sense. I don't mean that it was bizarre; many of my cases are that. I mean that it was illogical, or, at least, implausible. There seemed to be a kind of hidden agenda to the whole business.

Some years ago I was hired by the president of a trucking company to find out who was hijacking so many of his trucks. After a week or so I learned the identity of the chief hijacker: the president's son. When I presented my report to the client, I expected an argument. I was wrong. He simply paid me off and told me to turn my evidence over to the state's attorney. I realized then he'd known right along who was hijacking the trucks. He hired me because he wanted someone else to make the accusation. I had the same feeling about Lawson's assignment.

Lawson knew or suspected something about his grandfather, or the manuscript, or something related to the matter. It was something he found impossible to ignore, but also impossible to tell me about. I suspected it was not only the real reason he had hired me, but it was also the real reason he had never published the Cosgrove manuscript. Whatever it was, he believed I'd find it out on my own. I wasn't so sure he was right.

I tried out a lot of theories, each crazier than the one before. As it turned out, the one that happened to be the truth was the most outlandish. I never would have been able to prove it if I hadn't happened to find those receipts from the typing service Lawson's grandfather hired to transcribe his manuscript.

Globe Office Services went out of business in 1930, and its proprietor, Alonzo Hopkins, passed away six years later. However, his son is still alive. Now in his late fifties, he practices opthalmology in Oak Park, Illinois. When I visited him at his home there, I didn't even consider trying out the true story on him. I simply said I was trying to trace an heir in an inheritance case. He seemed happy to oblige by dragging out an old file storage box containing the papers from his late father's business.

From pay records I was able to compile a list of the twenty-seven women who had worked for the firm between 1902 and 1905 in the capacity of stenographer-typist. Fortunately I thought to note down the dates they left Globe and so saved myself a return trip to Dr. Hopkins in Oak Park. Most of the women had left to get married, and using the dates as a rough index to the wedding announcements in the local newspapers on file in the Providence library, I was able to learn the married names of eighteen of them, as well as the names of their spouses.

The State Division of Vital Statistics had death certificates on file for eleven of the ladies. I took the remaining list of seven and called in a big favor from an old friend in the Social Security Administration's computer center in Baltimore. He called me back that night to tell me about Matilda Greenly.

Mrs. Greenly—née Matilda Anderson—was the only one of the seven he was able to turn up in one bootleg pass through a portion of the total Social Security computer file. The lady never had contributed to the Social Security system herself, but she received survivor's benefits through her late husband, who had. The checks were currently being sent to the Montrose Retirement Home in Fall River, Massachusetts.

I drove to Fall River and found the Montrose Home on a quiet residential street. I stopped at the receptionist's office and asked to see Mrs. Greenly, using the same inheritance case story I had told Dr. Hopkins. An orderly led me to a glassed-in veranda, then went off to get the old lady. As I waited, I glanced around at several of the residents sitting in the late afternoon sunlight that streamed through the windows. One or two showed some curiosity about me; the rest seemed unaware of my presence or anything else around them. I wondered about the state of mind of the woman I had come to see. The receptionist had remarked that she was ninety-one.

I needn't have worried. Mrs. Greenly was a frail old lady who had to be moved about in a wheelchair, but she was clear-eyed and alert. As the orderly moved off she adjusted her eyeglasses and peered at me.

"Do I know you?" she asked with some urgency. "Have we met before?"

I said we had not. She seemed relieved.

"I was afraid I'd started to lose things, memories," she said, "like some of the others." She gestured toward the other residents on the veranda. "But I was sure I didn't know you. Everyone I know is dead, you see." She seemed to be mildly surprised by the idea.

"I'm glad your memory is working," I said. "I've come to ask you about something that happened over seventy years ago."

"Oh, I'm best at remembering those days. All of us are. It's remembering what happened last week that gives some of us trouble."

"Do you remember Nicholas Cosgrove?" I asked.

"Of Newport," she replied. "Yes, although I must say I'd quite forgotten him. I don't believe I've thought of poor old Mr. Cosgrove in fifty years. But listen to me—'poor old Mr. Cosgrove'—he must have been twenty years younger than I am now when I worked for him.

"Every Wednesday. He'd send a carriage for me or one of the other girls. It was quite an outing and we always looked forward to it. We'd be picked up in the morning and delivered back home in the afternoon. Served us lunch, as well; there was no question of us eating with the help. It was grand fun, but I don't know why he simply didn't send his work to our office to have it done. He seemed to enjoy limping about his study and looking over our shoulders while we typed."

"Mr. Cosgrove limped?"

Mrs. Greenly nodded. "Favored one leg, and often walked with a cane. It was an old injury, I seem to recall him saying, and I think the dampness from the Bay made it ache. But he had such a lovely estate there, right beside the water."

"Mrs. Greenly, there's someone I'd like you to meet," I said. "May I return tomorrow?"

"I haven't looked at my engagement calendar," she said with a twinkle, "but, yes, I'm sure I'll be able to make some time for you."

*   *   *

Bill Folsom teaches sketching at an adult education center in a suburb of Boston. Before he retired he was probably the best police artist in the country. I had worked with him several times and knew him well enough to ask a favor. He agreed, and the next morning I picked him up at his home in Weymouth and drove him to the

Montrose Retirement Home in Fall River. Mrs. Greenly was wheeled once more onto the veranda.

"Mr. Folsom is an artist," I said. "He's going to try to make a sketch of Nicholas Cosgrove for us. I'd like you to help him by telling him everything you can remember of how Mr. Cosgrove looked."

Mrs. Greenly was fascinated by the idea and joined in the project with enthusiasm. In answer to Folsom's questions she plumbed her memory for the tiniest details. She looked over his shoulder as he sketched, making frequent suggestions. Folsom wielded charcoal and eraser alternately until finally the old woman declared that he had captured a perfect likeness of Nicholas Cosgrove. She was so pleased with the result that I promised to send it to her after I was through with it. I thanked her for her help and we left.

I drove Bill Folsom back to Weymouth. I knew he was getting curious, and I hadn't explained anything about what I was doing.

"Did you find what you were looking for?" he asked.

"I don't know," I replied. "I may have. Tell me, is there any way you can take about forty years off this fellow?"

Folsom studied his sketch.

"Let's see, he's about sixty-five, seventy. You say you want to see how he looked in his late twenties? I'll see what I can do."

He tore the sketch from the pad, tacked it to a cork panel over his drawing board, and began a second sketch.

"First we tighten the flesh on the face and neck," he said. "Next the hairline—bring it forward and make the hair thicker."

"And add a mustache," I said. He did so, sketching quickly.

"Forty years on top of seventy," he said as he drew. "You seem to be into ancient history." He completed the drawing, tore it from the pad and handed it to me. There was no longer any doubt in my mind as to the identity of the author of the Cosgrove manuscript.

"Not ancient history," I said. "American history."

*   *   *

In its day Hopewell was among the most elegant of the estates that front on Narragansett Bay near Newport. During his lifetime Raymond Lawson spent his summers and Christmases here. Now it was closed up, part of Lawson's estate, to be auctioned by his executor. I decided not to call James Marsh in Washington to ask permission to enter the mansion. If he refused, as I thought he probably would have, then I'd really be in a fix if something went wrong. Carrying around a set of picks and tension bars was risky enough.

I decided to go right in in broad daylight, in case something did go wrong and I had to claim innocent intentions. Early the following morning I drove down the highway toward Newport, turning onto a side road a few miles past the bridge at Bristol Ferry. The large iron gate on the gravel drive that marked the entrance to Hopewell was unlocked. The mansion wasn't visible from the road, but came into view as the driveway rounded a knoll and emerged from a stand of pines. It was a stately Victorian building of three stories. I parked in front of the main entrance, stepped up to the door, and went to work on the lock. After about thirty seconds I felt the tension bar turn and the bolt slide from the mortise. I concealed the lockpicking tools in the trunk of my car, then entered the building.

It was a haunted house, smelling of dust and emptiness. Great pieces of furniture were draped with massive dropcloths. Cold, empty fireplaces yawned in every room. I started in the basement and worked upward.

I didn't really know what I was looking for, but I needed something more, something that would prove what I already knew to be true. The man who built this place, who lived here for over forty years, who spent his last years scribbling the Cosgrove manuscript was not Nicholas Cosgrove. He was undoubtedly Raymond Lawson's maternal grandfather, but he wasn't Cosgrove, because Cosgrove died in 1868, drowned in a storm on the St. Lawrence.

It was someone other than Cosgrove who was the sole survivor of that shipwreck, someone who needed a new identity and knew enough of Cosgrove's shadowy life to realize there was little chance of being found out if he became Nicholas Cosgrove. It was someone who knew the darkest secret of his age, a secret that could send the richest and most powerful men of the times to the gallows. It was someone who used that knowledge to insure his own life and buy himself riches.

The millionaire recluse of Hopewell lived a long and largely happy life. He was blessed with a loving wife, and if she was taken from him prematurely, he was consoled by a daughter and then a grandson. But as the years wore on, he was possessed by a desire to reveal the truth about the only truly important moment of his long life.

In the Cosgrove manuscript, he told as much of the truth as he dared, and that was almost, but not quite, the whole truth. He was an old man, and he arranged to keep his secrets until after he was gone, but he could not disclose, even then, the truth that would stigmatize his daughter, his son-in-law, and his grandson. So he remained Nicholas Cosgrove.

Somehow Raymond Lawson learned this truth. He was afraid publication of his grandfather's manuscript might lead others to the same discovery. He was the last of his line, and he knew no harm could come to the living if the manuscript was published after his own death. Still, he only gave history a sporting chance by hiring a detective with a reputation for more than average persistence, and turning him loose on the case. But I was sure that somewhere Lawson had hidden some document, some photograph, some object that would finally prove what otherwise remained only a theory. After three hours of searching, I found it in the attic.

It was a large, battered and very old trunk. Judging from the type of lock it had, I would estimate it to be well over a hundred years old. I dragged it into the light of a dormer window, opened it, and spread the contents on the dusty floor.

It was the detritus of a life upon the stage: playbills, daggers, swords and costumes of every kind. There was a toga, a crown, and an outfit that could have been used to play Hamlet or Romeo. The costume in which the actor had played his most dramatic role was at the bottom of the trunk. It was a riding outfit, and one of the cavalry boots was missing. The left one.

I replaced all the items but one in the trunk. The boot I took with me when I left Hopewell that day. I turned it in at the National Archives to the officials in charge of such matters, who had many questions to ask me concerning it. I have answered them all here.

People cling tightly to their myths, and only give them up with reluctance. Digging skeletons out of the national closet is not a sure way to win popularity contests. Still, the people in charge of the official record of our triumphs and follies may someday decide we are able to survive the knowledge of some rather ugly truths. If so, you may see the boot beside its torn mate in the Lincoln Museum at Ford's Theater.

Otherwise, you'll probably never hear anything more about it.

Appendix

Professor Haselmayer's Magic Tricks

Rather than remain in indefinite suspense as to how Booth/Haselmayer accomplished his tricks, and leave the reader in the same state, I consulted a student of stage magic for advice.

The disappearance from the balloon and materialization before the tent was done quite simply, he says. The basket of the balloon *did* contain a secret compartment, although not one large enough to conceal the magician. It was, however, of sufficient size to conceal a Zouave's uniform before the ascent, and the magician's costume afterward. Thus, after the magician had ascended out of sight of the crowd and rid himself of his handcuffs by means Cosgrove already explained, he simply changed clothing, became a Zouave, and stowed his magician's costume in the secret compartment. As the balloon neared the ground several of the Zouaves climbed into the basket. No one bothered to count them, so the presence of an extra Zouave when the basket was brought to the ground was not noticed. Neither was his speedy withdrawal from the scene, to hide in his tent, where he changed into a duplicate magician's costume, then stepped out to summon the crowd, which was still hunting for him somewhere in the basket.

The disappearance into thin air Cosgrove described in Chapter Eight is a familiar bit of stage magic, known in the nineteenth century as "Pepper's Ghost." It is accomplished by means of a mirror which projects the reflection of the magician, who is standing in a lighted recess beneath the stage, onto a glass screen, which is in view of the audience. When the light in the recess is extinguished, the figure appears to vanish from the stage.

As Cosgrove would say, "That, for the benefit of the curious and skeptical, is how it was done."

—M.C.

Bibliography

The following materials are sources of information bearing on the assassination of President Lincoln and related matters. The list is by no means complete, but it contains most of the items that proved useful in my efforts to verify *The Cosgrove Report*.

—M.C.

BOOKS:

Baker, Gen. Lafayette C., *History of the United States Secret Service,* privately published, Philadelphia, 1867. Revised edition, *The United States Secret Service in the Late War—Perilous Adventures, Hairbreadth Escapes and Valuable Services of the Detective Police— by General Lafayette C. Baker, Organizer and First Chief of the National Secret Service Bureau of the United States,* John E. Potter & Co., Philadelphia, 1889.

Bates, David Homer, *Lincoln in the Telegraph Office,* D. Appleton-Century Co., New York, 1907.

Clarke, Asia Booth, *The Unlocked Book: A Memoir of John Wilkes Booth by his sister Asia Booth Clarke, With a Foreword by Eleanor Farjeon,* G. P. Putnam's Sons, New York, 1938.

Crook, William, *Through Five Administrations,* Harper & Brothers, New York, 1907.

DeWitt, David M., *The Judicial Murder of Mary E. Surratt,* J. Murphy & Co., Baltimore, 1895.

Eisenschiml, Otto, *Why Was Lincoln Murdered?,* Little, Brown and Company, Boston, 1937; *In the Shadow of Lincoln's Death,* Wilfred Funk, New York, 1940.

Forrester, Izola, *This One Mad Act; the Unknown Story of John Wilkes Booth and His Family,* Cushman & Flint, Boston, 1937.

Hawley, J. R., *Assassination & History of the Conspiracy,* Cincinnati, 1865.

Horan, James E., *The Pinkertons: The Detective Dynasty That Made History,* Crown, New York, 1967.

Kimmel, Stanley, *The Mad Booths of Maryland* (Revised and Enlarged Edition), Dover, New York, 1969.

Milton, George Fort, *The Age of Hate: Andrew Johnson and the Radicals,* Coward-McCann, Inc., New York, 1930.

Mogelever, Jacob, *Death to Traitors: The Story of General Lafayette C. Baker, Lincoln's Forgotten Secret Service Chief,* Doubleday, New York, 1960.

O'Connor, Richard, *Gould's Millions,* Doubleday, New York, 1962.

Oldroyd, Osborn H., *The Assassination of Abraham Lincoln,* privately published, Washington, D.C., 1901.

Pitman, Benn, *The Assassination of President Lincoln and Trial of the Conspirators,* Moore, Wilstach and Baldwin, Cincinnati, 1865.

Poore, Ben Perley, *The Conspiracy Trial for the Murder of the President,* J. E. Tilton and Company, Boston, 1865 (three volumes).

Roscoe, Theodore, *The Web of Conspiracy,* Prentice-Hall, New Jersey 1959.

Smoot, R. M., *The Unwritten History of the Assassination of Abraham Lincoln,* J. Murphy & Co., Baltimore, 1904.

Townsend, George Alfred, *The Life, Crime and Capture of J. W. Booth,* Dick & Fitzgerald, New York, 1865.

U.S. House of Representatives, *Impeachment Investigation,* Government Printing Office, Washington, D.C., 1867.

Welles, Gideon, *Diary,* Houghton Mifflin Co., Boston, 1911.

ARTICLES:

Arnold, Samuel B., "The Lincoln Plot," Baltimore *American,* Baltimore, Maryland, December 8–20, 1902.

Gleason, D. H. L, "Conspiracy Against Lincoln," *The Magazine of History,* Vol. 13, No. 2, February, 1911.

Hall, James O., "A Noted Author Explains the Mystery of Lincoln's Guard," The Maryland *Independent,* Brandywine/Clinton/ Marlton, July 19 and 26, 1978.

Lincoln, Robert Todd, "Edwin Booth and Lincoln," *The Century Magazine,* April, 1909.

Porter, Dr. George L., "How Booth's Body Was Hidden," *The Columbian Magazine,* April, 1911.

Surratt, John, Text of "Rockville Lecture," Washington *Star,* Washington, D.C., December 7, 1870.

G. J. A. O'Toole was born in 1937 and worked for the CIA from 1966 to 1969. He was the author of several award-winning books, including *The Encyclopedia of American Intelligence and Espionage; Honorable Treachery,* a history of American intelligence; *The Spanish War: An American Epic 1898,* a Pulitzer Prize nominee; and *An Agent on the Other Side,* a novel. He died at the age of sixty-four in Mount Vernon, NY.